In the *Age of Myth and Legend*, the Lord's Arkon Thetan lost his faith, abandoned his honor and his solemn oaths, and betrayed the one true god — he who loved him above all others. Thetan's treachery threatened to bring down the very heavens and cast his name in infamy, forevermore.

When the mountain troll horde surrounded Lomion City, rivalry and machination paralyzed the High Council...until the mysterious Baron Jaros appeared offering salvation from the trolls. Salvation that came at a weighty price.

King Bornyth Trollsbane of the Darendor Dwarves was fearless, and confident that his people could withstand any siege, assault, plague, flood, or famine. Hardy were his Dwarves. Determined. Tireless. Patient. The problem was, the Draugar -- the dead that walked — were all of that and more.

Uriel the Bold had safeguarded the portal betwixt Midgaard and Nifleheim for untold ages. He'd repelled wizards, warlords, and hordes of howling barbarians. But what hope did he have to stop The Shadow League's cadre of Archwizards and the Nifleheim Lord that led them?

The Eotrus had suffered beyond all imagining:

1

family members dead, missing, kidnapped, their fortress, sacked. But now it was Ector's turn to take the battle to the enemy. To march on the troll city of Gothmagorn and exact his revenge…though it might cost him his very soul.

Captain Frem Sorlons was one of the toughest men to ever walk Midgaard. But deep in the heart of Svartleheim, when the drums of doom sound, even a brave hero can fall.

BOOKS BY GLENN G. THATER

THE HARBINGER OF DOOM SAGA

GATEWAY TO NIFLEHEIM
THE FALLEN ANGLE
KNIGHT ETERNAL
DWELLERS OF THE DEEP
BLOOD, FIRE, AND THORN
GODS OF THE SWORD
THE SHAMBLING DEAD
MASTER OF THE DEAD
SHADOW OF DOOM
WIZARD'S TOLL
DRUMS OF DOOM
VOLUME 12+ (forthcoming)

HARBINGER OF DOOM
(Combines *Gateway to Nifleheim* and *The Fallen Angle* into a single volume)

THE HERO AND THE FIEND
(A novelette set in the Harbinger of Doom universe)

THE GATEWAY
(A novella length version of *Gateway to Nifleheim*)

THE DEMON KING OF BERGHER
(A short story set in the Harbinger of Doom universe)

THE KEBLEAR HORROR
(A short story set in the Harbinger of Doom universe)

To be notified about my new book releases and any special offers or discounts regarding my books, please join my mailing list here: http://eepurl.com/vwubH

GLENN G. THATER

DRUMS OF DOOM

A TALE FROM THE HARBINGER OF DOOM SAGA

DRUMS OF DOOM © 2017 by Glenn G. Thater

ISBN-13: 978-1546392880
ISBN-10: 1546392882

Visit Glenn G. Thater's website at
http://www.glenngthater.com

May 2017 Print Edition
Published by Lomion Press

1

VAEDEN
AZATHOTH'S PALACE

THE AGE OF MYTH AND LEGEND

THE LORD'S ARKON THETAN

Azathoth, the one true god, sat stiffly upon his gleaming golden throne, flowing robes of white, wild hair and beard to match. Not at all young, but not terribly old. Chiseled features, granite hewn, mighty thews, and barrel chest. His milky hands rested on the throne's arms; his chin held high, jaw set. Eyes of gray simmered with the wisdom of the ages. A power wafted about him. A palpable thing beyond the ken of men. All in his presence felt it. Even to look upon him was hard; painful to the eyes, akin to staring into the midday sun, though he gave off no light. Not usually. Still, to set eyes upon him was joyful, uplifting, comforting, and frightful, all at once. Such it was to be in the presence of god.

Azathoth awaited the news that Uriel the Bold brought up from Egript-Mon, lately conquered by the heathen hosts of Asgard, that disbelieving barbaric rabble led by Wotan and his Aesir.

Seated to either side of Azathoth were his most trusted lieutenants. Their chairs grander than the thrones of Midgaard's greatest kings, yet, they were but pale shadows of their lord's ponderous perch. The lord's Arkon Thetan the Lightbringer sat to his right hand, armor of midnight blue, cape of black, weapons aplenty, somber and stoic, as was his wont. Mithron the Just to his left, in black and silver, mountainous and regal.

All of Azathoth's greatest Arkons were present; all stood to attention, shoulder to shoulder, arrayed along the central aisle that led to the lord's throne. Their armor, each to their chosen hue and style, their sigils and standards unique and unmistakable, proud and powerful.

Bhaal was there, all in black, so tall and broad, more giant than man, his heart, as hard as stone. Mikel stood near Thetan's chair, Gabriel beside him. Raphael was there. So too were Arioch, Azrael, Sidriel, Zophaniel, Steriel, Blazren, Hogar, Dekkar, Asmodeus, Belial, Iblis, Mammon, Mephistoles, Moloch, Rumael, Belphegor, Hecate, Bose, and more. Each, a legend among humankind. Champions. Heroes. Their deeds to fill volumes untold. Yet each hero's tongue was captive to the tension in the air, for their lord grew impatient. No doubt, he sensed he would not care for the news he'd soon hear.

Besides the Arkons, only one other was allowed in the lord's sight that day. Lasifer the Gnome, Azathoth's court wizard, lurked by the lord's knee, waiting to give good counsel.

Uriel marched down the center aisle, his plate armor gleaming to a near-mirrored shine. His left hand gripped a scroll sealed with wax. He carried his helmet in the crook of his right arm, his every movement precise and measured. Every booted step echoed across the great hall — so vast, it could have harbored a thousand folk and still felt empty. Its ceiling so high, its rafters, lost in the gloom. The Arkons' breath steamed and billowed above their heads like a cloud, for the air was ever chill in the lord's divine presence, though the god's breath produced no fog of its own. Incense hung heavy in the air, smoldering braziers clustered about the room. The clopping of Uriel's boots was the only sound to hear, save for the gong that Steriel tolled every second breath. That sound, distinct as it was, faded to the background, unnoticed, owing to its commonness.

All eyes were on Uriel as he approached unmolested to the lord's sandaled foot.

"What news, brother?" said Mithron as Uriel dropped to one knee before the lord.

Uriel handed the scroll to Mithron before he spoke, Wotan's stamp upon it.

"The Aesir will not give up Egript-Mon, my lord," said Uriel. "And Wotan will not let your people go. The plagues have not deterred him."

Mithron examined the scroll's seal, broke it open, and perused its contents. "It is as Uriel reports, my lord," said Mithron. "Defiance unto the last."

"Why does this self-proclaimed king defy me?" said Azathoth, his voice carrying with it a reverberation that set the men's throats to vibrating, though it was not overloud. "Is it stubbornness? Does he truly wish my people harm? Or to goad me to action?"

Uriel's face ran red. He steeled himself before

he spoke again. "Wotan claims he's saving them, my lord."

"Saving them from what?" said Azathoth, his eyes narrowed.

"From you, my lord," said Uriel.

"What does that mean?" said Mithron. "Why would the lord's own chosen people need protection from him? It makes no sense."

"Wotan says the lord is a false god," said Uriel.

As one, the Arkons gasped.

"He names you a mad demon born of the Nether Realms," said Uriel. "Says he will free all the people of Midgaard from your yoke and banish you to Helheim."

Azathoth's face grew dark. "So the barbarian reveals himself at last, my beloveds," he said as his eyes locked in turn on each of the nearest Arkons. "Power is what Wotan craves. Being king of all the northern lands fails to blunt his hunger. Being king of all Midgaard would not sate his boundless desires. He lusts for more. As all small and weak-minded men, he wants what he can never have. He wants to be a god."

"That is why he insults me," continued Azathoth. "Attacks me. Enslaves my chosen people. My people! Wotan fancies himself a god. And who could deny him that title if he defeated me? And so he must try. Or die in the trying. The ambitions of men hold no bounds."

"He fears the expansion of your kingdom, my lord," said Thetan.

"As well he should," said Azathoth. "I will not rest until all Midgaard lies safe in my bosom, until all the people hear the good word and rejoice. I will suffer the barbarians' false gods no longer. Their golden calves. Their obscene idols. Their witchery. Their abominations. Blasphemies. Merciless sacrifices. Mad bloodlust and base desires. Their fictions and humbug.

"The terrors that they inflict on all those they conquer and oppress must come to an end. But this, my Arkons, you all know well. You know my mind. You know my plans, such as I have revealed to you. I say to you, the time has come for Asgard to crumble under my might. We must liberate its people. Not only for the sake of our chosen folk that lie enslaved beneath their boots, but so too for all those other innocents who suffer under their oppression. We must do this thing, however hard the task."

"Wotan and his Aesir must pay the ultimate price," said Lasifer.

Azathoth's gaze snapped to the Gnome. "You would have me kill him?" he said. "Is that your counsel? Make him a martyr to be worshiped by those he leaves behind?"

"Only if it be your will and you see a value to it, great lord," said Lasifer squirming.

"All of Egript-Mon will pay the price," said Azathoth. "It must be a punishment that befits the crime. The nine plagues were but annoyances. Distractions to the Aesir. Wotan sat protected in his great hall while his people suffered. He cares not for them. For their suffering. For their very souls. And so the plagues I set upon them did no good. The barbarian lord sits entrenched. His heart, hardened to stone.

"Anticipating that it would be the common folk

that would suffer most, merciful was I in the plagues' crafting. No longer. Now all the heathen masses shall suffer under my wrath. The firstborn child of every family in Egript-Mon, from Wotan's own, to the most wanton beggar, to the most wretched prisoner in deepest dungeon, will die. In one fortnight this will come to pass. At the darkest hour, when the moons hang high, my will, will be done."

There was silence for some moments as the Arkons took that in.

"How shall it be done, my lord?" said Thetan.

"You, my Arkons, shall steal through the streets of ancient Egript-Mon that night," said Azathoth. "You will sunder every door, enter every heathen home and hovel. You shall pluck the firstborn child from their cribs or their mothers' bosoms and end their lives, swiftly, with as little pain as possible to complete the deed. There will be no mercy, no exceptions, no reprieves."

"A harsh penalty, indeed," said Azrael the Wise.

"The wicked Aesir have brought this upon themselves," said Azathoth.

"What of your chosen people?" said Thetan. "Their homes and hovels are scattered about Egript-Mon. How will we know them in the dark of night? Must they suffer too?"

"The doors of the faithful shall be marked in blood, be it of sheep or goat," said Azathoth. "The door frames, and the lintels above them, shall be swathed in the fresh blood of those animals. By their sacrifices, the households of my chosen people shall be spared. But no others shall be spared. Spread the word of the lambs' blood. Spread it in secret. Sariel, you will do this thing. Bose, you shall aid her."

"My lord, many innocents will die in this way," said Azrael. "Is there no other way?"

"The nine plagues that have failed to move the heart of the barbarian chieftain were the other way. Now stronger measures must be taken. Take heart, my Arkons, for these deeds, as terrible as they are, all fall into my grand plan."

2

LOMION CITY
HOUSE ALDER

YEAR 1267, 4TH AGE

MOTHER ALDER

"**W**here is Rom?" said Mother Alder, her voice slow and icy, her eyes trained on her grandson Dirk. "Where is my brother?"

Dirk Alder, son of Bartol, stood before her in House Alder's drawing room, sweating, his blue armor in disarray and covered in grime and yellowish gore. Gar Pullman stood a step behind him, hands at his sides, no expression on his face. Bald Boddrick was with them, towering over all and everything, his face paler than normal, sweat on his brow. Black Grint leaned against the wall looking bored as he picked dirt from his fingernails with a short blade. Sentry of Allendale lurked behind Boddrick and tried to go unnoticed.

"The Eotrus took him," blurted Dirk, the words dropping fast from his mouth. "A hostage."

Mother Alder's eyes narrowed. "How?"

"Trolls, if you can believe it," sputtered Dirk. "Trolls. Took us by surprise. Nothing we could do. Almost impossible to kill them. We tried--"

"Is it trolls that have my brother or the Eotrus?"

Dirk was not quick to respond.

"The Eotrus have him," said Pullman whose voice held no fear, only confidence; his tone, matter-of-fact. "But, I'm afraid, it gets worse than that. The Eotrus, they murdered Brock straight away when we arrived."

"What!" screeched Mother Alder. "My Brock? They killed my Brock?"

"A crossbow bolt shot from atop the wall," said Pullman. "Murdered him in cold blood. No warning or warrant."

"You're certain that he is dead?" said Mother Alder. "Could they have wounded him, and taken him alive?"

"We recovered his body," said Pullman, "there is no doubt."

"Did you bring him home?" said Mother Alder.

"Mountain trolls attacked our encampment that very night," said Pullman. "Hundreds of them. Scattered us in the dark. They wiped out most of the brigade. Rom and some men fled to the Dor; we and some others fled south. We left a lot of good men on that field that night, Brock's body with them."

"Yet *you* managed to make it back, none the worse for wear," said Mother Alder.

"We saw knife-work aplenty, I promise you," said Pullman. "That troll attack – it was no one-off raid. It's the start of an invasion. The trolls overran Dor Eotrus and the Outer Dor, and their folk fled to their Underhalls. We joined up with the Eotrus bannermen and retook the Dor from the trolls, but the Eotrus would not give up Rom. They figure that you won't move against them if--

"I know what they figure," said Mother Alder. "Is Rom alive? For certain?"

"A bit bruised is all," said Pullman.

"Who commands the Eotrus?" said Mother Alder. "Who is to blame?"

"Ector, the third or fourth son," said Pullman.

"Was it him that had my Brock killed?"

"That was Sarbek, the old Castellan," said Pullman, "but the trolls took care of him."

"I heard he died cowering in a corner, begging for his life, too scared to even defend himself," said Dirk. "They're all cowards, the Eotrus."

Mother Alder shook her head. "Dimwits and dullards, all my progeny. The Eotrus are many things, but cowards, I think not." She turned to Pullman. "You'll be coming up with a plan, Gar Pullman, to get my brother back. Alive. And in one piece. Do you hear me?"

Pullman stiffened.

"Should be doable," said Boddrick. "The Eotrus are marching north with all their banners. Out to sack the troll homeland. After their own revenge, they are. They've little more than a skeleton force manning their Dor."

"So the trolls broke and routed?" said Mother Alder.

"Not exactly," said Dirk.

"We wiped out the trolls camped at Dor Eotrus," said Pullman. "The problem is, the main troll force was already gone. Headed south. Headed here. It was all we could do to get here ahead of them."

"They're marching on Lomion City?" said Mother Alder.

"Aye," said Pullman. "It will be a hard slog to get past them and back up north."

"Then you'd best not waste any more time," said Mother Alder. "I want you to leave at once. Today. How many trolls are headed here?"

"Thousands," said Dirk.

"Thousands?" said Mother Alder.

"Thousands," said Dirk.

Mother Alder's head hung low as she sat her chair. She sipped a brandy and watched the fire crackling in the hearth. "Why didn't you tell me, Firstborn?"

Barusa paled. "I hoped that the reports were false. I wanted to spare you–"

"How long have you known? Was it a raven?" Mother Alder looked up to study Barusa as he responded.

"For a few days. A raven sent from Dor Eotrus carried the news. It could've been false. It could've been sent to demoralize us. How could I tell you that my brother, your son, was dead if I was not certain of it? I didn't want to put you through that."

Mother Alder nodded, her only response. They sat quietly until Mother Alder had finished her brandy. She stepped slowly across the room. Barusa met her near the exit, his face, sad.

Suddenly, Mother Alder punched Barusa squarely in the jaw. He fell back on his rump, dazed.

"Next time, Firstborn, best you tell me straightaway," she said, her voice calm and quiet.

She turned and headed off to her chambers.

3

FOOTHILLS OF THE KRONAR MOUNTAIN RANGE, NORTH OF DOR EOTRUS

YEAR 1267, 4TH AGE

ECTOR EOTRUS

Sir Ector Eotrus lay prone behind a fallen tree. He inched up his head, slowly, just high enough for his eyes to peer over the trunk and spy upon the troop of trolls that stalked through the woodland. To either side of Ector lay Captain Pellan, the Beardless Dwarf, and Sir Indigo Eldswroth, ranking knight of Dor Eotrus.

Several hundred mountain trolls led a ragged column of several dozen wagons through the trees, the entire train moving faster than a man's walk, but much slower than the usual loping gate of the trolls. No doubt, the wagons slowed them down – the woods unaccommodating to their passage. Stolen Lomerian horses pulled most of the wagons, but curiously, many were pulled by the trolls themselves. The horses gave them no end of trouble, skittish and wild owing to their fear of their captors.

"Dead gods," said Ector, "the scouts were right."

"I told you as much," said Pellan. "Stupid for us to get this close; if they spot us, there will be hell to pay. We can track these creatures from a mile back by their stench alone. No need to get up this close."

"I needed to see for myself," said Ector.

"We all needed to see it," said Indigo. "To plan whatever assault we decide on, if for nothing else."

"Now that we're here," said Pellan, "methinks we might be safe enough. Since that stench of theirs overwhelms even from this far out, they probably can't sniff us out, not even if we were upwind, which we're not."

"Wasn't it bad enough that so many of our people were murdered by these things?" said Ector. "Now, even in death they can't escape the troll. How many bodies do they have on those wagons? There must be hundreds."

"Hard to say," said Indigo.

"Four or five hundred, I'd mark it," said Pellan.

"Best not to dwell on it," said Indigo. "Nothing we can do for them now."

"I don't want to dwell," said Ector. "I want revenge. I want retribution. Those people, those bodies, piled one atop another are not just random nobodies. They're our people. Our friends. Our men. And they were under my protection."

"It's not your fault," said Indigo. "It's nobody's fault."

"They've been feeding on them," said Pellan. "Evil stinking monsters."

"That tells us something," said Indigo, "tells us

something important. We're food for them, we knew that, but they're not hauling this food off to the main horde, which went south by all accounts. They're bringing it back to the north. Why would they do that, I ask you?"

"They must need the food back in their homeland, whatever mountain they crawled out of," said Ector.

"And they're hauling ass to get there," said Pellan.

"Maybe they're desperate," said Ector. "Maybe their people are starving back home. Winter's coming on fast – maybe they don't have enough food stored."

"That's just what I was thinking," said Indigo. "It might mean they're even weaker at home than we hoped. Maybe we can finish them off – all of them. Rid the world of their scourge."

"Maybe this, maybe that," said Pellan. "It's all academic. If we knew the truth, if we knew their motivations, well, that might help us to understand them. There might be some value to that, but probably not. In the end, I don't give a darn. I'm going to kill them, the bastards. I'm gonna kill them all. For Sarbek. For Mindletown and my friend the Alchemist. For Old Cern. For everyone they've killed. Everyone they've butchered."

Ector and Indigo nodded.

"We have to take this bunch before we encounter any more in the mountains," said Indigo.

"We move tonight," said Ector. "We can't afford to wait; their scouts might stumble upon us. We don't want this horde coming down on us in our bedclothes. We need to catch them by surprise."

"Not tonight," said Pellan. "At midday tomorrow is when we move. We can't maneuver our horse to encircle them during the night. It'll take a few hours of daylight to do it right and proper. We hit them at noon tomorrow, no earlier. That's our best play."

"I'm glad to have your counsel, Captain," said Ector. "We can't let any of them escape. Not a single one. Otherwise, when we get up north, their folk will have a trap waiting for us – maybe as good as what we set for them in the Underhalls."

"And we'd all get dead," said Pellan.

"Best to avoid that," said Indigo.

"That's good thinking, Master Ector," said Pellan. "Trouble is, the Kronar Range goes on for at least two hundred miles east and west of us, and Odin knows how far north. If we can't sniff out a trail that we can follow, we might spend months slogging around those mountains and not find hide or hair of the trolls. Trust me, you don't want us stuck wintering up there, not in those mountains. So I say, let's let a few of them buggers get past us; let them slip through our lines all quiet-like; make them think they escaped clean. But we'll be watching. And our scouts will track them, they will. We've got men what can move through the woods mighty fast, mayhap not as fast as a troll, but fast. They'll follow their trail easy enough if it's fresh. Let the trolls lead us straight back to their home sweet home. Make our job a lot easier. A lot quicker. I'm just saying."

"A risky approach," said Ector. "But Sir Gabriel always said, *to achieve great victories, a man must take bold actions*. Let's make certain that we have the right men in position. Men that can follow whatever trail the trolls leave. And let's make certain that not many get through."

"We'll station two full companies behind our northern lines," said Indigo. "One of archers, the other, cavalry. With them will be our best rangers and scouts. They'll do as we've discussed. No better men for the job."

"We hit the main group on all four sides at once with equal measure," said Pellan, "but we keep in reserve the archers and cavalry that Indigo mentioned."

"Can we do this?" said Ector. "Can we win an open fight with these things?"

"If we fight them on our terms, in the daylight as we plan to," said Pellan, "then by Odin, we *will* destroy them. But whether some few that we can track get away, well, that's the gamble."

***

Indigo rode up to the gathered officers: Ector, Pellan, and the Eotrus's ranking bannermen: Lords Ogden, Lester, Brian, and Cadbury. "Three hundred trolls is our best count," said Indigo. "They've no outriders as far as we can tell."

"The bastards don't fear us," said Lord Ogden of Westforest.

"They'll soon regret that," said Ector.

"The men are jittery," said Lord Brian. "They

harbor more anger for the troll than any enemy we've faced in our lifetimes, but they're fearful too."

"They'll do their duty," said Lord Lester. "Of this, I've no doubt."

"Nor I," said Lord Brian, "but I too feel my nerves. I've fought in a hundred skirmishes over the years, and not just against men, as you well know. But I've rarely felt my stomach flutter like this. It doesn't make a lot of sense, for we outnumber the troll nearly forty to one. Our victory is assured."

"We're all feeling it," said Indigo.

"What's different about this," said Pellan, "is that the stinking troll can kill any of us. They're stinking tough. Their strength. The way they bound from tree to tree. Their speed. We've not fought a large force with skills like theirs before. Best we hit them hard and fast. One charge, then melee. Fight straight through until it's done. Until they're all down. That'll get us through this with least loss. And then onward to the mountains."

"To their homeland," said Ector.

"We'll yet have our revenge."

4

VAEDEN
MOUNT CANTORWROUGHT

THE AGE OF MYTH AND LEGEND

THE LORD'S ARKON THETAN

The campfire blazed at the center of the group of gathered men, crackling and sparking, sacrificing itself, all that it was, all that it ever would be, to give what fleeting aid and comfort it could to those old souls that surrounded it; that needed its warmth; its light; for however long it could provide.

Darkness came early atop the summit of Mount Canterwrought, the cold night air with it. Far colder than was the lush forest below. That chill harkened to the coming winter whose snows would soon strike. The mountaintop would lie deserted, gleaming virgin white, until the spring thaw. A last gathering of the season was it. At a place where great men sought solace. And quiet. Time away from their toils. Their responsibilities.

Their god.

From that lofty perch, one could gaze down upon all the lands of Vaeden, the great forest, and beyond, even unto the far reaches of Egript-Mon in the east, and mysterious Lum in the far west.

Canterwrought sat at the heart of Azathoth's empire, the sacred mountain from which the lord first appeared untold ages before. He sailed down from the heavens, the stories said, on a great winged ship of fire. And Midgaard was never the same again.

Seven men kept close about that campfire. Men unlike all others save for their brothers-in-arms. Arkons of Azathoth were they. The lord's handpicked lieutenants. Men of varied skills — of mind, magic, and muscle, but peerless amongst the common folk. They were the enforcers of Azathoth's laws. His edicts. His will. Both loved and feared were they, by all the people of Azathoth's demesne.

And rightly so.

Weighty deeds did the Arkons contemplate that night. Weightier than ever before or since. The fate of all Midgaard teetered on a razor's edge during their hours-long debate.

It was Thetan who pushed it over the brink, and forever sealed his fate, that of the other Arkons, and even Azathoth himself, and all Midgaard with them. That night, they set down a path from which there was no turning back.

Thetan and Mithron sat opposite each other across the fire. Around the perimeter were Gabriel, Azrael, Uriel, Raphael, and Arioch.

"The lord has given me the task of guarding Sariel and Bose as they search for the blood upon the doors," said Uriel, "so that we might correctly choose which doors to sunder and which to pass over."

"And what of all those families, of the chosen

26

people of Azathoth, that hear not of this strange method to safeguard their homes?" said Azrael. "What of them? And what of those who have no lamb, sheep, or goat to sacrifice? What becomes of them? Their children? How many will we kill in error?"

"A guilt weighs upon you," said Mithron. "So it should. It weighs so heavily upon me, that I can barely take a breath."

"We should not do this black deed," said Gabriel. "There is no good that can come of it."

"Wotan will likely still resist," said Raphael. "It may even steel his resolve against us. He'll never let the chosen people go. He's never given up territory before, except when pushed back by force of arms. He'll not change his ways now. Especially not if we kill a child of his own House."

"So are we suddenly wiser than the lord?" said Azrael. "We think we can predict Wotan's reactions, but the lord cannot?"

"If we do this deed," said Gabriel, "the stain upon our souls will mar us forever."

"Thetan," said Azrael, "you've sat silent long enough. Two hours we've gone around and around, and you've said not a single word, though I've no doubt, nor do any of us here, that you have much to say."

Thetan nodded and looked to each of his brothers before he spoke. "In times past, the lord destroyed much of Midgaard by flood. With our aid, he destroyed cities by fire. He has struck down his enemies by his own hand countless times, and by our hands countless more. Each time, he calls it justice. He says that it is good. He says it is part of his plan. A plan that is broad and deep, and complex beyond the minds of puny men such as we."

"Mayhap this is true," Thetan continued. "Mayhap I cannot understand his grand vision. That my sight is too narrow. Too focused. Too small. Maybe I don't understand. Maybe I never will."

"But what I do know — is the difference between a good deed and a black one. What were the lord's words, his exact words, about what we should do when we sunder those doors? Arioch, speak them back to us."

"Pluck the firstborn from their cribs or their mothers' bosoms," said Arioch, his voice mimicking Azathoth's, the impression, uncanny. "Kill them swiftly with as little pain as possible."

"Kill them," said Thetan. "The children. Kill the children, he said. Those words have echoed in my mind countless times since the lord spoke them. Mayhap I am a blind fool. I do not know. But to my mind, the lord orders us to commit an act of blackest, darkest, foulest evil, and as always, he calls it good."

"I say to you, my brothers, if any man were to give us such an order, or commit such an act, we would know it for what it was. Evil. But when the lord gives us that same command, we follow it. We resolve that somehow that black deed is good, even if we can't understand it. We accept that it is beyond us. We accept it because he tells us so, and because he is the lord."

"He *is* the lord," said Mithron. "The one true god. Who are we to disobey? Who are we to question? We who are naught but the instruments of his will. We are not his conscience or his keepers. And certainly not his equals. It is not for us to judge *him*."

"If not us," said Azrael, "then who? Who can question these deeds? Who can judge these actions? Who better than we?"

"I have never done an evil deed by choice," said Thetan. "I speak not of small slights, or callous words. I'm talking evil — a foul deed for selfish purpose or in anger unrestrained. Not once in all the ages that I've walked this world have I done such a thing. But I have ever followed the lord's orders. My heart has often been troubled by what I have done in his name. Deeds that I would never do in my own. And ever I resolved myself that I was too small to understand his grand vision. That it was beyond me. Just as he told me. Just as he has told us all a thousand times."

"But that's over now," said Thetan.

"Now I am done."

"Done?" said Raphael. "What are you saying? Will you petition the lord to relieve you of your position? There is no precedent for that. Surely, you will not openly defy him?"

"That is not what Thetan is saying at all," said Mithron.

"We venture onto dangerous ground here, my brothers," said Arioch. "Once said, some things cannot be unsaid. Let's speak carefully, but plainly, or else not at all. No matter what we decide amongst us here, we must have clarity. There should be no misunderstandings amongst us."

"I agree," said Gabriel. "Thetan, is there a plan that you can voice?"

"Rebellion," said Mithron. "The lightbringer contemplates rebellion. Open and grand. That's his plan. And has been for a long time. He's been waiting for the rest of us to come around to his way of thinking. Haven't you, brother?"

"If that is so," said Thetan, "how would Mithron react?"

Mithron's blue eyes bore into Thetan's. "I too am done," said Mithron, "and have been for a while now. I would join with you in this folly, brother, come what may."

"Join with him?" said Uriel. "I thought we lately agreed to speak plainly. Your words are not plain at all. What do you propose? Is it a rebellion to speak with the lord? To plead your case? To endeavor to change his mind? Or something more? Tell us your mind."

"As Mithron said, this has been a long time coming," said Thetan. "There has been too much evil done in Azathoth's name already. Uncountable evils. Though he calls each one good. The outcome is the same. The horror, the pain is the same. It must be stopped. He must be stopped. Once and for all time. I will stop him."

"You have often counseled caution and restraint," said Arioch. "The lord has not been deaf to your concerns. Gabriel has spoken similar words to the lord; I have heard him. Azrael has spoken much the same. The lord always hears our counsel, though, I agree, he does not always follow it. We have tempered his wrath many a time. Many a time."

"And we've failed to temper it a hundred times for every time we succeeded," said Thetan.

"But he is the lord," said Raphael. "All knowing. All powerful."

"He is unworthy of the loyalty that we have shown him," said Thetan. "The devotion. The trust."

"So what will you do?" said Uriel.

"I will kill him," said Thetan.

5

JUTENHEIM ANGLOTOR

YEAR 1267, 4TH AGE

URIEL THE BOLD

In the high tower of Anglotor, attended only by his beloved apprentice Kapte, stood Uriel the Bold, former Arkon of Azathoth, long fallen from his grace. Uriel's betrayal occurred in ages past, before recorded history, in the storied *Age of Myth and Legend*.

At the very top of the central tower were they, in a small room of stone and glass that boasted a panoramic view of the keep and its surrounds: rolling hillsides to the north, green forests to east and west, and the ocean blue to the south, for the southern side of the castle stood atop a rocky promontory that overlooked the sea and loomed high above the strand.

With a flick of his hand and murmured words of some forgotten tongue, Uriel tapped the Grand Weave of Magic and cast a wondrous charm of his own design. At his behest, the window glass turned gray and became as impenetrable as Dyvers steel, safeguarding Uriel and Kapte from any intrusions or attacks from without.

Before the windows, appeared an undulating

wall of fog called down from the Weave by Uriel's sorcery. Within those murky depths could be seen live images of another place, as if one were there, hovering about as a bird. Uriel could shift the view at will, from one place to another. *Farsight* he called it, that magic.

At the moment, the image before him was of the main entry hall of Anglotor's keep. The image focused on the great doors, solid steel: closed, locked, barred, and reinforced. The doors were under assault from the outside, the keep's defenses having been lately breached by Korrgonn and the dreaded League of Shadows.

Uriel's men thronged about the entry hall. In the main they were tall broad Jutens. But amongst them were Dwarves, Svart, Elf, Lugron, and even a few Ettin who towered above all the rest. To each side of the doors stood a rare and fabulous creature of high and ancient magic. Golems they were -- magical constructs built of solid cast iron by Uriel's hand and animated by his magics, via esoteric techniques long lost to the modern world, to do his bidding, and his alone. They stood ready to repel the intruders should they breach the doors.

"The children?" said Uriel.

"Secure in the hidden chambers," said Kapte. "Though there is little need. Magic will not avail the intruders against *those* doors. Or against the keep's walls. Every ward and rune known to Volsung, Dwarf, Elf, or Svart binds them. They will not get in."

A great crash sounded and the steel doors shuddered. A dent appeared near one door's center.

"They wield the brute as well as the arcane," said Uriel. "They have their own Golem and--"

"A primitive thing of stone, Master," said Kapte. "A pale imitation of your iron constructs. Iron will always shatter stone."

"Perhaps," said Uriel. "Though some stone be stouter than others. So too do they have a Red Demon of Fozramgar. No stronger beast of its size has ever walked Midgaard."

As Uriel conversed with Kapte, he shifted his *Farsight* view over and again, sometimes at lightning speed, surveilling his demesne from every possible angle. And on occasion, with some finger flick or small gesture of hand or wrist, his orders to maneuver his troops or spring this trap or that, were somehow transmitted to his minions positioned all about Anglotor. And thereby, he directed the battle and Anglotor's defense.

"The red demon will not breach our doors, Master," said Kapte.

"No matter our opponents' mettle, if confidence could win this day, my love, victory would already be ours, thanks to you and your good sisters. But confidence will not see us through. Not this time."

"Power will," he continued.

"Perseverance.

"And sacrifice.

"This is not a contest of wills or petty ambitions. We fight here for the very life of Midgaard. If the invaders win. If they tear open the olden portal to the Nether Realms, all Midgaard will fall. The world of man will come crashing to an end. I've staved off that end since before the very mountains were born."

"All the more reason that you will not fail," said Kapte. "You've defended this keep a hundred times--"

"A thousand times, mayhap more," said Uriel. "I've long since lost count."

"Some invaders were surely worse than these?" said Kapte.

Uriel smiled at the girl. "How lucky I am to have you. How blessed. Alas, though I have stopped men of great power from entering here -- warlords and wizards both — in small numbers, and in armies vast, never before has a Red Demon of Fozramgar come calling at my door."

"That changes things," he said.

"It changes everything."

"You can defeat it," said Kapte. "I know that you can."

"Perhaps I can. Perhaps I will. And if the demon were the worst of what was out there, I'd be down in the main hall now, ready to sally forth with our troops and duel it to the bitter end. But there is a thing of the Nether Realms amongst them. A scion of Nifleheim. It has not acted yet, lurking in the rear, letting its minions lead the way. It probes with its pawns. Testing our strength--"

"You already destroyed two Nether Warriors, my master — even unprepared, and lightly armed."

"Not two of what's out there. The ones that took Mysinious from us were merely Einheriar. Great warriors, tis true, of that there is no doubt. But little more than men were they. What's out there now is something altogether different.

"Something beyond any mortal.

"Perhaps, beyond any immortal.

"I can feel its power even from here, even without my *Farsight*. I can feel its hunger. Its lust. It wears the facade of a man, but it is no man. It is an otherworldly thing of power beyond my ken, more *god* than man. Perhaps it be one of the fabled Lords of Nifleheim, if such things are real. But whatever label we place upon it matters little -- for it is a thing of great power. A thing that intends to wrench the gateway open. A thing that will destroy all and anything that dares bar its path."

"Have you ever faced such a creature before, my master?"

"...Never alone. But during the *Age of Heroes* we hunted such creatures, cleansed Midgaard of them."

"You and the great Arkons of legend? The ones from your stories?"

"Aye, my brothers and I. In those days of yore, I stood against the darkness alongside Thetan the Lightbringer and Mithron the Just — the greatest of us all."

"Greater than you, Master?" said Kapte, her brow furrowed. "I cannot believe that. You are the greatest warrior I have ever seen. Far greater than any other."

Uriel smiled and placed a gentle hand on Kapte's cheek. "I spoke not of martial prowess, my love, but of other qualities that make men great."

"But in battle–"

"I was the better fighter than either of them," said Uriel, "though both were great in their way – possessing skills far beyond the most renowned of mortal men. But so too did others of our brothers: Gabriel the Hornblower, Azrael the Wise, Hogar the Strong, Bose the Swift, and more. We were giants amongst men. We strode across Midgaard as princes. As kings. The monsters of the world -- the dark and evil things -- they fled before us, cowering in terror, begging for their lives."

"But those days are long past. And they are all gone now, those heroes. Nothing but distant memories, fading from my mind's eye the more as each year passes. In truth, I say with sorrow that...I barely remember their faces, it has been so long."

"Nonetheless, I've prepared for *this* day for years beyond imagining, and yet here I stand, woefully unprepared. These invaders have done the impossible. They've broken through it all, layer upon layer of defense. They've laid low the stalwart Monks of Ivaldi, who have long guarded the entry to Jutenheim's interior on my behalf. They've destroyed the brave Svart of Starkbarrow. They've bested the jungles of Jutenheim itself with all its myriad dangers. They passed both the Lugron hordes and the Ettin tribes. And they found their way to our home — Anglotor. They've passed the outer bulwarks, the moat, the main gates, the inner bailey. They've conquered our muscle and our magic, survived our traps and our diversions. They repel or withstand everything I throw at them."

"Everything. And now they stand poised to

breach the door to this very tower, to our central keep. Your confidence in me and in our remaining defenses is admirable, my beloved, but I fear, misplaced. At long last, it seems, I may have met my match in these invaders."

"Many of theirs are down," said Kapte. "Many are dead."

"Only the pawns. The leaders endure. Archwizards — no fewer than five or six."

"I have never see you doubt before, Master."

"I had no reason to. Not in your lifetime."

"Will we survive this?"

"We will try," said Uriel.

"But will we?"

"Only if I find a way to bring down the Red Demon and the Nifleheimer. If there is a way, I will find it."

6

VAEDEN
MOUNT CANTORWROUGHT

THE AGE OF MYTH AND LEGEND

THE LORD'S ARKON THETAN

"**I** will cut out Azathoth's black heart and free us all of his evil influence," said Thetan. "Once and for all."

"Madness," said Raphael. "The lord is too powerful. Surely we have no weapon that could harm him, little less kill him."

"I will find a way," said Thetan. "There is always a way."

"Is there no less drastic approach?" said Azrael.

"We cannot turn him from his ways," said Gabriel. "If we openly defy him, and refuse to back down, he will destroy us. We've all seen his wrath; been instruments of it. He'll mark us traitors. He'll never suffer that. He'll kill us all."

"And we have no means to contain him," said Uriel.

"Even if we did," said Gabriel, "could we hold him forever? Whatever prison we forged, he'd escape from eventually. Thetan's words be true. Death is the only way to stop him."

"Our deaths, more than likely," said Uriel, "if

we plow forward with this folly."

"The lightbringer is not the only one who has had these thoughts," said Gabriel. "If he was, there would be shouts of *traitor* amongst us even now. Weapons would be drawn, and we'd have it out. As I look around to each of you, no hint of that is happening here. That means that we are all of similar mind, though before tonight, we lacked the courage to voice these thoughts, even amongst each other, perhaps even to ourselves."

"Thoughts they are, no longer," said Azrael. "Now they have life of their own. They are plans. A conspiracy. Each of us, co-conspirators. More than that, traitors. We've crossed a line that cannot be uncrossed. You've placed a weighty mantle upon our backs, Lightbringer, and you too, Gabriel. A mantle that threatens to crush us all to pulp."

"We must do this thing," said Gabriel. "We are the only ones that can. If we fail to act, how many more children will die? Cities will burn? Nations will fall? We must do this."

"The people will not support this action," said Azrael. "They believe the lord's words with all their hearts. They are in his thrall and always will be, no matter what we do."

"We can show them the truth," said Gabriel. "There is ample evidence. We have—"

"The truth has hung before our eyes for untold centuries," said Thetan, "yet we denied it. Even now, here amongst ourselves, we struggle with the truth. We will never convince the people to side with us. It is futile to try."

"If we betray the lord," said Uriel, "whatever

the outcome, our names will go down in history as traitors. They will curse us, forevermore. Demons they will mark us. Devils. The spawn of the Nether Realms. The Arkons that fell from grace. The fallen Arkons they'll call us."

"That and worse they'll say of us," said Thetan. "We cannot, we must not, let that deter us. We are unimportant, save for what good we can do for the folk of Midgaard. That is our first duty. Let them curse us down through all the ages. I care not. I will do what is right no matter the consequences. We have debated this long enough. Who is with me?"

"I am," said Mithron.

"And I," said Gabriel.

"And I," said Uriel, "though the whole venture is madness and cannot hope to succeed."

"I cannot believe that it has come to this," said Azrael.

"As you say," said Arioch, "it must be done."

Azrael nodded. "It must be done."

All eyes turned to Raphael.

"Many will stand against us," said Raphael. "Many of our brothers. Bhaal will never join this mad endeavor; he follows every order the lord hands down without question. Mephistoles will oppose us, I have no doubt. So will Iblis. And Moloch. And many others."

"But will you?" said Mithron.

"I will join you," said Raphael. "For the same guilt, the same regrets that Thetan has spoke of, have long troubled my heart. I have suppressed those thoughts, those fears, that guilt, for long years. Now that they reach the open air, and others echo them, I can deny them no longer. I too am done. But Thetan, my friend, I fear that you may be the harbinger of our doom."

"I fear that I am," said Thetan.

7

DWARVEN KINGDOM OF DARENDOR
IN THE DALLASSIAN HILLS

YEAR 1267, 4TH AGE

BORNYTH TROLLSBANE

"**B**y Odin," bellowed Bornyth Trollsbane, the Dwarven High King of Clan Darendon, as his axe cleaved through a Draugar's head. Blood and gore splattered the Dwarf king, though he was already covered in it, helm to boot. The Draugar went limp before him, collapsed to the floor, and did not move again. Bornyth turned about, wide-eyed, breathing heavily, looking this way and that, the sweat pouring off him. "Odin," he shouted, shaking from the battle rage that still gripped him. The torn dead heaped around him; filled the small chamber. Fifty bodies, mayhap more. Bloodied. Broken. Some few twitching. But no more of the dead things threw themselves at him. Not one was still on its feet. "Odin," he bellowed once more, his arms held high in victory.

And then he waited at the ready, breathing deeply, slowly calming.

Was it over?

Had he survived it? Or was another wave

about to rush in?

A handful of his best soldiers had been with him. Men he knew for years. Men that he trusted. That he loved. He couldn't see them. Not a one. Buried beneath the bodies, mayhap were they, those good men. Or else fled? Who could blame them? Better that than dead, he supposed. And anything was better than becoming a Draugar.

Bornyth stood alone in the Seer Stone's room, now naught but a charnel house. A chamber of blood. Death. Horror.

At least he'd gotten that message off. Warned Lomion City of the Draugar threat. By Odin, the stinking Volsungs had better believe him. The Elves needed warning too, but he hadn't had time to try.

The Draugar -- the dead that walk, that hunger, had come for him with little warning. Into his land. His tunnels. Into the very heart of Darendor, the ancient Dwarven stronghold of the Dallassian Hills. How those monsters had gained entry, he knew not for certain, but surely it was via the deeps. The far underhalls. It had to be. Even the Dwarves didn't know how deep they ran, how far afield their tendrils stretched, or all that lurked within their Stygian depths. But Bornyth had delved deep a time or two, deeper than any Dwarf lord in long memory. To his long regret, he had chanced upon some of what lurked way down deep. Horrors held over from *The Dawn Age*. Things best left alone. Best not spoken of. Not even contemplated. Bornyth could well imagine the Draugar clawing their way up from down there, having escaped from some ancient binding gone sour with long years.

The Draugar had taken Thoonbarrow, the Svart's capital city, from the deeps, or so claimed the Svart. Nearly wiped out the Black Elves, though Bornyth would shed no tears over that.

Had they done the same to the Dwarves?

The halls of Darendor were quiet. No horns sounded. No arms clashed. No boots pounded the tunnel floor. Had those miserable creatures destroyed his kingdom in but a flash? Was he the last? Dead gods, was he the last? Bornyth pushed those thoughts from his mind. Foolish thoughts they were, for Darendor was large and strong. It had withstood countless incursions over the centuries. This time would be no different.

The horror of the last minutes flashed before Bornyth's eyes. The Draugar charging wild, berserkers gone mad. Tooth and nail. No mercy or reason. No pause or respite. And the croaking! His ears rang with it, that horrid inhuman sound. No words passed the Draugars' lips, only that foul batrachian cacophony.

In life, many of the Draugar had been Black Elves. Small and spindly, light as toddlers. Easy enough to kill for a man of Borynth's skill, despite their uncanny speed and preternatural resilience. Others had been Volsungs. Larger, stronger. Tougher to put down. Tougher still to keep down. Some few had been Dwarves. His own folk. They were the hardest to fight. His own people, for Odin's sake! Some, his own soldiers -- no doubt, killed and turned only minutes or hours afore. Some looked familiar, though he couldn't put names to them, and he was happy for that. His mind muddled. It had all happened so fast. He'd been speaking to Barusa, the Lomerian Chancellor, and some hawk-faced noblewoman, through the Seer Stone, and then he'd heard the croaking and howling. They came on like an avalanche, those creatures did. His guards tried to usher him out at the first sound of their approach, to withdraw to a more secure area, the Seer Stone chamber being in a deep Underhall near Darendor's outermost border -- amidst of vein of rare mineral deposits that the Svart seer avowed would best serve her esoteric magics. He'd only lingered a few moments after the wardens raised the alarm. Just a few moments had he held his guards at bay.

But that was too long. That delay had gotten all his men killed.

A horde of the undead things barreled down the passageway and stormed into the Seer Stone's chamber before they'd even had a chance to close, little less bar, the door -- not that it would have held, the old, broken-down thing. If he had left at once, they would have met the Draugar in the passageway. Mayhap they could have fled to a defensible position. At worst, they would have battled them in the passage. His men would have formed lines, shoulder to shoulder, stout rock protecting both flanks. They'd have held that line, however thin it was, he was certain of it. They'd still be alive. Some of them at least. Their courage and sacrifice would have bought him time to get clear.

But would he have withdrawn?

Or stood the line with his men, come what

may? Against men, he knew he would have stayed. To the end. Even if it meant his death. But against the Draugar? He did not know. Or would not admit the truth even to himself. But no matter, for that test came not to pass. Trapped in the Seer Stone's chamber, he'd fought to the end with every ounce of his strength. And he'd prevailed. For the moment at least.

Bornyth heard a rustling from behind him, from the back corner of the room where few bodies lay. A whimpering.

Nothing lived there that he could see. Nothing moved, but the sound persisted. Not one of his men, for the voice was strange in pitch.

"Show yourself," spat Bornyth.

8

JUTENHEIM

YEAR 1267, 4TH AGE

SERGEANT PUTNAM

Sergeant Putnam and the remaining Pointmen trudged through the forest as quietly as they could manage. Over the last tenday, after escaping the deadly subterranean depths of Svartleheim, they'd successfully avoided conflicts, except for a brief run-in with a fierce horned beast twice the size of a bull, and a couple of close encounters with a pride of lions. By the luck of the Vanyar, they'd escaped each of those encounters unscathed.

There were only fourteen Pointmen left, even if you counted Lieutenant Bradik and old Ma-Grak Stowron. The Pointmen weren't quick to adopt, but them two fellows earned the men's respect. Great fighters both.

Ma-Grak kept to himself and didn't cause any fuss. The lieutenant, who hailed from Fourth Squadron, was smart, tough, practical, and liked by all - which was good, because he'd assumed command. The lieutenant taking over caused a bit of grumbling because Fourth Squadron were heavy foot, not Pointmen, but he was the ranking Sithian, so he got the duty. Nonetheless, when it came down to it, most of the boys looked to old Putnam to call the shots. The lieutenant didn't mind that much, because he knew how close the Pointmen were, and that they didn't mean him any disrespect.

Putnam figured, if they ever got back to the company, Ezerhauten would probably promote him. Lieutenant Putnam that would make him, and Ezer might even gift him command of the Pointmen. Putnam wasn't certain he wanted that; he liked being a working man, not an officer, but somebody had to do it, so he'd step up if asked. He also didn't care much for getting promoted only because he didn't get killed. That didn't seem the right way to go about it. But that's the way armies worked. He'd adapt. He always did.

The rest of the Pointmen what were left, were some of the Sithian's best. Four knights were still standing: Royce, Carroll, Lex, and Ward, bruisers and swordmasters all. Sergeant Grainer of Second Squadron and Trooper Maddix were still kicking. So were five of the Lugron: Torak, Wikkle, Borrel, Stanik, and Moag -- the Pointmen's Master Scout.

What Putnam couldn't get out of his head were the men that weren't with them anymore — the ones what got dead. There were a lot of them. Good friends. Old friends. Great soldiers. To Putnam, one of the biggest losses was Par Sevare Zendrak. He'd been the Pointmen's squad wizard — one of only a few in the entire company. And he was a real one, tried-and-true, no shifty-eyed card trickster or sleight-of-hand man was he. He was the real deal: a war wizard, trained up in the Tower of the Arcane. But he was a strange fellow.

Wasn't easy to like him or get to know him, but he was loyal and brave to the end.

Putnam would be dead, all the Pointmen would be dead, if it weren't for Sevare. Saved them all atop the great stair that led down to Svartleheim. Trapped between an army of Ettin and the Black Elf hordes of Svartleheim, only Sevare's magic and his heroic sacrifice had saved them.

Putnam had a hard time getting past the wizard's death. He felt a guilt over it — as if he should've found a way for the men to escape that slop without Sevare having to die. Felt he failed him in some way. Failed them all. They'd gone through hell in those tunnels — one of the worst slogs the company had endured in memory. To die at the exit, well, that was irony for you. Just not fair. But such was a soldier's life.

Worse than that, worse than anything for Putnam, was losing his Captain.

His leader.

His best friend.

Frem Sorlons.

Frem was the toughest darned fighter that he'd ever seen, except for maybe the commander himself.

Senseless death that crept out of nowhere was always the hardest to take, at least for Putnam. They won the battle. Sevare had saved their butts. And they were on their way out of the caverns. And then, of a sudden, four Ettin vaulted through the doorway. The first of them crashed right into Frem. Big as Frem was, and he was darned big, that Ettin outweighed him twice over, maybe more. When it barreled into him, running full out, Frem got knocked right off that landing. Right off.

He never had a chance. No man would've. Fell straight down into the black. Didn't scream, or cry out, or nothing. He went silent into Old Death's arms.

They couldn't even recover his body.

Mayhap he dropped all the way to the stair's base, which must've been four or five hundred feet. Most folks would figure that a gruesome end, but strange as it sounds, Putnam hoped he went to the bottom, because even though that would've given Frem a few seconds to think on what was coming and worry about it, maybe he could've made his peace in that time, and then when he hit, death would've tooken him all instant like, so he wouldn't have suffered. That's what Putnam hoped for, anyway. For his friend.

The men loved Frem. Heck, they followed him into hell already, and would do it again and not even gripe about it. So the Pointmen took apart those four Ettin. Didn't show them a lick of mercy. Not much left when they were done. Except for pieces.

By the time it was over, the main Ettin troop was fully engaged with the Black Elves. That battle raged far below; the whole stair shook and shuddered. Spells were flying – the Diresvarts were at it, so were the rock creatures they commanded, and who knows what else. The fighting was loud and furious.

Mayhap they're still fighting for all Putnam knew or cared.

The Pointmen got their butts out of there. And

they'd not go back. Not even to recover Frem's body. Not for nothing.

That was the worst of it — not being able to bury their friend and pay him the proper respects. But Putnam figured, nobody could say that Frem didn't die in battle -- after all, it was an Ettin what knocked him off the edge. A warrior's death it was, by any fair measure. Putnam would knock the lights out of any man what said otherwise. If the Valkyries dared venture down into stinking Svartleheim, they'd scoop up old Frem – Putnam was certain of it, or so he kept telling himself. They'd carry him up Valhalla way to drink with the honored dead -- the fallen heroes of ages past and of all their yesterdays. Frem deserved to be there amongst that lot. Deserved it as much as anybody did.

Putnam recorded all of it in the company annals. He scribbled in a leatherbound book for no less than a half hour every night, writing down everything that happened to the company. Some nights, he spent two hours on it before sleep took him. Every sight and sound of Svartleheim went down in that book. From the traitorous monks of Ivaldi, to the King of Svartleheim himself, to the wonders of the Black Elf city, and the horrors of their endless tunnels. He set it to paper, good and proper, just as he'd done throughout the entire mission, ever since they set out from Lomion City months prior. He'd started up a new volume when they left Lomion, and was already nearly through with the book — only a few blank pages left. If they ever got home again, that volume would take its place in the bookcase in their Chapterhouse where they kept all the annals going back to the founding of the Sithian Company.

Collectively, those annals served as a history, to record the deeds, great and small, that the members of the company had done — to remember those deeds, and the men that did them – for them, for their comrades, and for those company men what followed in years to come. Putnam was one of the few active members that had read most of the books, but even he hadn't got through all of them. Only Ezerhauten knew all the stories. Knew them by heart.

But that latest volume, likely as not, would be thought a work of fiction by future company men. There was too much in it that was fantastical, unbelievable. Too many things they'd encountered that were more myth and legend than reality. After all they'd weathered, their future brethren would think their volume no more than a bedtime tale to scare the new recruits. A bit of fancy that old Sergeant Putnam conjured up to push past the boredom of a soldier's life.

But maybe some few would believe it. Maybe they'd learn something from it. Maybe they'd remember the name of Captain Frem Sorlons, and that of Par Sevare Zendrack - and mark them as the heroes that they were. Maybe someone would even remember old Sergeant Putnam and what deeds he did in the shadow of greater men.

9

VAEDEN
MOUNT CANTORWROUGHT

THE AGE OF MYTH AND LEGEND

THE LORD'S ARKON THETAN

The Arkons sat quietly for a time, their eyes downcast, staring into the fire or at nothing at all. Thetan's feelings were confused; his thoughts, jumbled. He did not know if he had done the right thing. All he knew, just as Azrael cautioned, was that he could not take back his words. Not ever.

They could not be unsaid.

He felt free. For the first time in ages, the shackles of duty slackened. He might soon be his own man again. He was already that, in a way. But as Raphael had said, that decision was likely the death of him. And not only him, but those he called his brothers. And that is what they were. Not by blood. But by bonds stronger still: the countless years of serving together; of serving their lord; fighting side-by-side, protecting the people; carrying out the lord's will. After endless years of that, there was no stronger bond between men.

And Thetan's ideas now set his brothers on his reckless path. A path that surely led to red death and ruin, no matter what the final outcome. He

54

had condemned his brothers to suffer. To share in his fate. Likely condemned them all to death. At minimum, he'd made traitors of them all. Oathbreakers. Conspirators.

But what was he to do? Tell them now that it was all a mistake. That he'd been out of his head. That they must not move forward with their plans?

To save them, could he do that?

Did it make any sense?

He knew it did not.

The words could not be unsaid.

The plans could not be unmade. Not only had he brought that terrible decision upon his brothers, but he put himself, and the others, under the power of each one of them. In a way, he was more shackled than ever. If even one of the conspirators spoke out of turn, or turned them in to Azathoth, they'd all be rounded up and punished.

Azathoth was a vengeful god. Thetan dared not contemplate what the lord would do to him and his brothers should he survive their plans. A terrible risk it was. But a risk that he had to take. If he had not said his words aloud, not said them to the others, he might never have acted. He'd postponed taking action for all too long already. Only by great risk can a man accomplish great things. The problem was, would Midgaard be better off without Azathoth, or with him? For all the lord's flaws that Thetan could no longer overlook, he was a force for stability and order, and had established and spread the rule of law — all to the betterment of mankind.

But still, it had to be better without him. It had

to.

Or so he told himself.

The night was not overdark; one moon at half, the other at crescent. But it was clear. It had been so all day.

From the corner of Thetan's eye, he caught a fleeting flash of light. He looked up.

"Star fall," said Thetan. "A shower."

"A light show to mark our folly," said Raphael.

And so it was. A group of objects, blazing white hot, descended from the heavens toward Midgaard. Thetan and the Arkons had seen such things before. Star falls were not common, but neither were they terribly rare. Always a wonder to watch.

But this time, it was different.

"They look as if they're heading towards us," said Uriel.

"In the vastness of the heavens one cannot skillfully judge distance or direction," said Azrael. "An illusion of the eyes, it is. Star falls often appear to approach the observer, but then fall far in the distance, if even they fall to Midgaard at all. I have chased those things more than once, overcome with scientific curiosity, but I've never found the spot where they fell."

"This is different," said Gabriel. "They *are* heading towards us. See the flames about them? They boast no tail behind them. There is always a tail when the stars fall. We see no tails, because they are heading towards us."

"If that is true," said Mithron, "then let us have a bit of adventure to free our minds of weightier deeds. Let us watch where the stars fall and follow them. And then we'll see what there is to see."

"Mayhap it's a sign," said Azrael.

"A sign from who?" said Uriel. "From the lord? I don't think so."

"Perhaps it is," said Arioch. "The lord has eyes everywhere. Ears everywhere. Perhaps he knows our minds, our plans. Perhaps this is his way of letting us know that he knows."

"Worse than that," said Raphael, "perhaps he means to destroy us with those things. For I say to you they are not only headed in our direction, they are heading directly for us. Does he mean to smite us? Has he overheard everything? Has he already sentenced us to die?"

"The lord is rarely so subtle," said Azrael.

"Star falls are rocks that fall from the sky," said Thetan. "Nothing more. Nothing less. If they head towards us, it is no more than random chance."

"On tonight of all nights?" said Uriel. "I've never believed in coincidence. I doubt I'll start now."

"A fascinating debate my brothers," said Arioch, "but perhaps we should consider moving our tails from here so that those rocks don't drop on our heads."

"They will not hit us," said Thetan.

"How do you know that?" said Azrael.

"I just know," said Thetan.

The men watched as the star fall shower grew closer. They did appear to be headed directly for the summit of Mount Canterwrought, the narrow speck of land upon which they camped.

Mithron jumped to his feet, Thetan and Gabriel half a heartbeat behind him. "Move," said Mithron as it became clear that the stars were indeed falling atop them. "Scatter!"

And with a terrible crash, a bit of the heavens exploded into the earth only inches from Thetan's feet. The star hit the ground with a mighty crack. Dirt and stone flew in all directions. Thetan was thrown from his feet. So were the men closest to him. A moment later, another chunk of the sky slammed into the ground near Mithron. Then one hit close to Gabriel. And then to each of the others in turn, always just at their feet. And then several more fell into the campfire.

And exploded.

10

JUTENHEIM ANGLOTOR

YEAR 1267, 4TH AGE

JUDE EOTRUS

Jude Eotrus ducked his head lower when another explosion went off nearby, his face already cut, bruised, and bloody from its predecessors. Even hunkered down behind stone rubble, the flying gravel slashed and pelted him without mercy. The dust plume the last blast kicked up still hung so thick he could barely breathe, little less see. Teek Lugron was crouched close beside him, a powerful hand on the center of his upper back. Where Brother Donnelin was, Jude couldn't guess – they'd gotten split up in the chaos of battle.

Only minutes before, the jagged, broken three foot high piece of stone behind which Jude crouched had been a thirty foot tall pillar that supported a majestic archway not far past Anglotor's main gate.

Now it was a pile of rocks.

Nonetheless, Jude was thankful for the cover it provided. Death lurked on all sides. He wanted to be out of the line of fire, and for the moment, that pile of rocks was his best option. Before the assault, Ezerhauten had secured Ginalli's permission to unbind his hands, arguing that he might need to defend himself in the battle. They didn't want him dead after all. At least not until they bled him dry atop the unholy altar that they quested for. Or so was Jude's fear.

Problem was, they didn't give him a weapon. And not much armor.

More blasts went off on this side and that, the very ground rocking beneath him. Jude lifted his shirt over nose and mouth to keep the dust at bay.

Nearly all the fighting was out in front now, so he turned, put his back against the pillar, and looked back whence they came, Teek still beside him. The main gate was a twisted mess of ruined iron. The whole of the gatehouse, a crumbling wreck of charred and smoking stone.

Bodies lay everywhere. Broken, bloody, some hacked to pieces. The stench of the battlefield hung heavy in the air.

Leaguers were amongst the fallen, but most were Anglotor's defenders. Brave men were they, those guardsmen. Skilled at arms, impressively so. But against the sorcery of The League of Shadows, they could not stand.

Ezerhauten stationed a squad of his men behind the gatehouse to safeguard the line of retreat should such be needed, and to hold off any more hostile locals that might happen by. It was obvious enough that the Leaguers hadn't expected the level of resistance they encountered, though they were prepared for it.

In fact, it seemed that the League was prepared for anything.

The power that they wielded was unlike

anything Jude had seen before. Unlike anything he had even heard of — outside of song or story.

The keep's wall had been defended by at least a hundred trained fighters of varied race: Volsung, Dwarf, Lugron, and even Svart. While the wizards and Mort Zag tore apart the steel gate, out of the western woods marched a troop of Elves, perhaps two hundred strong -- bows, swords, and spears. With them, more than one wizard.

What a battle that was. It raged for nearly an hour before the Elves were fully overcome. Throughout the skirmish, Jude hoped for a chance to run, but the Leaguers kept him near the center of the expedition. Though the battle grew chaotic at one point and the battle lines blurred, the right opportunity to hightail it never presented.

Then came the Ettins. Jude had hoped he'd seen the last of them on the Plains of Engelroth. But another company of them came on, wild and crazed with bloodlust. No doubt, they'd discovered the fate of their fellows back on the plain, and lusted for revenge.

Nonetheless, it was clear enough to Jude that neither of those troops of locals came upon them at random. The master or masters of Anglotor had called on their aid, and on they came. How and why those diverse groups answered to Anglotor's Master, Jude could not hope to say.

Jude heard a commotion from off to his right. Immediately, Teek sprang to his feet, pulling Jude up by the arm. "Get up, Judy boy," said Teek, "here they come."

Teek placed a large knife in Jude's hand, a thing nearly as long as a short sword, and then turned towards the commotion. A squadron of men poured out of a hidden portal that had opened in one of the keep's towers. More sounds came now from Jude's left. A quick glance in that direction showed Jude a scene that mirrored the first.

Anglotor's defenders had sallied forth behind the League's lines.

They rushed headlong at the Leaguers, sword, axe, and mace.

Jude wanted to shout that he wasn't with the League, that he was their prisoner. But there was no time or opportunity for such parley. The scene was chaos.

Battle always was.

The defenders rushed toward him and Teek with the same anger, with the same intent to kill, as they rushed at any of them. And who could blame them? The League had invaded their home, and killed their folk on sight. They were just defending themselves. The same as anyone else would. And now Jude had to fight them. Had to fight them in order to survive.

Jude hated that.

Hated it.

11

VAEDEN
MOUNT CANTORWROUGHT

THE AGE OF MYTH AND LEGEND

THE LORD'S ARKON THETAN

Thetan opened his eyes, coughed, and sucked in a lungful of air. He instantly regretted it for the dust hung heavy; his breath drew it in. He coughed and gagged. Blinked his eyes. Tried to see. The dust was like a dense fog.

Then came coughing from this side and that. His brothers. Some of them had survived the star fall. His head was spinning. He saw the campfire's glow; not much more left than scattered embers. He pulled a water flask from his pouch, pressed it to his lips, coughing and gagging. Cleared his throat as best he could. Wrapped his scarf over his mouth and nose. Somehow his helmet was still at his side. He scooped it up, flicked it to dislodge the bulk of the dust, and dropped the visor down to keep dust from his eyes.

His limbs worked. More importantly, they were all there. Nothing seemed broken. He wasn't even bleeding, as far as he could tell. That seemed too lucky to be luck alone. It didn't make sense. He'd been pounded and pelted with rocks aplenty. Fire sprayed everywhere. His legs were half buried in dust. The star fall had impacted the ground only inches from his feet. Yet his boots were intact. He wiggled his toes, they wiggled back. Seemed to be there. They shouldn't be. He should have been in pieces. He knew it. It didn't make any sense. Something preternatural was at work. He had been wrong; that star fall was no random chance; nothing could convince him of that any longer. The heavens just happened to land at his feet after the treachery they had just planned? It was impossible.

Azathoth was behind it.

He had to be. Who else could it be? But if so, why wasn't he dead? Why weren't they all dead?

And then he realized, perhaps he was dead.

A ghost.

A phantom.

A shade of his former self.

He pulled himself to his feet. Forced his eyes downward. Peered through the dust as best he could. He would not have been surprised, not in the least, to see his broken body lying on the ground at his feet. He hovering above. Nothing but a soul, a spirit, a ghost — call it what you will.

But that's not what happened. Not what he saw. He saw no broken body. No blood.

He was alive.

Azathoth had spared him. Was this a warning? Was the lord giving them another chance? A merciful reprieve? If so, what did that mean? And what must he do now? How could he betray the lord, after the lord had shown them mercy; spared his life? And did that mean that he was wrong about the lord all long? That Azathoth was not evil? Not insane?

Or perhaps the lord had forgiven him, so that he could continue to use him as an instrument of his will. As an instrument of his evil. And so the mercy he showed them, was not mercy at all, but self-serving scheming. Something to further his evil aims. All these things rushed through Thetan's mind in but a flash of seconds. What the truth was, it didn't much matter. He was undone. They all were undone.

What would happen to him now? What would happen to all of them? Even at the summit of the sacred old mountain, he wasn't safe from the prying eyes of Azathoth, from that indomitable will, from his fearsome powers.

Then a tall figure appeared before him. Massive. Taller and broader than he, and he was amongst the tallest and broadest of men. Mithron. It could be no other.

"Are you hurt?" said Mithron.

"I should be, but I'm not," said Thetan. "You?"

"I have no injuries," said Mithron even as he coughed up and spat out a wad of dust and phlegm.

The breeze came over the mountain as it was wont to do. It cleared much of the dust. All seven men were still there. Not a one was injured, save for superficial scrapes and bruises. Eight fires burned atop that summit. Seven tiny, one larger.

Thetan looked down. One step from him was a hole in the ground. One foot in diameter. One foot deep. No more. No less. And at the bottom of that hole, pulsing white hot, glowing, wisps of flame trailing off of it, was a strangely shaped artifact. Of what it was made, Thetan could not say for it looked of metal, yet also of stone, but had a texture reminiscent of wood. Its shape was baffling. The hole it created was round, cylindrical. Just what one might expect from a thing that blazed through the sky. But the artifact was not rounded at all. It had the shape of a cross, bent, angled, and twisted a bit about itself. Whether that was its natural shape, or damage born of its travels, or its fall, Thetan could not hope to say. Yet there it was. And what it was, he had no idea.

Each of the seven Arkons had himself an artifact to match, fallen and flaming at their feet. Each one was different from the other. In shape. In size. In features. In texture. Yet all were of the same ilk. All different, yet all the same — just as were the Arkons themselves. And at the center of the summit, where their campfire had been, there was a larger hole, and within that hole sat six more of those strange relics. A total of thirteen altogether.

"What can this mean?" said Raphael.

"We are undone," said Thetan. "The lord has seen all. Heard all. Why he has spared us, I cannot yet say."

"I do not feel the hand of the lord in this," said Mithron.

"What does that mean?" said Uriel. "How can you know that? Even now he likely looks down upon us. But is it to seal our fate or to give us a second chance?"

"A second chance, we appear to already have," said Azrael.

"Mithron knows the lord's mind better than

any of us," said Gabriel. "If he says these things are not of the lord, then unless the lord reveals himself to us, I will believe Mithron is right."

"Then what can this mean?" said Thetan. "This is no random act. Someone, something sent these things down amongst us. Put them at our feet. Gifted them to us for some reason. Clearly, not to harm us. Anyone, anything that could do this, could just as easily have slain us all, here where we stood. So we know that whoever or whatever is behind this does not seek us harm. But what do they want from us? And who are they?"

And then a sibilant voice reached their ears. It came from here and from there and from all about and from nowhere. All at once.

12

DARENDOR

YEAR 1267, 4TH AGE

BORNYTH TROLLSBANE

"**W**ho's there?" shouted Bornyth.

A moment later, several feet from him, a cloak appeared from nowhere and spun about with a flourish. From behind it appeared the Svart Seer, cowering in the corner of the room. Bornyth didn't remember her name. She was tall for her kind, tiny of waist, long of limb, and gray of pallor, her neck twice as long as it should be, though that too was normal for the Black Elves. She'd been hidden by magic of an exceedingly rare sort. Invisibility magic. A wonder that Bornyth had heard tales of but not seen before, not in all his two hundred and fifty years. She appeared to be unharmed, the rickety thing, though speckled with blood and breathing faster than a spent horse. Scared out of her mind, no doubt, though you couldn't tell it by her face -- which held no expression to speak of. The Svart weren't capable of it, or so it seemed. Maybe they didn't feel emotions as proper folk do, or else, mayhap, their facial muscles just didn't work. Then Bornyth noticed the Orator, the Svart king's spokesman and translator. He was on his back, unmoving, beside the Seer.

"Dead, is he?" said Bornyth.

The Seer nodded. At least she understood the common tongue. She had a dagger in her hand. She knew what needed to be done. The Orator had been bitten. That's how the sickness passed. If left alone, he would turn in a matter of hours, mayhap, only minutes. He'd rise up as a Draugar. So would Bornyth's men. All of them.

"I will do it," said Bornyth.

The girl shook her head. She turned the Orator's head to the side, shuddering and shaking all the while. She looked up at Bornyth; he thought she'd lost her nerve, not that he'd blame her a bit, for it was a difficult thing to sink a blade into a man. How much the harder when it was a friend of years. But the girl hadn't lost her nerve. She plunged her dagger through the Orator's temple. Sunk it halfway to the hilt. She had some strength to her and some good sense. Hopefully, that made her more than baggage. Might be a tough slog to get back behind the battle lines. Any help she could provide would be a welcome boon. Bornyth wanted to do the same to all the Dwarven fallen, not only to keep them from rising again as Draugar but to spare them of the indignity of it, the horror. But he couldn't even do that for them, for there were no Dwarven bodies to be seen. All those visible were Draugar. Bornyth's men were buried underneath. He had neither the time nor the energy to spare to dig them out. That made Bornyth all the angrier.

The Svart girl stood. She held a bulging sack

that no doubt contained the Seer Stone.

"You bit, girl?" Bornyth said.

She shook her head. All she could do, for she spoke not a word of Lomerian as far as Bornyth knew, though she seemed to understand the language well enough.

"Did they claw you? Any scratches? Any at all? And don't try to bamboozle me, for I would know."

She quickly checked herself and shook her head.

Borynth felt no injuries save exhaustion, but he knew full well he might have a dozen lacerations about his body. No time to check. Trust to his armor and to fate, for the moment at least. Thank Odin for the armor. If not for it, the Draugar would've clawed him to the bone. Pulled him down despite all his skill and resolve. Jarn Yarspitter, his chief counselor and closest friend, had convinced him to wear the armor, and he had -- nearly every waking moment since the Svart had slithered up to his doorstep spouting dire warnings about the dead that walk. Bornyth was stubborn about the armor at first, arguing against it. Stubbornness was a Dwarf trait. Something in the blood, Bornyth figured. He knew he was afflicted with a stronger case of it than most, though milder than some. *The borders of Darendor cannot be passed without warning*, he had shouted to his counselors. But after endless haranguing, Yarspitter convinced him to wear it. *You'll not want to waste time putting it on if we're assaulted*, argued Jarn. *You'll want all your energies focused on tactics, not on getting dressed*. That was the point that had won him over. And giving in had saved his life.

For the moment at least.

"We've got to get gone from here, lass, before more of them nasties come calling. We won't be lucky enough that this was all of them. They're probably crawling all through the deep tunnels, swarming like ants or rats, the stinking vermin. We need us a stout door and stouter Dwarves to man it. Stay close behind me, but not too close. I need room to swing me axe."

She nodded.

He hoped that she understood. Old Guyphoon Garumptuss tet Montu, the venerable king of accursed Thoonbarrow himself, had left her in his charge. Bornyth was responsible for her, like it as not; so demanded his honor. Borynth knew at once upon hearing of the Black Elf king's approach that it meant nothing but bad luck for his kingdom. He wished he'd been wrong.

Bornyth stepped carefully toward the chamber's exit. Only a dozen feet away was it, yet a stressful and slow trek. The chamber's floor was nowhere in sight, buried beneath the torn dead. So each step he took was atop bodies heaped atop bodies. Blood, guts, entrails, and the nauseating stench that went with it all. Bornyth was immune to that while in his battle rage, but now it hit him. He breathed through his mouth to keep from retching. The Svart girl seemed unaffected. How that could be he didn't understand. Maybe the stinking Svart had no sense of smell. Who knew?

Bornyth moved slowly, prodding the bodies before and beside him as he went. He fully expected one at least to come alive again and lunge at him, teeth gnashing, claws raking. But they all lay still. He and his had done their work well. Sever the spine or the head — that's what keeps them down. That and fire — plenty of it. Consume the flesh — burn them to ash. Those are the only ways to keep a Draugar down. And even then, sometimes they'd still come after you, some spark of evil still in them. Or so the stories said.

Two steps from the exit, Bornyth heard a sound from the passageway beyond.

Something moved.

Something approached. It was close.

Bornyth planted his feet as best he could and raised his axe high.

A hand appeared and gripped the door frame from beyond the chamber's exit. A Dwarven hand by the look, though battered and bloody. Then the Dwarf stepped into view, obviously wounded. Yarspitter! It was Yarspitter! He'd been at Bornyth's side when the battle began. He'd thought him dead, buried beneath the corpses.

When Bornyth looked at Yarspitter's eyes, his stomach churned. His throat tightened. Yarspitter's eyes were black, no whites at all. His jaw hung slack, tongue lolling about. He was Jarn Yarspitter no longer. Now he was Draugar, the walking dead.

Bornyth's face scrunched up in anguish. That man was like a brother to him. He had thought him dead, but had shoved those thoughts away. Struck them from his mind and tucked them away until such time as it was safe to think of them. That was the warrior's way — what one had to do to cope. To survive. But now, with the thing that

Yarspitter had become standing before him, slavering, Bornyth could not but face the truth. His throat constricted in pain so much so that he could barely breathe. He wanted to turn away. To run. To tear that terrible image from his mind's eye. But he could do none of that. None of it. And he dare not attempt to slip past that creature. And even if he did, it might catch the Svart girl in its claws. He'd not abandon her to that fate, Black Elf or not. He'd see her to safety or die in the trying. Honor demanded no less.

Bornyth roared as his axe thundered down. Down to take the head of his oldest friend.

But the cut made no purchase, for the dead thing sprang back with shocking speed. The steel barely nicked its chest. And then, just as fast, it leaped at Bornyth's throat. The Dwarf king had no time to bring up his axe. It grabbed him by the shreds of his tunic. Its head led the way, jaws snapping: click, click, click.

Bornyth stepped back. Lost his footing atop the heaped corpses. He went down, the dead thing atop him, scrambling for purchase.

Bornyth twisted.

Dodged.

Barely avoided its teeth.

Bornyth planted his hand against the Draugar's throat. Wrapped his fingers around it. Held it fast, squeezing with all his considerable might, his toned muscles bulging with the effort. With his other hand, he batted away the creature's manic strikes. Strikes that pounded down on him, again and again.

All Bornyth's will was bent on holding its

throat. On keeping those jaws at bay. Thank the gods, Yarspitter still wore his greaves, so Bornyth was spared of any cuts by claws, if even, the thing had grown any of yet.

Yarspitter's arms were longer than Bornyth's. He could not strangle him with both hands without giving Yarspitter free rein to bash his face to bits. And then Bornyth realized, his attack was futile. The Draugar didn't breath. He could squeeze Yarspitter's throat closed and hold it there until the Valkyries bored of the battle, and yet it would profit him nothing. He had to throw the thing off, but he had no leverage, the bodies yielding beneath him. Already, he was halfway sunk beneath them. He couldn't roll. Couldn't get up. Couldn't throw Yarspitter off.

He had to call up the berserker rage. A power he'd long mastered to his advantage.

And then a dagger crashed down onto Yarspitter's forehead. Sank to the hilt.

No blood spouted from that terrible wound.

The Draugar went limp atop him.

Bornyth took a single deep breath, pushed Yarspitter off, and scrambled to his feet.

"Goodbye, old friend," he said.

The Svart girl bent down and retrieved her dagger.

"Useful girl, you prove to be," said Bornyth. "I thank you. If we survive this, you will be well rewarded. Well rewarded, indeed. Now, let us get gone before luck leaves us."

13

JUTENHEIM

YEAR 1267, 4TH AGE

FREM SORLONS

"**D**addy, aren't you forgetting something? Daddy!"

Frem opened his eyes but they were dry; everything, a blur. He felt half-asleep. In a daze. He sat up, turned toward the voice. Coriana's beautiful little face smiled at him the way she did. And he smiled back, just as he always did. No matter his mood, one look at her face brought him joy.

"Daddy, it's important that you remember. You have to remember. Try hard, please."

"Remember what, my love? I'm trying to sleep. Why did you wake me?"

"Think hard, Daddy. Think hard and remember. It's important. There's not much time left. I love you, Daddy, and I want you to stay with me, but it's time to get up now. Sleep time is over. You have to get up."

Her little hand touched his face and Captain Frem Sorlons jolted into consciousness. He couldn't see anything. Pitch black.

Was he blind?

Dead?

Or just in the dark?

His head throbbed. He took a deep breath; it hurt, but not that much — no broken ribs. Or else, he was so broken that he couldn't feel much anymore.

He wiggled his fingers and touched one hand to the other. Arms and hands still attached and in working order. Same for his legs.

That was good. Darned good.

He was groggy, could barely move, didn't dare stand up. His throat was parched; his mouth, dry; tongue, stiff. His eyes, crusty but intact; no blood dripped from them as best he could tell. There was a big lump on the back of his head. He'd been clobbered by something.

He lay on an uneven stone slab. Heard an echo after any movement he made, and felt the air stir. That told him that he was in a large space.

There was a faint smell of death. And blood - not just his. He couldn't tell from where it came.

And he had a bad feeling. A very very bad feeling that he was still in Svartleheim.

In Svartleheim, alone and with no light.

Dammit all, he'd rather be dead than that. The stinking choking tunnels that closed in on him from all sides. The creepy crawlies. The monsters. The walls, so close that he couldn't breathe. He didn't want to go through that again. Not ever again. Not if he lived to be a thousand years old, he'd never want to set foot in a cave or a narrow tunnel ever again. By the gods, he prayed that he wasn't stuck in that place. That hell.

Last thing he remembered, he stood on the

landing at the very top of the great stair that led from a surface cave down to the depths of Svartleheim — to the heart of the Black Elf city. Sevare had just died saving all their butts.

He remembered telling the men that it was time to get out of there, and how they all turned to leave, the coast clear.

But that's it. He didn't remember anything else. The blow to the head, whatever it was, had taken some of his memories. Mayhap a lot of them.

Had he lost a minute of time?

An hour?

A day?

A year? Who knew? And who turned out the lights?

Frem lifted his hands above his head, felt around. Nothing. No ceiling close above, just as he'd suspected. That was good. He felt to the sides, moving as silently as he could, trying not to dislodge any rocks, not to make any noise. Who knew what lurked about? If he was in Svartleheim, the Elfs could be near, and those buggers could see in the dark, which put Frem at a great disadvantage.

He found the edge of a drop-off. How far down it went, whether two feet or a mile, he had no idea. He'd figure it out eventually, dropping stones over the edge if he had to, but for the moment, he didn't want to make any noise, didn't want to give away his position. Better to size things up first as best he could.

His pack was still on his back. That was a great relief — it meant water, food, tools, gear, and light

— blessed light. All stuff he'd need to stay alive.

The place was mostly silent, but not entirely so. Time and again, he heard distant thumping. And sounds that could have been people moving about, but far in the distance.

He didn't move for several minutes during which he heard nothing close by. His sword was gone. His shield too. He still had daggers at waist and boot. Slim pickings in his pack as far as food and drink, but that was just as he'd left it when they fled from Svartleheim.

He was still there. He had to be. His worst fear come to pass. Probably something hit him on the way out, knocked him cold. But what happened to his men? Why would they leave him behind? Were they all dead? Or forced to flee?

His canteen held a few mouthfuls of water. His pack had two meals worth of beef jerky plus some odd-looking mushrooms that they'd picked up in the Svart city. As for gear: a bit of rope; flint and tinder; his cutlery; his medical pouch, somewhat depleted; a lodestone; a small flask of brandy, nearly half full; small tools; blanket and clothes wrapped in a waterproof sack; three torches (two more attached to the outside of the pack along with empty canteens) and the miscellaneous warrior wares and survival gear he always carried.

Unless there was a way out nearby, he needed to find water, and soon. But for that he needed light. Had to take a chance on lighting a torch.

But not right away. He waited. Listened. A half hour, mayhap more. In all that time, as best he could tell, nothing and no one was anywhere close-by, unless whoever or whatever it might be, lurked even more silently than he. He couldn't worry about that. Not any longer. He had to get his bearings. Get moving. And find a way out.

Or else, that place would be his tomb. He couldn't let that happen; he had to make it home for Coriana – she was counting on him. He wouldn't let her down. Not ever.

It took him but a few moments to get the torch lit. He was on a rocky outcropping about ten feet deep and half again that long. A decent-sized tunnel led into the rock face, thank the gods. That meant, at minimum, he wasn't trapped on that ledge, even if there were no other way off. He might die in Svartleheim, but he wouldn't die stuck on that stinking ledge. That was good.

About fifteen feet away was the great stair. It may as well have been a mile. There was no way to get over to it. Nothing to catch a rope on, and no way to jump that far.

The top of the stair was about ten feet above him, so that was how far he'd fallen. That made sense given his minimal injuries. He could only see the stair from the very edge of the outcropping. That's where he must've hit and then rolled down under the overhang. His men wouldn't have been able to see him even with torches. They probably figured he fell all the way to the bottom. The way the cavern wall curved, there was no way to climb up, unless one had the climbing skills of a spider, which Frem did not. And he had no climbing gear left, save for that bit of rope.

There was no evidence that his men were still around to lend him any help. The battle between the Ettin and the Black Elves was obviously over before he awoke. He must've been out for hours. Mayhap more.

Bodies littered the stair. The torchlight revealed little, given the distance, but he saw one dead Ettin for certain, several dead Elves, but none of *his* men, as best he could tell. Reckless or no, he chanced a whistle -- a signal to the company men, but got no response.

He focused his thoughts and reviewed every possibility for escape, for any chance to avoid heading down that tunnel -- which seemed to grow smaller every time he glanced at it. He dreaded where it might lead. Or what might come howling out of it as he sat there thinking.

He concluded, his only chance to avoid the tunnel was to run from the far edge of the ledge, leap as best he could, arms outstretched for the stair, and hope that he managed a handhold.

The idea was lunacy; he knew he couldn't jump that far. Knew it from the first moment he'd gauged the distance. More than likely, he'd fall a few feet short. And if somehow he leapt far enough, at best his fingers or hands would make it to the stair's edge. And then he'd have to grip the edge strongly enough that he didn't fall outright. Then, feet and body dangling in the air, pull himself up onto the ledge.

It was impossible. He'd never make it. No chance of it. Maybe Moag could, mayhap even Borrel, but not him, or any of the other Pointmen. Had his men been there on the stair, he could've thrown the rope to them. They'd have held it taut or tied it off and he could've swung or climbed over. A harrowing passage it would've been, but it would've worked. He'd have tried it in an instant to avoid braving those tunnels again. But alone, and with only the gear that he had, there was just no way. If he tried to leap, he'd fall to his death.

That left him no choice but to enter the tunnel and follow it wherever it went, hoping against hope that somehow, someway, he could find a way out of Svartleheim before his light or his strength ran out. He knew that he might get lucky – a few steps down that tunnel might be a way up. After all, the top of the stair was no more than a dozen feet above him. There had to be a way up there from here. But Frem knew that there wouldn't be. Things just never worked out that easily. Not for him.

He had to duck to enter the tunnel, and walk stooped-over within, but the passage was amply wide. The problem was, it sloped downward from the start. He was less than twenty feet below the surface, so close he could taste his freedom, but no way to get there.

He'd gone but ten yards down that tunnel when he first heard the drums. Black Elf drums. Their call to arms. More than likely, they'd either seen his light or heard his whistle, or both. And if so, the Elves knew that there was a man still left in their caverns.

They'd be hunting him.

And from recent experience Frem knew that they'd never give up until they found him.

14

VAEDEN
MOUNT CANTORWROUGHT

THE AGE OF MYTH AND LEGEND

THE LORD'S ARKON THETAN

At first, Thetan thought the voice nothing but a figment. Something in his head. A bit of imagination or a pestering byproduct of the blast he'd just experienced.

But it persisted.

Coming from everywhere at once.

A whispering on the wind.

Magery.

And of a high order. It had to be.

Yet it could not be, for no one, wizard or not, could reach the summit of Cantorwrought without the Arkons' notice.

A woman's voice, it was. Strong, yet soothing. The words at first, indistinct. More humming than speech.

And it was . . . familiar. As if he'd heard that voice countless times throughout his life. As if he knew it better than his own. Like the voice of a beloved daughter, a cherished wife, an adoring mother.

And then the humming became words.

"I have called down these Ankhs to aid you,

my beloveds, in the struggles to come," said the voice.

In something less than a single blink of an eye, all seven Arkons had in their hands their weapons of choice, their stances at the ready. Instinctively, they moved back to back, in a tight circle, the remnants of the fire at the circle's center. These men were not accustomed to fear. They were not accustomed to the unknown. It was they whom others feared. They were the will and the good strong hand of the lord — the swords of god himself. No one snuck up on them. No one had power over them.

No one save for the lord himself.

Who then was this woman that could approach them unseen? That could pluck stones from the heavens and cast them down upon them? Who had such power? What witchery was behind it? Their hearts raced. They made ready for anything.

And in those moments, as the woman's voice echoed in the air, they smelled...springtime. That could not be, for winter was not yet there, spring far-off in the new year. Yet the scent was unmistakable: flowers in bloom, the grass in the fields, pollen in the air. For men who lived ages beyond count, they knew the scents of the world just as well as its sights.

Spring — the new beginning of the natural year. And so too with that smell they smelled the good earth. Fresh tilled soil. It came on the breeze. Wafted about them. Just as had her voice.

"Do not be afraid," she said.

Thetan and all his brothers were startled out

of their heads. They spun about. Weapons ready.

She was behind them!

Standing tall in the middle of the circle they had just formed, their backs to her. Standing where the fire had lately been, but no longer. She should have been skewered by seven weapons in that first instant, yet each of them stayed their hands for reasons they could not explain.

They paused. Gave look to her. Harkened to her words.

She was beautiful, that woman. Tall. As tall as the men, every one of which was tall even for their kind. Soft but solid of limb with curves where a woman should have them. Her skin was of such strange hue, like the greenest grass of springtime. Her hair was flaxen. Her eyes, large and piercing blue. Barefoot and barehanded was she. The wisp of a green and yellow dress that flowed about her covered her enough for proper eyes to look upon her, but no more than that.

"Who are you?" boomed Mithron, the first to break their silence.

"Do you not know me, my dear?" she said. "Think back. Think carefully. Do you not know my voice? My face?"

"Yours is a face I would not soon forget," said Mithron. "There is a familiar air about you that I cannot explain away, but I have not seen you before."

She smiled and laughed. It was not a mocking laugh and rose no anger in Mithron or the others. "How predictable you are, my Mithron. Your words almost exactly the same every time. What about you, Thetan? Do you also claim to not know me?"

This time, sarcasm dripped from her voice.

Thetan did not respond. He merely stared at the woman.

Gabriel spoke. "Raphael, Arioch – look to our flanks. Let no one else approach without our leave."

"Always the tactician, dear Gabe," said the woman.

"Mithron asked who you are," said Uriel. "We await your answer."

"Patience you still must learn, Uriel," said the woman, "or the struggles ahead will be all the harder."

"What do you want with us?" said Thetan.

"Your name?" said Mithron.

"I am who I am," said the woman. "I have many names. You have often called me the Woman on the Wind. I fancy that. It has a nice sound to it. A bit too long though, don't you think? Instead, you may call me…Midgaard."

15

JUTENHEIM ANGLOTOR

YEAR 1267, 4TH AGE

JUDE EOTRUS

Before launching their attack on Anglotor, Father Ginalli had worked the Leaguers up into a foam-mouthed frenzy. Of all the speeches that Jude had heard Ginalli spit out since the start of his captivity, the one the priest gave before the attack on Anglotor was perhaps the most rousing of all. He had told the men about how the holy gateway was under the control of the most vile wretched creature alive in Midgaard, save for the Harbinger himself, of course. And with that creature stood an evil regiment of its vile minions. Their sole purpose in life, to keep the holy pilgrims, the beloved followers of the one true god, Azathoth, away from their holy site, and keep closed the wondrous and beautiful gateway to the glorious realm of Nifleheim. Their core purpose – what they lived and trained for their entire lives – to keep the lord from his chosen people. To bar his path back to Midgaard.

What profound evil must they represent to devote their lives so. And how the Leaguers reacted to Ginalli's words. True believers every one. Even more than a few of Ezerhauten's bought and paid for mercenaries shouted in support of Ginalli's words, raising their fists on high as he spoke and thumped the base of his staff to the ground.

He had them all under his thrall.

Ginalli laid it out so clearly. He made you believe that anyone of good and true heart had to strive, even unto death, to fight against the evildoers that held closed the holy portal that barred the lord's return. How every goodly man had a right and duty to stand against them. To fight, to die, to reach that olden portal, and to wrench it open on behalf of the lord himself. And that any who would stand opposed to such actions, revealed themselves as almost inhuman in their wickedness. Some, no doubt, must be demon possessed, the most foul and base creatures that ever dared roam Midgaard.

There could be only one choice for the Leaguers. To fight, to kill. And in so doing, complete their quest and return the lord home to Midgaard, to usher back his divine kingdom to the world of man.

By the time Ginalli was done, the Leaguers' eyes were closed, and they rocked slowly back and forth, repeating Ginalli's words in a mumble. Jude's mind felt cloudy. Ginalli's will tugged at the outer reaches of his brain, eroding his will, demanding him to listen. To believe. To obey.

But Jude resisted. And curiously, for him, that was no difficult task. For whatever reason, the sorcery that Ginalli commanded had little effect on Jude. He kept it out. Barred the priest's words from his mind. And so, he remained true to himself. Few others amongst the expedition could do the same.

Jude wondered if Brackta was susceptible to Ginalli's sorcery, or was she above it as an archwizard? He could not see her face from where he stood, nor those of the other archwizards. Were they all affected? Or only some? Or all immune due to their powers? Jude knew not, but he hoped that Brackta wasn't immune. He hoped that she was under Ginalli's thrall. For if she were, there was hope for her.

Hope for them.

Hope that what they felt for each other was real. Hope that Brackta was a good person at heart. That she was only with the League because Ginalli had beguiled her. Oh, if only that were the truth, then Jude need only discover how to break the spell. To free Brackta's will. And then she would help him escape. And they could go off together on the homeward road. Back to Lomion. Back to the North. Back to Dor Eotrus and his family.

And then Anglotor's best were on them.

Teek interposed himself between the Anglotorians and Jude. He stopped cold the first three of them. He put his sword's tip through the throat of the first – a short Juten, young and rangy. Teek parried a sword thrust from a second Juten. And then tripped an onrushing Dwarf.

And then Jude was in the thick of it. He backpedaled from the fallen Dwarf who swiped at his ankles with an axe. And then a young Elf was at him, his sword swinging from side to side, back and forth, looping this way and that — a display Jude knew was designed to intimidate and put him off balance. But Jude had seen skillful swordplay before. Impressive though it was, he did not fear it. Jude dodged a thrust, spun out of range of a slash, and then, just as quickly, stepped in and grabbed the swordsman's arm. The man tried to pull away, but Jude's arm was iron. He sent his dagger into the man's armpit. Sunk it deep. The Elf immediately dropped.

And Jude scooped up his sword.

A broad smile spread across his face. Having that weapon in hand changed everything. Two more Anglotorians came at him — tall Jutens both. Stab and slice, slash and whirl. Jude dropped one with a dagger pommel to the back of the man's head. The second, he took with a slash to the throat. As the man fell, he lopped off the top half of his head.

Magical blasts went off on this side and that: cones of fire, bolts of lightning, streams of crackling plasma -- blue, silver, yellow, and gold — the League's wizards at work. They ravaged the enemy. Blasted the Anglotorians back whence they came.

Jude found himself running. Running for the gatehouse. A pang of guilt struck him, for leaving Teek and Donnelin behind. But that was his chance, mayhap his only chance, to get clear of there, to escape the League and the gruesome fate they had planned for him. He leapt over the rubble by the gatehouse. Ducked around the mangled iron of the former gate itself.

And then outside the gates he witnessed the

last moments of another skirmish. A squad of Ezerhauten's men were finishing off the last of a troop of wild Lugron locals. Two score fresh corpses littered the field. Nearly all, the locals. Upon seeing Jude approach, the Sithians barred his path. A dozen stout mercenaries stood between him and escape.

He had to chance it, no matter the odds.

Sword raised, he leapt for the Sithian sergeant that barred his way.

And then he froze.

In the air.

Hung there as if plucked by an invisible giant's hand.

16

VAEDEN
MOUNT CANTORWROUGHT

THE AGE OF MYTH AND LEGEND

THE LORD'S ARKON THETAN

"**M**idgaard?" said Azrael.

"It's as good as name as any other," said the woman. "And fits me well."

"Quite an ego you must have," said Azrael, "to name yourself the world. Think you so great? So grand?"

"Test and probe," said Midgaard. "Question and confuse. Push and shove. Good and bad. I know your techniques. Your motives. Your methods. I have no time for them this night. And they do no good on me. So let's get down to business, shall we? First of all, put down your weapons. I do not find them amusing. And do not care to be pricked."

"But you are a bit prickly," said Uriel. "It's not with a sword that I would—"

"Spare us," said Azrael to Uriel. "Have you no manners at all?"

"A little humor goes a long way in this dismal life," said Uriel. "You would do well to embrace a bit of it now and again."

"Enough," said Mithron as the men lowered

their weapons — not because Midgaard told them to, but because each one of them thought it the right thing to do. After all, with the strange powers that Midgaard exhibited, their weapons may well do them no good. That fact did not escape them.

"Tonight," said Midgaard, "at long last, you have banished the fog from your eyes. You've accepted the terrible truth about Azathoth. About his evil. His menace. His madness. And you have put yourselves on a fateful path. A path that will determine the fate of much, perhaps of all, the world. It has been a long time coming. But I knew that one day you would reach this point. And I have prepared for it. I will help you in such ways that I can. That is why I am here. That is why I have sent these Ankhs to you. They have many powers, which you will discover in due time. Trust in them. Rely on them. But even more so, rely on yourselves. On each other. You must be united in your plans, and your deeds. Only together can you accomplish your goal. Only together can you defeat Azathoth and rid the world of his menace."

"Who are you?" said Thetan. "And how do you know these things?"

"What you need to know is that I am a friend," said Midgaard, her voice growing softer. "I have always been your friend, Thetan. Always and forever. I have appeared to you and these others many times before. I have aided you when you most needed aid. More than once, it's fair to say, I have saved you from ruin. I am here now to aid you again."

"I have no memory of you," said Thetan.

Midgaard waved her hand. Turned about. And

waved it in front of all the men. And then they remembered. They remembered all the times that she had appeared to them. The wisdom that she had imparted. The aid she had given. The grievous hurts that she had mended. They still didn't know who or what she was. That was something she had never revealed to them. But they remembered those previous interactions. All of them. They had known her as long as they had known each other. Some of them had known her longer. Thetan had known her longer still. Much longer.

"And now you'll ask why you have failed to remember all this until now," said Midgaard. "And Azrael will counsel, that perhaps you're not remembering anything, that the strange woman has bewitched you, and these memories that you now have are false. And then you argue that point around and around and around until I finally tell you all to shut the heck up. I don't want to spend time on that again. The reason you didn't remember all the times we've spent together is because I took those memories from you at the end of each of our meetings. I have done this for very good reason. There are powers in this world, in this universe, that are far beyond any man, far beyond any wizard human born. Some of those powers are my enemies. And if they knew that I aided you, that you were my allies, that would make you their enemies. And they would smite you one way or another. So I take your memories of me, and only of me, so that they can never discover this connection between us. So that they will not act against you or against me in this way."

"You fear them?" said Azrael. "These powers?"

"There are rules that must be abided by," said Midgaard. "Rules that bind me for reasons I cannot and will not explain. But I bend the rules. I stretch them to aid humankind whenever and wherever I can. There are others who stretch them to aid other causes. A constant battle throughout time and history. A battle I aim to win."

"So is it we that are helping you, or you that are helping us?" said Azrael.

"By helping me you help yourselves," said Midgaard. "Azathoth does not belong on this world. He is an intruder. He has no claim to it. To rule this world's every acre with an iron fist is what consumes him. To be worshiped by all is what he desires above all else. I will not have that. You must put him down. You must carry out your plans just as you have discussed. The ankhs will help you."

"How will they help us?" said Thetan. "What can they do? Are they weapons?"

"They will protect you from his magic," said Midgaard. "He can rain down all the fire and fury from the Outer Spheres that he wants, but with those Ankhs in your pockets, or hung about your necks, he cannot touch you. This protection, I give to you to aid you in our common struggle. But mark my words well, you must never let Azathoth's eyes fall upon the Ankhs. If he sees them, he may know them for what they are and take them from you. But even if he does not recognize them, they will arouse his suspicion. If he touches one of them, you are all undone. One

94

touch will tell him all. He will know them for the threat that they are. He will know that a higher power has entered a game to which he thought he was the only player. I cannot have this happen. Not at this juncture. Keep the Ankhs safe and secret from all. But keep them on your person: morning, noon, and night; when you sleep; when you bathe, always. These talismans are your one advantage against him, save for surprise. Use them wisely. Keep them secret; keep them safe."

"You said that the Ankhs have many powers," said Thetan. "What can they do besides protect us from his magic?"

"When held in your hand, when you are of clear and thoughtful purpose, they will reveal to you not only the presence of magic, but will mark it as of good or evil will. So too can they reveal things cloaked by magic and otherwise invisible to common sight. They are also powerful wayfinders. And they can gift you a bit of luck when you most need it. And everyone needs luck from time to time. You fellows more so than anyone. There are other powers unique to each Ankh, some of which are unknown even to me, but the ankhs will reveal them to you in time as your needs require."

"So the Akhs are no craft of yours?" said Azrael. "You did not make them, did you?"

"They are artifacts of the Outer Spheres," said Midgaard. "Who made them, I cannot say."

"You won't say or you don't know?" said Azrael.

"I don't know," said Midgaard. "Probe and jab, question and redirect. I tell you only what I want to, know that well."

"What does that mean, things of the Outer Spheres?" said Uriel.

"They are things born not of this world," said Midgaard. "Such things as them are needed to combat a creature of the Outer Spheres, which is what Azathoth is. He is not of this world. He is from somewhere else."

"From where?" said Thetan.

"I am not the fountain of all knowledge," said Midgaard.

"Azathoth is not what you fear," said Azrael. "There is something else. Someone else. Tell us."

"Azrael the Wise, your name, fairly given," said Midgaard. "Azathoth is not the only creature of the Outer Spheres to walk this world. There have been others in the past. There may be others in the future. Besides Azathoth, there is at least one other here now. One other of power. Those two are my enemies. I cannot not act openly against Azathoth or his ilk without them acting openly against me and mine. Hence the binding of which I spoke. A status quo if you will, to prevent mutual destruction. Know this, I am on your side. I have always been on your side. I'm here to help you. The Ankhs will help you. And this help you gravely need. Without it, you will not survive your fateful encounter with Azathoth. Do you all understand that? Do you believe it? You must."

17

DARENDOR

YEAR 1267, 4TH AGE

BORNYTH TROLLSBANE

Bornyth knew Darendor's passages, both the public and the secret, like no other. Fifty yards down the tunnel from the Seer Stone's chamber he halted, the location nondescript, no different to the untrained eye than any spot along the way. He ran his fingers over the wall's stony surface, left bloody streaks behind. It was only then that Bornyth noticed the blood and gore that clung to his gauntlets and arms. He turned his head whence they came and spied the trail of bloody boot prints that followed in his wake. His eyes lingered on the clutch of bodies heaped about the entry to the Seer Stone's chamber. Praise Odin, there was no movement there or anywhere in the dim corridor. Bornyth put his hand back to the wall and soon came a barely audible click. A hidden door popped open. Silent darkness beyond. In stepped Bornyth without hesitation, the Svart seer but a step behind, though that was too close for his comfort – for the closer she got, the queasier went his stomach, owing to the strange emanations of the Seer Stone that she carried.

Pitch black was that place they'd entered.

Bornyth eased the door closed behind them, sealing out the light. They waited some moments, listening, but the only sounds they heard were a muted clamor far off in the distance. Bornyth lit a lantern he plucked from a hook near the secret door. It illumed a passage much like the main, though smaller in all dimensions. A wall niche held a small trove of supplies: water, weapons, dried food, another lantern, flint, rope, and more. The Dwarves were always prepared and kept such caches scattered about the perimeter of their demesne and far beyond. They'd learned their lessons through the endless struggles against the Lugron, the Svart, and even darker things of the forbidden subterranean depths. Bornyth quickly filled a satchel with what he needed, then emptied a water flask in one plunge. The Svart girl waived off his offer of another.

She stared at him as if looking for reassurance. Some promise that they were out of danger or that they'd survive the day. He had little comfort to give.

"Stay as quiet as you can," said Bornyth. "Few amongst my people know of these tunnels, but some may have fled within when came the Draugar. We might find friend or foe or both within these sorry walls. Be ready to battle or to flee, however I command you."

The girl nodded and they were off. The Dwarf king moved quiet enough for a man in armor. The Svart was quieter still, and that did not escape Bornyth's notice. They made their way through long passages and up several ladders and rough-hewn flights of steps, narrow and steep. At first, they went slowly, but as sounds of battle reached their ears, Bornyth picked up his pace. He was anxious to help his people, to throw himself back into the fray. But though the battle sounds became louder, they remained distant, or so it seemed in the eerie corridor.

After a time, Bornyth spied a dim, flickering light in the passage up ahead. There was no way around and no way to approach unseen or unheard, for Bornyth had to keep his lantern lit to see his way. He and the Svart girl drew closer to the light. It was two of his soldiers. One was on his back, the other seated against the passageway wall.

"Who goes there?" spoke the seated soldier.

"Your king," said Bornyth as he stepped close.

The Dwarf soldier's eyes went wide and then a smile appeared on his face. "Forgive me, my lord, but I'll not be getting up to greet you. I'm glad to see that you are well. That gives me hope that we can still beat these bastards back."

Bornyth put down his lantern and took a knee beside the seated soldier whose leg was heavily bandaged -- but still the red ran through. "What happened, son?" said Bornyth

"I'm with Lord Malbec's battalion, southern border patrol, first squadron. We couldn't hold them. Tried as best we could, I swear it, but they kept coming. They've no regard for themselves. They don't care if we stab them, hack them, skewer them, or cut off their limbs, it don't matter. They just keep coming, fearless and crazed. Worse than berserkers. They don't die. And they had our people amongst their ranks – our folk, not just Dwarves, but our own clansmen. When our line broke, me and Drilk slipped in here, but Drilk was bit bad, bleeding like a stuck pig. I couldn't leave him out there. Not to get eaten; not by those things. While I was pulling him inside, one of them got hold of my leg. Got me good. Took a chunk out. I put my hammer into its head. Crushed the bastard's skull to mush. And then I dragged my sorry ass in here. Drilk died of blood loss not two minutes later. I had to put my dagger through his ear to keep him from coming back as one of them. I had to kill my own friend -- Helheim, I don't know what to call it since he was already dead. But I had to stab him. Now I'm soon to follow," he said pointing to his leg. "It's not much of a wound. Something like that, if it don't go septic, it would be mostly healed in a couple few weeks. But the bites of those things," he said shaking his head, "those aren't normal. They got a poison to them, them things do. A poison. Just a little wound, that's enough to kill a man, I think it is. I've already got a fever; it came on almost at once. That don't make no sense to me. But I know what can happen. Great King Bornyth, is there any treatment for this? Any way to survive it? Any way at all?"

Bornyth shook his head, a sad expression on his face. "None that I know of, lad."

"I won't become one of them," said the soldier. "I won't have that, no sir, I won't. I don't want to die, but if there's no way to survive this, I'd be honored, King, if you would finish it for me, because I can't do it for myself. Would you do that? Could you?"

Bornyth's eyes were wet. "Aye, lad, I will. Close your eyes, son. I'll be quick." Bornyth pulled a dagger and plunged it into the soldier's temple. The old king's hand trembled after the deed was done. To kill one of his own, a man that should not have been on death's door, was a hard thing, even for an old warrior. The Svart seer looked on, expressionless, as always.

After that, Bornyth advanced his pace – jogging through the tunnels – a pace that seemed his fastest, given the fatigue of the recent battle, the weight of the armor he wore, and his advancing age. "They've got us killing our own, dammit all," muttered Bornyth as he went. "That's the worst of it, killing our own."

Three times their passage was blocked by dead ends or barred doors, though they ran into no one else along the way, living or dead. Bornyth always had a way through any blockage — whether by key or hidden lever. At last, they reached a series of stone steps that wound upward in a tight spiral. Up and up they went, no less than two hundred feet.

"This will drop us out at Darendor's uppermost level," said Bornyth, "far behind and above the fighting. I'll marshal our forces from here and beat the Draugar back if I can, or bar their entry into the city's heart if I can't. Stick close to me, girl; it will be chaos out there. I may have need of your Stone."

Bornyth opened the small stone door that marked the apex of the spiral stair, bending over double to get through. They found themselves on a concealed stone balcony, high up on the wall of a vast cavern — the cavern that housed Darendor's city center. From below, obscured from their sight by a tall balustrade, came groaning, wailing, and screaming. Smoke hung heavy in the air. Bornyth's eyes grew wide. He rushed to the balustrade's step and rose to his full height, his eyes reaching just above the railing's coping. His face twisted into a mask of anger, shock, and fear. His knuckles turned white as he gripped the balustrade. The breath caught in his throat, but only for a moment, and then came a long, anguished groan.

Darendor was on fire.

And its streets were a slaughterhouse.

From so high aloft, Bornyth could not make out individuals on Darendor's streets, but by their loping gates he spied the Draugar that polluted his streets and that preyed on his people. They howled as they raced down the avenues, leaping onto any Dwarf they came across. Ripping. Tearing. Killing. Infecting their victims. Making them become Draugar. Such an insidious enemy were the Draugar. For each of your own that fell to them rose up to join their ranks and fight against you.

Bornyth sidestepped from one end of the balustrade to the other and back again, on his tiptoes all the while. He studied the scene below. His gaze shifting here and there. And then his gauntleted fist crashed down atop the balustrade so hard that stone shards broke off and tumbled over the edge. Then his chin dropped to his chest and he stepped down to the balcony floor. When his eyes met those of the Seer's they were watery.

"I've lost my kingdom. Darendor has fallen."

The Svart girl's face was expressionless as always, though her mouth was open, and her breathing was quick. She said nothing.

18

FOOTHILLS OF THE KRONAR MOUNTAIN RANGE, NORTH OF DOR EOTRUS

YEAR 1267, 4TH AGE

ECTOR EOTRUS

The only warning that the troll had, were the sounds of Eotrus horns as they signaled to begin the attack. By then, there was nowhere for the trolls to run, save into the advancing Volsung troops. And they only would've done that had they feared the Eotrus, which they didn't. So the trolls stood their ground. And that made the Eotrus job the tougher, for the trolls weren't gathered in an orderly circular encampment. They were spread out along a ramshackle line that stretched for more than a quarter of a mile along a woodland game trail.

The Eotrus cavalry sounded like thunder and the very earth shook beneath their hooves. They came in from all sides, galloping out of the woods, and blasted into the troll ranks.

And everything went to chaos.

Such was the way of battle.

Ector knew that as commander of the Eotrus army, he should've stayed well back from the front lines, protected by a stout contingent of bodyguards. Leading from the rear some called it. It was perhaps the best way to control his troops and react to the battle's progress.

But Ector wouldn't have that. He was a man of action just like his father.

The trolls had sacked Dor Eotrus. Laid waste to it. Killed thousands of his people. Many that he called friend. Many that he loved. One of the last to fall at Ector's side was one of the dearest to him — old Sir Sarbek, one of the greatest men Ector had known.

He would have his revenge for Sarbek, and for all the rest.

So he charged with the troops, leading all that remained of Dor Eotrus's knights. Captain Pellan was at his left hand astride a small gray charger. Sir Indigo Eldswroth was on his right, atop a huge black destrier.

When they drew close, Ector saw why the troll's pace was slow. It wasn't just the weight of the wagons that they hauled. These trolls were the old, the sick, and those injured beyond their abilities to heal. Many of them walked stooped over. Many limped. Some were missing a limb or an eye; some were missing more than one. These were the ones that the troll commander didn't need in his battle force, so he sent them home carrying food aplenty — the spoils of war.

No matter, figured Ector. They got their wounds in battle with the Eotrus, so these deserved death as much as the rest. He felt no guilt in killing them. As they closed on their enemy, the northmen all called out the same battle cry, just as they had planned.

"Dor Eotrus," shouted the men. "Dor Eotrus!" Those were the last words they wanted the troll to hear.

As his horse charged, Ector lowered his lance, and crashed its tip unerringly to the center of a troll's chest. The lance shattered with the impact. The troll went flying. Ector was thrust backward, but kept his seat, his shoulder screaming in pain from the terrible impact.

Ector urged on his horse and its front hooves crashed against a second troll, knocking it back on its rump, and then trampled it underfoot. A moment later, the horse's shoulder caught a third troll and knocked it aside. Another rider hit it and trampled it. Ector's horse stumbled. He thought it would go down, but it righted itself. He couldn't turn his mount, for other horses advanced to either side.

Then another troll appeared in front, its claws swiping. Ector felt the blow as the thing's claws rended his horse's barding. Ector threw the remnant of his lance at it — a clumsy toss that likely did no good. Without waiting to see whether it hit, he drew his sword.

The troll tore at his mount and shredded its barding. The warhorse snapped its jaws and tried to bite its attacker even as it kicked wildly; Ector struggled to keep his seat.

And then a terrific blow hit the horse from the rear. As it staggered, Ector pulled his feet from the stirrups and leapt off, praying that another charging rider wouldn't run him down.

A troll loped toward Ector.

Ector slashed his sword in a wide arc from on high and scored a powerful hit to the troll's shoulder. But somehow, the steel sword snapped in two, the upper fragment embedded in the troll's chest, the lower part still gripped in Ector's hand.

The troll kept coming.

It crashed into him. Powerful claws sank into his tunic. Ripping. Tearing. Its mouth, open. Teeth reached for his neck. Saliva dripped. Foul breath washed over him.

And then Pellan's spear's tip sank into the troll's back: one, two, three times.

The troll immediately went limp, though it still growled and its eyes were open and wide, filled of fire and hatred.

Its spine was severed. Paralyzed.

Ector pushed it off him and scrambled to his feet.

Pellan was already dueling another. Trading blow for blow. And then two soldiers rushed in to help the Dwarf.

Ector pulled a dagger with his left hand, his right still gripped his broken sword. He saw Indigo and three other soldiers hack a troll to pieces a few feet away.

Ector turned a full circle. Groups of men were all around. Three, five, eight of them on each troll — they hacked and slashed, wild and fierce; horses stomped, kicked, bit; war cries and curses sailed on the wind. No more trolls loped toward him, toward anyone. All in sight, surrounded by men, most already down.

The battle was over.

Only the killing continued.

When it was done, they severed the heads of every troll in the troop. Piled the bodies in a dozen heaps, poured oil on them, and set them ablaze — mindful to keep the fire from spreading to the woods.

They stuck the troll heads on pikes and carried them with them as they rode from the field.

More than fifty brave northmen died in that skirmish, more than twice that number of horses. They counted 312 troll corpses altogether.

"Did any of them run?" said Ector. "Did they get through our lines?"

"Most fought to the death," said Indigo. "Brave or stupid go the trolls. The rangers say no fewer than a dozen fled, no more than a score. Our men are tracking them, just as we planned, all heading north."

"Woe to the troll nation," said Pellan. "They'll suffer the same fate as these. This I vow."

The northmen burned their dead — both those killed in the battle, and the poor souls whose corpses the trolls had carried north. Not far from the battle site was one of the hot springs that dotted the foothills of the Kronar Range. 'Twas a shallow isolated pool of bubbling water too hot to touch. The northmen made camp for the night nearby. Someone came up with the idea of tossing the troll heads into that hot water.

And they did.

Boiled them all night long. The next morning, before dawn, a group of men fished out the heads, the flesh sloughing off, white bone left behind. They collected the skulls. Nearly three hundred of them and attached them to pikes and spears, and carried them amongst the army's vanguard as they rode — a gruesome warning to any troll that spotted them.

19

EGRIPT-MON AESIR ENCAMPMENT

THE AGE OF MYTH AND LEGEND

THE LORD'S ARKON THETAN

Thetan stepped silently into the Aesir command tent. The place was warm and smoky, much of the tent's skin long blackened of ash and soot. Lanterns hung about, yet shadows abounded. The place smelled of meat, mead, and men.

King Wotan sat at the far side of the great table that surrounded the central hearth, roasted turkey leg in hand. The Aesir king's face was lined and scarred, his hair and beard full but white as winter snow; his armor, strong and polished, though, as was the custom of his people, it left bare his massive arm muscles, the better to instill fear in his enemies.

Other Aesir chieftains, most of them, sons or kinsmen to Wotan, crowded around the table, drinking and feasting, laughing and boasting. Big men were they. Tall, long-haired, barrel chested, and much thicker of limb than Azathoth's people. Wotan's eldest son, Donar, sat at his right hand, Loki at his left. Heimdall was there. So too was Balder, Bragi, Njord, Hoder, Tig, Vidar, Vali, Vale, and several others whose names Thetan did not

110

know.

Wotan's eyes immediately flicked to Thetan. "What ho," shouted Wotan over the men, "by the peaks of Asgard, look who fronts us now."

The men jerked around in surprise, eyes wide at the sight of the newcomer. No one should have entered the command tent, at the very heart of the Aesir encampment, unannounced and unescorted, save for others of Wotan's inner circle. Something was amiss. The room fell silent. A smile came over more than one face when they recognized Thetan. Others darkened.

"The Lightbringer himself looms before me, long absent from my table," said Wotan. "Long missed."

"Not by all," whispered Loki.

Thetan stepped forward and approached Wotan, a hint of a smile on his face.

"How does a wolf pass my guard with no word or call?" said Wotan.

"Who would stop me?" said Thetan.

"Who indeed," said Wotan as he stood and held his hand out.

Thetan stepped close to him and clasped his hand and shoulder. The grips of those two men were like iron vices, so strong as to crush a normal man's hand. They were a match, those two, in height, muscle, and girth.

"There are matters of import that we must discuss in private," said Thetan quietly so that only Wotan might hear, "and our time is limited."

"Is it now?" said Wotan loud enough for his men to hear. "From where I stand, I have all the time in the world. Azathoth's forces are on the run."

"Azathoth," shouted Loki, his voice mocking the style of Azathoth's priests. "The one true god! Bow down before him and worship no others, ha, ha."

The men laughed uproariously, banged their mugs together, and drank deeply.

Wotan raised his hand to silence them. "Egript-Mon is liberated," he said. "We will not give it back to the false god. I told as much to the last emissary — Uriel, I think his name was. Would my response have been clearer if I had sent back only his head?"

"That one was prettier than your wife, Donar," said Heimdall as he slapped Wotan's eldest across the back.

"And your daughters followed him out of town, licking his boots all the while," said Donar to more laughter.

"Fancy men in fancy armor are Azathoth's Arkons," said Loki. "Their hair just so," he said mockingly as he primped his own lengthy locks. "More like women than men."

"Perhaps they are women," said Vali. "What lies under that steel, emissary?"

Thetan's face hardened. His jaw set and he locked his eyes on Vali.

"Enough!" boomed Wotan. "You fools know not whom you provoke. Thetan is my friend of old times and he is welcome in my camp, so hold your tongues lest you lose them."

"As I said, we should speak in private," said Thetan.

Wotan paused, considering, then nodded.

"Leave us," he said, gesturing to his men. "All of you. And waste no time about it."

The Aesir warriors rose and filed from the room, drinking jacks in hand, grumbling at the interruption to their feast. Most took their plates with them, piling high more food atop them in a flash. For a brief moment, there was a struggle over the last turkey leg, Vidar and Vale gripping it for dear life, before Wotan's glare sent them to flight, Vidar with a handful of meat and skin, Vale with the lion's share. Several of the men patted Thetan's shoulder as they passed, nods of respect exchanged. Loki merely grinned at him, an evil look in his eye.

Donar remained seated at his father's side, though that was expected. He was the heir apparent to the throne of Asgard should his father ever pass or abdicate.

When the last of the men left, and the tent flap swung closed, Wotan spoke again. "Does Azathoth think I'll give you a different answer than I gave Uriel, old friend? For if he does, you've wasted your journey."

"I come of my own accord," said Thetan. "Not to bargain over Egript-Mon."

"That is good," said Wotan, nodding. Was that relief on his face? Wotan grabbed up a great mug, ornate with runes, studded with jewels: emerald, ruby, and sapphire, filled it to the brim from the mead barrel beside the table, and passed it to Thetan, motioning him to take the seat next to Donar.

What a sight were those three. Each of shoulders as wide as two common men. Bulging muscles. Armor thick and gleaming. Weapons aplenty.

"Bear you bad news, as did you the last?" said Donar, his father responding with a disapproving look.

"Weighty news," said Thetan. "And a plea for aid."

"Aid?" said Donar. "Then your trip is wasted after all, for to Azathoth we will offer no aid or comfort, whatever be his troubles."

"Not for him," said Thetan. "For me."

"Whenever you darken our door," said Donar, "you always ask something of us. Just because my father was your mentor and teacher of years long past does not put him at your beck and call whenever your coffers or larder runs low. You presume too much."

Thetan raised an eyebrow and turned his gaze to Wotan. "So you were *my* teacher?" said Thetan.

"I never told him that," said Wotan.

Donar's face stiffened. He looked surprised. His mouth dropped open.

"He assumed as much, and I did not correct him."

"Perhaps now would be the time," said Thetan, his voice icy cold.

"Perhaps," said Wotan, nodding. "Son, it was Lord Thetan who was *my* teacher," he said to Donar. "Thetan was my mentor. Taught me the Old Way of the Sword. Taught me the axe, the hammer, and the bow. Taught me of ancient mysteries. Of wonders beyond belief. Of magic and sorcery. And more. Most of all, he taught me how to be a king."

114

Donar was astonished. Disbelieving. Wordless, as if waiting for his father to say it was all a jest.

He did not.

"But you are the oldest of the old," said Donar. "You walked Midgaard before any other living man."

"Thetan came before me," said Wotan. "Long before me. And so too did others, but they are all gone from this life, as best I know, save for Lord Thetan."

Donar shook his head, looking dazed. "My head spins from these words," he said. "But if you say this is the truth, then it must be so." He turned to Thetan. "I gaze upon you with newfound respect, Lord Thetan," said Donar. "And gratitude for all that you taught my father for he has passed that knowledge on to me. Forgive my foolish words. The mead weighs heavy tonight and my tongue has wagged afoul."

Thetan patted Donar on the shoulder. "I have been your father's friend of long years; I would have it so with you as well."

Donar nodded. "As would I."

"And now to the matter at hand?" said Thetan.

Wotan nodded.

"I plan to kill Azathoth," said Thetan. "And I need your help to do it."

20

JUTENHEIM ANGLOTOR

YEAR 1267, 4TH AGE

JUDE EOTRUS

As he hung suspended in midair, Jude felt the crackling energy about him, invisible though it was.

Magic.

Sorcery.

One of the League's wizards had trapped him.

Par Rhund it was, the quiet one. The mage stepped up beside the Sithians, straining from the effort of holding Jude aloft.

"Disarm him," said Rhund. "Tie his hands. Guard him closely, bring him to Ginalli at once."

"This has taken far too long already," said Stev Keevis to the other wizards as Jude was pulled before them. "Who knows how many more troops of locals they have marching toward us. We can't hold off unlimited numbers."

"Then get the blasted doors open," said Ginalli.

"What are we supposed to do?" said Par Keld. "We've been cut to the core. There's hardly any of us left and we've no idea what's behind that door."

"We do have an idea," said Par Brackta. "A wizard. One with greater power to bar doors then we have to sunder them. More than likely, that means he's got other powers greater than what we have."

"That makes me feel much better," said Par Keld. "Wait, what if there's more than one archwizard in there? A whole cadre of them? For all we know, this castle could be *their* Tower of the Arcane." Keld looked about furtively and scurried away.

"Ever the coward is Keld," muttered Stev Keevis.

"He has his uses," said Ginalli.

Keld stopped in his tracks. He was far enough away he shouldn't have heard Keevis, but he did. "Don't call me that. I'm no coward. I'm not worried about myself. I'm worried about the mission. I'm worried about keeping safe Lord Korrgonn. That's all that matters to me. All that I care about. Seeing the mission done, that's what I'm about. And don't ever say that's not true. Don't ever."

"If there be as many troops inside as we've faced out here," said Par Brackta, "this will not go well. We've little sorcery to spare if we want to face the wizard with any magic left. We must hold the core of our remaining power in reserve."

"What are you suggesting?" said Ginalli. "We're doing all we can. Most of our muscle is dead. Only a fraction of Ezerhauten's troops remain."

"I am loath to do it, for it will greatly weaken me," said Master Glus Thorn, "but I can call forth more reinforcements to aid us. I planned to hold this back, unless and until the Harbinger and his minions caught up to us. But it seems, our need is already great."

"More Stowron?" said Par Brackta.

"But you don't have the coach," said Ginalli. "It's back on the ship."

"The coach is merely a conduit for my powers," said Thorn. "An aid, a tool, no more than that. I can accomplish the spell without it, though it will be all the harder and more tiring."

"Stev Keevis," said Ginalli, "call your Golem off the door. Have him stand guard over Master Thorn beside me. You do the same."

A few moments later, Mason marched up and stood protectively beside Thorn, Mort Zag, the red giant, a few steps behind.

"I can breach the door," said Mort Zag in his deep booming voice. "The Stev's last spell weakened its bindings. I can tear apart the rest of what holds it in place. After that, it's just iron and stone. I can bring that down, however thick it may be."

"Wait until Master Thorn's conjuring is complete," said Ginalli. "Once we have a troop of Stowron positioned before that door, then you may take it down."

"Once you're inside," continued Ginalli, "destroy whatever defenders lurk within. Let nothing stop you," he said looking to each of the Leaguers in turn. "Let nothing stop you."

"We can't run headlong inside," said Par Keld. "There could be anything in there. Death could await us."

"It does," said Korrgonn breaking his silence. "The guardian of this place is ancient and strong. I can feel him even from here. He lurks up high in the tower. He watches us even now via olden magics. Leave him to me. He is an evil far beyond you."

"My lord, you must not risk yourself," said Ginalli.

"What risk is there to the son of Azathoth?" said Korrgonn.

"It is not fitting," said Thorn, "that you should fight petty mortals. Let us destroy this creature for you."

"The master of this place is no mortal," said Korrgonn.

"Then what is he?" said Keld. "A demon lord? A devil from the Nether Realms? Another of the Harbinger's minions?"

"You need only know that I will defeat him," said Korrgonn. "With the aid of the Heartstone, the task will be all the easier."

"That's the thing you plucked from the big lizard's chest?" said Keld.

"From Dagon of the Deep," said Ginalli. "Careful, Keld, speak not so lightly of gods of the Outer Spheres."

"Do not disturb me until I speak again," said Korrgonn. "Meanwhile, Thorn -- you shall prepare your conjuring. But do not call your Stowron forth until I give you leave."

21

EGRIPT-MON AESIR ENCAMPMENT

THE AGE OF MYTH AND LEGEND

THETAN

Wotan grimaced. He smashed his fist to the table, the mead hopping from the men's cups. "You mean those words? You mean to kill Azathoth?"

"I do," said Thetan.

Wotan's entire body shook. His voice quivered. His fist again smashed against the tabletop. "Long have I yearned to hear those words escape your lips. I knew. I knew if I but had patience I would see this day come to pass. Tell me that the fog has finally lifted from your eyes. Do you know him now for what he is? Do you?"

Thetan nodded. "He does evil and calls it good. He says that if I could grasp the complexities of his divine plans, I would know them to be good and proper and just. He says that I must put all my trust in him. That I must have faith."

"And so long as you believe those words," said Wotan, "he can get away with anything. And he has."

"Aye," said Thetan. "To my everlasting shame, he has."

"Why did you follow him in the first?" said Wotan. "You who have never bent the knee to any man before? You have never told me how he ensnared you, though I have asked you many times. Now you must tell me the truth of it. Why?"

Thetan paused for some moments before he responded. "I wanted to make sense of creation — of the universe. To understand our place in it. My place in it. I wanted answers to questions that could not be answered by any but a god, if such a person even existed. Someone greater than myself. Greater than any man."

"We thought we were alone," continued Thetan. "That all the universe was a barren expanse of nothingness save for twinkling lights in the night sky. That only Midgaard harbored life. And then one day, *he* sailed down from the heavens upon a ship of fire. From the heavens!"

"You were alive before him too?" said Donar. "Before Azathoth first appeared?"

"Aye, long before," said Thetan, nodding. "Though your father was as well."

"Thetan is older than the mountains," said Wotan. "He is more ancient than the seas. He is...the first of men."

Donar's eyes were wide, his face paled.

"No sooner than had he arrived, Azathoth proclaimed himself our creator," said Thetan. "The guiding force behind our history and heritage. The architect of our hearts and minds. The sculptor of our souls. He displayed powers beyond all others. Knowledge beyond all knowledge. I thought that with him I could find the answers that I have long sought."

"What are these questions that bewitch you so?" said Wotan.

"Who I am," said Thetan. "And where I came from."

"Where *did* you come from, first of men?" said Donar. "Would you have us believe that you sprang full grown from the ground? Who birthed you? A woman? An ape? What?"

"That portion of my mind is cloaked in shadow," said Thetan. "A shadow so deep and dark that I cannot penetrate it despite countless years of trying."

"This I do not understand," said Wotan. "Your memory is sounder than any man's I have ever met. You often quote me the exact words of conversations that we had centuries ago."

"Those things that I cannot remember," said Thetan, "I have not forgotten. Those memories were taken from me. Memories of my origin. My youth. My family. Stolen. All my knowledge and memory of those early times is gone. And my memory has other holes in it that I cannot explain."

"Who could do that to me? Who has that power? I need to know. I need back what was stolen."

"A mystery unsolved," said Wotan. "Perhaps unsolvable."

"That's why I followed him," said Thetan. "I thought perhaps a god could unlock the binding magic that clouds my mind and reveal to me the truth in all its glory or horror. Which it is, I didn't even care. I just wanted to know. Needed to know."

"And if someone is behind your memory loss?" said Donar.

"Then there will be a reckoning," said Thetan.

"Woe is them," said Wotan.

"Did Azathoth refuse to help you in this?" said Donar. "Or did he fail in the attempt?"

"He tried once when I first joined him," said Thetan. "He put his hand upon my brow. He closed his eyes and mumbled words of a language unknown to me. His hand lingered upon my forehead for long moments. At last, he said that there were reasons for the holes in my mind. And that the truth could only be revealed to me slowly, in the fullness of time. He said that it was part of his grand plan that I be restored. Made whole in mind and memory. But that I must have patience. That in the end, all would be revealed."

"And you believed this?" said Donar.

"How easy now to see his lies for what they were," said Thetan. "But at the time, I wanted to believe. I needed to. He knew just what to say. And how to say it. And every time I questioned his actions, if even but in my own mind, my thoughts drifted to his call for patience. That all would be revealed to me in due time. And those lies clouded my thinking. Stayed my hand. And paralyzed my tongue."

"But you are free of his yoke now?" said Wotan.

"The veil of lies has been lifted," said Thetan.

"And your memories?" said Wotan.

"Still lost," said Thetan.

"Have you given up hope that Azathoth could restore what you have lost?" said Wotan.

"It doesn't matter even if he can," said Thetan. "For the price is too high. I will not pay it."

22

DARENDOR

YEAR 1267, 4TH AGE

BORNYTH TROLLSBANE

Bornyth opened the balcony's door and exited into a corridor where Dwarves dashed this way and that, weapons to hand. And then Throgden was there, a retired general from Bornyth's father's court, a dozen stout Dwarf soldiers with him.

"My lord," said Throgden, "praise Odin, we thought you lost."

"Report," said Bornyth.

"They came at us from all directions. All at the same time. A coordinated assault like no other that we've seen. They came through every hole. Every tunnel. Through the aquifers. The sewers. The air shafts. From above and from below. Before we even knew they were upon us, they'd cut the city off. Broke all our lines of communication. Within minutes they were in the city center. We didn't even have time to marshal our forces. We barely got the alarm sounded. We still don't know how many there are. Just that they're everywhere. Our people are turning—"

"Into them, I know," said Bornyth. "Where are Ragneer, Talmik, and General Charp?"

"I don't know," said Throgden. "Anyone outside the city center when the attack began was unable to return. The streets were overrun so quickly. There are battles up and down—"

"I know, I saw," said Bornyth. "Any word of Galibar, of my son?"

"None that I know of, my lord," said Throgden. "Hopefully, he's still far from the city; his best chance to escape this."

"What troops do we have?" said Bornyth.

"I held the citadel guard in reserve, but minutes ago I deployed half their number. The dead have broken through the main doors. I sent down the guard to slow their advance. To give us time to set up barricades. The remainder of the guard are setting them up."

"Where did you place them?"

"Two levels down, one level down, and on this level," said Throgden.

"So you've given up not only the city, but the citadel itself? We're trapped here on these top levels only?"

"You don't understand, my lord," said Throgden. "Those things are unstoppable. They've broken through everything we've thrown at them. General Sidon led an entire regiment across the courtyard not five minutes ago to guard the citadel doors. He set a line of spear and sword ten men deep. Look," he said leaning over the railing and pointing down. "Look. They're gone. Gone. The entire regiment in minutes. What are we supposed to do against that? Now, that regiment is fighting against us."

"So we've no refuge? None but the secret

tunnels?"

Throgden shook his head. "Not even that."

"We came through there," said Bornyth. "They were clear."

"Then you were lucky, my lord, for the Draugar are in there too, we've had several reports of it. Not as thick as they are in the main passages, but they're in there. There's little chance of escape through those tunnels and certainly no refuge to be found there. We're doomed. The gods have forsaken us. We have but two choices. Die today in battle or barricade ourselves within the stoutest room we can find and hope that the things go away before we run out of food and water. I say, hiding in a hole is no way for a Dwarf to die. No way for a soldier. No way for a king."

Bornyth nodded. "We must stop them here, no matter how extreme the measure. You know of what I speak," he said as a group of Dwarves staggered by -- four men, wounded and bleeding, bandages hastily wrapped about vicious wounds.

"How fare the stairs?" said Throgden to the men.

"They're through the first barricade, my lords," said one soldier, a grizzled sergeant. "The fighting's thick at the second. Half of the dead, they are our men. Our own guardsmen. Coming back up the stairs at us. We can't hold. We don't have enough men left."

Bornyth and Throgden's gazes followed the men as they staggered off. "They will die, those brave soldiers, just like all the rest," said Throgden. "First one will turn, and then he'll kill the others. We are undone. Darendor is dead. Our clan is finished."

"I will stop them here," said Bornyth. "They will not get beyond this mountain. That is what Bilson's Drop was designed for a thousand years ago. Let us get to the perch while we still can."

Sounds of battle reached them from this side and that. There was already fighting on their level.

"How could they have breached the third barricade so quickly?" said Throgden.

"It's not the barricades," said Bornyth as they rounded a corner and came upon a grisly scene. "It's the wounded. Some have turned." Before them in the corridor was a soldier, bandages wrapped about his arm and leg; his face, sallow; his posture, stooped. He bent over slavering. Beneath him, the twitching body of a Dwarf woman, blood spurting from her neck where he had bitten her. Bornyth raised his axe and plowed forward but before he reached the Draugar, a flash of yellow light erupted in the corridor and the Draugar's head exploded. From around the hallway's next bend came the Svart king, his bone staff glowing with mystical energy. With him were what remained of his retinue, a dozen battered Svarts, several wounded. None of his Diresvarts – his wizard priests – were with him.

"That way is blocked," said Guyphoon Garumptuss tet Montu, the High King of storied Thoonbarrow, in a thick accent as he pointed back the way he had come.

"Turnabout," shouted Bornyth to his men without hesitation. "We'll go around. There is another way."

As they started back, two Draugar, lately,

Darendor Dwarves, raced down the corridor towards them, jaws clacking: click, click, click. Bornyth's guards quickly hacked them to pieces.

"We must fly, my lord," said Throgden, "before we're trapped."

Twice more were they assaulted before they reached the seldom-used room that was their destination. Once by a single turned soldier. The second time by a half dozen. Two of Bornyth's men were killed outright. Three more were bitten or scratched. They knew their fate. They would not endanger their king. They stood guard in the hall, beyond the door. Waiting for more Draugar to come. Waiting to die. Four wounded Svart stood with them. Bornyth, Throgden, the Svart Seer, seven Dwarven soldiers, and six Svart entered the room and barricaded the door.

23

JUTENHEIM
TUNNELS OF SVARTLEHEIM

YEAR 1267, 4TH AGE

FREM SORLONS

The eerie tunnel that led from the ledge upon which he'd awoken grew narrower and steeper as Frem walked, every step taking him farther and farther from where he needed to go – up and out – out of that forsaken place -- the tunnels of Svartleheim -- never to return. And the Black Elfin drums hounded his every step. He hadn't gone far before he doubled back and searched every square inch of that tunnel, desperate to find any small shaftway or side tunnel that would lead up and out. He even checked for hidden doors in the rock, but found nothing.

There was nothing he could do except continue along the main route. But it offered him only one way to go — down and down into the depths of that accursed Elfin underworld.

After a time, the tunnel turned so steeply downward that he had to climb, hands and feet -- bracing himself along the walls as he went. Walls that grew so close, his shoulders barely cleared them on either side. Time and again, he struggled to keep hold of the torch as he made his way. He could not afford to lose it, for without light he was finished.

After what seemed like hours, the passage leveled out. The air was colder and still. But the Elfin drums still plagued him.

He came to a split in the passage — a side tunnel led off from the main, but low it was and it angled downward — he'd have to crawl through it. He had no desire for that, so he passed it by and remained on the main track. Twenty feet farther on, another small side tunnel. Then another. Several more, one smaller than the next. All going off this way and that, small and uninviting, filled of creepy crawlies and spidery webs. None of them appeared to turn upward, so far as he could see, so he passed them by. He walked as softly as he could, his ears straining for any sound, but all he heard were his own footsteps and the incessant beating of the Black Elfin drums.

After a goodly time, he heard other sounds behind him. Some distance back. Scurrying feet he marked them and mayhap, voices too.

He froze.

Was something there or did his mind play tricks on him?

He waited, listened, but heard nothing more. After a time, he continued on. But some minutes later, came the sounds again.

Closer.

Unmistakable this time. Scurrying feet on stone. Behind him. Following him. Stalking him. Perhaps on the main course, or else skulking through some parallel side tunnel — one of the many he'd lately passed.

He picked up his pace. Walked faster and faster still, but the sounds did not abate.

They grew closer.

And closer still.

And then Frem flew through tunnel as fast as his feet could carry him, head ducked down to avoid the uneven ceiling, torch outstretched before him, dagger in opposite hand.

The Black Elves had his scent. He had no doubt of it. They stalked him, waiting for their chance to strike.

Frem didn't know what to do.

Turn and fight?

Slip down a side tunnel and hope that they'd pass him by?

Or run headlong until he found an exit, or reached the limits of his endurance, or until they pulled him down from behind?

If the tunnel were tall enough for him to stand up straight, and if he were armed with sword and shield, he'd stop and make a stand — and give them what for. But stooped over, alone and ill equipped, he was too vulnerable. The odds too grim. So small were the Black Elves, that even in that narrow passage they could come at him two at a time from front and rear. Surrounded like that, he'd be in sorry shape, indeed.

And he dared not hide, for if they found him tucked in some tiny warren – he'd be trapped. He'd never have a chance. All his strength and skill at arms would do him no good. He didn't want to die.

He refused to.

So on he sped for the better part of an hour,

the passage still heading steadily downward all the while, the drumming never quieting. No side passage did he pass, save for those same tiny tunnels, too small for him to brave.

He stopped a moment to catch his breath, and to listen. Closed his eyes and grimaced, praying that he'd hear nothing. That he'd lost them. That he'd have some blessed time to rest. But almost immediately, the sounds of myriad scurrying feet assaulted his ears, echoing through the tunnels accompanied by the very drums of doom. This time, the Elves were closer than before. They'd gained a lot of ground on him despite all his effort. A lot of ground.

Still, he had but two choices: run full out and try to lose them, or turn and fight and be done with it.

He had no stomach for another battle. Not with the fatigue he felt. And not in that place. Not in that dark. Not with the knowing that if he lost his torch, he'd be done, he'd be dead. But if he ran full out, eventually he'd have no strength left. He'd double over, he'd drop. Too tired, too winded to fight. They'd make short work of him.

If he was going to die, he'd die fighting, not lying exhausted on his back.

So he made his decision.

Frem Sorlons turned and made his stand. He stood his ground, torch before him. He plucked another torch from his pack, lit it with the first, and tossed it a few yards behind him. That way, he'd have a backup light in case he lost the first.

He stood there, winded, breathing heavily, waiting. Waiting for death to charge out of the darkness for him and for the Valkyries to carry him home to Valhalla.

24

EGRIPT-MON AESIR ENCAMPMENT

THE AGE OF MYTH AND LEGEND

THETAN

"Your mind is set on killing him?" said Wotan.

Thetan looked surprised at the question. "Do you counsel against it?"

"I want that foul bastard dead more than any man alive," said Wotan. "But sorcerers of great power are not easy to kill. Some cannot be cut by sword or axe, or pierced of arrow or spear. Some others are immune to fire or magic, poison or plague, and who knows what else. A dangerous thing to go against men like that. And worst of all, they have a habit of coming back after you think they're dead."

"You believe that Azathoth is a wizard?" said Donar.

"What else could he be?" said Wotan. To Thetan he said, "You've seen him do wonders, haven't you? Great and terrible?"

"More terrible than great," said Thetan. "If he's not a god, then he's a man. A man with magic more powerful by far than any I have seen."

"Even such a man can be killed," said Donar. "Any man can be killed."

Wotan nodded. "Why not just strike him down? No one has better access to him than you. There must be opportunities. Why come to us? I've never seen you hesitate before once you've set your course."

"If I strike alone," said Thetan, "and I fail, Midgaard will remain under his yoke. I would not have that. The world must be free of him. We must destroy him on the field. Break his armies. Without them, his power is greatly diminished. Without the Arkons, and his armies, he cannot maintain control of his empire. For all his powers, he'd have to flee."

"How many of the Arkons will side with you?" said Wotan.

"One third of Vaeden's host, or thereabouts," said Thetan. "The rest will remain loyal to Azathoth, come what may."

"And the armies?" said Donar.

"A few units may follow the rebel Arkons, but the bulk, if not all, will remain with Azathoth."

"Are you asking us to stand against his armies?" said Donar.

"I'm asking you to assault them," said Thetan. "To focus Azathoth's full attention on dealing with you. That will be the distraction I need to catch him unawares."

"In this, even victory will come at a terrible cost," said Wotan. "The Aesir losses will be unimaginable. A battle to end all battles."

"But imagine the glory," said Donar. "To put down that monster and all his minions in one great strike. Our names would be remembered down through the ages. The Aesir would be revered as gods ourselves. What greater thing can a warrior aspire too?"

"We have waited for such an opportunity for long years," said Wotan. "Now that it presents itself, we cannot but take it. But you knew that."

"I hoped as much," said Thetan. "Now let us formulate a plan."

"First, tell me why you've taken this step now?" said Wotan. "What has changed?"

Thetan stared at the ground. Took a deep breath before he spoke.

"He has ordered the death of every firstborn child in all of Egript-Mon. Only his faithful to be spared. A lesson to the Aesir and all who follow you."

"What a foul thing is he to order the murder of children?" said Donar. "What a coward."

"Does he think we keep no watch over this city?" said Wotan. "That your armies could march in and do this black deed without resistance?"

"The Arkons could do it," said Thetan.

Wotan shook his head. "Not while I live."

"And that is why we're talking," said Thetan.

***

"This could all be a trap," said Donar as he and his father sat alone in the command tent, Thetan lately departed. "Everything he said could be a lie."

"I do not believe that Thetan would betray me," said Wotan.

"The false god likely thinks the same," said

137

Donar. "If he ensnares us, and destroys us, there will be little to stop Azathoth from taking over all of Midgaard. His power would be absolute."

"What I fear," said Wotan, "is that Thetan has been duped by Azathoth into taking these actions. The trickery of the false god puts our dear Loki to shame. But even if it is as Thetan says, this will be a battle unlike any other. The cost to our warriors will be staggering."

"We will be victorious," said Donar. "We will crush them beneath our boots. This is what we've wanted for countless years. To finally free all Midgaard of the false god and his minions. It is everything we've been working towards."

"We're not ready for an all-out battle," said Wotan. "Up until now, we've attacked where they were weak and spread thin. Our victories resulted from sound planning and strategic maneuvering even more than through skill in the field. In this way, we've been wearing them down. My whole strategy has been to avoid a pitched battle. To bide our time, chipping away at them. And then when they're weak enough, crush them. Now we're blundering into a single battle that will decide the fate of all. It's reckless."

"We gave Thetan our word," said Donar.

"Foolish was I to do so," said Wotan.

"Then why did you?"

"I never imagined that someone else would kill Azathoth for us," said Wotan. "I always thought that in the end, it would be he and I facing each other, the winner take the world. But when Thetan said that he and his Arkons would kill Azathoth and his inner circle, it sounded like a dream come true. How much easier would be our victory without Azathoth and his magic on the field? How could I let such a chance go by? I had to agree."

"Thetan knew that," said Donar.

"Of course he did," said Wotan. "Every move that man makes is planned. Friend he may be, but so too, I fear that he is the harbinger of our doom."

25

JUTENHEIM ANGLOTOR

YEAR 1267, 4TH AGE

URIEL THE BOLD

Kapte stood at Uriel's side, weeping. "The Wood Elves are all dead," she said, her voice quaking, her eyes red. "The last of them fell by the moat: Burget, Ronnet, Maldet, and even First Sword Torbet. Old Norby and all the Rock Dwarves are dead too. And the Lugron tribesmen, even the Dragon Fighters Clan — they fought to the last warrior down by the stone palisade."

"Even if we win this, Master, things will never be the same. All the warriors of Jutenheim have fallen. Without them, the common folk will be defenseless. The wild will take them all."

"A terrible day this be," said Uriel, "but I have been through this before. We will rebuild. We will–"

Uriel's head snapped back and his body stiffened.

Startled, Kapte spun toward him but stepped back in fear when she saw the look on his face.

"I am here," said a disembodied voice, deep and raspy. The sound filled the chamber. Kapte spun this way and that, searching for the speaker, but no one was to be found. She and Uriel were alone in the high tower's uppermost room. Uriel stood transfixed.

"Who are you?" said Uriel.

The voice responded, "I am Korrgonn, son of the one true god, Azathoth. Open your doors, lay down your arms, and I will show you mercy. No one else need die today."

"Azathoth has no son," said Uriel. "You are a deceiver. A charlatan that weaves tales to fool the foolish into following you. Who are you really? Give me your name, wizard."

"You feel my power, just as I feel yours," said Korrgonn. "I have a cadre of archwizards at my side and warriors with skills far beyond yours. I need no parley. I can take this keep with little more effort. I do you this boon out of respect, to preserve life. To limit unnecessary bloodshed. Stand down, mage, so that you and yours can see the morrow."

The *Farsight* mist that swirled before Uriel and Kapte changed color toward the red. It went wild and chaotic for some moments, swirling about against Uriel's will. And then finally it coalesced, coming again into focus. This time, it was Korrgonn's aspect that was visible within the mist.

Shock fell over Uriel's face. His mouth dropped open, and for several seconds he could not speak. "Gabriel Hornblower," he said at last. "Can it be you? Or do my eyes deceive me?"

"Uriel the Bold!" said Korrgonn, his eyes wide with surprise. "Is it you? Is it truly you?"

"It is I, Hornblower. Your voice is not as I remember. I did not recognize it at all."

"An old injury that never healed," said Korrgonn pointing to his throat. "I thought you long dead, brother. I thought I was the last."

"Then why do you besiege this temple of power?"

"I thought you minions of the dark powers," said Korrgonn. "I feared that you were a demon lord that slipped through some hole in the ether from the Nether Realms. And with good reason, so did I think: you command the Svart, and wild Lugron, and more. I sought to free the temple from your grasp. And guard it with my own, to keep it safe from those who would violate the gateway, that would tear it open to all our ruin. Thank the heavens that it is you. How long have you guarded here?"

"Too long, brother. Too long."

Korrgonn's face looked panicked and he turned aside shouting to others unseen through the mists. "Stand down," he shouted. "Have all our forces stand down at once. It is not what I thought. They are not our enemies. Stand down. Kill no one else." And then Korrgonn turned back toward Uriel. "Forgive me, brother, for I knew not what I did. I sought to liberate this holy place from evil. And instead it was I that brought the evil here. I am so sorry. I don't know what else to say. How to make amends for this."

"Why the charade?" said Uriel. "Why call yourself the son of Azathoth?"

"Because the name Gabriel Hornblower holds no power anymore," said Korrgonn. "Very few remember my name, and most of those mark me a villain. A traitor. So announcing myself properly either gets me nowhere or gets me violently assaulted. The name of Azathoth, on the other hand, is still feared and respected. And in some quarters, revered. A necessary duplicity."

"But doesn't it put you at odds with any true and honest defenders of these olden temples?"

"Of course it does," said Korrgonn. "But I thought it a small risk. I thought all the defenders of the temples were long since gone to dust. A costly mistake that I will long regret."

"Was it *you* that sent the Einheriar against me?" said Uriel.

"At my command, that was done. I wanted to avoid bloodshed. I thought a decapitation strike against the wizard that ruled this fortress would end the conflict before it started. Again, I say that I am sorry. There is no way to make up for the losses that you've suffered here, though my own forces have suffered too. How foolish it was for me to not seek parley at the outset. This could've all been avoided. I am at fault and I accept responsibility for it."

"Parley would've put you at a disadvantage had it not been me ruling this place," said Uriel. "You did what you needed to do, just as you've always done. Unfortunately, this time, we've both suffered for it. We shall find a way to put this behind us. But these revelations will take some time to explain to my people. No doubt, it will be the same for you. We must tread carefully to avoid any further unpleasantries."

"The towers of the inner courtyard are well equipped," said Uriel. "You may take your ease there — finding food, drink, and bunks. When I have things sorted, I will come out to greet you. We shall speak again soon, brother." With a wave of Uriel's hand, the undulating fog went dark and the connection was broken.

"His mouth never moved the entire time that he spoke," said Kapte, "but I heard his words."

"A quality of the magic that he employed," said Uriel. "A form of telepathic projection -- olden magic seldom remembered in modern times. Only we two could hear him– which was his intent so as not to give himself away to his followers. He needs to tell them in his own way, on his own terms, in his own time."

"You know him?" said Kapte. "Is he truly one of your Arkons of legend? The one called Gabriel?"

Uriel looked at her for some moments, but his thoughts were elsewhere. He turned back toward the swirling mists and worked his will on them. Korrgonn came into focus once more. "Brother," said Uriel speaking through a magical mist. Korrgonn turned and nodded.

"At R'lyeh, after we were split up, when Thetan the Lightbringer emerged from the citadel, who was at his side?"

Korrgonn's head tilted, his eyes looked away. "Sendarth," he said after some seconds. "It was Dark Sendarth."

"Aye, it was, brother," said Uriel. "It is good to see you again."

"And you, brother."

Uriel broke the connection.

EGRIPT-MON

THE AGE OF MYTH AND LEGEND

THETAN

The night that Azathoth's Arkons crept into Egript-Mon, blades bare, was a blacknight -- a night where the cloud cover was so thick that the moons' light was completely blocked out — the first of its kind since the Aesir had taken the city. By tradition, the locals doused their lanterns and turned in early on such nights, fearful of drawing the attention of dark spirits said to roam the black. Spirits intent on mischief and mayhem.

Some old folk were even more fearful. They warned that demons and devils of the Nether Realms prowled the streets on such nights, hunting for hapless victims to sate their ravenous appetite for blood and souls.

On that night at least, those stories weren't far from the truth.

On blacknights, the good citizens of Egript-Mon ignored noises on the commons.

Cries.

Screams.

Pleas for help.

Nothing more were they than the siren calls of restless spirits, warned the wise. Tricks to ply the foolish from their beds. Entreats to lure them out into the cold night where the specters ruled. The wise folk of Egript-Mon would not be fooled. They hunkered down on those nights. Kept their shutters shut. Their doors locked and barred. Their lanterns dim. And most of all, they stayed quiet. No matter what they heard outside. They stayed quiet.

Thetan didn't believe for a moment that the timing of the Arkons' mission was random chance. Somehow, the blacknight was Azathoth's doing.

The better for his assassins to succeed in their mission.

Ages before, Thetan had lived through the great deluge that Azathoth called down to punish the people for their wickedness. Weeks of continuous rain that drowned hill and valley alike certainly took more power than manipulating some clouds on a single evening. But Thetan often wondered whether Azathoth had truly caused the deluge or merely knew of its coming.

Did he have a way to predict the weather and other such things and then use that knowledge to his advantage? Perhaps he had no power to stop the great storm and save his people. So he named them wicked and claimed the storm was his wrath. Ingenious. Instead of the storm diminishing his power in the eyes of the people, it greatly enhanced it. Who but a god could do such a thing?

Or perhaps he did cause it; perhaps he did have the power. Thetan didn't know. All he knew for certain about it, was that he'd never know the truth.

But Thetan had seen Azathoth defraud the people with an eclipse. Most men didn't know that eclipses of the sun and of the moons were natural occurrences that recurred periodically according to some esoteric celestial schedule. When the light dimmed, the people mistakenly thought that it was a sign from the gods, usually an ominous one -- a bad omen that brought on fear and dread. Some even thought it the beginning of the end of the world.

Thetan had stood at Azathoth's side long ago when the lord put the fear in an enemy nation by predicting an imminent eclipse, which came to pass even as his booming voice threatened them. Thetan had known that that eclipse was coming, for Azrael the Wise, the greatest scholar and tinker amongst the Arkons and an expert at such matters, had forewarned him.

Somehow, Azathoth also knew that the eclipse was coming. Knew its timing down to the precise moment that the sun's light began to dim. The lord had made certain to be in just the right place at just the right time to convince the people that he'd caused it. That he was in control of it. That only he could restore the sun to the heavens. An effective tactic if you wanted to convince folk that you were a god.

That's when Thetan started to suspect that Azathoth was a fraud.

A charlatan.

A con man.

At the time, Thetan put those doubts aside and told himself that the lord had wisely used his foreknowledge of the eclipse to his advantage.

Why shouldn't he? What was wrong with that?

Thetan pushed back the nagging questions. Why deceive the people? Isn't deception, in itself, a wrong? A sin? And why would an all-powerful god, the self-proclaimed one true god, have need of such tactics?

It didn't make sense to Thetan.

A lot of what Azathoth did didn't make sense to him.

But it all came down to faith. To trust. To belief.

Did Thetan have faith that every action that Azathoth took -- more than that, that everything that happened in the world by luck, chance, or happenstance, was all part of Azathoth's grand plan? That he was behind it all? And that that plan was good?

Thetan kept that faith for a long time.

For too long.

And now he knew why. Deep down, he always knew, but denied it, suppressed it. He didn't want to face that truth.

It wasn't for love. For honor. For duty. For loyalty.

He kept the faith because he wanted those promised answers about his past, his memory. He wanted his memory restored. His life restored. His identity, restored.

Azathoth had played him for a fool.

And a fool he was.

But no longer.

No longer.

Thetan would not kill children. Not even if Azathoth were the one true god.

27

DARENDOR

YEAR 1267, 4TH AGE

BORNYTH TROLLSBANE

Bornyth's room of refuge was filled with crates and barrels of various supplies. At the back wall, a ship's ladder extended from floor to ceiling, ending in a hatch fifteen feet up. One by one, Bornyth and his party climbed the ladder and crawled through the hatch while those waiting barricaded the door with stacks of crates. By the time the last of them squeezed through the hatch, they heard a skirmish outside the storeroom's door. From the sound of it, the men they left behind were set upon by a large contingent of Draugar.

Inside the shadowy upper chamber, which was known as the perch, they lit wall sconces that revealed an oddly shaped high-ceilinged room with stone walls and ceiling, one side of which was filled with great metal gears that reached to the chamber's full height. Those gears were but a small part of a much larger machine built within the wall beyond their sight. Towards the back of the otherwise bare room was a great iron lever that extended up through a hole in the floor. The lever was tied back to the wall by several thick steel chains that locked it in position.

Bornyth went to the lever, studied its chains. "Throgden, see what you can see out there," he said pointing to a window high on the front wall. That wall curved as it rose, part of the roof of the cavern that overlooked the city below. Throgden scampered up a ladder with agility that belied his age until he reached the perch for which the room was named – a narrow walkway that accessed the wide window. The window was indeed an overlook, much like the balcony that Bornyth and the Seer had stood on when they exited the secret corridor, except here they were higher up. Throgden looked out the portal for a time but said nothing.

"Is there no hope?" said Bornyth.

Throgden shook his head as he turned back toward his king. "Beyond, I hear only the wails of the dying and the croaking of the dead. I see only chaos, horror, and despair. Our beloved clan is no more. Darendor is dead. And all Midgaard teeters on the brink of destruction."

"Then we've chosen well in coming here," said Bornyth. "For in our dying we will yet have our revenge."

The Svart king stepped forward. "What be this device?" he said pointing at the lever and at the geared machine in turn. "What devilry do you plan?"

"I'm planning to destroy them all. We will take them with us. Every last one of them." Bornyth turned toward the Seer. "Raise the Lomerian witch-woman, if you can. I would have them know what we do here today. What sacrifice we make for them and for all others. Get her on your stone now; do not fail me."

The Svart Seer set down her satchel and pulled from it her Seer Stone. The Dwarves and the other Svart, save their king, all backed away from her. She sat the floor, the stone set between her knees. She put her hands to its surface, which now glowed in vibrant colors, swirling patterns of red, yellow, and brown. She spoke words in her olden tongue, unknown to the Dwarves. Her call went unanswered for some time.

"They're at the storeroom door, King Bornyth," said one of the Dwarven soldiers guarding the top of the ladder as he looked through the hatch.

"Will it hold?" said Throgden, still at the perch.

"Not for long," said the soldier. "They're pounding it but good, bending it in its frame. Eventually the hinges will fail. Our barricade will fare little better."

"Close and block the hatch," said Throgden.

"No," said Bornyth, "that will just slow them down. Drop the ladder so they can't reach us at all."

At last, Mother Alder's face appeared within the smoky depths of the Seer Stone.

"Can she hear me?" shouted Bornyth.

"Of course I can hear you," said Mother Alder. "What happened? Before our earlier transmission was cut off, it sounded as if there was a battle about you? What's going on over there?"

"Is Barusa there?" said Bornyth. "I need to speak with your chancellor."

"He's not here at the moment," said Mother Alder. "You can speak to me. I will convey whatever message need be conveyed."

"The Draugar have taken Darendor," said Bornyth.

"I don't understand," said Mother Alder. "Isn't Darendor a great city? A fortress? Your armies, legend? We spoke but a few hours ago."

"The Draugar are swift in their killing," said Bornyth. "Darendor has fallen."

"I...I am sorry," said Mother Alder. "Are you safe?"

Then came a great crash. The Draugar broke through the storeroom's door and several crates from their makeshift barricade had fallen over. The soldiers slammed the hatch closed.

"Is the ladder down?" said Bornyth.

"We couldn't get it fast enough," said a soldier. "We don't have the tools."

"Block the hatch," said Throgden. "There's a crossbar – set it swiftly, men."

Bornyth turned back to the Seer Stone. "I stand before you now to warn you," he said, "of the seriousness of the Draugar threat."

"And I want you to know why they won't be on your doorstep on the morrow. I want you to know of the sacrifice the Dwarves of Darendor are making on your behalf. On all Midgaard's behalf. I will stop them here. Every one of them within my caverns. Problem is, there surely be others outside. Beyond my reach. Those will continue to spread their plague. And they will come for you. For Lomion. Mayhap in a month. Maybe in a year. But eventually they will come. You have to be ready for them; you have to be prepared. We will lay low their main horde. Mark our sacrifice well.

152

It needs to be remembered. We deserve to be remembered." Then Bornyth's voice grew softer, slower. "You will remember, won't you?"

"How will you stop them?" said Mother Alder. "You've already said that you are defeated. I don't understand."

"Watch. Watch for as long as you can, Seer. Keep your line open until the last."

The hatch rattled and buckled. The Draugar were on the ladder pounding at the hatch from below. The soldiers, Dwarf and Svart alike, stood about it, weapons ready, jaws set. They would fight to the end to protect their kings.

"No need for swords or axes any longer, my lads," said Bornyth. "Tonight, we drink in Odin's halls amongst the gods and the honored dead."

"What mean your words?" said the Svart King. "What plan you?"

"Bilson's Drop," said Bornyth. "The last weapon of the Dwarven kings of Darendor. A safeguard designed by our ancestors to ensure that no enemy force will ever hold our city. Our caverns will remain sacrosanct from the foulness of the Draugar or any other. Forevermore."

"This lever and these gears," said Bornyth, "and much more that you don't see, will bring down these caverns and crush all and everything within beneath a million tons of solid stone. That is our sacrifice. All that we are will be lost to the world, forever."

"No need," said the Svart king. "Position here we hold. One by one up ladder they come. We hold. We fight. We survive. No need, collapse stone."

"If we don't bring down the cavern," said Bornyth, "the Draugar horde will move on to the next town, the next city. Everyone and everything in their path will fall. We can't let that happen. We have the power to stop them here and stop them I will."

"We die, you do this," said the Svart king.

"A hero's death," said Throgden.

"What more can any man aspire to?" said Bornyth. He narrowed his eyes. "But you, you are not men. Maybe you don't understand these things. Honor. Duty. Sacrifice. I don't know if they mean anything to you but they mean everything to us, to me." Bornyth undid the chains that restrained the lever.

"Die here, I will not," said the Svart king. Swift as could be, the Svart king lowered the tip of his bone staff.

Pointed it at Bornyth.

Yellow fire blasted from it.

And Bornyth Trollsbane fell.

28

JUTENHEIM
TUNNELS OF SVARTLEHEIM

YEAR 1267, 4TH AGE

FREM SORLONS

The Black Elves slithered from the shadows into Frem's view. Those Elves were all similarly clad and equipped with strange black and silver garments of cloth and metal, garb unlike any other Black Elf Frem had yet encountered. Perhaps they hailed from another Elfin town or city, or else were a special military unit. They carried swords and axes, black faces hidden in the darkness, the glow of their eyes against the torchlight the thing most easily seen. They massed before him, beyond the edge of his light, gibbering and jabbering. What they said, Frem had no idea.

What held them back, Frem knew not.

Did they await an officer or champion to take his place at the fore? Or were they gathering their numbers and girding their courage before they advanced on the big Volsung?

The Black Elves, for all their skills, had lost their armies when they sent them against the Shadow League expedition. The Elves were left broken and bloodied, what few of them that survived. So perhaps they feared Frem. He didn't know. He'd never know. And in the end, it didn't matter. For every moment that they held back, Frem caught his breath and grew stronger, recovering from the run. Sweat poured down his brow and his back, his shirt clinging to his skin. He held a dagger in one hand, a torch in the other. Ready and waiting for what could only be his final battle.

Frem wanted to charge. He wanted to shout a war cry and rush towards them, but he held himself back. Not out of any fear but out of hope. Hope that they had a good reason not to attack him. Perhaps they wanted to parley and awaited one of theirs that spoke the Volsung tongue. Or else, perhaps they just didn't have the nerve to attack him at all. Perhaps he could still walk out of there, the Elves merely monitoring his progress.

He waited and waited some more. The minutes ticked by. The Elves' chattering grew louder and louder. Frem couldn't understand their words but he thought he began to understand the meaning.

They were afraid.

They were gathering their courage.

That's when he knew he had to charge. If he did, there was a chance that he'd rout them. That they'd run fleeing if he swiftly took the life of the first few that he engaged. The rest may well turn tail. Then, mayhap he'd have a chance of escape.

"Odin," shouted Frem. "Odin!"

And then he charged.

When he did, a startled scream went up in the Elfin ranks, and a few of their number turned and fled outright. But most held their ground, screeching and howling — and then, they charged at him.

As he reached them, Frem threw a side kick at the lead Elf; his huge boot smashed against its head, and that of the Elf next to it, and sent them careening backwards into their fellows who tripped over them and went down in a heap. Frem lunged with his dagger. A quick triple thrust with both took down more Elves.

Frem backpedaled as the Elves poured over their fallen fellows. And he tried the same tactic again: a side kick followed in quick succession with multiple thrusts at any Elves within arm's reach. Again it worked. Svart blood showered the tunnel floor, and their screams echoed against the stone.

But on came more of them.

Dozens more.

Frem backpedaled again; stabbed, sliced, and clubbed with his dagger and repeatedly thrust his burning brand to keep the devils at bay. Then an arrow whooshed out of the black and impacted his shoulder, finding purchase at the joint between his armored plates. A second shaft smashed into his breastplate, followed immediately by a third. Several more flew wide and broke against the tunnel walls. He stepped back again and more arrows crashed into his legs, two at least taking hold. Frem's armor was thick and stout as was the padding below it. The arrows, what few reached his flesh, did not sink deep. The wounds were of no threat to him, save if the weapons had been tipped with poison. Frem prayed that they were not.

Despite the manic chaos of that melee, Frem's strikes were carefully aimed, measured, and precisely executed. He wasted no motion and no energy. He moved when he needed to move. Blocked when he needed to block. And struck when he needed to strike. There was no wild frenzy about him, no hint of the berserker. Frem was a swordmaster, born to the blade, a titan amongst warriors. With each dagger swing or thrust, he sliced or skewered another Black Elf and sent them on to Helheim.

But they kept coming.

They jumped and dived for his legs, sacrificing themselves in attempt to trip him up or pull him down. They stabbed, bit, and clawed his legs, his stout armor all that kept his flesh from being torn to the bone.

They jumped atop one another to get at him, attacking in a wild frenzy, climbing atop the corpses piled higher and higher before Frem.

One Elf grabbed his helmet and managed to rip off his visor and face guard. It lunged and in its frenzy tried to bite Frem's neck.

But Frem bit first.

Clamped his teeth around the Svart's throat and tore it out. Blood sprayed into his mouth, across his face and eyes.

He pummeled the Black Elves that clung to his legs with the base of his torch and his dagger pommel. He dared not hit too hard with the torch for fear it would extinguish, but the pommel he used with abandon. Each strike crushed the skull of whatever Elf he hit.

And then they came at him from behind. He knew it when he felt a spear slam into his back. So powerful was that strike, its tip passed through the metal plate but then stuck, never penetrating through the armor's padding.

Frem felt as if he hefted tree trunks, so heavy with fatigue were they. He took a deep breath, steeled himself, and punched and thrust and sliced all the faster, all the harder, all his power and will behind each attack, grunting and groaning with the strain, calling out, "Odin! Odin! Odin!"

The Black Elves swarmed like ants around him. His adrenaline pumped, his heart pounded. Neither by skill nor force of numbers could they pull him down. He pounded and pounded away, the broken bodies piling in heaps about him. He fought like Thor himself, destroying his enemies with inhuman might.

At last, he lost his dagger. He grabbed the closest Black Elf by its upper arm, picked it up, and swung the creature as a bludgeon, over and over into its fellows. He turned and swung and turned and swung again and again, slapping that Elf from one side of the tunnel to the other, hitting two or three of its kind at a time. He stopped only when the thing's arm tore off.

He grabbed the last dagger from his belt and went back to work in a flash, slicing and stabbing, still with precision and power.

A moment later, without word or warning, the Black Elf horde melted away. They disappeared; slithered back into the darkness whence they came.

They were done.

By the gods, they were done.

Frem heard the scurrying feet as they fled, never stopping until the sound of their passage faded to nothing.

At first, Frem didn't believe it. He stood at the ready, alternately looking before him and behind, waiting for the next charge or some other attack, some subterfuge, something. Anything.

But the Elves were gone!

They had fled from him.

Fled from him in terror.

He had won. Dead gods, he had won.

"Odin," he shouted.

29

EGRIPT-MON

THE AGE OF MYTH AND LEGEND

THETAN

No one in Egript-Mon had reason to suspect what was coming that night. Not with the tight cordon of troops that the Aesir had stationed about the city perimeter and the scattered troops they had encamped about the interior. The northerners had taken over the palace, the main barracks, and various other government buildings, though, by and large, they preferred to sleep in their tents. The tall northmen weren't at home in the ponderous stone buildings of Egript-Mon -- so different from the smaller wood structures of their northern homeland.

Despite the occupation, the citizens were happy to have Azathoth's troops gone. Notwithstanding its close proximity to Vaeden, Egript-Mon had ever been a free city that ruled itself and the fertile river valley that extended for untold miles to the south. Only lately had Azathoth annexed the place. He'd moved his armies in so quickly and in such force that the Egripts didn't dare resist. A nearly bloodless campaign that lasted less than a day after the Arkons and their troops arrived. Mithron had led the attack.

The conquerors claimed they'd come to free the people from their false gods; to put them on the path to enlightenment; to save their souls. The Egripts didn't understand that. They didn't think that they needed saving and they'd always thought that they were free. Free to say and do most anything they wanted, so long as they didn't run afoul of the great Faroun, what they called their king -- he whose dynastic line ruled over them for untold eons, generally benevolently, so long as they paid their share of taxes and behaved themselves.

The Azathothians had changed everything.

They instituted martial law.

Set curfews.

Imposed strict religious laws on the citizenry. They set stone tablets inscribed with the laws on the street corners and other prominent places.

There were many laws. Some obvious. Others obscure or downright odd. The Azathothians punished lawbreakers with a heavy hand. Although, if one repented and begged forgiveness, mercy was often granted.

The Egripts were smart enough to realize that resistance to Azathoth's rule was futile, so in general, they complied with the new edicts -- outwardly, at the least. Over the weeks and months, as life again became routine in Egript-Mon, Azathoth's armies withdrew. They were needed elsewhere. It was, after all, a large and growing empire.

By the time the Aesir showed up, the Azathothian occupation was down to only four brigades of regulars, each led by an Arkon. With no sign of rebellion fomenting in the city, even that was overkill. No one expected a foreign invader to strike so deep within Azathoth's territory.

Which was why Wotan did just that.

The Egripts had had no dealings with the Aesir before they attacked the city. But they'd heard of them.

Everyone had.

Northern barbarians, the civilized folk called them. Some thought them raiders. Marauders. The superstitious marked them giants or ogres, not men at all. But the wise knew that they were much more than that. Like Azathoth, Wotan and his Aesir were building an empire, one that stretched from the northern snow caps, down along the coasts for hundreds of miles. They were a different breed than the southerners. Taller. Broader. Wilder. More unpredictable. And warlike. Their culture was one of battle. They were born and bred to it. Where Egript children played with toys, Aesir children played with bows and axes.

When the Aesir came, there was no siege. No lengthy battle. There was simply a charge. Wild. Loud. And frightening.

They came through open, unsuspecting gates, and over the walls on all sides of the city at once. They rushed headlong at anyone that dared oppose them. The Azathothians were caught off-guard. Within minutes, the Aesir controlled the streets. Within hours, all of Azathoth's forces had fled, gone into hiding, been captured, or slaughtered.

The people cowered in fear. Some in the great temples. Some in their homes. They didn't know what the barbarians planned for them. Slaughter? Slavery? Subjugation?

What they got was freedom.

The great king of the Aesir, Wotan himself, called on the people to assemble in the central square. Thousands upon thousands gathered there to hear his words. Fear filled their faces. They held their children close, expecting the worst. But Wotan told them that he'd not come to conquer them or to harm them in any way. He'd come to free them from Azathoth's clutches. That the Aesir's quarrel was with the Azathothians, not them. He would not sack their city. He wouldn't steal their goods. Life could return to normal, as it was before the Azathothians came, save that the Aesir would remain. They'd occupy the city, but only to hold it against Azathoth.

True to his word, Wotan had done just that. Still, some of his men took matters upon themselves. The Aesir were a wild, verile people. Drunken brawls were routine. Assaults against citizens, though unsanctioned and often harshly punished, were all too common. Women were abused. When that happened, Wotan had no mercy for the culprits. He lined up three of his men who had defiled two young women, and had their private parts sliced off. Then, with a great two-handed sword, Wotan himself cut off their heads. Behavior amongst the troops showed marked improvement after that.

That was one month to the day before the Arkons crept into Egript-Mon on Azathoth's orders.

30

JUTENHEIM ANGLOTOR

YEAR 1267, 4TH AGE

"**W**ho is he, my lord?" said Par Keld, the other Leaguer wizards looking on. "Who rules Anglotor? A Nether Lord? A beast from Helheim? Or some rogue archwizard?"

Korrgonn made an esoteric gesture with his fingers, tracing a runic symbol in the air. From his mouth, strange clicks and whistling issued forth, barely audible, barely noticeable except by those knowledgeable of such things. Sorcery it was, subtle yet sublime. A protective shield, an invisible mystical barrier to keep sound in or out – a cone of silence, if you will.

"He is a monster," said Korrgonn. "A traitor with a black heart. There is no good in him. No honor. No loyalty. He lives only for his own selfish desires. Midgaard will be a better place when it's cleansed of him. In my father's holy name, I will destroy him. But never fear, I have duped him. Convinced him that he and I have common cause, even that we are old friends. To restore the lord to us, a bit of subterfuge I think is warranted."

"Indeed," said Par Keld. "The lord must be brought back, no matter what it takes."

31

VAEDON

THE AGE OF MYTH AND LEGEND

THETAN

"**H**ow can we allow this?" said Gabriel. "This culling cannot go forward. To murder the firstborn of every family -- I can hardly imagine anything more evil than that. We agreed to take a stand. To put an end to this madness. We cannot now stand by and let it happen."

"We have to do that," said Uriel. "And worse, we have to participate. The lord will suffer no defiance in this. His orders were clear, as is our duty."

"The Aesir need time to ready their forces," said Mithron. "They are not ready to assault Vaeden. Not nearly. As horrible as this culling is, it will give the Aesir time, and perhaps more importantly, it will give them motivation."

"How much time?" said Azrael.

"As much as it takes," said Mithron. "Patience brothers. The right time will come."

"Wotan has only a foothold in Egript-Mon, albeit a strong one," said Uriel. "The bulk of his armies are scattered about his empire. It will take months to bring all his forces into position."

"Months!" said Azrael.

"We cannot wait that long," said Gabriel. "This madness must come to a stop."

"So where does that leave us?" said Raphael.

"It means that we cannot avoid the culling," said Thetan.

"Then we should go it alone," said Gabriel. "Forget the alliance with Wotan. Forget battling the lord's armies. We deal with the lord ourselves, in the palace. This very night. Let us be done with it."

"And if we fail, all Midgaard is lost," said Thetan. "No one could hope to stand against him. He'd reign unchallenged. Imagine what he'd do with absolute power."

"Even if we fail, Wotan can still attack," said Gabriel.

"Without us working from within," said Uriel, "the Aesir, for all their strength and courage, would not have a chance. I agree with Thetan. Only working in conjunction with the Aesir can we succeed in this."

"Then I'll do it myself," said Gabriel. "I will act alone. If I succeed, then it's over. If I fail, our plans with Wotan can continue. You need only claim no knowledge of my betrayal."

"No," said Thetan. "I've thought of that. I would strike him down myself. I would already have done it. But the risk is too great. Even acting alone, if I fail, Azathoth will be on the alert. If I, or any one of you, betrayed him, he'd suspect all the rest. He might even kill us all, and start over with a new retinue of Arkons, just to be safe. Even if we escaped his wrath, he'd not let any of us get close to him again. Not for a long time. Years. He's always been paranoid. How much more so, then?"

"The lord would not murder us," said Arioch, "just by association with a traitor. You can't believe that."

"You were not here for the great flood," said Thetan. "I was. So was Mithron."

"Nearly all life on Midgaard was wiped out within a fortnight," said Mithron.

"If I strike, I will not fail," said Gabriel. "I will put my dagger through his black heart. I will end him with one blow."

"What if that doesn't kill him?" said Thetan. "Have you thought of that? What if his magic turns your blade or heals him? He'll call the alarm. Then, if he doesn't smite you, the guards will. When he's done with you, he'd smell a conspiracy and be after all of us."

"Then you be there," said Gabriel to Thetan. "And you too," he said looking to Mithron. "If I fail, leap to the lord's rescue. Strike me down. Then you'll be heroes. He'll never suspect you. You'll be trusted more than ever before. Then, you can go forward with the Aesir or some other plan of your making. We must do this."

Thetan, Mithron, and the other Arkons hesitated, surprised by Gabriel's plan.

"My life in trade for all those firstborn of Egript-Mon," said Gabriel. "A small price to pay to save so many. And if I succeed, then there'd be no sacrifice at all."

"There is logic and wisdom to these words," said Azrael. "A selfless sacrifice to be admired. But it puts a heavy burden on Thetan and Mithron or any other that takes that duty. A weighty burden indeed."

"Say that you will do it, if it comes to it," said Gabriel.

"Perhaps they could just subdue you," said Raphael.

"And leave him to Azathoth's torture?" said Mithron. "No man could resist that forever. No offense, my brother, but in the end, you'd give us all up. Everything would be undone."

"I know this," said Gabriel. "If I fail, you must kill me, and do so quickly. Say that you will and then let us proceed."

"The lord would still suspect Thetan and Mithron, even if they struck you down," said Azrael. "His mind sees many moves ahead, far more than we ever could. We cannot out-think him. We cannot hope to trick him. What say you, Lightbringer?"

"I say…no good comes of an evil deed. Killing a brother is an evil, even if done for the greater good."

"Isn't that exactly what we're rebelling against?" said Mithron. "Refusing to do the lord's evil even though he says it's for the greater good?"

The men nodded.

"You're right," said Gabriel. "If you did as I said, you would become what Azathoth is. That cannot be. My head spins."

"This leaves us no option," said Azrael, "then to let the culling occur, and then bide our time until we can act."

"Still, I will not harm an innocent," said Gabriel.

"Nor will I," said Thetan.

"I have an idea," said Uriel. "The lord ordered that the faithful paint their doors with the blood of lambs and sheep. That is how the Arkons will know which homes are to be passed over and which are not."

"What of it?" said Arioch. "You cannot warn the Egripts to paint their doors too. Our brethren would figure it out in no time, and surely some of the Egripts will give us up. Again, we'd be undone."

"Paint the doors ourselves," said Thetan. All eyes looked to him. "Every tenth door we come to, we paint with the all-clear. We could save hundreds of families."

"Someone would see," said Arioch.

"We brought the paint to protect the homes of those innocents that Sariel and Bose were unable to contact," said Thetan, "but of whose homes they knew."

"There is risk to this," said Mithron. "Perhaps too great a risk, but, as you say, we could save many innocents."

"I would take that risk," said Raphael.

"As would I," said Gabriel.

No one disagreed.

"Then so shall it be," said Thetan.

32

LOMION CITY HOUSE ALDER

YEAR 1267, 4TH AGE

MOTHER ALDER

Mother Alder gazed deeply into the Alder Stone, sweat glistening on her brow from the effort of holding open the connection to Darendor. Barusa was two steps behind her, hand over his mouth, another clenching his belly. He didn't have the stomach to get any closer. He didn't have the stomach to stand where he was, but Mother Alder had urged him forward when he arrived. Luckily, the servants had caught him before he'd gotten too far off – on his way to a High Council meeting. He needed to see what went on in the Dwarven kingdom.

"Is Trollsbane down?" said Barusa.

"They're all down," said Mother Alder, "except for the Black Elf king himself and one of Trollsbane's officers. Those two are locked in a fight to the death."

"They're fighting each other?"

"Trollsbane tried to collapse the caverns, to stop the Draugar in Darendor, but the stinking Elves are not having it. The Elf king put down Trollsbane with a magical blast and then he and

172

his went after what few Dwarves Trollsbane had left."

Mother Alder winced and reared back from the Alder Stone. "That's it then, it's over. The Elf king just gutted the last of Trollsbane's men — a graybeard, but by Odin, did he put up a fight. Stood with the king Elf shot for shot since before you entered the room. But in the end, the Elf's dark magic was too much for him."

Barusa chanced to move in closer to get a better look. "What is the Svart doing with the bodies?"

"Piling them atop that hatch in the floor to keep the Draugar out. No bigger than a child, but do you see how strong he is? Drags armored Dwarves as if they're toys. He's worthy of the evil legends about him."

"If the Draugar head straight this way," continued Mother Alder, "how long until they're on our doorstep?"

"As little as a fortnight, *if* they came straight on."

"We can't repel both them and the trolls," said Mother Alder. "If we're lucky, the Draugar will take care of our troll problem."

"Don't count on that," said Barusa. "This siege will not hold. In a fortnight's time, Lomion City will either have fallen to the Troll or we will have beaten them back. If we win, we'll be weakened, perhaps greatly so. We'll be in no position to take on a horde that rolled over Darendor in a day."

"I might be able to do something," said Mother Alder.

"Farseeing is a useful skill," said Barusa, "and

speaking through the Stone the more so, but such powers will not stop this threat."

"Firstborn, you know not of all the powers that I possess. Let me try something." She put all ten fingertips to the Seer Stone. Streaks of white, blue, and yellow light flashed within the Stone, reaching up from its depths to her fingertips, on and off, one after another.

"Bornyth Trollsbane," said Mother Alder, "get off your butt and kill that stinking Elf. Pull that lever and bring down the caverns just as you planned. Do not let the Elf stop you."

"Can't the Elf king hear you?"

"I sent that message straight into Trollsbane's head. If he's not dead, and if his thick skull didn't block me, then mayhap he heard it."

"I think he's dead," said Barusa.

Mother Alder cupped her hands together, intertwining her fingers and laid them against the Seer Stone. She leaned closer and closer to it until her lips brushed against it. Then she blew a puff of air against the Stone. And then a second. "I gift you this bit of life," said Mother Alder. "Don't you dare waste it, you bastard, for it costs me dearly. Get up now, Dwarf, and see this through. Midgaard needs you." Mother Alder's eyelids fluttered, and both hands shook. She steadied herself and blew a third time against the Stone.

A moment later, Bornyth opened his eyes, gasped, and bounced to a sitting position.

Mother Alder's eyes closed and she slumped forward, unmoving.

33

MOUNT TROGLESTYRE
TROLL CITY OF GOTHMAGORN

YEAR 1267, 4TH AGE

ECTOR EOTRUS

The northmen had some of the best trackers and scouts in Midgaard amongst them. Their skills enabled the Eotrus men to follow the fleeing trolls through the rocky foothills of the Kronar Mountains and then deep into the stately and seldom-visited Kronar Range. The Eotrus column could not keep apace but they had scouts aplenty to track the troll and maintain contact with the main Eotrus force.

"Seven days in these mountains," said Indigo as he sat before the crackling campfire with the other officers. "Do they lead us to their lair as we hoped, or into the endless wilds of the frozen wastelands, and thereby, to our deaths?"

"We don't even know if they know we're following them," said Ector. "Not for certain."

"They know," said Pellan. "They have to know. The way those things tracked me through the woods, they have senses as sharp as bloodhounds."

175

"Then can we trust their trail?" said Indigo. "Would they be so foolish as to lead us to their home? Or are we walking into a trap?"

"I think they're scared," said Ector. "I think they're running home to whatever help or comfort they think they'll find there."

"If we hadn't let those trolls through our lines," said Indigo, "we could've spent months in these mountains and found nothing. I never knew there was this much wild land up here. This range goes on forever. If they aren't leading us to their lair, then we'll never find it."

"We will find it," said Ector. "We have to."

Lord Lester approached the campfire, a grin on his face. "We just got word from the scouts," he said, "the trolls are heading up the peak that lies straightaway north -- the tallest peak in the entire range. There's a hidden trail, well used. And there are caves."

"By Odin," said Ector as he slapped his hand to his thigh, "we have them!"

***

Ector stood near the entry to the great cavern of Gothmagorn, his sword and shield in hand; both dripped of troll blood. Blood spatters marred his tunic, helm, and pants. A trickle of blood still dripped from his nose where something had hit him during one of several skirmishes over the prior few hours. Captain Pellan and Indigo were with him, along with several score knights and soldiers.

Structures of stone, wood, and thatch filled the cavern. The howls and screams of hundreds, no — thousands of frightened and dying trolls filled the air. Northmen breached every door, every structure, their weapons bloodied. No less than two thousand men battled in that single cavern with whatever troll resistance remained. Thousands more men prowled the myriad tunnels that branched off in all directions.

"After we took those what guarded the entry tunnels, and those that fought us here at the gates of their city," said Pellan, "the battle was over. Now it's just the slaughter. Them that is left are noncombatants. Females. Old folk. Children. Thousands of them. That's all that's left here. Of their soldiers, only the token force that we've already put down, was here."

"That much is clear," said Ector. "Victory is ours. Our revenge is at hand."

"Are you suggesting that we stop?" said Indigo. "That we break off the attack? We knew what we'd find here. We knew their army was afield."

"I just want to make certain that we understand what we're doing here," said Pellan. "Do we really want to kill their noncombatants? Is that what we truly want? Is that who we are?"

"I've been asking myself that since the moment we took down their guards," said Ector. "What would my father do, I've asked myself. What's the right thing to do? The honorable thing? The just thing? The good thing? The wise thing? That's all that's been in my head these last hours."

"What *would* Lord Aradon do?" said Pellan. "I

177

really don't know. I was never with him in a situation remotely like this."

Ector looked toward Indigo.

The big knight shook his head. "Lord Aradon never killed noncombatants that I ever saw or heard of. But these are not men – they are monsters. They eat us. All of them – combatants and noncombatants. They eat us. It's different, isn't it?"

"I don't know," said Ector. "To kill noncombatants is a dishonorable act. It's against the rules of war. Mayhap, it is even an evil thing, regardless of circumstance. But as you say, these are not men. They are as animals––"

"Are they?" said Pellan. "They built this place. They wear clothing of their own make. They forge armor and weapons for their warriors. They have a language—"

"Grunts, groans, and howls," said Indigo.

"What does it matter that we don't understand it?" said Pellan. "Mock it if you will, but it's a language all the same. And they have a culture. Can we say the same for bears or lions or saber cats? I think not. These trolls, they are people. Not like us, but they are people. And just because they're not like us, does that change the rules? The rules of war? The rules of civilized behavior? Of common decency? Of morality? Does their *otherness* make it okay to kill their women, children, old folk, and their sick? Their babies?"

"They're monsters," said Ector. "What they did, their atrocities. All the people that they killed. Killed and ate. They killed Sarbek. They sacked the Dor; they destroyed our home, for Odin's sake."

"They did," said Pellan. "But not these ones. Not the civilians."

"They're the same," said Indigo. "One and the same. These ones would have done the same to us as their army did if they could."

"Maybe so," said Pellan. "But if these were men -- Volsungs, Dwarves, Gnomes, or Elves — would we kill them to the last? Wipe them out? Even the children? Would we?"

Ector paused and thought long before responding. "If any men behaved as the troll does — if they killed us to eat us, then yes, I think we'd kill them to the last, and rightly so. I think we'd have to. Because if we didn't, someday they'd be standing over our folk — our women, our children. Do we want that fate for them? If we finish it here, wipe them out to the last, or nearly so, that terrible day will never come again. Our people will never have to suffer the horror of a troll invasion again."

"With such things," said Pellan, "sometimes there are unintended consequences."

"What do you mean?" said Ector.

"Killing them all may set in motion events of which we cannot now predict," said Pellan. "Events that might be worse for us than if we let them live or came to some understanding or treaty with them."

"And if we show them mercy," said Ector, "we may live to regret it...I think I'll take my chances."

"They attacked us," said Indigo. "They started this war, they began the atrocities. If we finish them here, they're getting what they deserve."

"I say again," said Pellan, "is killing their noncombatants really what we want to do?"

"No," said Ector. "It's not what *we're* deciding here. It is what *I* am deciding here. Unless and until my brothers return, I am the Lord of Dor Eotrus. I am the Warden of the North. This burden, this responsibility, falls on me and me alone. History may call me a hero for what we do here today. Or my name may be remembered in infamy. Ector the slaughterer. Ector the mad. Ector the villain. Mayhap that will be my fate. But it is *my* fate. These people, these trolls, whatever they are, they started this, just as Indigo said. I will not have another Volsung family murdered in their beds. Torn apart and eaten alive. Never again. Never again. We will kill them to the last, infant to crone. Every one. Spare not one of them. Those are my orders."

Indigo's face was grim, his jaw set. He nodded slowly.

Pellan's chin dropped to her chest, her eyes downcast. "So will it be, Lord Eotrus. But this is not on you alone. What we do today will live in the memory of every soldier here for the rest of his days."

A small group of men ran up to the officers, sweating and out of breath, covered in troll blood. "My lord," said the eldest of the soldiers, addressing Ector, "we have the troll queen."

34

VAEDON

THE AGE OF MYTH AND LEGEND

THETAN

"**I**s all in readiness for tonight?" said Azathoth as he and Thetan strolled along the palace's terrace that overlooked the City of Vaeden and the surrounding lands. Azathoth stood as tall as Thetan, all in white, robes flowing about him.

"It is, Lord," said Thetan, bedecked in full battle armor.

"You will lead, of course," said Azathoth.

"I will lead the vanguard," said Thetan. "We shall insure that all the faithful are passed over and safeguarded from any retribution by the Egripts. Bhaal will follow, in command of the assault forces. Your will, Lord, will be done, just as you decreed. The Aesir and their Egript lackeys will pay for their defiance."

"And Mithron?" said Azathoth.

"With my vanguard," said Thetan.

Azathoth halted, turned to Thetan, and placed a gentle hand on his shoulder. "I know that what I have asked you to do tonight is difficult. To mete out such a harsh punishment must weigh heavily on your soul. I know this. And I wish that it were not necessary to burden you and my Arkons with it. But alas it is, and though I cannot deny that the role you've chosen for yourself for this mission is the one most important, it is not the one that suits you best. You are a warrior, Thetan, not a bodyguard."

Thetan's mouth opened as he prepared to speak, but Azathoth's other hand came up to stay him. "I will respect your decision. Never forget that all my faithful are as sons and daughters to me, not only because it was my hand, my divine will, that put the spark of life and the miracle of a soul in each of you, but because of the love I have long developed in watching you grow, thrive, and prosper. But of all the faithful, *you* are the one most like a true son to me, no different than if you were of own my body and of my own blood. And so I support your decision. You may keep your hands clean during tonight's culling. So too may your lieutenants who hold the same concerns. Safeguard the faithful tonight, Thetan, that will be your task. I put my trust in you and your wards to do that."

Thetan was at a loss for words.

Azathoth smiled. "You did not expect that reaction from me?"

Thetan shook his head.

"You expected me to be angry. To demand that you lead my avengers into battle. So long have you known me, sat at my right hand, and listened to all my teachings, and yet, so little do you understand me. I am the lord. I know your heart and your mind better than you know yourself. I know your doubts. Your temptations. Your fears. Though you may conceal such things even from yourself, you cannot conceal them from me.

"I know all.

"Do not doubt me, Thetan. Do not let your faith waiver, no matter the cause. Never forget, that everything that happens, be it good, or though it appears evil, is part of my plan for mankind and for all the world. Every action, every happening all plays into those plans in a grand dance whose complexity is infinitely beyond human comprehension. It is all for a reason. You must have faith in me. Faith in my plan.

"But know well that I do not control free will. That is what makes mankind special. It rises you above the animals of the fields, the birds of the skies, the fish of the sea, and all lower beings. You are more than instinct and desire. You can reason. You can choose your own course, be it for good or ill. You can stand with me and the faithful or against us. Choose wisely, my beloved, as you have always chosen. Do not stray from the true path, for that dark road leads only to sorrow and ruin."

Thetan nodded.

They did not speak again as the terrace took them slowly around the perimeter of the entire castle, each lost in their own thoughts, or so it seemed to Thetan, and paying little heed to the majestic gardens and fine stone buildings below. At last, they returned to the spot where they began. Before they parted, Azathoth again put his hand on Thetan's shoulder. The lord's face lacked its usual warm glow. His eyes looked sad and his voice was soft. "Thetan, though I love you best of all," said Azathoth, "never forget that I am a jealous god. Keep true to me. Keep true to your faith." And then Azathoth's voice became stronger, filled of menace. "And do not dare to break my heart."

35

JUTENHEIM ANGLOTOR

YEAR 1267, 4TH AGE

URIEL THE BOLD

Uriel walked slowly down the tower's stairs, Kapte in tow.

"You cannot trust him, Master. I don't know if he's the man that you once knew, but you cannot trust him now. He is even more than he seems, and he seems a great deal."

She looked to Uriel as they walked, but he made no response.

"You called him a Nifleheimer when you first detected him. That's what you felt. Not an Arkon of old. But a Nifleheimer — a thing that slithered down from the Outer Spheres by wicked ways and wily magic. A thing not of Midgaard. A creature of the Nether Realms. Please tell me that you are not now deceived?"

"He has Gabriel Hornblower's face," said Uriel.

"But not his voice," said Kapte. "His appearance may be but an illusion, a high level sorcery designed to trick you, to give you pause; to make you hesitate, even if you doubt his words."

"He explained his voice well enough," said

Uriel. "He knew the answer to my question about R'lyeh. Very few could answer that correctly, and probably all but he are long since dead. No one could have guessed that answer."

"He's a powerful sorcerer, that one," said Kapte. "Even I can feel his power. He's brimming with it. Isn't it possible that he used those powers to read your mind? To pluck the correct answer from your own head?"

Uriel stopped in his tracks. "That's worth considering." He looked Kapte in the eye and smiled. "What a marvelous girl you are. How lucky I am," he said as he kissed her on the forehead. "Mayhap he did use some charm or cantrip to play false with me. But he was as surprised to see my face as I was to see his. If he didn't know who I was, why appear wearing Gabriel's face? It doesn't make sense."

"I cannot explain that, Master, but I cannot shake the feeling that his appearance was disguised. Like a costume. Like a false skin. I feel it."

"My Ankh would safeguard me from most sorcery that could do as you suggest, that could blind me from the truth."

"But not all?" said Kapte.

"Not all," said Uriel. And then Uriel's eyebrows rose up. "Gabriel Hornblower would go nowhere without his Ankh. Did you see one about his neck?"

Kapte shook her head. "I did not notice, Master, but I was not looking for it."

Uriel closed his eyes and played back the scene in his mind's eye before he spoke again. "He wore no Ankh, no hint of a chain about his neck. Perhaps it was well hidden under his clothes. Perhaps he carries it in his pocket these days. Perhaps it was destroyed. Perhaps even stolen. We have far more questions than we have answers."

"So even without the Ankh," said Kapte, "he could be the Gabriel that you knew of old?"

"He could be," said Uriel.

"What of the strange creature that you detected from afar?" said Kapte. "A thing of evil you called it. A thing of vast and incredible power. You thought that it remained back at their ship. Why would Gabriel Hornblower travel with such a thing?"

"I don't know what that creature was," said Uriel. "Or if even it was a creature at all. With so many archwizards amongst their number, plus Gabriel, and a Golem, and a Red Demon of Fozramgar — all of those powerful auras, the Weave of Magic so strong amongst that group, who knows what I felt. I can make little of that now. But I agree that that man is a powerful sorcerer. And that may explain everything."

"How so, Master?"

"Sorcery corrupts the soul," said Uriel. "It's an old saying; I'm sure that you've heard it."

Kapte nodded. "What of it?"

"Olden sayings are often grounded in truth," said Uriel. "Excessive use of sorcery affects one's mind. One's sanity. It is a slow process. It takes many years to do its insidious work. A mortal sorcerer rarely uses powerful magic often enough for it to significantly affect him. But sometimes,

187

with great age, a sorcerer's mind becomes muddled. He grows angry and corrupt. Develops a contempt for others. For all life. Paranoia rules him. He becomes a danger to all those around him. To any that oppose him. Friends become enemies over an artless turn of phrase or sidelong glance. But when a sorcerer's life is unlimited – when he's an Eternal, an immortal, the magic has ample time to do its work. It chips away at a the wizard's mind. Slowly. Slowly but inexorably does it chip away. Does it corrupt."

"*That's* why you're so reluctant to cast your charms," said Kapte. That's why you only throw the most minor of cantrips. We've tried to understand that for years, Master. Why you held back your sorceries. Why you would not demonstrate your magics to us, but only describe them. Why didn't you tell us?"

"Because it would never affect you, my love. You are all mortals. If you follow all that I have taught you, and use your magics sparingly, you will never suffer that terrible affliction. That madness. And also...I didn't tell you because I feared that you and your sisters would begin to fear me. To question my deeds, my actions. Were they my own or born out of madness? Paranoia? Or some evil plot hatching in my deluded addle-pated brain? I never wanted such thoughts to cross your minds, so I kept the truth from you. Now you know."

"It changes nothing, Master," said Kapte. "You are the bravest, truest man in all Midgaard. I do not question you. None of us do."

"Thank you. It seems that together we have

worked out the answer. The man that leads our attackers, more than likely, *is* Gabriel Hornblower. He has practiced sorcery, too often, too powerful. He is compromised. Perhaps he struggles with bouts of madness. Perhaps he is always mad. And in his delusions he convinced himself he is something greater than he is. Not a man. Not an Eternal. Not even a great Arkon of Azathoth. No, none of those things are great enough for an immortal archwizard. So he became the son of Azathoth himself. The son of the monster that we rebelled against. That would explain his actions: why he allies with those who he brought here; why he killed our folk."

"But why reveal himself to you?" said Kapte.

"Perhaps he truly was surprised to see me. Perhaps, in the shock of that, he became himself again, if only but for a short time."

"But then surely we cannot trust him," said Kapte.

"No, we cannot trust him. Through my *Farsight* spell, you saw the holy symbols worn by one of their mages. You saw the standards that they carry. No matter what Gabriel has in *his* mind, those men with him, they are true believers. They are disciples of Azathoth; a half dozen archmages. No matter what Gabriel does, those men are here to wrench open the gateway. If Gabriel is on our side and tries to stop them, be he their leader or not, who knows what they will do. They are here to destroy us. To destroy all Midgaard by bringing that monster back. And Gabriel stands with them. He is their leader. In some ways, he *is* their god. It can be nothing but madness that drives him. I cannot explain it otherwise."

"Is there no hope for him?" said Kapte. "Is there no way that we might cure him? Restore him to the man that he once was?"

"The only cure for that madness is death," said Uriel.

"So what do we do?" said Kapte.

"We do what we've been doing," said Uriel. "We kill them all."

36

EGRIPT-MON

THE AGE OF MYTH AND LEGEND

THETAN

Like shadows were they, Thetan and his Arkons, as they skulked through the streets. Harbingers of death and doom. Quick and quiet went they, despite the dark. Silent and stealthy as the wolf. The perfect killers. Unmatched instruments of Azathoth's divine will.

But for the occasional lamppost along the thoroughfares, the dark was absolute. It cloaked their passage, though it hindered them as it would any man. The boon the blacknight provided was streets where not a soul would venture.

The people huddled in their homes. Behind their closed doors. Shutters shut, curtains drawn. Lamps down low, voices too. Superstition kept them captive.

That left the Arkons free to do their duty that night, unimpeded. Or so was the plan. Unlike many of their brethren that followed behind under Bhaal's lead, the thirteen men in Thetan's party did not see the mission as a duty.

To them, it was an atrocity.

An evil, unspeakable.

Unforgivable.

Unthinkable.

The only solace they had was that they could save a few innocents. A few that otherwise would not be saved. That was something.

A precious something.

Uriel skulked up to a door to someone's home. All in black: breeches, boots, and hooded cloak; even Thetan would not have recognized him. Not in that darkness. Like all of Thetan's vanguard, Uriel wore no metal armor that night, for their mission called for the utmost stealth. Where the Egripts might cower in fear of the blacknight and what bogeymen they imaged it harbored, the Aesir did not. At the first sign of trouble or trespass, the northern warriors would rush howling into the night, weapons bare, battle ready. Thetan had to avoid that. The last thing he needed was to kill Wotan's men. Or have them kill his brethren. Though the common Aesir soldiers knew it not, they were all soon to be allies in the greatest conflict of their time, and Thetan feared that he needed every one of them.

No blood sign marred the first door, a modest house of a tradesman. Likely, he and his were native Egripts. What gods they worshiped, Thetan knew not. Or mayhap they counted themselves amongst Azathoth's faithful, yet had failed to hear or heed the warning to mark their door.

One in ten would be spared, this the first of those. They could spare no more than that, otherwise, they'd surely be found out, and have no defense for their actions.

Uriel took out a horsehair brush from his pocket and dipped it into a bucket brimming with a mixture of red ochre and water, close enough to pass for blood. He spread it across the top of the doorframe in a thick line, hard to miss, even at a casual glance.

One family saved.

The next three homes all had smears of lamb's blood about their doors. The next dozen did not. Uriel managed to mark one of those doors before Bhaal and his men drew close. Thetan and his squad withdrew to the shadows. They stepped far back from Bhaal's men, as if that would somehow disassociate the two groups.

Bhaal, the tallest of all the Arkons at nearly nine feet, lumbered toward the first door, his massive frame dwarfing even the likes of Thetan and Mithron. The scion of a proud lineage from a far-off land, Bhaal had the blackest skin that Thetan had ever seen. He'd left his bright white plate armor at home that night, in favor of chainmail and dark clothing. Mikel was at Bhaal's side. So was Mammon, Iblis, and Tergon. Dozens more Arkons backed them. Even more fanned out and guarded the perimeter against any locals or Aesir that came out to meet them. Bhaal kicked down that first door himself and rushed inside. The screaming began seconds later. The Arkons were in and out of that door in under a minute and on to the next and the next.

"I can't watch this," said Gabriel. He turned as if to leave.

Thetan grabbed him by the arm. "You must stay. We cannot have suspicions raised." Thetan turned toward his men. "Do not look away, any of you. Watch whatever there is to watch. Listen to the pleading, the screaming, every bit of it. Let it sink into your soul. It will fuel the fires of our vengeance. Remember this night when we take up arms against the lord and his loyalists."

"We ourselves have done almost as bad as this in times past," said Raphael.

"Just as bad," said Bose.

"Never again," said Mithron. "Never again."

37

DARENDOR

YEAR 1267, 4TH AGE

BORNYTH TROLLSBANE

Bornyth Trollsbane, the last king of Darendor, opened his eyes and looked about, bewildered, gasping for air, and dizzy. He felt as if tendrils of electricity shot through his head, back and forth, over and again.

What in Helheim?

Had he passed out?

Had someone hit him in the head?

There was blood everywhere.

The Svart Seer lay a few feet from him, dead – cut down by some bladed weapon, the poor thing.

Who could have done that?

He didn't see any Draugar about. Had one of his men or one of the Svarts turned Draugar?

Then he saw the Svart king. The Black Elf stood by the hatch, covered now with a heap of corpses, Dwarf and Svart alike. The Draugar still pounded on the hatch from below; they hadn't gotten in. The perch was still secure.

The Svart king was without his precious bone staff. Bornyth had thought he never put the blasted thing down.

And then Bornyth remembered the Svart's treachery. His heart raced and his breathing quickened.

By luck alone he found his axe in but a moment and scrambled to his feet even as the Black Elf king bounded into action.

The runt raced for his staff.

Bornyth tried to beat him to it.

He failed.

The Svart spun the staff and made to level it towards Bornyth. Bornyth dove forward, his axe slicing down with all the power that he could muster. The two weapons collided -- the mystical and otherworldly versus honest Dwarven steel.

And on that singular occasion did the steel prove the stronger. The bone staff snapped in two from the terrific impact. Both the Dwarf and the Svart went down, rolled, and scrambled to their feet.

Bornyth still felt dizzy, disoriented. The room was dark and hazy. His eyes were not as sharp as they should be, his hearing was off; all his senses, dimmed. But he was a soldier, born and bred to action, he moved through instinct and memory as much as iron will. His axe, firmly in hand, but the Svart was ready for him.

Swift and sure was the Black Elf, and possessed of uncanny senses. A blade, a foot long, gripped in his hand – an obsidian dagger of ancient Svartish make.

Bornyth swung his axe in an arc. That blow, well aimed, should've bit deep into the Elf's chest, ripped him open, and been the death of him.

But it was not.

The Svart danced back so quickly it shocked Bornyth.

And then the Svart darted back in, dagger thrusting.

Bornyth deflected the blade with his greaves, and then sidestepped. With every step he moved, and every breath he took, Bornyth's head cleared and his strength returned.

Then the Svart produced a second dagger, this one but half as long as the first; no doubt, just as sharp.

He advanced.

Bornyth had never faced an opponent so swift, so agile, in all his long years. For each swing of his axe, the Svart struck twice.

The ancient enemies, Dwarf and Black Elf, dueled one last time. And in that battle, Bornyth shuddered with the knowledge that if all the Svarts still possessed their olden, pure bloodlines as did their king, woe to the Draugar, the Dwarf, and all the peoples of Midgaard, for an army of creatures with the Black Elf king's skills would be nigh unbeatable.

But Guyphoon Garumptuss tet Montu was the last of his kind. Some bane had polluted and corrupted the ancient bloodlines of his once stalwart people. Time had weakened them, leaving flimsy things behind – shadows of their former selves.

When the Black Elf king came calling on the Dwarven Lord
  One last time,
  Treachery and deceit,

Ever his mind.
Two great kings they were,
Blood and bone,
Grit and iron,
Each fought alone,
Hack and slash,
Grunt and moan,
Stab and whirl,
Death's seeds were sown,

Fifth Scroll of Cumbria
Verses 946-947

The two great kings fought on, until at last, Bornyth's armor failed him. The Elf king's thrust pierced Bornyth's mail and plunged deep into his abdomen.

But the last Dwarven lord of Darendor could not easily be undone.

Bornyth grabbed the Svart's wrist in a grip of iron. Held it fast while his other arm brought down his axe upon the Svart's unprotected neck.

'Twas a downward slice that took the Svart king between neck and shoulder. Six inches deep sank that blade.

The Black Elf king staggered back. Collapsed to his rump and then fell backward. Gasping for air. His life's blood drenched the floor.

Bornyth turned and staggered toward the great lever.

He found Throgden, his back against the wall, sword still in hand, but the old soldier was cut to pieces. A score of wounds afflicted his body, head to foot. The Svarts had trouble putting that old Dwarf down, and that made Bornyth proud.

When Bornyth reached the lever, he looked back at the Black Elf king. The lord of Thoonbarrow still lived, but lay where he fell.

Their eyes met one last time.

Bornyth grinned at him as he pulled the lever. The ancient iron did not readily yield to the Dwarven king's will. It moved, but even with all Bornyth's strength, it moved slowly. But move it did.

And when he had pulled it to its end, the great iron gears began to move, to turn, with a fierce grinding of metal.

Bornyth dropped to one knee as blood streamed down his legs. The wound the Elf gifted him burned like fire, perhaps poisoned by its evil blade. Bornyth grew cold to his core, and shivered. He knew the life was draining from him. But it didn't matter. He was dead either way. He had done what he needed to do.

The great gears turned faster and faster still. There was a thundering crunching and cracking of stone. A rumbling like an earthquake.

"A hero's death it is," said Bornyth. "Ha, ha ha — open the gates of Valhalla," he shouted, "for a Dwarven lord approaches. Break open the casks; I will drink my fill tonight at Odin's side, ha, ha, ha," he shouted as the cavern collapsed around him.

38

JUTENHEIM
TUNNELS OF SVARTLEHEIM

YEAR 1267, 4TH AGE

FREM SORLONS

The Black Elf bodies heaped four feet high in front of Frem; a dozen more corpses lay strewn behind him. Svart arrows and spears pincushioned Frem's legs and torso — more than he'd realized during the melee. He staggered against the tunnel wall. He didn't know how he was still alive. Still standing. He'd been hit so many times.

He bent over in a world of pain and picked up his torch. When he had dropped it, he knew not. He scanned the broken Elfin bodies -- searching for any that played possum. But he saw none. A few still lived — wheezing, bleeding, moaning, and crying in pain, but they were out of the fight. Frem staggered down the tunnel, giving the dying Elves wide berth.

He pulled one spear from his armor and then another. Then two spear tips, their shafts broken off during the battle. He extracted several arrows, the worst from his right shoulder, though even that wound wasn't deep. Praise the gods for thick armor and even thicker padding. None of the wounds demanded immediate attention, so his thoughts turned toward supplies. He needed them desperately.

He took the risk of approaching the fallen Elves; searched the bodies of more than a dozen. Not one carried any provisions: water, food, or medical supplies. All they had were their little weapons, for which he had no use, and the clothes on their backs. He gathered up several little cloaks, rolled them up, and tied them to his pack, ignoring their Elfin stench. He'd burn them if he ran out of light, or needed heat. Frem looked over the other Elves, searching for any packs, bladders, or other evidence of provisions, but found none. So he turned from them.

Started off again; made his best walking pace down the tunnel the way he'd been going. On he went for a mere ten minutes before exhaustion overcame him. He could go no farther.

He grabbed the last torch that hung from his pack, lit it, and threw it whence he came. It landed some twenty feet from him. Then he slumped down on his rump. That torch enabled him to see anything approach from some distance, giving him precious time to react.

He shook all over: hands, arms, even his legs. He was covered in blood; his eyes stung from it and twitched. His breathing was heavy. He didn't know how badly wounded he was. He was afraid to check, but he had to. He had to treat the wounds as best he could, with what meager supplies he had. And he had to do it fast, while he had the chance – for the Black Elves could come again at any time.

He couldn't believe that he was still alive. He

had no way to explain it. How he fought through that pummeling. How his strength held up. Only in song and story had he heard tales of warriors that had done such things. And almost always, those men were berserkers, and died soon after the battle. But he was no berserker. His mind was his own. He knew exactly what he was doing, every movement and maneuver, every swing of his weapon, every punch and kick. He was in control. He just couldn't grasp how he had kept it up. It was, unbelievable.

Stout Lomerian armor was the only answer – worth its weight in gold, a hundred times over. That and freakishly strong endurance.

What to do? Continue on until he dropped? Treat his wounds and move on? Or treat and rest?

He had to see to the wounds, he'd put that off too long already. His legs first, for without them, he was done. He took the armor off one leg, cleaned every scape with alcohol, and stitched up and dressed two gashes using the supplies from his medical pouch. With shaking hands and poor light, that was a task that took a goodly while. Too long for Frem's comfort. He put back the armor and repeated the same with his other leg. Then both arms. His shoulder wound took nearly all the gauze he had left, but he got the bleeding stopped.

He counted no fewer than forty wounds about his body but, by the luck of the Vanyar and the grace of the Aesir, not one wound was overly deep, not one life-threatening, or even debilitating. Barring infection, he'd be fine. Or so he told himself.

He pulled the canteen from his pack and drank it one mouthful at a time until half his meager supply was gone. Then he took out the brandy and swallowed one mouthful. He ate one meal's worth of jerky and took a final few sips of brandy to wash it down and dull the pain that radiated across his entire body. He extracted a few dried leaves from his medical pouch and placed them in his mouth, between his cheek and gums. They too would dull the pain and help to stave off infection.

He pulled himself up and continued on, fearing to remain in that spot for any longer. As he went, the tunnel narrowed further and the ceiling grew lower. He had to crouch more and more the farther that he went.

He needed to stop every one or two hundred feet to rest, so hard was it to walk so crouched over in such a space.

After a goodly time, perhaps a couple of hours, the ceiling grew too low, and he could walk no more.

He'd have to go on hands and knees to continue.

Dead gods, the horror of that was too much to bear.

He had but a few mouthfuls of water left. A few ounces of brandy, a few bites of dried meat and a few mushrooms. A few more torches, and then he'd be done. Dead in the tunnel, in a tomb of stone on the far side of the world.

He was beyond exhaustion. He wasn't thinking clearly, his mind muddled. He needed sleep, if only even for a few minutes. He slumped against the wall. Put his pack between him and the direction he had come — to serve as a rudimentary shield between him and anything he needed shielding from. Thank the gods, still he heard no sign of pursuit. Mayhap the Elves had fled for good. Could he dare hope for such luck?

He closed his eyes. In but a few minutes, fell off to sleep. When he awoke he was still alone. And he thanked the gods for that. How long he slept, he knew not. His best guess, judging by what was left of his torch, was a few hours.

His body hurt from the hair on his head to the bottom of his feet. He was achy stiff and burning all over.

But he was alive.

He had the use of all his limbs. And his mind was reasonably clear. Better than he could've hoped for, given the circumstances. He had to keep moving. Had to find a way out or find fresh water. There had to be water in the tunnels, for the Black Elves needed it just as much as he.

On hands and knees he continued. Slow and painful going.

The passage meandered up and down and then went flat again, over and over, endlessly. Sometimes, the ceiling rose high enough that he could walk stooped again, though never high enough for him to stand tall. Then after a goodly time, it dropped down low, so low that even on hands and knees he could not pass. He'd have to crawl to go on.

What to do?

Continue on or turn about? This was his last chance. Once he crawled into the narrow part, he'd never be able to turn around again, not unless the passage widened, and who's to say it ever would?

But what to turn back to? There was nowhere else to go? No sizable side passage that he'd seen during the entire trek from the ledge he awoke on so many hours previous.

Going on was the only choice and his only chance at survival.

But he didn't want to go into that narrow piece of tunnel.

The weight of it pressing in on him, trapping him, suffocating him. Dead gods, the horror of it was too much to bear.

He'd almost rather die.

Almost.

He grit his teeth and crawled.

He crawled and he crawled and he crawled some more. So slow it was and yet so tiring. It gave a man time to think. Too much time to think. To ponder it getting worse. Narrower. Lower. Closer. Tighter.

He tried to focus his thoughts on movement. Nothing but movement. Think only of that. Move and breath. Move and breath.

When the tunnel narrowed further, his shoulders scraped the walls on both sides. He wanted to scream. Wanted to curse the gods. The Elves. The Norns. And his own darned bad luck.

He fought to control his breathing. To steady it. To stay calm. He had to take his helmet off. Clipped it to his pack. He took some deep breaths then he pulled himself through the tunnel by his arms and legs. Moving that way was beyond exhausting even over a short distance.

When the tunnel grew still lower he couldn't raise his head any longer. He couldn't think about that. He wouldn't let himself. To see, he tossed the torch out in front of him and then crawled forward until he reached it. Then repeat. Over and over. It was all he could do. He had to keep his breathing steady. Move and breath.

He had to keep his head level with his shoulders. There was no view but the flickering fire of the near expended torch and the rocky tunnel floor between him and it. Thus, he couldn't see where he was going. He couldn't turn around. He couldn't raise his head. Dead gods, he had to get out of there. He never should have gone down that tunnel. He should've tried another way. There had to be another way.

His breathing went fast and sharp. His heart pounded in his chest. He felt as if he were choking. He couldn't get enough air. He couldn't think. "Odin," he screamed. "Odin."

He wished he'd died in that last battle with the Elves. He should have. If he had, he'd already be up Valhalla way, drinking and eating his fill. Instead, he was in Helheim. Crawling through a tunnel to nowhere. Choking to death. Dead gods, please, please...

He lay there for a time, not knowing what to do.

There was no way out.

He was hundreds and hundreds of feet below the surface now.

There were no more side tunnels. There hadn't been any for a long long time. And the main tunnel, such as it was, was barely larger than his body.

He couldn't continue.

Eventually, the tunnel would grow too small for him to push through, no matter what he did. But it was already far too late for him to go back. He couldn't turn around in the tunnel, the confines too narrow. He couldn't crawl backwards uphill.

And he couldn't go on.

And he couldn't go back.

There was no way out.

And then he knew it. He knew where he was.

He *was* in Helheim.

"Oh, dear gods," he shouted, "deliver me from this terrible place, from this evil. Do not forsake me. Please, gods, do not forsake me."

He still had two daggers. One he recovered from the battle, and another in his pack.

He could slit his wrists.

Or his throat.

Or plunge a blade into his heart and end it.

But, dead gods, he didn't even have the room to properly plunge the dagger.

But still, there were his wrists. There was room for that. He could end it reasonably quickly. There were worse ways to die. Many worse ways. Better that than dying of thirst in that place. Better than slowly suffocating to death.

He could end it.

How did it come to this? he thought.

How?

39

VAEDEN
AZATHOTH'S PALACE

THE AGE OF MYTH AND LEGEND

THETAN

A knock upon his chamber's door surprised Thetan. Rarely did anyone bother him unexpectedly after he'd retired for the night. And he always heard people coming. Was he that lost in thought? Or did his visitor move with that light a step? Perhaps Uriel? Thetan opened the peep hatch but no one was there. The only thing in sight, the thick stone wall across the hall.

"Down here," came an anxious voice, not much louder than a whisper. Thetan stepped closer to the opening and looked down. There stood gnarled old Lasifer the Gnome, a steaming mug of tea in hand. No one else in sight. "We must talk," said the Gnome as he turned his head to one side and then the other, as if checking to see if anyone lurked in the hallway, watching.

Who could be watching, there, at the penultimate level from the top of Azathoth's great palace, only the lord's own chambers above?

Only a few of the most senior Arkons resided on Thetan's level. Few others had rank or status enough to even visit without prior permission.

Captain Zardren and his guardsmen saw to that.

Thetan pulled back the deadbolts, lifted the crossbar, and pulled open the thick wood and metal door. He stepped aside to permit the Gnome entry.

After Thetan had closed the door behind him, the Gnome glanced at the elaborate locking system.

"Expecting an invasion?"

"It helps me sleep," said Thetan nodding toward the door.

"We are alone?" said the Gnome as his eyes turned toward the room.

Thetan nodded.

The Gnome stopped in his tracks as he took in the place for the first time. The large chamber was a greatroom with a high vaulted ceiling of polished wood beams and planks, floor to match. Large leather couches and chairs were arranged in circular fashion about a central hearth lined with stones. Stunning tapestries and artwork hung from the walls. So did weapons and shields of various types, all polished to a shine. Heirloom furniture pieces from various cultures were placed about the room in complementary and functional manner. Large windows looked out upon a generous private terrace with unimpeded views of all the surrounding lands. Before the windows, on a raised platform, was a bathing pool large enough for a dozen folk. Despite the greatroom's size, it was cluttered, yet meticulously kept. Wide hallways to either side led to Thetan's bedchamber, library, kitchen, watercloset, training, and storage rooms.

The room was cooler than it could have been, though the pleasant woodsy smell from the hearth hung in the air.

"I doubt even the lord's chamber tops this," said Lasifer.

"I haven't seen it," said Thetan. "Mithron's is its twin, though his style is much different from mine."

"I gaze at you now with new eyes," said Lasifer. The Gnome pointed to the door. "Best to lock it."

Thetan did. He would have anyway. "What trouble brings you here?" he said as he pointed to the couches before the hearth where but a lone log glowed.

"Nothing yet," said Lasifer as he shuffled toward his seat, "but much will very soon."

"You have my attention," said Thetan.

Lasifer spoke in a quiet voice, barely above a whisper. "I'm here to offer you my help, for without it, your plot cannot hope to succeed."

Thetan didn't move, didn't take a breath for some moments, his eyes locked on the Gnome's.

"I'm not one for plotting," said Thetan. "Speak plainly."

"Just as you," said Lasifer, "I have been the lord's faithful servant for untold years. I've done whatever he's asked of me. More often than not, without question. You know this."

Thetan nodded.

"What you don't know," said Lasifer, "is that just as you, I have been troubled by many of his commands. Though I've been spared participation in the latest campaign, it tears apart my heart. To attack the innocent in the dead of night? To kill children? He can tell us a thousand times that doing so is good, and part of his plan, but every time, it will be a lie. I don't know why he is so cruel, but it doesn't matter. I can't be a part of it any longer."

"You spoke of a plot," said Thetan.

Lasifer's face grew red, sweat appeared on his brow, he squirmed in his seat. "Am I mistaken?" he said, looking over his shoulder, first this way, and then the other.

"If I were involved in a plot of some sort," said Thetan, "how would you know of it, Gnome?"

"I am an archwizard," said Lasifer. "I can sense things. I have powers unknown. Parts of your mind are open to me."

"You are lying," said Thetan, his voice cold as ice.

Sweat dripped from Lasifer's brow.

"Let the truth fall from your lips, and make no false moves as you go about it," said Thetan, "or you will not leave this chamber alive."

The old Gnome took a deep breath, and then another. Then he sat up straight in his chair and composed himself.

"On the lord's orders," said Lasifer, "I have long surveilled your visits to Mount Cantorwrought. But I've told him nothing of your plot, and I will not. I'm on your side."

"Speak what plot you know," said Thetan.

Now Lasifer's voice was a whisper and he leaned toward Thetan as he spoke. "You will betray the lord. You and a small group of Arkons: Mithron, Gabriel, and Azrael amongst them. You will kill the lord if you can. Wotan and his Aesir are your allies, that is, if your recent visit to Egript-Mon was successful. Of that, I do not know."

"How have you spied upon me?"

It was clear enough that Lasifer didn't want to answer, but he was trapped. Felt he had too. And he did. "I have a seeing stone," he said, "and other powers. The lord acts as if trusts you, but he does not. Not fully. And he never will. It's not his nature. He's had me spy upon you for long years."

"And you heard our discussion on the Mount?"

"Every word," said Lasifer, "until that meteor shower came down. Somehow, it interfered with the Magical Weave, and the very ether itself, and confounded my sorcery. Until you all appeared back here, I thought you dead. I wondered for a time if it were the lord's wrath that brought that shower down upon you."

"Does he suspect anything?" said Thetan.

"If I had told him all that was said at your previous gatherings," said Lasifer, "then he'd know your mind, just as I do. I have seen this day coming for a long time and have carefully weighed what I reported to the lord and what I did not. I did that at great risk to myself, as I'm certain that you can imagine."

"So he suspects nothing?" said Thetan.

"Nothing."

"What aid do you offer?" said Thetan. "And why do you think I need it?"

"You need it, because Azathoth cannot be killed by any craft of man or any thing born of Midgaard. He is a god. A being of the Outer Spheres. Only something from there can kill him."

"And you just happen to have such a weapon?" said Thetan.

"None exists on this world, as far as I know," said Lasifer. "But we can banish him. Send him on a one-way trip back to the Outer Spheres whence he came."

Thetan leaned forward. "How?"

"There is a magic that can do it," said Lasifer. "At the heart of the palace, in the holy of holies, lies a black sphere of mystical power. That sphere has the power to banish him."

"I have seen it," said Thetan. "Azathoth called it the Sphere of the Heavens. An artifact of great power that he brought down to Midgaard."

"Another half truth," said Lasifer. "Great power, it has, though it has existed on this world long before the lord arrived."

"What is it?" said Thetan.

"Of its full nature, I cannot say," said Lasifer. "The lord may not even know. But it's a focus for the magical weave, channeling and enhancing mystical energies. The lord uses it to enhance his magics, or so I have long believed. And it is only one of many positioned at points of power around Midgaard."

"Who placed them and to what end?" said Thetan.

"I do not have those answers," said Lasifer, "but I have studied ancient scrolls that claim that, upon the completion of the appropriate rituals, if a Sphere of Power is broken, a doorway will open to the Outer Spheres. A portal that offers passage from here to there."

"Does Azathoth know of that power?" said

Thetan.

"I cannot say. After you obtain the sphere, I will conduct the rituals," said Lasifer. "and you will get the lord to go through the portal that we open."

"How?" said Thetan.

"I don't know," said Lasifer. "You're the muscle-bound warrior, not me. Shove him through. Kick him in the rear. Or better yet, pick him up, and throw him through. Whatever you do, know well, you'll only get one chance. If you fail, no doubt, he'll kill you where you stand. Then he'll root out the rest of us, and finish us too. This is the only way, Thetan. Nothing else you could do can stop him or contain him. This is the only way."

"The holy-of-holies is locked, even to me," said Thetan.

"I can get you in," said Lasifer, "but once inside you'll have to deal with the guardian yourself."

"I saw no guardian when I was there," said Thetan.

"Because you entered with the lord," said Lasifer. "Enter alone and it will attack. An invisible creature. A spirit of some kind. Brought over from another realm by the lord, to stand the watch for all eternity."

"How can I defeat such a thing?"

"The same way you defeat any foe," said Lasifer. "With your wits first, your brawn second."

Thetan sighed in frustration. "Let me be clearer. If weapons will not work against Azathoth because he is of the Outer Spheres, will they also not work against this guardian?"

"Must you always be so direct?" said Lasifer.

"Gnomes don't like to admit when they don't know something. Gnome wizards, doubly so. You'll have to find a way to defeat it. And quietly so as not to rouse the lord. Never forget, there is always a way. Oh, and whatever you do, don't dare touch the Sphere of Power with your hands. It resides in a glass and metal box. Keep it in there."

"What happens if you touch it?" said Thetan.

"You die," said Lasifer.

When their meeting was over, before they parted at the door, Thetan asked, "Who does the lord have watching you, Gnome?"

Lasifer narrowed his eyes and slowly nodded his head. "There you go being all direct again," he said before he turned and shuffled quietly down the hallway.

40

JUTENHEIM ANGLOTOR

YEAR 1267, 4TH AGE

URIEL THE BOLD

"**O**ld friend," said Uriel as he spoke once more to Korrgonn through the undulating wall of fog in the tower's high chamber, "though I am the leader here, the people with me are free folk. They are not my minions, servants, or slaves. You have explained your error, but you and yours killed many of their friends, many loved ones. They held a vote and they will not open their doors to you. They do not believe that you are a friend."

"What do you believe, Uriel?" said Korrgonn.

"If I didn't believe that you were Gabriel Hornblower, we would not be having this conversation. I have a way to prove your good intent to my people. I can bring you up to my tower using a bit of art, a small tapping of the Weave. Once we've had a chat, perhaps a brandy or two," said Uriel smiling, "we can walk down the steps to the main hall together – arm in arm as brothers. As we were of old. That will go a long way to convincing them. And if all goes well, tonight, you and yours, and me and mine, will dine together in the great hall and mourn our lost friends."

"There is wisdom to your plan," said Korrgonn, "but perhaps also a bit of craftiness, more characteristic of Azrael or Dekkar than you. You ask me to put myself at your mercy. To walk alone into the heart of your power."

"Gabriel, it was you that knocked down *my* gates," said Uriel. "It was you that killed *my* people. And now you worry about trusting me? Is that fair? I seek no revenge against you. You explained yourself. A mistake it was. A terrible, costly mistake. But a mistake is what it was. Had you known it was me that occupied this keep, would you have attacked?"

"Of course not," said Korrgonn.

"Then you have nothing to fear from me," said Uriel. "If you do not believe me, then simply turn about and walk out my gates. I am not holding you here. Go. You and all with you; go if that is what you wish. I will not pursue you."

"And even if I did, why fear it? If I had sufficient forces to overwhelm you in the field, do you think I would've locked myself in my tower? Go or stay, it is your choice."

"You bear no hatred in your heart for me?" said Korrgonn. "For what we did here? The terrible crime that we committed against you, however unintended?"

"Hatred?" said Uriel. "I am not capable of that emotion. But anger? Yes, I do feel anger. How foolish it was for you to attack not even knowing who you were attacking. A costly mistake, you say? Yes, yes, very costly, and far more so to me and mine than to you and yours. High crimes you've committed here however pure your intent. I have anger. Anger that I will not get over for a long time. But time...that is what you and I have the most of. Is it not?"

"I bear you no ill will," continued Uriel. "And we will get through this in time just as we both said afore. I tire of talking through this fog. I will open the portal by which you may step through. And if you do so, know well that I am still Uriel the Bold. The man that you once called brother. I have not changed much in these many years. Gabriel Hornblower has nothing to fear from me."

"And as I said, if you disbelieve, you are free to go."

"Open the portal, brother," said Korrgonn.

***

Korrgonn turned toward the Shadow Leaguers. He gestured his magics once more, to keep Uriel from overhearing his words. "By olden magics," said Korrgonn, "I shall soon leave you and appear within the tower, by the side of the evil wizard himself. I must do this thing and I must go alone. Guided by the lord's mercy, I shall make one last attempt to stop this conflict before it goes any farther, but I fear that my chances of success are slim. And if I fail, as soon as battle begins, and trust me, you will know when that is, renew your attack on the tower's door. Do not stop until you're inside."

"With a heavy heart I tell you," said Korrgonn, "that all those who stand with that wizard against our holy mission betray themselves as both foul and corrupt, unworthy of mercy -- unless they repent and beg the lord's forgiveness, which I fear they will not. Thus, the burden of the lord's justice falls to us. Harden your hearts, my friends. For the Lord Azathoth is a just but vengeful god. For their crimes against him, we must put them all to the sword. Down to the last."

"You cannot do this, my lord," said Ginalli. "Not alone. Let me--"

A thick mist appeared directly before Korrgonn. In he stepped.

And disappeared.

41

VAEDEN
AZATHOTH'S PALACE

THE AGE OF MYTH AND LEGEND

THETAN

"**H**ow many?" said Azathoth as he sat rigidly upon his throne, his hands bawled into fists, his voice reverberating in the huge chamber.

"Two hundred thousand troops is our best estimate," said Uriel who stood at attention before the lord.

"Two hundred thousand?" shouted Azathoth. "Are you certain? Can it be so many?"

"We may well be far off, lord," said Uriel, "though more likely, our estimate is low rather than high. Wotan's troops are spread out far and wide; hard to count them all. He's mobilized all of the north against us."

"All the north against me," said Azathoth as if to himself. "Never before has such a host been raised against my people. Are they a rabble of no consequence? Conscripted farmers? Slaves?"

Uriel shook his head. "They march and ride in orderly fashion for barbarians. Trained men and women mostly, if not all. Half the horde approaches from the north, mostly footmen. Forty to fifty thousand advance from the east, many of them on horse. Wotan's allies, the Vanir, approach from the West; fifty thousand strong. Several thousand Vanir cavalry advance from the south."

"The south?" said Lasifer. "How could that be?"

"How did Wotan move so many troops to our northern border without our knowledge?" said Azathoth as his Arkons stood at attention before him. His voice boomed louder than usual, an edge to it, his cheeks flushed. "And how did he get thousands of northern barbarians within our realm undetected? Even to our south? How can this be?"

"They could not have passed our defenses unseen," said Mithron. "We've lost contact with at least six of our forts. Probably more. It may be that they were taken unawares in the night. Perhaps through trickery or magic. With those forts taken out of communication, the barbarian marched in."

"It's more than that," said Thetan. "We have been betrayed."

All eyes turned to the Lightbringer.

"Betrayed?" said Azathoth. "Betrayed!" he boomed. With that shout, the Arkons were knocked backward, one and all, from a sonic force that emanated from Azathoth. The great hall shook and creaked; chandeliers swayed. "Who has done this? Who has betrayed me?"

"I do not know, Lord," said Thetan, "but with your leave, I will find out. As you say, it would not be possible to bring up such forces without our knowledge. Someone eliminated our border forts and our scouts. Accomplished undetected, the barbarians had to have help from within your kingdom. There are traitors amongst our forces.

Of this, I have no doubt."

Azathoth stood. His face went bright red, his hands too; his eyes glowed crimson. "I am the lord your god," boomed the lord with another sonic blast that rocked the hall. "Put no other gods before me!"

Then Azathoth went quiet and stood there glaring at the Arkons as they pulled themselves to their feet. Many winced in pain and blood dripped from many an ear.

"Harken to my words," said Azathoth, "for this be my will. We must quickly dispense with these barbarians, once and for all time. I will not have Vaeden besieged. It must be a clean, decisive stroke for all the world to see. We shall send out our forces to harass the barbarian and lead him through the hill country to our north. We shall meet him in the Gnorak Valley, in the shadow of Mount Rahg. The barbarians will never leave there. Not a one of them, for I will take to the field myself to destroy Wotan. I will make an example of him. All of you will be with me."

"The Aesir wish to steal my followers? My chosen people? They dare wish to be worshiped as gods? Perhaps as gods they will be, but their ascension will be brief. This battle will mark their twilight. Once they are destroyed, no force in Midgaard can stop the spread of my good word. Now, go, all of you. Begin your preparations."

Azathoth signaled Thetan to remain. The lord did not speak again until the hall was clear and the great doors closed.

"I want you to root out the traitors," said Azathoth to Thetan. "Use every method available to uncover their identities and their plot."

"I'll need the aid of several of my brethren, handpicked for their skills and loyalty."

"Assemble your team as you will, but make certain that no traitor infiltrates it. Include Lasifer amongst your agents. His loyalty is beyond reproach and he is too old to take the field for a battle of this magnitude. His magic will serve you well."

"Aye, my lord," said Thetan.

Azathoth stepped down from his throne and walked up to Thetan. He put a hand on Thetan's shoulder. "Dear one," he said, "in the battle to come, I wish you at my side above all others, but you are best suited to root out these traitors."

"Mayhap, I can do both," said Thetan. "If I mark the traitors well, they can be dealt with later. If I finish the job quickly enough, I may be able to join you in the battle."

"The traitors have escaped even my notice up until now," said Azathoth. "Unlikely that you'll be able to uncover them quickly enough."

"I will try, lord."

42

DOR EOTRUS

YEAR 1267, 4TH AGE

GAR PULLMAN

When Gar Pullman stood at the base of Dor Eotrus's outer wall, he wished that Bithel the Piper were still alive. Bithel was the right man to scale that wall. He could've done it with both eyes closed and one arm in a sling.

Instead, Sentry of Allendale, their next best climber, got the duty. Sentry barely made it up in one piece, the wall tall and devoid of handholds as it was. He slipped a couple of times, and got stuck more than once; had to work his way down and start over. Pullman expected him to fall from on-high, and maybe get dead.

But in the end Sentry made it. A darned good climber he was, just not in Bithel's league.

So far, the mission wasn't going quite as Pullman had planned it. It started out better than he expected in that by circling far south before turning north they were able to bypass the troll horde. Never even got close enough to spot the troll scouts. And as best he knew, the troll scouts hadn't spotted them — thank the gods. That was better luck than he could've expected.

Things started going downhill when they

reached Dor Eotrus. Pullman figured he'd saunter straight through the gates at midday as if he owned the place. Just put on a hood so that he wouldn't be easily recognized and in he'd go.

But that didn't work out. With everything that happened of late, the Eotrus had stepped up their security. They permitted no entry into the Dor proper save for those known to the guards and that had valid business. There was little chance Pullman and his men could've talked their way through that, so they didn't even try. They waited until the wee hours of the morning and scaled the wall like criminals, which, by and large, is what they were.

Once Sentry got atop the wall, the next challenge was hauling up Bald Boddrick.

The man insisted on coming along. Wouldn't take no for an answer, the stubborn bastard. Pullman figured that if he pushed it, things might come to blows, and that wouldn't do anybody any good. So the bald blowhard went along, more trouble than he was worth. The man had no climbing ability whatsoever. If the wall had been only six feet tall (which was well shorter than he), he still wouldn't have gotten over it — not without a step stool and a heave-ho. All they could do was put a foot loop in the rope and haul his big butt up, hand over hand. That was no easy task since he outweighed the next biggest man by nearly one hundred pounds. Pullman figured that on the way out, Boddrick could jump if he couldn't climb down the rope. If he broke his stinking neck, that was his problem.

The Eotrus were stretched thin — beyond the

wall, their security was pathetic. The battlement guards were grandfathers and young and middle teens. Not a young or middle-aged adult amongst them.

And they weren't accustomed to guard duty, that much was clear. Half of them were nodding off. The other half were snoring. If the trolls came back before Ector and his Bannermen, they'd take the Dor again, this time, all the easier.

Anybody would.

And then Pullman wondered whether he should order an all-out assault. He'd traveled up north with his entire mercenary company. They might have enough men to take the place. If they got the gate up, it would be theirs in an hour.

But then he thought better of it. Wasn't worth the cost of his men's lives. And what did he have to gain? He'd never be able to hold the fortress. Not against the northern army — if they returned from their troll hunting campaign, of which there was some doubt.

Pullman decided to go in quiet and stealthy with a small crew, despite the fact that stealthiness and Bald Boddrick were mutually exclusive. The rescue party was Pullman, Boddrick, Black Grint, Sentry, Pike the Gnome, and Jak of Ravenshollow. He figured, if that bunch of nasties couldn't handle the Eotrus overnight guards, a few more mercs wouldn't make the difference, but might get them noticed, and that wouldn't be good. Not good at all.

They made it down to the courtyard all stealthy like, even Boddrick, believe it or not. The problem was getting into the Underhalls. There was only one way in — through the Odinhome, and it was well guarded — those men, actually awake.

They scrounged some Eotrus colors from an unmanned guard station along the wall – shields and cloaks and a couple of helmets. That would get them past any casual notice in the dark. So long as they didn't happen upon any officers, they likely wouldn't get stopped, which is why they went in during the wee hours of the morning. What few officers the Eotrus had left would be in their beds.

Though they knew it was in the Odinhome, it took a while to find the entrance to the Underhalls. There were two guards on duty. Black Grint put a dagger through one's heart before either man saw Pullman and company coming. Boddrick snapped the neck of the second one before his sword was out of its sheath. They dumped the bodies in a shadowed corner and hoped they wouldn't get found anytime soon.

Pike made short work of the lock. Had it opened before the others cleaned up the murder mess. The Underhalls were deserted except for the sixth level — where the Eotrus kept their dungeon. There were two more guards there. These they jumped but didn't kill. There was no one within earshot to hear, so Pullman took the risk of taking them alive. It went so fast, neither had a chance to give a shout or raise any alarm. They tied and gagged them and left them for the shift change guards to find.

"Pike," said Pullman, "skedaddle down that hall and around the bend and see what there is to see.

Consider this a reconnaissance mission, so don't go killing anybody, or tripping any alarms. You got it?"

Pike nodded and scurried off. Came back a minute later.

"There be no lanterns lit along dungeon row," said Pike. "But there's a table set way down at the end, some candles on it burning bright. At least one man sitting there, talking all casual-like to whoever is locked up tight in the last cell. Must be Rom, I figure. The rest of the place be midnight dark and tomb quiet."

"How far down the hall is it, where he's sitting?" said Pullman.

"Seventy or eighty feet I'd mark it," said Pike. "There be 'bout ten cells on each side, the party's outside the last.

"Too far for a dagger toss, unless I go skulking to get closer," said Black Grint.

"With the echoes in these halls, he'd hear you coming," said Pullman. "And the ceilings are too low to count on an arrow shot at that distance."

"I bet there's an alarm down at that end," said Sentry. "A pull rope attached to a bell on the floor above. If he sees us coming, he'll set it off, and there will be Helheim to pay to get out of this place."

"In most buildings, I'd chance it," said Pullman, "but there's only one way out of these Underhalls."

"What about the escape tunnels?" said Boddrick.

"Locked and barred with heavy duty hardware," said Pullman. "The Eotrus were

228

working on that before we left. Planned to make certain that no trolls or anybody else would ever get in that way, now that half the North knows about them. We don't have the right tools to get through that quick enough. The way we came in is the only way we're getting out. That means no alarms or we'll be rotting in the cells next to Rom."

"So what we do?" said Sentry.

"We keep close the Eotrus colors and march down the hall as if we own the place," said Pullman. That should fool him until we're up close and personal."

"Unless he calls out," said Black Grint. "Asking for a password or maybe just what we're about."

"I think we've got to chance it," said Boddrick.

"I think so too," said Pullman. "If it comes to it, Sentry can use that silver tongue of his to buy us some time. Let's move."

The group carried two lanterns. Angled the light from one to face forward, away from them, and the man in the rear, Pike, had his lantern facing backward. Doing that, the man down the hall would only see them in silhouette and shadow. Boddrick walked next to last, stooped far over so as to conceal his height.

It worked perfectly. The man at the end of the hall saw and heard them coming, paused for a moment, looking, and then continued his conversation with Rom or whoever was in the last cell.

When they got close, they confirmed that at the table sat a single guard — a man of rather impressive girth. The table before him, set up for a game of Mages and Monsters.

He was playing against Rom Alder.

"What's happened?" said the man to them as they approached. "Some trouble?"

"We were told to come check on the prisoner," said Sentry, his voice casual.

And then Jak had an arrow pointing at the man's head.

That's when they realized the man was no common guard.

It was old Lord Nickel, one of the Eotrus's leading Bannermen — the man folks called the Lion of the North. He'd earned that title decades previous when he was a young man, fighting alongside Aradon Eotrus and his father before him in every significant border skirmish or incursion over the previous fifty years.

But the man that sat before them was long past his prime. Near eighty years old was he and struggling with the accumulated injuries an old warrior racked up, not to mention the routine ravages of age. The man had trouble walking and wheezed when he breathed. But his mind was sharp and his voice was strong and commanding. He sized up things quick enough.

"Gar Pullman," he said. "Back to spring your employer, I see. How many good northmen did you kill getting this far? Tell me true, how many?"

"Only those we had to," said Pullman, "and I regret even that. But we're here to bring Rom home, and that's what we're going to do. Make no trouble and I'll put you quietly in that cell and you can have a nice rest until the guards find you in the morning."

Lord Nickel stood up. He was a short man but

probably near three hundred pounds, and moved like it. Rom stood up too.

"Nickel, don't do anything foolish," said Rom. "There are six of them that I see, and killers all. No man can stand up to that bunch alone. Nothing you can do here. Stand down."

"I can't do that," said Nickel. He smiled a broad smile. "So I'll have my warrior's death after all."

Pullman reached out, put his hand on Jak's bow arm, and lowered it.

Nickel pulled his weapon, a big two-handed bastard sword, forged in the old style of the northern knights. He kicked the table aside, Mages and Monsters figures went flying. He raised the sword on high and yelled his war cry.

Black Grint stepped forward. Before Nickel was able to take a swing, Grint stuck his saber a foot deep into his belly.

Nickel took the blow with little reaction, save a grunt. His sword slammed down and knocked the saber from Grint's hand. The old man staggered forward and swung wildly.

Grint dodged to the side. Nickel's sword screeched as it tore into the wall, dust flying.

Jak stepped forward, sword in hand. Jak's sword and Nickel's crashed together. Nickel's olden blade sheared the mercenary's sword in two. And with a backhanded return, sliced Jak across the neck. Blood spurted like a fountain.

Grint leaped forward and thrust his dagger up under Nickel's chin. Sank it deep. Up into his brain.

The old knight collapsed backward. Grint pounced on his chest and plunged the dagger through Nickel's heart. Held it fast until the old man moved no more.

"By Odin," said Pullman as he looked down at Jak seated on the floor, hand to neck, futile fingers attempting to staunch the blood. Jak's eyes fluttered. Pleaded. Blood spurted. Then Jak slumped forward and moved no more.

Pullman shook his head. "The old man must've been something in his day."

"A terrible thing we did here," said Sentry.

"No it wasn't," said Rom. "Old warriors like Nickel deserve to die a warrior's death and thereby earn their place in Valhalla. You men just secured a spot for him. And if you hadn't, he might have lived a few more years, only to die sickly in his bed, Valhalla forever lost to him. You did him a service today. Don't feel bad about it. Let's get ourselves out of here before enough Eotrus show up to send us all to Valhalla."

43

JUTENHEIM
TUNNELS OF SVARTLEHEIM

YEAR 1267, 4TH AGE

FREM SORLONS

Lying alone in that tunnel, that hell, Frem figured, maybe he was already dead. Maybe something had killed him on that stair and he'd been judged unworthy of Odin's Halls, unfit to dwell in Valhalla in the demesne of the gods and amongst the great warriors of Midgaard's storied history. Instead, he was dumped into Helheim as punishment for some perceived inadequacies or slights against the gods. Cursed to spend eternity in endless combat and claustrophobic madness.

Maybe that's why the Black Elves couldn't kill him. For the dead cannot die. Was he now but a shade, a specter of his former self, cursed forever to roam the forsaken tunnels of dread Svartleheim?

His own personal hell.

He tried to rid his mind of those thoughts, those fears. To steady his breathing. Deep breaths, one and then another, and more, over and over, slow but steady. Soon, his heart slowed; his nerves calmed.

He tried to think happy thoughts: Coriana's

beautiful little face; her loving smile; holding her hand; carrying her in his arms; her laugh; the sound of her voice when she said, *I love you daddy*.

When he'd calmed enough, he opened his pack, ate the last crumbs of jerky and mushroom. Determined was he to gird himself with every bit of strength available to him. He drank the brandy, all but a few sips. And then he downed every drop left in his canteen.

He hardened his mind to the present, anchoring himself to what he must do.

He was a knight.

A Pointman and Captain of the Sithian Company, the foremost mercenary unit in all Midgaard. And more importantly, he was Coriana's father.

The tunnels might kill him.

The Black Elves might yet kill him.

But neither would drive him to kill himself. Not then. Not ever. He'd never give up. Never give in to fear. To hopelessness.

Never.

But it was so hard to go on. If he knew, if he only knew for certain that that way led to salvation, to freedom, it would be easy to keep going, no matter the physical strain or hardships. Knowing, if you just kept going, you'd make it. You'd survive. And escape. But he didn't know that. All that effort, all that strength expended, and he might be pushing himself toward a dead end, toward a hole he'd never fit through.

The only way to go on was to drive those fears from his mind. To believe with all his heart that the way forward led to freedom, to the light, to the surface world. He had to believe that. The only way.

He started to crawl forward again. One arm and leg at a time, over and again, and again. He counted each crawl as he moved forward. Counted to fifty, then a hundred, two hundred. More. He rested a few minutes but kept his mind focused recounting his progress.

Then he began again. Fifty. Sixty. One hundred. One fifty. Rest again.

Another hundred. Rest again.

And by then, the tunnel had grown so narrow that he needed only to grab the rough sides in front of him and pull himself forward with his arms while pushing against the walls with his legs, the narrowness, strangely now making the passage all the easier.

He kept moving. Pull and push. Pull and push, over and again, a thousand times and more. His strength, his endurance so far beyond that of a normal man as to be nigh unbelievable. His constitution almost godlike. Driven perhaps by his incredible physique or by his indomitable will to return home to his daughter, or more likely, by a combination of both.

As he went and the tunnel continued to narrow he fought a continual battle with himself, to force himself from thinking about what would happen when he could advance no farther. When he got stuck. Every time those thoughts leaped into his mind, he pushed them back, pushed them to the side, denied them, pretended it would never happen, and kept going. Frem was a veteran soldier and survivor, he knew well that during such trials, the mental war was every bit as hard and often harder than the physical. He steeled his will and pushed on. Push and pull, push and pull, on and on and on forever.

And then the tunnel grew wider.

A momentary reprieve or the start of a trend?

He knew not. But hope took hold, and his strength momentarily surged.

He struggled to reach the sides. Then the tunnel grew taller. And taller still. Dead gods, was there hope? Soon he could sit up, and he did. And rested.

And he smiled and daydreamed of Coriana.

He wished he had more jerky. But he rewarded himself with half the brandy he had left — a pittance, but something to wet his tongue and warm his throat.

A hundred feet farther along the tunnel and the ceiling rose to where he could walk stooped.

His torch was dying. He took his last three spares from his pack, lit one, and tied the other two to the outside of the pack, so they'd be ready at quick notice.

Now the tunnel sloped upward. Then steeply so, then gently again. But up and up it inevitably went.

Dead gods, perhaps there was still hope for him. Hope for escape from that hell. He banished those thoughts as quick as they came. He had to, for he knew the danger. If he grew too excited, too hopeful – and then, the tunnel narrowed again or turned steeply downward — that would crush him. It would break his spirit. And then he'd be as good as dead. So he only allowed the merest spark of hope to take hold in his thoughts and help drive him forward. Even that was a great danger, but he took the risk.

44

VAEDEN
AZATHOTH'S PALACE

THE AGE OF MYTH AND LEGEND

THETAN

Lasifer mumbled strange words and gesticulated oddly as he stood before the ponderous metal door that led to the holy of holies, a secret and sacred chamber situated directly below Azathoth's throne, one floor down. His words echoed off the stark stone walls, ceiling, and marble floor. The Gnome's breath fogged before him, for the antechamber was strangely cold. More than that, the place had an unnatural feel to it, an odd atmosphere. Alien. Foreign. Other. From what that stemmed was impossible to say, yet any that entered that place felt just the same.

Several feet behind the Gnome, Thetan paced, bedecked in full battle armor, falchion and shield at the ready.

Standing straight and tall, the Gnome was not quite three feet tall, though he appeared shorter still, owing to his stooped and bent posture. Wrinkled as an old prune was he; white hair, thick and full; clean-shaven face; skin that tended toward gray; and bright white teeth, straight and true, the envy of men a fraction of his age. He wore a gray robe that dragged the floor and swallowed his arms in oversized sleeves. A tall pointy hat decorated with glowing esoteric script of some forgotten language sat askew atop his head; how it stayed aloft was anyone's guess. And yes, he carried a wand of sorts: a wooden staff some two feet long, gnarled as he was, and covered in runes drawn in blood or something that resembled it. In later times, people would have marked Lasifer the very caricature of a wizard and poked fun at him.

But stereotypes are oft founded in truth.

Lasifer was the first of his kind: the sorcerer supreme upon which all others were modeled. A wizard of skills surpassed by no living man or mage of legend. Many of those who came later, even those of great fame and storied reputation, were but feeble imitations of him in both knowledge and power. He sat at the pinnacle of his art, a perch to which the greatest wizards of earlier and later days endeavored unsuccessfully to ascend.

Or so he had most everyone believe.

"You said you could open the door," said Thetan, frustration in his voice, his first words since the Gnome had set to work.

"There are spells coiled, knotted, and twisted about other sorceries here," said Lasifer, "the complexity of which I've never before seen. I cannot unravel one without unraveling them all – all at once. That is no small feat, not even for me. I did not expect this," he said, his gaze fixed on the door as his fingers danced. "It will take a bit more time to unravel. The lord has taken great pains to suffer no intrusion into that room, that much is clear. Who or what he's guarding it against, I cannot say, though surely it cannot be me. After all this time, he must trust me. But if not me, then who?"

"You said you could open it."

"Patience," mumbled Lasifer.

"That ran out after your eighth spell failed," said Thetan. "Is there another way in, or no?"

The Gnome ignored him. "I am close."

A moment later there came and went a clicking sound. Suddenly, a sparkling light burst from the door with unavoidable speed. It struck Lasifer in the chest. At first, the old Gnome didn't react; stood motionless for several seconds.

Then he toppled backward as a felled tree.

Hit the floor hard. Thetan heard the back of his head hit the stone.

The great door remained shut.

Thetan's sword was out, but what purpose that served even he didn't know. No more bursts of light appeared. There was silence in the anteroom. After some moments passed, when it seemed that nothing else would happen, Thetan knelt at Lasifer's side.

The Gnome was unresponsive to name and nudging.

His chest neither rose nor fell with breath.

A moment before Thetan gave him up for dead, the Gnome's eyes popped open. He sat straight up, his eyes, glassy.

"How long?" said Lasifer. "A moment or an age?"

"Less than two minutes," said Thetan.

"Welcome back from the dead."

"We are undone," said Lasifer as his eyelids fluttered. "The energy blast that hit me was an alarm of sorts." The Gnome tightly gripped Thetan's forearm. "He knows someone is trying to get in. No one else but me could breach that portal. He'll be after me now; he'll mark me a traitor. He'll be coming."

"Try again," said Thetan, unperturbed. "If we can get inside, we'll use the Sphere of the Heavens here and now. Send him back to the Outer Spheres where he belongs." Thetan reached out to help the Gnome up, but Lasifer waved his hand away and pulled himself up, moving as if none the worse for wear.

"It's open," said Lasifer. "My sorcery succeeded, just as I promised. You have only to pull the door open, if you have the strength. I cannot help you with what lies within. You should have brought the others. You cannot face what's in there alone. This will be your end."

"I will do what needs be done, Gnome," said Thetan. "If you will not aid me further, then find yourself a hole to hide in until we're ready to use the sphere. Do not let the mad god catch you."

Without another word, Lasifer turned and was off, a spring in his step that belied posture, age, and injury.

Thetan approached the door. Pulled on the great iron handle. It did not yield. He sheathed his sword, anchored his shield, and pulled the door handle with both hands, straining. The door budged, but barely that.

He strained anew, bringing all his power to

bear, muscles bulging. And then the door moved, not much, but it moved. Once he got the great mass moving, his task grew easier, and the door opened slowly but smoothly, pivoting on its hinges.

The cold that lingered in the room beyond was unmistakable, and clearly the source of the antechamber's chill. Thetan felt it the moment the door began to open. An eerie, unnatural chill that leached the heat from his bones and sapped his energy, head to toes. Thetan hadn't experienced that during his previous tour of the chamber with Azathoth, but the lord warned of it. *The icy breath of Nifleheim*, the lord called it. Said that he held it at bay, for *no human could survive the great frost wind of the Nether Realms*. Even as that icy touch accosted Thetan, he heard a strange and unexpected humming from the adytum: a high-pitched ringing, unexplainable in origin.

As the door swung fully open, two feet thick of solid stone, Thetan felt an unexpected warmth against his chest. A warmth that grew stronger by the moment and spread across his body, accompanied by a strange vibration. His hand reflexively went to his chest. His breastplate, hot to the touch. And then, he deduced the warmth's source: the Ankh that hung about his neck by a leather cord, tucked under his breastplate and out of sight. That strange relic, recently fallen from the night sky to land atop Mount Canterwrought, at Thetan's feet. What it was, he had no idea, though certainly it was no mere rock, no simple stone. He instinctively knew that even before it grew hot of its own accord.

And why must it remain secret?

He knew that it must, but the reason for it lay hidden in a hole in his memory.

One of many.

Before he took a single step into the room, his lungs ached from the chill and he began to shiver, despite himself.

Before him was revealed the holy of holies. Why it was called that, Thetan did not know, for the room harbored no religious icons, treasures, or relics. It harbored nothing save for the black orb, the so-called Sphere of the Heavens, that Thetan sought. The sphere lurked within a glass and metal case that resembled a large lantern, handle and all. It sat atop a carved stone plinth at the room's center.

The sphere was black. No shine to it at all. It devoured all light that dared fall upon it, and left nothing behind but its own blackness. Most oddly, the sphere hovered within its case, floating several inches above the glass bottom. By what craft it did that, Thetan could not begin to guess.

The adytum was otherwise bare. Gray stone walls and floor, ceiling to match. Nothing else.

Save perhaps for the invisible guardian that Lasifer warned of.

Thetan prayed it was a bogeyman only: a story to frighten away the curious but with no real teeth.

His prayer wasn't answered. How could it be?

45

JUTENHEIM ANGLOTOR

YEAR 1267, 4TH AGE

URIEL THE BOLD

Korrgonn stepped through the mystical wall of fog and emerged in Uriel's tower. Such an uncommon journey would bewilder the best of wizards and befuddle the wisest of men and the most storied of heroes, but Korrgonn weathered the journey unperturbed. He presented with his hands down, his palms empty and facing Uriel, as if to show he posed no threat and carried with him no ill intent.

With a flick of a finger, Uriel closed fast the magical portal. A moment later, the mystical fog disappeared. Only the gray stone of the tower's wall remained. Korrgonn would not leave that chamber the way he entered. That much was certain.

And that was part of Uriel's plan.

Uriel stood tall in full battle regalia; one hand on sword's hilt, the other held a majestic shield -- all in his colors of orange and black on a field of sky blue. His sigil, at center of shield and tabard — an orange lion devouring a black winged serpent.

Tension filled the air.

The two beings gazed silently at one another for some moments before Uriel spoke. "You have Gabriel's face," he said. "A face I once knew as well as my own. A face I loved as a brother of my own blood. So too do you have his mannerisms, such as I remember. But your eyes – your eyes *are not* Gabriel's. I could not see that through my wizardry. But here in the flesh there can be no doubt."

"You are *not* Gabriel Hornblower. Who are you?"

"I told you true from the start," said Korrgonn. "I am the son of Azathoth. Here to open the ever-barred door. To bring back my father. To restore his kingdom to Midgaard. To revive his glory of old."

"Why the charade?" said Uriel. "Why seek to trick me but for motives foul and black? You ventured here to battle the guardian of the gateway, so face me now with courage not cowardice. Draw your weapon, sir, and let fate decide the day."

"Your death be not my purpose," said Korrgonn, "though your wagging tongue may yet bring it about. I seek parley in this meeting, not blood. Common ground and common purpose we may find we have, if we but search a moment for it. Hear me out, will you?"

"I've heard a good deal already — all trickery and lies. I've no more patience for it–"

"No more trickery will there be between us," said Korrgonn. "As you say, through your sorcery, my measure you could not take, nor I, yours. We needed to stand before each other in calm and quiet and have these words. My trickery served that purpose well, for here we are. So I say again, hear me out, will you?"

"Tell me first," said Uriel, "what has become of Gabriel Hornblower? And let your tongue be true this time or hold it still, for you will not fool me again, not here at the center of my power."

"Alas, Gabriel is gone from this world. He died heroically fighting against all odds. As the son of the lord our god, my true appearance varies from that of mortal man. Too much attention would it draw. Too much interest that would delay my purpose. Too many enemies that would thwart me. And so I choose to wear this face, that of one of Midgaard's greatest heroes, as a fitting replacement, and to honor the memory of the good man that Gabriel once was."

Korrgonn continued, "It is not too late for you, Uriel the Bold, once beloved of Azathoth."

"Not too late?" said Uriel. "For what?"

"My father can be a harsh and unforgiving god," said Korrgonn. "His laws are strict but just. His penalties, harsh and swift. A jealous god is he. But more than anything, he believes in redemption. He believes that any person can be restored to a life of goodness and faith no matter how far or for how long they have fallen.

"Faith, Uriel. That's what you lost. But it need not stay lost forever.

"You can come home.

"You *can* come home. Let us have that brandy. Let us toast to olden times and friends long lost. Let us trade joyful stories of the lord.

"And then, when trust we've built between us, let us walk down the tower steps, just as you suggested, arm in arm, as brothers.

"And then stand with me, and lend me your power, so that together we can open the ever-barred door. We can bring the lord back, just as I was brought here from blessed Nifleheim.

"And never fear, Uriel, for all will be forgiven."

Uriel tried to hide his surprise at those words, but his face betrayed him. His mouth sought to make words, his jaw stuttering, but the words were slow to come. At last he said, "If I do as you suggest, if I help you, and if we are successful — if Azathoth returns to Midgaard, then what?"

"You shall beg his forgiveness," said Korrgonn. "And I shall stand at your side and vouch for your sincerity. The lord will see your heart, he will know your mind, and he *will* forgive you. Of this I have no doubt."

"I'm not asking about me," said Uriel. "I am asking what he will do on Midgaard?"

"You fear his wrath? His retribution against a world that forsook him? I see no need for that. Most of those who betrayed him have likely gone to dust long ago. There is no one for the lord to be angry at. Those who betrayed him are gone. Those who besmirched his reputation, that denied him, that disparaged him, all long gone.

"He cannot blame those modern folk that look down upon his memory, for they have been fed falsehoods all their lives. They've been taught only of pagan gods, myths, and legends.

"The lord will reveal himself to the people once more, just as he did so long ago in the days of

247

yore. And the people will know his glory, his wisdom, his justice, and most of all, his love. His kingdom will be restored to Midgaard and will be again just as it was in the days of old."

"But what will he *do*?" said Uriel. "What will he do for mankind?"

"He will do as he will, for he is the lord," said Korrgonn. "It is not for us to question. Not even for I."

"And that's the trick, isn't it?" said Uriel. "He will do as he will. Whatever he wants. Whatever he thinks is right, to Helheim with any differing opinion."

"It is not for us to judge the lord," said Korrgonn, "but for us to have faith. Faith in his goodness and mercy, in his glory and justice, and most of all, in his unconditional love. By following in his path we give him glory and we find everlasting love. Peace. Joy. All that we could ever want and more."

"When he destroyed the world by fire," said Uriel, "was his heart filled with love? With joy? What about when he destroyed it by flood? Was that to demonstrate his love? His wisdom? His mercy? When he killed so many for the slightest misdeeds, even those done by accident, was that justice? When he ordered his Arkons to slay innocent children, was that out of love?"

Korrgonn shook his head in frustration. "After all the eons that you've had to contemplate your misdeeds," said Korrgonn, "still you do not see the light. You do not repent. Still you wander in darkness, blinded by your limited understanding of creation. You *have to* have faith, Uriel. It is

248

beyond any man to understand the full purpose and intent of creation. The lord's plan is so vast, so complex, so deep, that it is beyond human comprehension.

"Faith is essential.

"Sometimes, bad things must happen so that in the fullness of time, the greater good can come to pass. Sometimes things, that from our limited perspective, which appear to be evil or bad, must be done, even at the lord's behest, for the greater good — to make us stronger, to make us better, more faithful servants.

"If such things did not happen, we would not learn, we would not grow. We would be static. Life would be barely worth living.

"Free will, Uriel. Much of the evil in the world is done by the hand of man, not the whims of chance, or the will of the lord.

"The lord grants us free will. To be free beings, created in the image of the lord himself. That is our gift. That is what separates us from the beasts of the field, the birds of the air, and the fish of the sea. Without free will we are nothing. No more than a rock, a plant, or an insect.

"But with free will, we are free to pursue the light, and equally free to do dark deeds. To sin. To transgress against each other and against the lord.

"And many men do. All men do to some extent, but some fall far from grace, and do nothing but evil. They commit terrible villainies. Savageries. Atrocities.

"And when they do, the lord's wrath can be severe, just as it was in those terrible tales that you remember and that have troubled you down through the long years.

"But it was all necessary to maintain mankind's free will.

"And to maintain justice.

"To balance the scales.

"I know this is difficult to understand and in truth the details are beyond any of us, even me.

"Faith.

"That is what it comes down to. We must fall back on it. We must hold it close to our hearts and never let it go. For only with faith can we remain with the lord, blessed in his grace and his love.

"Your faith must be restored, Uriel.

"Come back.

"Come back to the lord.

"And let us bring *him* back to Midgaard together."

Uriel's face looked confused. He wanted to speak. To counter Korrgonn's arguments, but the words did not come.

"All the battles that you fought in the *Age of Heroes*," said Korrgonn, "against the minions of the dark — those came not about by any will or deed of Azathoth. They came about by the deeds of the traitor, the Harbinger of Doom -- he whose name forever lives in infamy. It stains my very tongue to speak it.

"It was he that opened the gateway, not to the paradise of Nifleheim, but to the Nether Realm of Helheim. It was its scions that invaded Midgaard and laid it to waste. It was the traitor's madness, his jealousy and contempt, that brought that about.

"A terrible crime, for which you and your brothers spent millennia making amends. Battling against the darkness. All that, because of the traitor's misdeeds, the chaos that he wrought, that he wanted to bring about for his own avarice and pursuits of glory.

"How the world suffered because of him. Because of one man's vanity, pride, and ambition.

"Do you think that I came here today by happenstance after all this time?

"I did not.

"The timing of my arrival was no chance, no accident.

"I come here now because *he* is coming here.

"Thetan, who was once called the Lightbringer. *He* was the one that corrupted you and your brothers. *He* was the one that beguiled you.

"The trickster.

"The Prince of Lies.

"The Harbinger of Doom.

"Even now, he journeys here to destroy this holy portal. To prevent the lord from *ever* returning to Midgaard, from *ever* living amongst, protecting, and loving his chosen people.

"He will soon be here, the Harbinger. And that is why the lord has sent his own son down to Midgaard.

"I am to stop him. That is my purpose. To stop him at all costs, even at the expense of my own life. And in so doing, to give the lord's people a chance to choose whether or not to bring the lord back.

"And the great men that have so chosen are those who I brought with me. You must take your

251

place amongst them, I beseech you. You must stand against the darkness with them, with me.

"All can be as it once was, Uriel. You can stand at the lord's side once again. This time, at his right hand, as his First Arkon. No longer will you have to live in this exile, alone here in this tiny corner of the world doing nothing of any importance save existing for existence sake.

"You can make a difference again. Like a giant you can stride across Midgaard once again, doing great deeds, fulfilling the lord's will. You can help raise his kingdom back – to restore Vaeden to all its former glory. And you can help teach the people the ways of the lord. The ways of goodness -- all the principles of honor, justice, law, order, and civilization.

"You can help bring the people back from the brink of barbarism and the terrible toils of war.

"The world is in chaos, Uriel. It has wallowed there for untold ages. That happened not by accident, but by the absence of faith, and the absence of the lord.

"You can bring it all back.

"The lord needs you, Uriel.

"The lord our god needs *you*.

"Do not let him down. Do not forsake him. Once again, embrace his love. Embrace your redemption. Stand with me. Stand with the lord."

Tears streamed down Uriel's cheeks.

"What say you?" said Korrgonn. "Are you with me, brother?

"Are you with the lord?" said Korrgonn as the heartstone pulsed with otherworldly light beneath his tunic.

46

VAEDEN
AZATHOTH'S PALACE

THE AGE OF MYTH AND LEGEND

THETAN

At Thetan's first step inside the holy of holies, the invisible guardian attacked. Strange that was. He'd been there before with Azathoth. Surely, the creature would've remembered him and not immediately marked him an enemy. It was as if it were waiting for him with ill intent. Hiding in ambush. Ready to pounce. Ready to kill. Was Lasifer right? Did an alarm go off when he cast his enchantment to open the door? Did Azathoth know of his plot? His treachery? Was his plan undone even before it began?

Wisely, Thetan didn't blunder into that chamber blindly or foolishly. He went in with weapons drawn. Shield held close to his breast. Helmet on. Visor down. Muscles tensed. All at the ready.

And well that he did.

He didn't see the thing coming. He couldn't. It wasn't merely fast or stealthy, and it was no chameleon. It truly was invisible. How that could be, of course, made no sense. It defied the natural laws of science and alchemy. Some scion of sorcery it had to be. Something from outside the natural world. Beyond Thetan's ken.

So be it.

He would face it, come what may.

He sensed movement. Perhaps, the slightest shifting of the air, or else some small vibration and attendant sound. Warning enough was that. He braced. Raised his shield the higher.

And well he did, for the creature's blow struck the shield's center. Buckled it. Nearly staved it in two. What power that took! For Thetan carried no common wooden shield; no fragile flimsy thing of oak or elm. His was metal; forged in molten fire, heat treated, tempered, and folded in flame five hundred times by an expert smith. Not banded or studded with steel was it, but solid. Thick. Strong. Its edge, sharpened and honed, a tool as much for offense as defense. Five times the weight of its pedestrian counterparts, yet it hardly encumbered Thetan, such was the strength of his mighty thews.

That shield had withstood ten thousand blows by sword and axe, hammer and mace, fist and talon. It bore its battle scars proudly: gouges and dents aplenty, but that strike bent it badly across its span. The blow wrenched down Thetan's arm. Pulled him forward. Even as it did, Thetan's lightning thrust sailed straight and true overtop the shield.

And it struck home. The creature screeched -- a high-pitched whine that lasted but a moment and sounded like nothing Thetan had heard before.

His sword came back bloody. Though not with

the blood of any natural beast. The stuff that clung to the blade was milky white. Thick. Sticky. More like tree sap than blood. A stench to it so sour as to make a man retch.

Thetan did not hesitate.

The thing lurked before him, though invisible still. Somewhere close.

Hurt. Bleeding.

He advanced.

Spun his sword with blazing speed.

Chopped down at where the creature should be.

But struck only air.

Thetan turned this way and that. Sword swinging in measured strokes, faster even than the eye could follow. First, to this side. Then to that.

More empty air.

He advanced two steps. Swung again and again.

And then once more.

Empty air is all he caught.

He spun about. Struck behind.

A thrust.

A spin.

A slice.

Nothing.

No contact.

He couldn't see it. Feel it. Hear it. No blood trail. No droplets. Only the sour stench of the otherworldly blood. He couldn't localize that odor.

It was everywhere at once.

And yet nowhere to be found.

Thetan struck high, over his head.

Nothing.

He struck low. Spun about in full circle. Came up ready for a charge. Nothing. Nothing.

Nothing.

The chamber was too small, it could not have fled far. It should be there. He should have struck it already. Finished it.

Thetan's heart raced the faster as he questioned himself. Had the creature been there at all? Was he bewitched? Ensorcelled? Imagining it all? Losing his mind to a curse long lurking in wait by Azathoth? Had he been entrapped? Mesmerized?

He refused to believe that.

He swept his sword around again. Backpedaled until he bumped the wall. With honest stone behind him, he crouched, shield before him, such as it was. Weapons poised. Ears straining for the slightest tell.

But all he heard was his own breath and the thumping of his heart in his breast.

The creature had to be there. It had to be real. His mind was sound. His vision, clear. It had to be there, somewhere.

Then the thing crashed down. Fell atop Thetan's head and shoulders without warning.

The creature must have been clinging high upon the chamber's walls like a spider.

Thetan's knees buckled, the thing's weight beyond belief. He hit the floor hard. Rolled. The thing straddling him. Had to get it off; gain space to maneuver.

His sword clattered across the floor. Far out of reach.

Thetan ignored the pain of the impact. He rolled and twisted until he got clear. Made his feet in a flash. Punched with his shield even as he thrust his dagger.

Neck throbbing. Head spinning. Legs like jelly.

The shield grazed the thing. The sharpened edge bit.

The dagger sliced empty air.

A terrific impact to his wrist sent the dagger tumbling away. It too, far out of reach.

No time to retrieve it.

Thetan shot forward. Punched with his shield again.

Bash.

Advance.

Bash.

Nothing. No contact.

Where was it now? No shimmering of the air. No scent. No footprints on the stone tile.

He felt naked and vulnerable, his back now exposed.

No way to see the creature. Sense it. Track it.

Thetan was blind to it. But he knew by then that it was large. Probably larger than him. Heavier too. And strong. Fast. Agile. A foe unlike any other that he had faced.

His eyes flicked to the chamber's door. For a fleeting moment, he thought to flee. To put aside his mission. To run.

To live to fight another day.

Only for a moment did he ponder such thoughts, for he was no common man. No common soldier. No uncommon man for that matter. He was a singular being unlike any other.

257

Over his long years, he stood witness to the sad pattern of life, as civilization after civilization crept up from obscurity, grew to maturity, then depravity, decrepitude, and self-loathing, until at last, one and all, they imploded in fire and blood, their ruins slowly wasting away until all memory of them -- their knowledge, culture, wisdom, and grand achievements -- everything that they had been and ever would be, were forever lost from the world. Such things took a long time. Other things took far longer. And so too, in the fullness of time, Thetan witnessed mountains born, and oceans dried to dust. Such vast perspective had he. And for that reason, amongst others, unlike nearly all other men, fear did not rule him. He fled from no man or beast, ensorcelled or not.

47

LOMION CITY
TAMMANIAN HALL
HIGH COUNCIL CHAMBERS

YEAR 1267, 4TH AGE

REGENT BARUSA ALDER

"**T**he mountain trolls have us in a stranglehold," said Guildmaster Slyman from his seat in the councilors' mezzanine where Lomion's High Council met in closed session – as they had so often in recent days. "All trade and travel other than by river has been cut off. Caravans wiped out, guarded or no, messengers and couriers lost — even the raven system has lately failed us. Commerce has ground to a halt on all fronts. Potentially the worst economic disaster to hit our city since the reign of King Thrabakdill over a hundred years ago." He turned toward Field Marshal Balfor. "I told you in no uncertain terms that the western and southern roads had to be kept open; they're the lifeblood of this city. The northern and eastern roads are less important–"

"What of the northern road to Kern?" said Lady Dahlia. "My city needs—"

"Kern can fend for itself for the time being," said Slyman. "No doubt, the roads to Kern's east remain open and free of the troll. Your folk will be just fine for the present, dear lady, but against all reason and wisdom, the good Marshal spread Lomion City's forces thin. He had to flex his muscles and keep *all* the roads open — and in his arrogance and stupidity, now Lomion City is cut off. Every overland route is closed to us. Our people will soon be starving."

"Starving?" said Balfor. "Your penchant for exaggeration grows even faster than your waistline."

Slyman smashed his fist to his chair's armrest, then rose to his feet, fuming. "I will--"

"Sit down," shouted Chancellor Barusa. "I will not have this chamber spiral out of control. Not ever, but not now, least of all."

"The southern or the western roads must be reopened," said Slyman. "I want to know how you're going to accomplish that."

"What of the Hudsar?" said Lady Aramere of Dyvers. "Last I heard, the trolls have no command of the river. Most of our supplies come via the water anyway, so as long as that route is open to us, why sacrifice more troops in opening land routes?"

"Those ships that keep to the deep water are safe enough, it's true," said Lord Jhensezil, "but any captains foolish enough to venture near the shallows risk their ships and their lives, for the trolls have little fear of the water."

"They have no ships, do they?" said Lady Aramere. "They can't blockade the river. How big a threat to shipping can they be?"

"They attack passing ships en masse if they

260

can wade or swim out to them," said Jhensezil. "More than a few barges and private craft have been lost that way over the last few days. When word of those attacks spread downriver, most river captains chose to keep their ships south, putting to port at Dor Malvegil or Dor Linden, biding their time, waiting to see what happens. They don't have the stomach to test the trolls. If we can convince them that the river route is safe, so long as they keep to the deeps, and keep their ships moving swiftly, we can be resupplied indefinitely."

"But unless and until that happens," said Slyman, "either the western or southern overland routes must be reopened. Food must get to the city. Supply lines for our troops. And aren't we still waiting for reinforcements from Dor Caladrill?"

"We need a way out for our people," said Lady Dahlia. "We can't rely only on the river. There simply are not enough ships to evacuate even a fraction of the population if it comes to that."

"Councilors," said the Vizier, "there are harsh realities that we must come to grips with. We are not prepared for a long siege. And truth be told, Lomion City is not prepared for a siege of any length. It is outside of our experience. Our capital has not been threatened in this way in years beyond memory. We're not equipped for it. Soon there will be chaos in the streets. If the trolls breach the walls as they did at Dor Eotrus, anything might happen. The streets would run red with blood. We would lose control."

"We all know this," said Barusa.

"The walls will not fall," said Marshal Balfor.

"My men will hold the battlements. We will not cede a single street to the troll. Not a single one. And once they give up and withdraw, we'll chase them back to the mountains whence they came. Wipe them out, once and for all."

"So said the Eotrus," said Slyman. "Their walls fell in a single day. A single day, councilors! And meaning no disrespect to our fine troops, but those Northmen – those Eotrus – have much more experience dealing with such threats than do our regulars. If they couldn't hold the troll back, not even for a day, will we be able to? Even with the strength of our numbers? Even the Eotrus's underground tunnels fell. Nothing is safe from the troll."

"We have the largest, best equipped, and best trained standing army in the known world," said Balfor. "We can handle the trolls even if–"

"But you haven't," said Slyman. "Our troops are overmatched. You have to admit that. You can't let your ego or your pride get in the way of the truth. It's only our vastly superior numbers that give us a chance and that have kept the trolls at bay up till now."

"We don't even know how many trolls are out there," said Jhensezil. "The reports we've received are incomplete and contradictory. We don't know if we're dealing with a few thousand trolls, or tens of thousands, or even more."

"There have to be tens of thousands of them to have encircled us and cut us off the way they have," said Balfor. "I've sent out more scouts. We will get a better reading on their numbers and disposition within the next day or so. Then we'll know if we can sally forth our armies and bring this assault to an end, or whether we must stay hunkered down and fight a defensive action."

"We must be prepared to transfer the flag," said the Vizier.

Several councilors gasped at that suggestion. Bishop Tobin's eyes opened and he leapt to consciousness at the very thought of it.

"Are you saying that we should abandon Lomion City?" said Barusa. "Abandon our capital? Yield it to animals?"

"Certainly not," said the Vizier. "What I'm suggesting is that we consider moving this Council to safer environs. This Council and the Council of Lords are the glue that holds our nation together. We cannot chance its fall. Especially not at this time of crisis after we've lately lost our king."

"Two kings," muttered Jhensezil.

"There is a wisdom to these words," said Lady Aramere. "A wisdom that must be considered."

"Never," said Marshal Balfor.

"Would we all leave under this scheme?" said Bishop Tobin. "Or would some few of us remain to...oversee things? The defense and such?"

All eyes turned to the Vizier.

"I had not thought through that point," said the Vizier. "But since the good Bishop brings it up, it *would* make sense for one of us to remain here. Someone must be in charge; after all, we are not abandoning the city, we are merely contemplating temporarily moving the highest ranks of government to a safer environment."

"One could argue," continued the Vizier, "that the Tower of the Arcane is the safest location in all of Lomion City. As its grandmaster, I would have little fear in remaining there. So if it is the wisdom of this Council to have some token member of government remain, if only so that the people do not feel abandoned, I would agree to be that one."

"Would it not make sense for Marshal Balfor to remain?" said Lady Dahlia. "To command the troops?"

"If we were to transfer the flag," said Balfor, "someone of high rank must remain to command our armed forces. That must be me. Not that I agree with this idea. I think we should all stay. I think it's our responsibility."

"So long as the city is not overrun," said Slyman, "I will not abandon my guilds, my mercantile interests."

"The nobles," said Lady Dahlia, "will they stay or will they flee?"

"Those inclined to flee," said Barusa, "have already done so. Dozens of their yachts and barges have fled downriver. But they are in the minority. Most of the nobles, the olden bloodlines in particular, will not abandon our fair city, no matter the threat."

"Until the walls are breached," said Jhensezil. "Then you'll see the rats scurrying to the river to hop on whatever floats."

"The Church Knights will not forsake Lomion City, come what may," said Bishop Tobin. "They will remain and fight to the last man. Such is their duty. Honor demands no less."

"Duke," said Lord Jhensezil, "you have been strangely quiet. What is your counsel regarding transferring the flag?"

Archduke Harper Harringgold slowly leaned forward in his seat, wincing – obviously in pain from his recent injuries: an assassin's arrow and shortly thereafter, a dose of poison that nearly killed him. His voice lacked its normal volume and vigor. "If this Council abandons Lomion City in its time of dire-most need," he said, "we will lose the loyalty and the respect of the people. They will look elsewhere for leadership and gift their loyalty to that one courageous councilor who remained with them — our dear friend, the Vizier. And when we finally beat back the trolls, it is he that will be the recipient of the people's love and gratitude. And when we councilors return to the city, the Vizier will welcome us in with open arms and toothy smile. He'll tell us that it's his city now; that he's taken over. He'll promptly cut off most of our heads, leaving one or two of us alive to spread the tale of his iron-fisted rule. That's what I think."

"Your ignorance and your evil thoughts never cease to amaze me, Harringgold," said the Vizier. "Even in times of war you cannot put aside your petty politics. Your jealousies. You still see all of us as rivals, as villains. We are Lomerians. Patriots. Every one of us, despite all our differences. And yet you still pit us one against the other, even now, during this terrible crisis. Shame, Harper. Shame on you. The sooner you retire from your position on this Council the better off the realm will be."

"I stand behind my words," said Harringgold, "and I reject yours. I will not abandon this city or my position. Not now. Not ever."

"I think it noteworthy," said Jhensezil, "that the recent attempts on the Duke's life were no doubt orchestrated by men of like mind to the good Vizier."

"What are you implying?" said the Vizier. "If you're to accuse me of something, speak plainly – don't hide behind vague words. A coward's tactic."

"His implications were plain enough to me," said Dahlia.

"To all of us," muttered Bishop Tobin.

The Vizier's face twisted in anger. "You're as corrupt and dangerous as Harringgold," he said scowling at Jhensezil. "I will not be defamed. I will–"

"Now that I've raised your ire," said Jhensezil, "I suppose I'll need to double my security to make it through the week."

"Enough," shouted Barusa. "Put your squabbles aside, councilors. The fate of the city hangs in the balance. We must focus our attentions to that."

Bishop Tobin cleared his throat to gather the attention of the others. "No Bishop has left his post in Lomion City in times of war in over one thousand years," he said. "I will not be the first."

"And House Alder will remain in the city as well," said Barusa.

"So that is our decision then," said Lady Dahlia. "How can we open the trade routes? Marshal, is there a way?"

"On open ground, the trolls destroy our troops by the battalion," said Balfor. "Even the Myrdonians are no match for them. I cannot keep a train of wagons safe. I cannot even keep my cavalry safe."

"So then what?" said Slyman. "We cannot sally forth to face them, for we are not their match in close combat—"

"Unless the scouts confirm that their numbers are much smaller than we fear," said Jhensezil.

"We also cannot withstand a siege," said Slyman. "We cannot properly resupply. Then what are we to do? What are our options?"

"That my friends is the question," said Barusa. "They'll be no rest for us until we find its answer. And I fear I must burden you all with more dire news. News that mayhap is worse than this troll invasion though not yet on our doorstep."

That grabbed every councilor's attention.

"I've been in contact with the Darendor Dwarves of the Dallassian Hills," said Barusa. "With their king, to be precise."

"Bornyth Trollsbane?" said Jhensezil.

"One and the same," said Barusa. "They've been overrun by a plague that they call Draugar."

The Vizier and Bishop Tobin stood up from their seats at the same moment, astonishment on their faces.

"Did you say, Draugar?" said Bishop Tobin.

"You've heard the legends?" said Barusa.

"The church records have dire warnings about Draugar," said Tobin. "An evil from a dark and distant past best forgotten. We must investigate these reports at once. They must be confirmed or not. You are well to call this threat more dire than the trolls. More dire indeed. By Odin, I pray that what you've heard is wrong."

"I spoke to Trollsbane myself," said Barusa,

"through the Alder Stone. There can be no doubt. The threat is real. And the Darendor Dwarves are no more."

"No more?" said Jhensezil. "Are the Dwarves trapped within their halls or have their caverns been breached, their armies defeated?"

"It seems," said Barusa, "that those Dwarves that are not dead, now walk Midgaard as Draugar."

"How can that be?" said Jhensezil. "That we had no reports up until now? The Darendor Dwarves are many, with a formidable force of soldiery. They are a militant people, and always have been. Nearly every member of their society is trained in the arts of warfare. They would not go quickly or quietly into defeat. How could we not have heard of this invasion or plague or whatever it is?"

"It came on them quickly," said Barusa. "They were assaulted from all sides with little or no warning."

"What is this, Draugar?" said Lady Aramere. "You just said that they were assaulted, but before you called it a plague. Is it a sickness or an invading army?"

"If it is Draugar," said the Vizier, "then it is both, dear lady."

"If the legends be even half true, the Draugar are worse than anything you can imagine," said Tobin. "The old scrolls warn us, when Helheim is full, the dead will walk Midgaard and their name will be Draugar."

268

48

MOUNT TROGLESTYRE TROLL CITY OF GOTHMAGORN

YEAR 1267, 4TH AGE

ECTOR EOTRUS

Four burly soldiers dragged the troll queen — Terna, mate of Gotrak, the High Chieftain -- before the northern lords. They had hogtied her with iron chains. She had no chance of escape. No chance to defend herself. Unlike most female trolls, she was nearly as large as the males, tall, and muscular. Battered and bruised was she, but not severely injured as far as Ector could tell. But he wouldn't expect her to be, for the trolls healed so quickly that if an injury didn't kill them outright, usually it would shortly pass, leaving little more than a bruise or dried blood behind. She exhibited plenty of that.

"Her clothing is more ornate than that of the others, the jewelry and such, but beyond that, how do we know this is their queen?" said Lord Lester.

"One hundred of them died protecting her," said Lord Ogden, "and took more than a few of my men with them. I was there. There is no doubt in my mind that it was this one that they were protecting. This one, that they were dying for. She's either their queen or high priestess or witch-woman. Someone revered above all others."

"Do you understand my words?" said Ector to the troll woman.

Terna did not respond. She gave no indication that she understood. She looked angry and defiant to Ector's eyes, but who could read emotions in the face of a troll?

"Not afraid of us, is she," said Pellan, "even now. Even trussed up like a Wintersfest goose. Brave things these trolls."

"Or stupid," said Indigo.

"They're nothing but animals," said Lord Brian. "They don't know how to fear or hate or love or anything else. It's all instinct with them. Hunt, kill, feed, and reproduce, that's all they know– same as a lion or a saber cat."

"There are many men amongst us that would kill this witch slowly for the crimes her kind committed against our people," said Lord Ogden. "There are many that would flay the skin from her bones and chop her to pieces. I'm a civilized man, but I understand those feelings. We cannot communicate with her. She cannot surrender. We cannot negotiate terms or extract information. She can do nothing but growl and spit at us."

"We will not make sport with her," said Lord Lester. "As you said, we are civilized men. We should do onto her no different than we would have done to our own."

"We would have our own freed," said Pellan. "Is that what you suggest? For if it is, the notion may be foolhardy or else, mayhap, it may be wise. Spare her life and the lives of those who remain in these tunnels — that may be the spark that ignites peace. Mayhap, the *one* chance of peace between our peoples."

"If we kill them all," said Lord Cadbury, "we don't need to worry about terms and surrenders. Or peace."

Ector drew his sword and stepped toward the troll queen. "It ends here."

"In future years," said Ector, "our folk will never know the horror of the troll. They'll never be stalked in the night by these things. They'll never be hunted. Eaten. They'll never have their homes invaded; their lands destroyed. Not by them. Soon the trolls will pass into legend." Ector raised his sword high.

The troll queen raised her head, her eyes boring into Ector's, hatred on her face.

Ector brought his sword down with all his strength.

Severed her head with a single blow.

Ector looked at each of his officers. "Send men down every tunnel, search every chamber, find every hidey-hole."

"And kill them all," he said. "Kill them all. Every one."

49

VAEDEN
AZATHOTH'S PALACE

THE AGE OF MYTH AND LEGEND

THETAN

The beast barreled into Thetan again. At the last moment, he sensed it. The slightest sound, the movement of the air. But that did him no good. He had no time to react for the thing came on too fast.

It hit him as hard as a charging bull.

Took him off his feet.

Carried him through the air.

Crushed him to the floor.

All its weight slammed down on Thetan's chest.

Blasted the breath from his lungs. His strength, instantly sapped. For a moment, he couldn't move; no strength at all.

It was in such moments that warriors died. He knew that better than any. But luck was with him. After but a moment, his limbs responded. He twisted. Pulled his arm free of the battered shield, now more hindrance than help.

The creature's invisible hands were at his throat. Icy fingers clamped down, though his armored collar thwarted its grip. That steel plate was there to safeguard his neck from any blade that sought it. It served near as well against a stranglehold.

But still, Thetan couldn't breathe. The thing's weight was unimaginable. Compressing his chest. His whole body. It didn't even need to choke him. Seven, eight, perhaps nine hundred pounds was it, squarely atop him. He couldn't raise his chest to take a breath, but the creature's icy breath washed over him. No stink of death did it harbor. No foul scent at all. Just cold. Unnatural, bitter cold. In but a moment, Thetan's nose and cheeks went numb from it, the icy frost of Niflehiem.

Thetan knew at that moment that what he faced was a thing not born of his world. Until that instant, he believed it a man or beast ensorcelled by Azathoth's magic with unnatural strength and speed and to walk unseen.

But nothing that lived was so cold to its very core. That could mean only one thing. That it *was* a creature from the beyond. A thing of the Nether Realms. A demon, or devil, or some such. Thetan knew of such creatures. He knew that they were more than mere myth and legend. More than tall tales to frighten misbehaving children. He'd faced them before, those outre creatures. Faced them and lived, as few others could boast. They could be called over to Midgaard, across the ether, by dark sorcerers of terrible power but poor judgment. So too could they cross over to our world at certain special locations where the veils betwixt the worlds are thinnest, but only when the stars lie in blessedly rare and proper alignment.

Thetan knew that the demon spawn that

accosted him, as did all its kind, lived only to destroy. To take life. To defile it.

And yet there it was, in the service of the so-called one true god who claimed to be all good, all holy. What a crock. Even in that terrible moment, at the brink of death, Thetan took solace that he was doing the right thing. Anyone that brought such a creature over to Midgaard, regardless of purpose or intent, had to be stopped.

One of Thetan's arms was free, the other, hopelessly pinned between his torso and the beast's. He brought his hand up. Guessed where the creature's chin would be. Struck with the palm of his hand.

The thing's head flinched back.

Its grip did not slacken.

Thetan tried to push up on its chin. Twist its neck. But the creature buried chin to chest.

It fought to protect itself. That meant that it was intelligent. That it could reason. It was no mere magical construct or mindless wild beast. That meant that it could feel pain. That it was vulnerable.

And if it were vulnerable, then it could be killed.

Thetan struck at its face. Over and again. Fast and faster still. Poking. Jabbing. Using all the strength that he could bring to bear. Went for its eyes. Its nose. Whatever vulnerable area he could reach. He sensed the thing's head bobbing and weaving from this side to the other, trying to avoid his pointed strikes.

Thetan felt and heard his neck armor bend and buckle under the superhuman grip of the invisible

274

creature.

There was no escape.

His vision blurred, the last of his oxygen gone. He kept striking. His indomitable will refused to yield. Refused to give up. But the darkness closed in. His vision grew narrow. All sounds, muffled. The end was near. Death beckoned.

50

LOMION CITY DOR LOMION

YEAR 1267, 4TH AGE

LANDOLYN MALVEGIL

Lady Landolyn Malvegil, ink quill in hand, carefully annotated the large street map rolled out on the tabletop, a big leatherbound ledger open next to her. She labored in a seldom-used suite on a seldom-used floor within the great fortress of Dor Lomion, the central seat of power of House Harringgold. Her husband, Lord Torbin, lay in bed in the back room, recovering from the life-altering wounds inflicted upon him by The Black Hand assassins.

All but a handful of people thought her husband dead, killed along with many others during the assassination of King Tenzivel.

Torbin escaped death — but at a terrible cost. Paralyzed from the waist down. Unable to walk. Unable to move or even feel his legs. A warrior that could never fight again.

But he was alive.

And of sound mind.

And that was what mattered most to Landolyn.

"Come in," she said in response to a knock at the chamber's door. A dozen Malvegillian soldiers stood the guard night and day outside that door; picked men every one, many others down the hall, guarding every stair and entry. The Malvegils had two thousand of their best soldiers stationed in the city. Several hundred were guests of House Harringgold.

Master Karktan of Rivenwood opened the door when Landolyn gave her leave. Karktan was Weapons Master of House Malvegil and one of her husband's closest friends. His brother, Stoub, died protecting Torbin during the assassination attempt. It was Karktan that led the Malvegil troops against The Black Hand assassins, in revenge. And under his fine leadership, they sacked Black Hall, The Hand's base of operations, and wiped out its leadership. In that single bloody night they killed nine tenths of that nefarious brotherhood. But the remainders proved elusive and caused them no end of trouble.

Karktan looked a mess. His black cloak and breeches were crusted with dried blood. His face was bruised; his nose, bloody.

"Dead gods, what happened?" said Landolyn.

"The Hand hit us at five different locations, all at once. We lost sixty men."

"Sixty of ours?" said Landolyn, shock in her voice. "Dead gods, how can that be? I thought we killed almost all The Hand's agents."

"It seems that Weater the Mouse only gifted us a partial roster of their membership. At least a hundred Handsmen were involved in those five attacks. We thought they had less than half that number left."

"Probably that was their full complement," said

Landolyn.

"It wasn't," said Karktan. "I saw the last bit of one attack and chased after them. Caught them eight blocks later in a dead end square. They were waiting for us. A trap it was. I went in there with one hundred and fifty men and came out with one hundred and twenty. That's thirty more than the thirty they killed at our bases. If I'd have had a single squadron with me, you'd be in need of a new Weapons Master tonight."

"How many assassins were in that square?"

"No less than a hundred. They hit us from all sides with arrows, bolts, and poisoned darts. My guess is that each of the other Hand attack squads had a similar trap set up to deal with any pursuit."

"Then they must have several hundred men or more left in Lomion City," said Landolyn.

"And Odin knows how many more they can call in from other cities," said Karktan. "There's enough of them to do us grievous damage – tonight was proof of that. They know this city so much better than we do, it counters our advantage of numbers. They're going to keep hitting us. They're going to keep coming."

"So we must continue to take the fight to them," said Landolyn, "just as we have been doing." She pointed to the map on the table. "Based on the information that we've collected and that Grim Fischer and his Orphan's Guild have shared with us, I've identified five or six of their safehouses that we haven't raided. The Grandmistress may be holed up in one of them. I want you to hit them all - at the same time, just as they hit us tonight. I want you to find her and bring her before me if you can, or kill her if you must. She must not escape us."

"I will plan the attack just as you've ordered," said Karktan, "but I fear that the Grandmistress will continue to elude us. And even if she doesn't, even if we kill her, I don't believe that will be the end of it. These criminal brotherhoods, they're not dependent on a single person. Another leader will rise."

"We can't let The Black Hand continue to exist," said Landolyn. "Not after what they've done. They have to be stopped. They have to wiped out."

"In a straightforward battle," said Karktan, "the two thousand men we have are more than enough to finish The Hand — even if there be five hundred of them left. Even if there's a thousand. We would crush them. But in the streets of this city, with its narrow alleys and innumerable hidey holes—"

"How many men do you need? Three thousand? Five? Ten thousand? Tell me."

"It's not just numbers," said Karktan. "We're not trained for these kinds of battles – the street warfare with an enemy that fades into the populace and hides from view. Even with ten thousand men, I don't think I could get them all. I'm sorry, my lady, but I don't know how to fight this kind of war."

"Then you're going to have to learn," said Landolyn sternly, "and waste no time about it." Karktan stood silently as she poured them both a goblet of wine. "Did you capture any tonight?"

"Three, but each bit down on a poison pill.

Killed themselves rather than be taken, just like all the others. That's their way. That's how their brotherhood has remained so secret for so long, how they're able to exist in a civilized city like Lomion."

"Why don't you think we'll find the Grandmistress," said Landolyn.

"It won't matter if we do," set Karktan. "As I said, another will rise. Unless we kill them all, this will never be over, at least not as long as we remain in Lomion City."

"We can't exactly leave," said Landolyn, "with the trolls in siege. But if we could — is that what you'd advise me to do? To run?"

"To survive," said Karktan. "The moment the siege is lifted, assuming it ever is, we must flee back to the Dor with all our people, and make no secret of it. We'll leave word for The Hand, telling them that we've satisfied our revenge and that we're calling an end to the feud."

"Would they honor that?" said Landolyn.

"I don't know," said Karktan. "But it won't matter either way. You and Torbin will be back at the Dor, safe amongst our people, and guarded more closely than ever before. I will remain here with a contingent of our best fighters. We'll take off our insignia. Our coats-of-arms. Anything that would trace us back to House Malvegil. We'll wait a few weeks and then we'll begin our assaults again, but this time, we'll use different battle tactics, different styles from anything they've seen from us so far. They won't know who we are."

"To what end?" said Landolyn.

"We'll put rumors out, that there's a new

power rising in Lomion's underworld," said Karktan. "A new faction looking to take over from The Hand now that their power has ebbed. We'll be that faction. That will cover Malvegillian involvement, at least for a time. It will distract them. Keep their focus off you and the Dor even as we continue to pound them. In the end, even if I don't finish them off, I may weaken them to the point that they're no longer a threat."

"And in the meantime, while we wait out the siege?" said Landolyn.

"We're vulnerable," said Karktan. "I can't even be certain you're safe here in this room, not even with a dozen Malvegils outside the door. As you say," pointing to the map, "so long as we are trapped here, we must continue to take the fight to them."

"We must," said Landolyn. "I don't want them hunting us."

"My lady, they've been hunting us since the day we entered this accursed city."

"**Y**ou understand that when the siege is over," said Landolyn, "I'm not leaving Lomion City, your plan, notwithstanding."

"What?" said Karktan.

"There are votes coming up in the Council," said Landolyn. "We came here because Lomion needs the Malvegils."

"Forgive me, my lady, but we came here so that Torbin could convince the government of the Duergar invasion. Our best proof of that – the Svart orb – was stolen by The Hand, and we've not been able to recover it. But we've already told Harringgold all that we know. And he believes us. Our mission here is over save for the revenge that we seek."

"We also came here," said Landolyn, "so that Torbin could speak before the Council of Lords — convince them not to support the mad provisions that the High Council is contemplating – the rewriting of the Articles of the Republic, the abolition of our god-given freedoms."

"He can't do that any longer," said Karktan. "Maybe not for months. Maybe not ever."

"When the time comes, if Torbin is well enough, he will do it."

"And if he's not?" said Karktan.

"If he's not," said Landolyn, "*I* will speak in his stead.

Karktan looked shocked.

"You think they will not hear from the consort of a Dor Lord?" said Landolyn. "That they will not suffer a woman of the blood before them?"

"That is not for me to say," said Karktan.

"The Malvegils will not abandon the Kingdom of Lomion in its time of need," said Landolyn, " injuries, assassins, or prejudices against Elves, be damned."

Karktan nodded. "I'm proud to serve you, my lady."

51

JUTENHEIM
TUNNELS OF SVARTLEHEIM

YEAR 1267, 4TH AGE

FREM SORLONS

Frem saw a light ahead, far up the tunnel, but whether it emanated from a torch, luminescent lichen, a natural light well, or even an exit to the outside, he could not tell, owing to the distance.

In normal times, he'd have doused or hidden his torch and stood silent and still, waiting to see whatever there was to be seen before advancing. That was the safe play. The prudent move. But he had little patience left and even less energy to wait things out. That was one of the dangers of being lost in the wild. Conditions forced you to blunder forward when caution was the better tactic.

He knew the risks. There might be a Black Elf encampment up ahead, filled with who knows how many of the little buggers. Or perhaps, an enclave of some other subterranean dwellers even less hospitable. But all things considered, he judged it better to advance and deal with whatever needed dealing with rather than expending his energies waiting and watching. But whether that was sound reasoning or impaired, he didn't know for certain.

He couldn't trust himself any longer; not fully — he was too tired, his head too muddled.

He consoled himself with the thought that if enemies lurked up ahead, that might mean food, water, and other provisions were available for the taking. Given his dire straits, that was worth another fight.

It took much longer than he expected to reach the light, for the tunnel was long and straight and sloped gently upwards all the while. When close enough, he discerned it was a light well: a circle of light, some three feet by three feet in size, projected onto the floor of the tunnel through a shaft in the ceiling. Deliverance might well be at hand.

He hurried forward until he reached it. When he looked up, his mind was at once elated and his spirit broken. For above him, he saw the light of day projecting down the rocky shaftway — wide enough for him to climb up, thank the gods, but so terribly long and steep a shaft it was — a hundred feet or more to its top, and nearly vertical. Only the noonday sun could have ventured to its bottom. Had he passed that point at any other time of day, he might not have noticed any light at all, and might have passed the shaft by, unknowing. By the gods, he might've passed other such shafts already, Odin knows how many.

Did he have the skill for such a climb? Did he have the strength for it? His best chance was that the shaft was narrow. He could brace himself on either side as he climbed up.

He would do it. He had to. It was his one

chance of escape.

He resolved to take a quick look farther up the tunnel, just in case there was an easier way that led up. But then he heard a clicking sound from behind him. A jittering clicking sound, as an insect might make, but louder.

The whole cavern system was filled with bugs. Cave crickets, beetles, spiders, all manner of creepy crawlies, large and small. He'd become almost immune to their presence. But he hadn't heard that clicking before.

And then he saw movement in the distance, beyond the limits of his torchlight.

Shadows swayed.

Something or someone lurked there. He pulled another torch from his pack, lit it from the first. Threw the nearly spent one towards the movement.

And there it was. A cave creature that should exist only in darkest nightmare or fireside tale. A multi-legged fiend — but whether insect, lizard, or an unholy cross between the two, he knew not. As tall as he, it was; its gray torso, six or eight feet long; its limbs, spindly with jagged ridges; its hide, like armor plating, a long tail dragging behind. Big eyes it had, jagged crooked antennae, and a gaping maw with one huge fang on top, two to match on bottom.

It skittered away from the torch, afraid of the fire, as are all natural beasts. But no doubt, it saw Frem as a savory meal not to be missed.

It leapt forward, braving the torch's flames. Frem had no time to climb into the shaft, little less escape up it. If he'd had a spear or pole axe, he would have stood his ground, but with naught but dagger and torch for weapons, he had no interest in fighting such a thing. Instead, he turned and ran up the tunnel. He'd rely on speed and endurance to escape from it. He'd find another way out, or else circle back in his own time and take the thing unawares.

A mere twenty feet down the passage, the main tunnel abruptly dead ended! Several small passages branched off from it near its end — but so small were they, Frem might not be able to crawl through. He wasn't going down any of them, even if he could; not with that thing nipping at his heels. Knowing he was cornered, he had no choice but to fight. He turned and rushed forward, torch before him, dagger poised to thrust.

The thing reared back, afraid of the flame. But it lashed out with one multi-jointed leg. Frem ducked, then heard the tremendous impact when its kick struck the stone wall beside him and sent dust and rock fragments flying. The creature screeched a high-pitched wail that rattled Frem's ears and plumbed the depths of his courage.

Frem thrust the torch at its face, lunged forward with his dagger, but the thing's iron-like exoskeleton turned aside the steel blade, sparks flying.

One leg battered Frem's shoulder, the strike so powerful it lifted him from his feet, slammed him against the wall, and pinned him there.

Frem dropped his forearm with all his power onto the thing's leg. The creature's bone snapped with a thunderous report.

Undeterred, it reared up again. Opened its

maw.

Suddenly, some indefinable instinct took over in Frem – perhaps owing to a deeply embedded racial memory stored in his very bones and carried down from time immemorial — and caused him to turn about and duck, giving the thing his back.

A spray of sizzling venom shot from the creature's maw and Frem screamed.

52

JUTENHEIM ANGLOTOR

YEAR 1267, 4TH AGE

JUDE EOTRUS

Jude had seen enough to know that Master Glus Thorn was extraordinarily powerful, even for an Archwizard, but he never expected to see the man conjure an army from thin air.

Thorn held his staff between his hands and raised them high overhead. He spoke eerie words of a strange tongue akin to the *Magis Mysterious,* though of some distant dialect or archaic variant foreign to Jude's ears. The other Leaguers gave him wide berth as he called down the sorcery from the Grand Weave of Magic. Concern filled the wizards' faces as they watched.

When Thorn spoke his mystical words, Jude didn't just hear them with his ears -- he felt them throughout his body -- pressing, squeezing, constricting, weighing him down on all sides. Jude felt the words penetrate his skull and assail his senses. Felt them invading his brain, boring ever deeper, leaving nothing private, nothing clean. His entire body vibrated owing to some preternatural resonance in Thorn's voice. Fear welled up inside the young Eotrus. He'd never experienced anything like that conjuring. His stomach roiled; the bile rose in his throat; his head ached; he strained to suck sufficient air into his lungs.

Jude backed away, the others did much the same, though he didn't recall willing his legs to move. His intellect told him, distance would not save him. Not if that magic sought to destroy him. There was nowhere to hide from it. Nowhere to run, for its tendrils reached out across Midgaard to accomplish its unnatural purpose. After Thorn's words stopped, Jude was surprised that he still stood; surprised even that he still lived.

He witnessed a rectangular area of utter blackness, of pure darkness, appear at arm's length before Thorn. Small it was, too small even for a man's fist to pass through, but it hung there in the air, as real as anything. In but a few moments, it expanded -- taller and wider – soon the size and shape of a small doorway.

Thorn's arms, still upraised; his jaw, set; his eyes, wide; his body, rigid. He stood motionless throughout the remainder of the conjuring. And from that black doorway, boldly stepped a Stowron -- a match to those others Jude had seen amongst the Leaguers. The last time, they'd slithered through Thorn's coach, though that was left far behind, stowed within *The White Rose's* main hold.

A step behind that first Stowron came its twin. And then a third. A fourth. And then a multitude flooded through that cursed portal.

They came by the hundreds.

The courtyard filled with them.

And after a time, Thorn's strength faltered.

Vibrating and sweating from the strain, his face red, his legs unsteady; Thorn's arms dropped to his sides, and the portal snapped closed. One Stowron was only partway through the portal when it collapsed. It cut him in two.

Thorn staggered to the side and then dropped to one knee. Par Keld rushed in to steady him. Ginalli came forward as well.

"Get me inside, you fools," spat Thorn before his eyes closed and his chin dropped to his chest. Ginalli waved some of the mercenaries over, and they carried Thorn's limp form into one of the stone buildings near the main gate as Par Keld and Ginalli followed behind.

53

VAEDEN
AZATHOTH'S PALACE

THE AGE OF MYTH AND LEGEND

THETAN

Thetan threw one last strike. Hardly any strength to it, but it caught the creature's nose at just the right angle. Snapped it. Blood poured from it. Milky white and sour as before. That foul stuff, colder than any fluid that Thetan had ever felt. How it failed to freeze solid was beyond his comprehension.

The thing howled. A guttural, apelike howl. It pulled one hand from Thetan's neck and attacked his breastplate. In its pain and fury it knew not how close Thetan was to blacking out. How close it was to victory. Sparks flew all about as the thing's unseen claws repeatedly raked Thetan's breastplate.

Still, Thetan could not throw it off. It was too heavy. Too strong. And at the moment, he was too weak. Barely conscious. But still fighting. Still struggling. He would never give up. Not so long as the merest spark of life remained within him.

With the beast's grip slackened against his throat, and its attention focused on ravaging his armor, Thetan had a moment to take a breath, to gather his strength. Only a fleeting moment was it, until he heard the skirling rending of metal, for the creature's claws did not just scrape against his armor, they tore into it, cut through it, shredded it like common cloth, though it was Valusian steel, tempered and tough – the stoutest armor known to man; thrice as thick as most. And yet the beast's claws carved it like a festival fowl.

Of what unholy substance must those claws be made?

Thetan struggled anew to throw the thing off.

Failed again.

He felt the claws bite into his flesh.

The searing pain.

The blood.

The beast's grip tightened. It tore away the breastplate, snapping the stout leather straps that held it in place.

Thetan reached his hand up. Fumbled for the thing's invisible wrist.

He had to grab it. Hold it fast. Or else its claws would rend him to the bone and beyond. It would rip his beating heart from his breast. And that would be his end. Even he could not survive that.

By luck as much as anything, he found its wrist, thick and hairy to the touch, and gripped it soundly before the thing's claws shredded his fingers or forearm. Thetan poured every ounce of strength he had into holding it fast, keeping those claws from his chest. But he was weak from loss of oxygen. Beaten. Bloody.

And the thing was powerful.

Stronger than any foe he had ever faced, and filled of a rage that could not be sated, at least, not as long as Thetan lived.

It pushed back Thetan's hand. Inched it ever closer towards his chest, his throat. The warrior could not hold it back. And he knew not how long its claws were. How soon they'd rip into him again.

Thetan's heart pumped wildly in his chest. Panic. This could not be. He could not be defeated. Such a thing could not come to pass. He would not allow it.

And then the thing's claws found his chest again. Cut his flesh.

But this time, when they did, for a fleeting moment, the beast at last became visible; roared in pain; bucked back.

When Thetan saw that scion of the Nether Realms, his blood ran nearly as cold as its. An otherworldly beast, it was, of no denying. A fiend of the Outer Spheres. Its aspect akin to both man and ape, but a natural cousin of neither breed. Its skin, a sallow, sickly gray -- near to white. Nose, overly broad and flat. Mouth, larger than a man's; teeth, even the larger. Its eyes, deep set and black, the sclera, a deep yellow. Brow, heavy and ridged. Bald of head, but its body was covered in light gray fur, thick and shiny, face to fingertips. Its eyes shone with an intelligence beyond that of any beast, perhaps on par with a man, though who could say. And in those inhuman eyes, Thetan saw fear. Pain too; its face was covered in it. But the fear was what was important. He could use that to defeat it.

The fiend recovered its wits and its courage in but a moment and pushed down again, claws extended, thirsty for blood. It struggled to sink those claws anew into Thetan's chest. But this time it shifted its grip; moved over, away from the center of Thetan's chest for no good cause.

Why? His breastplate was gone, flesh exposed. His blood already spilled. Easy prey. Why move?

And then Thetan knew the truth of it. For against his chest lay the misshapen Ankh that lately fell from the heavens, still attached to its metal chain.

He knew then, it was that strange relic that the beast feared, for it no longer stared into his eyes, but instead, stared at the Ankh, its eyes wide, fear ruling them.

Perhaps the Ankh possessed a magic that forced it visible. And the Ankh's touch caused it pain.

And so, Thetan used all his strength to shift the thing's hand back toward the center of his chest, braving its claws. The very moment its claws touched the Ankh, it became visible again and remained so. A searing sound. Smoke rose from the thing's hand. It howled in agony and sought to pull away. But this time, Thetan held it fast. He lunged forward, opened his jaws wide, and sank his teeth into the beast's neck. Despite the creature's thick hair, he broke the skin, and tasted its sour blood. It burned like acid. The creature howled, mad with fear and pain. It leaped backward and tore free of Thetan's grip, even as Thetan spit its blood from his mouth.

At once, the creature began to fade from view.

54

LOMION CITY
TAMMANIAN HALL
HIGH COUNCIL CHAMBERS

YEAR 1267, 4TH AGE

REGENT BARUSA ALDER

A Myrdonian commander pushed open the doors to the Council chambers and strode towards the petitioner's dais.

"What news, commander?" said Marshal Balfor.

"A stranger seeks an audience with you, my lords," said the knight. "A foreigner of regal bearing. They say he approached the walls unmolested by the trolls. My men saw this through spyglass and their own eyes. We cannot account for it."

"He's in league with the trolls," said Slyman. "That's obvious enough. What else could it be?"

"Sent on their behalf to present terms to us?" said Balfor. "A messenger or a lackey, mayhap."

"Perhaps merely lucky or swift," said Lady Aramere.

"A wizard he could be," said the Vizier, "to pass the trolls unaccosted."

"A foreigner, you said?" said Barusa. "Is he a

Volsung?"

"He appears to be," said the knight commander.

"What be his name?" said Barusa. "Who does he claim to represent?"

"He'll speak only to the High Council," said the commander. "Given how he rode into the city, I brought this news to you at once."

"Wise," said Barusa. "Send this man in, heavily guarded."

The Dramadeen commander stepped from the shadows and took up position at Barusa's right hand. Other Dramadeens gathered protectively around the Regent. A squadron of Myrdonian knights hovered closely about the other councilors.

Minutes later, ushered in by a full squadron of Myrdonians, came a curious figure. A middle-aged man, broad and muscled, well past six feet in height, with dark close-cropped hair, and a meticulously groomed mid-length beard black as pitch. His armor was archaic in design, battered and weathered, with a flowing red cape that fluttered behind him. He paused overlong to look around the room, noting each councilor, though ignoring the guards about him. Then he strode to the petitioner's dais, a broad toothy smile on his face.

"Wise was it for you to receive me so promptly," said the man in common Lomerian, no accent detectable, "for there is precious little time to spare. The trolls will soon mount your walls and then all will fall to chaos."

"Are you their messenger?" said Balfor, "here

296

to treat with us?"

The man shook his head. "No, no, no, certainly not. I am here to aid you against them, for they are the enemies of all humankind. You do know why they are here? Why they are at your gates?" he said.

"You tell us," said Barusa.

"For food," said the man. "They are here for food. A supply that will last them indefinitely."

"Plenty in the forests, in the mountains, is there not?" said Slyman. "Why come here? Why start a war? Incur terrible losses?"

"You don't understand," said the man. "They're not looking for fruit or vegetables. Apples will not stave them off. Chickens will not satisfy."

"Then what?" said Bishop Tobin. "Our cattle? Goats? Sheep?"

"It's you they want," said the man. They eat...people."

"Surely you jest?" said the Vizier. "We've all heard the olden tales, but certainly there can be little truth to them."

"There have been rumors of this," said Lord Jhensezil. "Rumors in recent times. Tales from northern woodsmen."

"The survivors of the brigade we sent to Dor Eotrus suspected as much," said Barusa. "They saw many bodies gnawed upon. But how do you know these things? What gives you such insight into the ways of trolls?"

"I've watched them," said the man. "I've witnessed their atrocities. They don't want your land. Your riches. Your gold. Or even your livestock, though that they'll take. They want you.

And they will not be satisfied with anything short of all of you. The entire population of the city will be their larder."

"Madness," said Lady Aramere. "There are more than a million souls in Lomion City. Many more if you count the surrounding villages, towns, and hamlets, and all the farms."

"If this is true," said Slyman, "then how can we negotiate with them? How can we buy them off?"

"Or reach some accommodation?" said Bishop Tobin.

"Negotiate with a lion?" said the man. "Negotiate with a snake? Reach an accommodation with a cave bear?"

"So you're saying they are nothing but animals?" said Barusa. "Acting on instinct, nothing more? Driven by hunger in their bellies, not envy or avarice?"

"I believe so," said the man.

"Why are you here?" said Duke Harringgold. "What is your name? Who do you represent? Answer me quick, man."

The man raised an eyebrow and stared at the Duke before responding. "I am here to help you," he said. "I represent myself and only myself, though I do possess a smattering of followers. As for my name, I am called Baron Jaros."

"Baron of what land?" said Jhensezil. "You are no Lomerian. Where do you come from?"

"My title has been handed down through the generations; my House, of an olden bloodline. From well south of Dover do I hail."

"How do you propose to help us, Baron?" said

298

Barusa.

"I should think the information I've already conveyed would be considered of some help," said Jaros. "But that help I've freely given. What I offer now is much more valuable." He paused a moment before continuing. "I shall rid you of the trolls."

Slyman leaned back in his chair and rolled his eyes. "This can only be some ploy to extort coin from us," he said. "This man is either a thief or he's in league with the troll."

"I am neither," said Jaros, his tone even and calm. "I will rid you of the troll by killing them in the main and running off the rest. I will do this using my own forces, though I may ask some small support from you and your troops. But either way, I will rid you of them. Whatever remains of their forces, I will drive back to the northern mountains. Afterwords, I expect they will not trouble you again for a goodly time."

"Your forces, you say?" said Lord Jhensezil. "What forces are those?"

"Does it matter?" said Baron Jaros. "Isn't the important thing that the trolls be beaten back? Defeated? Who and how many does this thing, does it matter? Really? I will do this. I will rid you of the trolls. And you will pay me handsomely for this service."

More than one of the councilors shook their heads and looked displeased.

"What? Did you think I'd offer this service for free? Put my troops to the field without pay? Who would?"

"What is your price?" said Barusa.

"You will not bring foreign troops into Lomion

City," said Marshal Balfor.

"And I don't propose to," said Baron Jaros. "Your city will remain sacrosanct."

"I ask again, what is your price?"

"When I rid Lomion City of the troll threat," said Baron Jaros, "this Council and the Council of Lords will vote, legal and proper, and you shall elect me as your new king. I will take my place on the granite throne."

The councilors were dumbstruck.

"Harrumph," went Bishop Tobin. "The man is a jester. He jests."

"I don't think he's jesting," said Jhensezil.

"Good councilors," said Jaros, "I can assure you, I am not jesting. I will save Lomion City. I will save this kingdom. And in return, you shall lawfully anoint me as king of the realm. This is my price. I will accept nothing less. But do not fear, my friends. For I will be a benevolent king, acting always in the traditions of this grand Republic, for the good of all its people, just as have my predecessors for these many centuries. And fear not for yourselves, for I pledge to you that after I take power, each and every one of you shall remain in your current positions as valued counselors to the king. All will remain much as it has been, much as it is now. The good Regent of course must have a different role, for when I am king there will be no need of a Regent. However, I will need a good right hand. A man experienced in Lomerian politics. I plan to name Barusa, Archduke of the Realm."

"This is madness," said the Vizier. "We don't even know who this man is. What his loyalties are.

300

He's not even a Lomerian. He cannot be king. He must not be king."

"The king cannot be elected by this council," said Harringgold, "when a queen sits the throne, and a queen we have."

Jaros looked surprised. "I thought that matter resolved," he said. "Your fair daughter was queen for but a day. And as I understand it, the marriage was not yet consummated, and the king not of sound mind when the marriage took place. I am no expert on Lomerian law, but don't those facts invalidate Miss Harringgold's claim?"

"The facts," said Bishop Tobin, "are in some dispute."

"No matter," said Jaros. "If the throne is vacant, you can elect me. If Miss Harringgold sits it, I will marry her and assume the throne in that manner."

"You will not," said Harringgold, voice raised.

"In times past," said Balfor, "such arrangements have been struck."

"You support this idea?" said Barusa.

"If this man is serious, and can do what he claims," said Balfor, "then we must consider his proposal, however distasteful it may seem at the outset."

"Millions of souls depend upon us to keep them safe," said Bishop Tobin. "We must not be hasty, for whatever decision we make here today will outlast us all. It will change the course of Lomerian history."

"But for better or for worse?" said Lady Dahlia.

"It is beyond the power or purview of this Council to decide who the queen will marry," said

Jhensezil. "Only she can decide that."

"That is only relevant if this Council declares her claim valid," said Slyman. "We are far from that decision, and agreed to set it aside until the matter of the trolls is resolved."

"It cannot wait," said Jaros, "since the resolution of the trolls depends on it. If you accept my offer, you will be alive to contemplate your history and debate anything you like until you drop. That is what I offer."

"Words," said Barusa. "All we know of you, Baron Jaros, is that you allegedly passed through the troll lines unaccosted. Perhaps you did. Perhaps you did not. Perhaps you are lucky. Perhaps you *are* in league with the trolls. Or perhaps you are more than you seem. I don't know. But I do know, I will not entrust the fate of Lomion City to a man unknown, based upon words and promises alone. Show us your army, Baron. Show us what power you have over these trolls. Prove to us that your words are true and we shall give them close consideration."

"Close consideration?" said Jaros. "Hmm. How kind of you. How thorough. I tell you what, have your scribes draw up a writ. A writ that promises that if I rid you of the troll, that you will lawfully elect me the king of Lomion or offer me the hand of your queen if that be the outcome of your debate. And that if I fail, I will be exiled from your realm, forevermore. Produce that writ. Sign it in private — letting no one know of it outside this chamber, save Miss Harringgold who must also sign. Each and every one of you, put your name and your oath to it. Do that, and I will give you your demonstration. If it does not impress you, tear up the writ and forget it ever was. Throw me from your walls if you care to. But if I succeed, if I prove to you my power, you will file that writ and read it aloud before the Council of Lords, and have every herald in the city speak it on every street corner. Do this and I will rid you of the trolls as I have promised. Will you agree to this?"

"Why do you want to be king?" said Jhensezil.

Jaros rolled his eyes. "A man of little ambition you appear to be, good sir. Who would not want to be king of the greatest realm in all Midgaard? We've debated this long enough, my friends. The trolls are at your doorstep. Soon they'll be in your house. Soon they'll be slaughtering your people. Feasting upon them on your very streets. Your walls will not hold them back. Your armor will not save you. No hidey hole you find will safeguard you. The hour grows very late, good councilors. Make your decision. Draw up the writ. And ensure Lomion City's continued existence."

55

VAEDEN
AZATHOTH'S PALACE

THE AGE OF MYTH AND LEGEND

THETAN

Why he did so, Thetan could not say, but as the creature began to fade from view, he placed his right hand upon the Ankh, gripped it tightly. When he did, the creature's aspect became solid again. Somehow, the Ankh held sway over the creature's magic.

Thetan stepped forward, smashed his fist against the beast's jaw. A blow with power enough to fell an ox. The thing shook its head wildly but held its ground, growling. Thetan's fists fired into its jaw, its nose, its eyes -- a flurry of blows too fast to follow.

The thing didn't budge. Didn't back up a single step.

It lashed out with its arm; Thetan blocked it, but his arms were knocked aside. The creature's next blow caught his jaw. Thetan stumbled back, his knees weak, his legs barely supporting him. The room spun. He gripped the Ankh again even as the creature began to fade once more. He had to keep it visible; his only chance. Even still, he felt overmatched. It was too strong. Too resilient.

The creature charged at him, head down. From a sitting position, Thetan leaped aside at the last moment. The beast barreled into the chamber's wall. Stone cracked. A large panel broke, smashed to the floor. Thetan scrambled to his feet, his eyes seeking his weapons. In but a moment, he found his sword. Raced for it. He heard the creature rise. Felt it at his heels. He grabbed the sword. Spun, swinging. His blade cut into the creature's shoulder. But the beast clubbed him across the back. That lifted him from his feet and sent him crashing to the floor again.

Groaning, Thetan pulled himself up, falchion raised. The beast came on again, not slowed by its wound. Injured or no, Thetan was prepared for it that time: he could see it, and he had his sword at the ready. Thetan's overhand chop sliced the creature open from right shoulder to left hip. Thetan spun and sidestepped as the creature's momentum carried it forward. As it passed, he buried the falchion deep into the creature's back, all his power and leverage behind the slash. He barely managed to dislodge and keep hold of the sword as the creature turned and backpedaled.

He tightly gripped the Ankh again. Had to make certain the beast remained visible. Stepped forward to finish the monster. The battle had gone on far too long already. He had to secure the Sphere of the Heavens and be off before he was found out. He'd take the creature's head to make certain that it would stay down.

Thetan's eyes widened and he stopped in his tracks when he saw the terrible wound he'd inflicted across the creature's chest close of its own accord. It fully healed in barely a moment.

Thetan's hesitation was his undoing.

The creature stepped forward, smashed both fists against him, shoulder and hip, as it howled. The blow sent Thetan flying through the air. He crashed against the chamber's wall a dozen feet away. Slumped to the floor.

For a moment, all his strength was gone. All breath expelled from his lungs. Every bone in his body felt rattled, broken, pulverized.

The creature roared again, baring its teeth. Pounded fists to its chest, thumping it like a drum. It had won.

Thetan struggled to get up. He'd die on his feet, fighting to his last breath, staring death in the eye. But his muscles betrayed him. He could not rise. Could barely hold the sword before him. He'd skewer the thing as it came in if he could, sink the blade straight through its heart. But he needed to see the thing coming. He gripped the Ankh as tightly as he could.

And then it vibrated in his hand.

It grew warm.

Began to glow.

Vibrated more.

A humming sound.

The creature noticed it at once. Its eyes went wide with fear again. But undeterred, it charged. Roaring. Slavering.

Instinctively, Thetan held the Ankh out before him. And then…a wonder happened.

A bolt of energy -- akin to lightning -- erupted from the Ankh and shot at the creature. How that happened, where that power came from, Thetan could not fathom.

The numinous bolt struck the beast, center chest and all at once: there was a blinding flash of light; the creature froze in place; a burst of smoke exploded about it; and a booming sound rang out that rattled Thetan to his core. The lightning departed as suddenly as it came. The creature teetered for a moment, then fell face forward to the floor. When it hit the cold stone, a burst of dust and smoke erupted from its body, and a foul scent of burned flesh accosted Thetan's nose.

Thetan blinked and waved his hand before his face, the dust hanging heavy in the air.

The creature lay still and silent.

After a few moments, as Thetan watched, its body spontaneously burst into flame, consumed from the inside out.

Thetan pulled himself to his feet. Held out the Ankh before him with wonder, and then a broad smile crept over his face.

56

JUTENHEIM NEARING ANGLOTOR

YEAR 1267, 4TH AGE

CLARADON EOTRUS

Claradon was startled when Ob spat, "By Odin! It sounds as if old Mister Fancy Pants has stirred up another hornet's nest. All we need."

Though he heard nothing himself, the young Eotrus knew better than to question Ob, for the Gnome was famous for his hearing even amongst his own kind. Claradon, Ob, and Glimador were at the fore of the Eotrus line, the balance of the expedition closely following, all moving at a fast walk, the best pace they could manage and stay together given the fatigue and injuries that plagued them from their travels and ordeals. Due to Ob's short legs, he had to jog to keep up with the others. He did that with no complaints.

The Eotrus expedition was on the last leg of their long quest, fast approaching their ultimate destination – the temple of power in Jutenheim known as Anglotor, wherein could be opened the ever-barred door – a mystical gateway to the fabled otherworldly realm of Nifleheim. From a sacked guard tower high on a hill, the Eotrus had spotted Anglotor miles away — apparently under attack, smoke and fire pouring from several of its buildings. Not knowing whether they'd arrived just in time or a bit too late, the Eotrus made their best pace towards Anglotor.

Lord Angle Theta; his manservant, Dolan; Milton DeBoors – the Duelist of Dyvers; and The Wild Pict – Kaledon of the Gray Waste, had gone on ahead, sprinting towards Anglotor, far faster than any of the others could move.

"How far up ahead are they?" said Claradon.

"Half mile, give or take," said Ob as he cupped his hand to his ear. "Get your butts in gear, men," shouted Ob over his shoulder, "up ahead, there's knife work what needs doing. Mister Fancy Pants has stepped in some slop and we're to be the cleaning crew."

The expedition broke into a quick jog, the officers making certain that the men stayed in formation, and that no one was left behind.

"A full-blown charge, it sounds like," said Claradon as they drew closer to what was obviously a skirmish, though they could not yet see it.

When Ob and Claradon reached the top of the next rise they were shocked at what they saw. Hundreds of strange little men adorned in deep-hooded cloaks of black, wooden staffs in hand, bore down on Theta and his squad. The attackers moved hunched over with a strange side-to-side gait, reminiscent of a jungle ape. The Eotrus men had never seen their like – though if they had, they would've marked them as Stowron, an ancient and reclusive breed that hailed from -- or rather, under, the deep mountains of the far north, not over-far, in fact, from Eotrus demesne.

The Stowron shouted their war cries as they charged toward Theta, their vanguard not more than one hundred yards out. No fewer than a score of Stowron – likely an advance patrol – already lay dead about Theta's squad who all still stood.

Theta's men turned about and sprinted northward up the trail, back toward Claradon and the rest of the expedition.

But on came the Stowron troop. As they raced forward, they broke formation, the fastest of them outpacing the rest. Dolan and Kaledon fired arrows into their ranks as they ran, each shaft dropping a Stowron, though the inexorable tide continued forward.

From just beside and behind Claradon sounded Artol's battle horn. No doubt, he sounded the blast to distract the Stowron. To give Theta and the others a better chance.

Claradon looked over his shoulder at the sea of shining helmets that gathered behind him. His men were ready, bunched around him several rows deep, close to sixty men in total — all that remained of the Eotrus expedition and those from *The Gray Talon* that had joined with them. These were some of the most loyal and skilled warriors Claradon had ever known.

Par Tanch Trinagal was there, winded and weak, but he would do his part – he always did; Claradon would never underestimate him again. Claradon's knights were there: Glimador, Kelbor, Ganton the Bull, and Trelman. So were Sergeant Vid, Seran Harringgold, Little Tug, Captain

Slaayde, and squads of Kalathen Knights, Harringgold regulars, Alder Marines, Malvegillian archers, and Eotrus troopers. A motley crew of battle-hardened warriors, ready to charge once more into the fray at Claradon's behest.

There was no time for strategy. Or tactics. Or uplifting speeches. Only swift, direct action. No matter the risk. No matter the cost.

"Charge," shouted Claradon.

And they did, every one.

57

VAEDEN
AZATHOTH'S PALACE

THE AGE OF MYTH AND LEGEND

THETAN

Breathing heavily, pale and shaken, Thetan reached high and carefully grabbed the handle of the lanthorn within which sat the *Sphere of the Heavens*. The moment he touched the brass handle, the Sphere's strange vibrations sent bolts of electricity shooting up and down his arm, shoulder to fingertips. At the same time, an unnatural chill poured off the Sphere; the same frigid cold that afflicted the entire chamber, though Thetan's gauntlets shielded him well enough from that. He let go the lanthorn, but then realized that the electricity had done him no harm. Tentatively, he put his hand to the handle again; felt the electrical stream pulse through him. It tingled but caused him no pain. He bore the discomfort; picked up the lanthorn again. When he turned toward the exit, he half-expected Azathoth to be standing there, either a disappointed or an angry look upon his face.

But Azathoth was not there. The antechamber was empty. No shouts of alarm in the distance. No pounding feet approached. He had done it. Stolen the unstealable from right under Azathoth's nose.

Or so it seemed.

Was it too much to believe, to hope, that Azathoth was unaware of his theft? Of his loss of faith? Of his wanton betrayal?

Perhaps he'd get away clean. He hoped to, but he didn't expect it, for the lord knew all, or seemed to. Only far afield atop Mount Cantorwrought did he feel free of the lord's gaze. Why that old mountain shielded him from the lord's sight, why the lord relied on Lasifer to monitor him there, he knew not, for it surely was neither the distance nor the height, for Azathoth saw much that occurred in far-off lands, even those across the great oceans. In the very heart of the holy palace what chance did he have to go unnoticed? He was on the road to ruin, and he'd led his brothers there with him.

He was responsible for whatever happened to them. That guilt and fear hung heavy over him.

But there was no going back. Only forward.

He was committed. The plan was in motion. Others were carrying out their parts.

And he'd do his.

No matter the consequences.

Thetan pushed the doubts from his thoughts and girded his courage. He pulled a silken cloth with a precut hole at its center from a deep pocket, and placed the cloth over the lanthorn, effectively disguising it. It appeared as if Thetan carried nothing more than a large box with an ornate handle. He stepped from the chamber and pulled the great doors closed, checking to make certain that nothing in the antechamber looked out of place, then pulled his cloak tightly about him in a futile effort to conceal his ravaged armor. When he did, he felt sharp pains across his chest and belly, and a wetness where his shirt pressed against his skin. He looked down. No blood pooled about his feet; that told him enough. He was cut but not bleeding out. He'd dress the wounds later. More pressing matters were at hand. He made for the stairs.

Lasifer lurked in the shadows at the top of the stairwell. He stood so still and silent that Thetan failed to see him until he stepped forward and spoke.

"You've got it?" said the Gnome, rare excitement on this face.

Thetan nodded.

"I must see," said Lasifer.

"We've no time to waste," said Thetan.

"I need but a moment," said the Gnome as he bent down and uncovered the lanthorn. "A wonder it is," he said breathlessly as he caressed the lanthorn's surface. "Do you feel its power? The vast energy that it harbors? Can you?"

"I feel a terrible cold pouring off it. And a strange vibration that tingles my fingers and hands."

Lasifer raised an eyebrow. "You feel more than that, I think. Tell me."

Thetan hesitated before he spoke, reluctant to say more. "It's as if the thing is alive. It wants to leach the very life from me. To suck the strength from my very core."

Strangely, the Gnome smiled and chuckled.

Thetan narrowed his eyes as he gazed down

upon the Gnome. "An evil thing, this Sphere. The sooner we are done with it, the better."

"What of the halo of colors that dances about it?" said Lasifer. "You do see that, don't you?"

Thetan shook his head.

"And its music?" said Lasifer. "Do you hear it? Surely you must."

"What music?" said Thetan.

"The music of the spheres. No more beautiful sounds have ever graced my ears."

"I hear a faint monotone humming, nothing more."

"A shame," said Lasifer.

"Does he know?" said Thetan. "Did that alarm you tripped alert him?"

"I don't know," said Lasifer. "It may have only alerted the guardian. The lord is in the throne room. The place is full, as best I can tell. I dared not enter in case he was on to us."

"If he was, he'd be turning over the entire palace to find us."

"He's distracted," said Lasifer. "Wotan is on his doorstep. The barbarian has several full corps on the approach."

"He's early?" said Thetan.

"If the Aesir keep Azathoth occupied until we can get clear with this, then early is most welcome. I have two Targons waiting for us on the low tower's roof."

"I'm not leaving without my men," said Thetan.

"Gabriel, Mithron, and Arioch are in the throne room," said Lasifer. "Perhaps some of the others as well, though I did not see them amongst the throng. He summoned all the Arkons upon word of the Aesir's approach. They'll be looking for you as well."

"Take it," said Thetan pointing to the lanthorn. "Take it on a Targon or by some other means if need be. Stop for nothing. We will meet you at the appointed place. Do not fail to be there. And don't be late."

The old Gnome's eyes went wide. "How am I supposed to carry this thing on my own? It's half as big as me. This wasn't the plan."

"The plan has changed. Wotan is early and now I need to extract my men from the palace, which may be no easy task. Use your magic to carry it. Or get some help. But waste no more time about it." Without awaiting any further response from the Gnome, Thetan turned and was off.

58

JUTENHEIM
TUNNELS OF SVARTLEHEIM

YEAR 1267, 4TH AGE

FREM SORLONS

Most of the cave creature's venom sailed over Frem's head, but some doused his helmet and back. Praise the gods, none found bare skin. Then came a sizzling sound akin to an egg dropped into a hot frying pan. Acrid smoke billowed, and a terrible heat afflicted Frem's head and back. But he saw no flickering light, no flame, no fire.

And then he understood. The thing's spittle was concentrated acid. Fearing it would eat through his armor, he pulled off his smoking helm, spun, and threw it at the thing's face. Frem stumbled against the tunnel wall and rubbed his back along the stone hoping that would somehow counter the acid. He felt and heard his armor crack and break like an eggshell, embrittled somehow by the acidic spray.

The cave creature lunged toward him again. One leg slammed into each of his shoulders. Simultaneously, it head-butted him in the chest, and bowled him over, the thing atop him.

Frem stabbed it over and again with his dagger, even as the creature's claws rent into his armor, ripping and tearing.

The thing tore the armor plating off his right shoulder, no doubt taking flesh with it.

Frem's dagger sparked ineffectually against its exoskeleton as he frantically searched for a vulnerable spot. Simultaneously, he tried to angle his torch to burn the thing, but the torch was pinned. Acrid smoke rose up all about him, the fumes burning his eyes and choking him.

The creature reared up again, legs flailing.

Frem thrust his dagger up under the creature's chin, up into its neck, and found purchase at last. He stabbed and sliced over and again at the same spot as black ichor spewed over his chest and neck and spattered his face.

The thing tried to back off, but Frem grabbed one leg, held it fast in an iron grip, held it fast, and stabbed and stabbed again into its neck. He pulled himself up, still holding the creature as it thrashed wildly. Frem plunged his dagger into one of the beast's great eyes. Pulled the blade out and plunged it into the other. Then he pushed the thing's head down and slammed the dagger into the base of its neck. This time, the blade shattered against its exoskeleton. So Frem kicked it in the head, a dozen times or more, as hard as he could, blows powerful enough to crush stone, though he was unable to stave in its head. The creature rolled over, thrashed wildly, legs flailing in all directions, screeching its high-pitched wail.

After several moments, its struggling subsided; its lifeblood drenched the cave floor from the dagger wounds. Finally, it went still.

Frem hurriedly pulled off his breastplate and

the padding below, the armor still smoking, the acrid scent burning his nose. He looked the armor over – a ruin. The rear of the breastplate had multiple holes, and what was left was so brittle that pieces broke off in his hand. The padding was smoking and burnt, essentially useless. That left him in naught but shirtsleeves above the waist, with scattered burns on his back, neck, and arms.

Frem had to step on and over the creature to make his way back to the light well. When he did, its legs flailed chaotically — perhaps some life yet remained in it. No matter, it was no longer a threat. Frem picked up his torch and staggered back toward the shaftway with all he had left: ragged pants with the battered remnants of leg armor, bracers, a mangled backpack, and burns, bruises, and scrapes aplenty. Few that saw him at that moment would've thought him a knight. A vagabond they'd mark him, a homeless bum.

The shaftway awaited him just as he'd left it. He tied off his lit torch to his pack such that it would provide light but not burn him or require him to hold it. He prepared to climb up into the shaft -- no easy task, for the base of it was above his head.

That's when he heard more clicking. For a moment, he wondered whether the creature had arisen, only stunned from its wounds. But then he realized, this time the clicking came from the opposite direction. It was a different beast, another of its kind. And then as if in answer to that clicking, came more, this time from yet another direction and farther away.

Frem nearly panicked. By the gods, had he

stumbled into a hive of those things?

Then came a screeching not unlike the death throes of the beast he'd felled. Another screech in answer. Then more. Soon, came a chorus of screeching from all around. There must have been dozens of them, all scurrying about the tiny side tunnels.

Frem repeatedly tried to heave himself into the shaft, but fell back down, unable to get a good grip. On the fourth attempt, he made it, and using all his strength — strength that dwarfed that of a normal man — he pulled himself up by his arms alone until he was able to find purchase with his legs. Braced to each side of shaft with both arms and both legs, he found a stable position even as the creatures' clicking and screeching drew closer, no doubt investigating the fate of their fellow.

Owing to the light from his torch and that which filtered down from above, he was able to assess his surroundings, if only for but a moment. The shaft's walls of stone were rough and uneven, offering plenty of hand and footholds along the way.

Frem knew he had only one chance for survival — to get up and out of that shaft before the cave creatures found him. So he climbed like he had never climbed in his life. Using every ounce of speed and strength in his body, while being measured in his movements. No doubt, he rushed faster than caution allowed, but he wasn't reckless, wasn't wild. He knew if he were, he'd lose his grip. He'd fall. And he'd die for certain.

He made it up ten feet, the creatures' shrieking growing louder. They had to be close.

Would they find him? Would they look up the shaft? Track him by scent? Or might he go unnoticed?

He made it up twenty feet. Then thirty. Forty. Fifty — halfway to the top, his muscles burning, his fingers going numb, his breathing heavy, head pounding. He dared to hope that he'd gone unnoticed. That he'd soon be free.

Of course, that's exactly when they found him.

59

LOMION CITY HOUSE ALDER

YEAR 1267, 4TH AGE

MOTHER ALDER

"**W**e must get him to agree to keep his troops, whatever they be, out of Lomion City," said Mother Alder.

"Of all people," said Barusa, "I expected you to oppose Jaros's proposal."

Mother Alder smiled. "I do oppose it, but I fear for our city. For our people. For our House. Let's say we send this Baron away or throw him in the dungeons, and face the troll on our own, as we have been. Even if we win, and I do think that in the end we would win, for we certainly have the numbers on our side, would it be worth the cost? How many thousands will die? Tens of thousands? Even more, mayhap? Our army will be decimated. Can we afford that? Can we afford to be so weakened? What will our rivals and our enemies do when they become aware of our weakened state? Is it not wiser to strike a bargain with this man and let him and his do the fighting?"

"I say back to you," said Barusa, "at what cost? Is it worth the granite throne? Is it worth my position on the Council?"

"Do you think he'll agree to keep his troops out of the city?" said Mother Alder.

"Balfor already raised that objection," said Barusa. "The marshal will never allow foreign troops on our soil. I can support that position. Make it a condition of the agreement. Jaros would have to agree. But once it's done, once the trolls are gone or dead, and he's the king —no matter what that writ says, it won't matter. He'll be able to do anything he wants. He'll be a hero. He'll be the king. He'll bring his troops and whatever else he wants into the city and no one will be able to stop him. If we cede power to this man now, all will be lost. The city will be saved. But not House Alder. And not the Council."

"I don't trust him to keep his word," continued Barusa. "To keep the Council in place. A purge is what we'll see, I expect. He'll have all our heads on pikes, and he may even have the people behind him, having saved them all from the trolls. He may even blame us for their arrival; an excuse for doing away with us."

"Firstborn, you must learn to think less linearly. Strike the deal. Agree to make him king. Just so long as he brings no troops or forces of any kind into our city until after the trolls are destroyed. If he agrees to that, sign the writ. Sign it with a smile on your face. Give him your warmest handshake and a pat on the back. Hell, even give him a hug. And let him do our fighting for us. And if the trolls destroy him and his, they'll be all the weaker for it, and that much easier for us to withstand. But if he wins, at what cost to him and his? Won't *he* be that much weaker? What strength will he have left?"

"You counsel betrayal?" said Barusa. "After he saved our city? Our people?"

"Don't be naïve," said Mother Alder. "The moment it's clear that the trolls are defeated, we will slay him. Whether that be by the Black Hand, or by the Dramadeens, or mercenaries that we employ. Or by your own darned hand if need be. Kings and would-be kings are dropping like flies about Lomion these days. What is one more? That man will never sit the granite throne of Lomion. Not while I live. And not while you live, Firstborn."

"Won't he be expecting such treachery?" said Barusa. "That man is no fool. He will take measures to safeguard himself."

"Firstborn," said Mother Alder, "he has already told you what he'll do to safeguard himself. Having the writ in writing, signed by all, spoken before the Council of Lords, read aloud by the heralds on every street corner of the city — he thinks that if everyone knows about the deal, that we will have to abide by it.

"That honor will demand it.

"That the law will demand it.

"That the people will demand it.

"He is a fool. When he gives us this victory, we will give him death.

"And what will the law say?

"We are the law.

"The Council is the law.

"You, the Regent, are the law. The lords have no interest in a foreigner on the throne.

"And what will the people do? Let them protest. Let them cry. Let them march up and down Main Street and Commoners Court. Why should we care? If things get out of hand, we will spin a story to expose Jaros as a villain. We will find a way to quell whatever conflicts arise.

"And Lomion will stay with the Lomerians.

"You will keep your position.

"And House Alder's fortunes will rise.

"Do you understand, Firstborn? Has any of this sunk into your stinking soft skull? Or is this too dangerous a game for you? Too bold? Too frightening? These are the moves one must make to stay in power in this game of kings.

"To preserve our House.

"To safeguard our way of life.

"I hope you're man enough to see it through."

"Thank Odin," said Barusa, a bewildered look on his face, "that you are on my side."

"Never forget that," said Mother Alder. "And never take it for granted."

60

VAEDEN
AZATHOTH'S PALACE

THE AGE OF MYTH AND LEGEND

THETAN

Thetan knew the faces but not the names of the throne room's two door guards. They pulled open the heavy doors and stood aside as he approached, their eyes downcast. That at once made Thetan suspicious, for those men always looked at the great Arkons as they passed -- a sign of respect. The center of the great hall was empty, as was Azathoth's throne and its surrounds, but a great throng gathered by the overlook on the south side, the mammoth doors open, exposing a panoramic view of the countryside far below. As Thetan moved to approach, he heard the throne room's doors open behind him again. A cohort of soldiers marched in, armor gleaming. Azathoth's honor guard, the Einheriar they were called, greatest of all warriors save for the Arkons. They were close to the lord, the Einheriar were, one and all. His strongest. His best. The most loyal.

Something wasn't right.

Thetan should have heard that group coming from afar, but the corridor was quiet only moments before when he passed through. They must have been hold-up inside one of the guard chambers just outside the throne room. Had they been waiting for him to appear? Were they there to block his retreat? To capture him and throw him in irons? Did the lord know everything? What a fool he was to think he could conceal his treachery from Azathoth.

He ignored the Einheriar and headed straight toward the overlook.

As Azathoth paced, he gripped his golden staff, a thing of wood and metal inscribed of esoteric runes, and topped with a white diamond a full hands-breadth across.

A Targon, one of the thin, translucent, batlike creatures that served as aerial steeds for the Arkons, flew through the overlook and landed, bearing the Arkon Mammon securely clutched about the chest by its forelimbs and gripped about the legs by its rear claws. As all its kind, the Targon's body was nigh invisible, save for its great white feathered wings, such that when it carried an Arkon, it appeared from a distance as if the Arkon were winged himself and flew — as if the Arkon were half man, half bird — less a thing of Midgaard and more of the heavens.

"What news?" shouted Arioch from Azathoth's side as Mammon's Targon made its landing. Mammon landed lightly on his feet despite the discomfort of his journey. He was taller than most of the Arkons, of lanky frame, and skin near as dark as charcoal.

"More northmen approach from the south," said Mammon. "Several brigades, mayhap more. But from the west marches death. A great host of barbarian footmen, shirtless heathens bearing axe, sword, and hammer, a great supply train behind them, well protected."

"More than one battalion?" said Guiron, the Warden of Western Vaedon.

Mammon shook his head. "They stretch all through the Courwood, to the very borders of Vaedon. A host unlike any that I've seen."

"Another full corps?" said Guiron.

"Three or four corps, no less," said Mammon.

"Your eyes must have played tricks upon you for no nation on Midgaard boasts an army so large," said Guiron.

"Wotan does," said Mammon. "Unless foul sorcery afflicted my eyes. Only the east lies open to us, though through the south we can still pass if need be."

"What do you mean, pass?" said Azathoth.

The hall fell silent.

Mammon hesitated, his jaw dropping open. Azathoth stared at him, expressionless. Waiting.

"I only meant that if, if, there were some reason for us to leave Vaedon, the east remains open to us. We can yet pass that way unmolested."

Azathoth shook his head slowly, a look of disappointment on his face. He paused some moments before he spoke. "Vaedon is my holy kingdom on Midgaard," said Azathoth, his voice calm and soft. "Here dwell my chosen people. We will defend Vaedon and her faithful against all my enemies, those from without, and those from within. We will not abandon her. There will be no withdrawals. No retreat. No surrender. This will be over only after we send the northmen fleeing back to their mountains or we crush the last of them beneath our boots. Do you understand that?" He looked from one Arkon to the next. "All of you, do you understand?"

"Aye," said the Arkons, heads nodding.

"We will fight unto the last," said Bhaal.

"Unto victory," said Mikel, a muscled man of fair hair and skin and chiseled jaw.

"Unto victory," shouted the Arkons.

It was then that Azathoth took notice of Thetan.

61

JUTENHEIM NEARING ANGLOTOR

YEAR 1267, 4TH AGE

CLARADON EOTRUS

Upon Claradon's order to charge, the Eotrus expedition raced down the rise, close in formation.

Their opponents did not hesitate, but kept up their charge. It was as if they were not surprised to see the Eotrus.

And had no fear of them.

And that told Claradon all he needed to know. This was no chance encounter with hostile locals. These were the defenders of the ancient keep, sallying forth to destroy them on approach. Did that mean that they'd already destroyed the Shadow League expedition? Was Korrgonn already dead?

Arrows flew from the Eotrus ranks: Malvegil archers and Harringgold crossbowmen at work. They could hardly miss, the mass of little men so thick before them. Many fell to their missiles, though it had no effect on their charge.

As they ran, Claradon conjured a mystical shield – a glowing translucent field of shimmering blue energy that safeguarded him, foot to helm, back and front. It would not make him invulnerable, not by any stretch, but it would deflect certain attacks, absorb others, and possibly deter some Stowron from attacking him at all, and thereby, give him that bit of battle edge that Theta so often spoke of. Most men that called themselves "wizard", a title that Claradon would never subscribe to, could never accomplish such a feat – to cast an enchantment while running downhill, with the stress and heat of battle looming. But such was Claradon's training; such was the advantages of the *Militus Mysterious*, the sorcery mastered by certain knightly orders. Glimador, at Claradon's left hand, cast a similar charm – Claradon sensed the sorcery, felt the Magical Weave open just beside him, and felt the energy pour down at Glimador's command.

At one point, Theta and DeBoors stopped and turned about, ready to face the onrushing Stowron. They timed their maneuver precisely, for the Eotrus reached their position at the same moment that the Stowron charge caught them, the war cries deafening, so close at hand.

The two sides came together with a thunderous crash. The Stowron, for all their numbers, were stopped in their tracks by the Northmen, their bulk, their mass, too great for the spindly Stowron to overwhelm.

Artol fought on Claradon's right, Kelbor just beyond him. The other Eotrus knights were close around, Kayla in their midst -- blade in hand, as fierce, tough, and ready as any of the men.

As always, the battle went quick to chaos.

So outnumbered were they, Claradon knew it would be a tough fight unless the little men proved to be no warriors. The opening moments of the melee made clear enough, the Stowron were warriors true – battle hardened and eager killers, as agile as the Svart, swift as the Gnome, masters of staff and short blade.

Fearless.

They would not retreat.

Not give ground.

And like as not, had no concept of surrender.

Each Stowron, a match for most Lomerian warriors.

But luckily, Claradon's Northmen were no common Lomerians. No common warriors.

Within moments of the initial clash, the screams and howls of wounded and dying men accosted Claradon's ears from all about. Thank the gods, they were Stowron voices in the main, higher pitched were they than most Lomerians'.

Blood spattered Claradon's tabard from some source, and then more sprayed his face when he slammed his sword into a Stowron's neck. So closely packed about him were his comrades, Claradon could only strike up and down with his sword, cleaving over and again, his physical shield protecting most of his body, his magical shield safeguarding the rest.

From all around, he heard the thunderous clanking as the Stowron staffs slammed again and again into stout Lomerian steel — shields and armor alike. A chaotic din, as if an army of smiths had gone mad.

The Stowron came on as fiercely as any opponents he had ever faced. They had little regard for their own lives. They were all about the attack, wild, swift, and relentless – more berserker than disciplined soldier.

Within moments, they began to push the big Lomerians back.

Claradon knew what he must do.

From the Grand Weave of Magic, he called down one of his most potent sorceries. It only took a moment. A few words of the *Militus Mysterious*, and a moment of deep concentration — no easy feat amid a battle, and called it up he did. An expanding cone of blue fire erupted from his fingers' tips. It spread and stretched out as it went. It did no harm to Claradon's allies, but it set ablaze whatever Stowron it touched, as if they'd been doused in oil and lit with a torch. That unforgiving sorcery carved a channel fifty feet deep and several feet wide in the Stowron ranks. A score of them fell dead, another twenty rolled about on the ground, wailing and on fire.

Bolts of blue and yellow fire sliced through the Stowron ranks just off to Claradon's left – Glimador's work, of that he was certain. Those mystic bolts exploded on impact, taking off arm, leg, or head with equal effectiveness.

From Claradon's right came a ball of fire that sailed over the Stowron ranks in a great high arc and came down a hundred feet behind the front lines. That could only be Tanch's work.

When it hit the ground, the explosion rocked the battlefield. The concussive blast nearly took Claradon from his feet, and did take down nearly everyone around him, save the sturdiest. Shrapnel flew, body parts careened through the air. Claradon raised his shield to protect himself,

ducked his head behind it, and kept fighting —
cleaving up and down with his sword. Up and
down, again and again.

When the blast passed, Claradon realized the
Stowron did not break. They did not run even in
the face of such overwhelming power. They came
on howling like madmen, but madmen so very
skilled at arms.

Was it that they had no fear?

Were they truly mad?

Or were they so sophisticated in the ways of
magic, that they knew the Lomerians could not
keep up such mystical attacks for long?

Claradon didn't know. And in the end he
supposed it didn't much matter. So long as the
Stowron came on, the Eotrus would fight them –
to the bitter end.

62

VAEDEN
AZATHOTH'S PALACE

THE AGE OF MYTH AND LEGEND

THETAN

"**W**hat news, Lightbringer?" said Azathoth. "Have you unmasked the traitor?"

"The palace is compromised, my lord," said Thetan as he stepped toward Azathoth's right side, his usual place, a place of honor, respecting his high station. "I spied a cloaked figure skulking about the lower levels. When I gave chase," said Thetan as he pulled open his cloak and displayed his ravaged armor, "I was sorely beset by a thing of magic — a fierce creature of great power. 'Twas a thing not of Midgaard. A beast conjured up from the Nether Realms by he that fled me."

"A wizard?" said Bhaal. "A summoner here in the holy palace? Are you certain?"

"The northmen boast of sorcerers of great power," said Uriel. "Bonesmen, they call them. Tricksters of the highest order. Perhaps they could affect such a conjuring."

"How could one such as that breach these halls unnoticed?" said Mikel.

"Not unnoticed," said Mithron. "Thetan sniffed him out."

"Did you slay him?" continued Mithron. "The wizard?"

"He fled as I battled his familiar."

"Long gone by now, I suspect," said Bhaal. "A weakling. A coward."

"Or skulking about still," said Azrael, "intent upon spying or mischief, great or small."

"I agree," said Gabriel. "The wizard was here with some purpose. He either accomplished it and has fled, or seeks to do so still."

"Accomplished or not, he may have fled after Thetan spied him out," said Mikel. "No heathen wizard would dare face the Lightbringer in battle."

"We should leave nothing to chance," said Gabriel. "I will scour the palace, top to bottom, to find this wizard if he yet lingers, or uncover any misdeeds he has done," he said turning toward Azathoth. "With your blessing, my lord."

Azathoth nodded his approval. "Who shall join you in this?" said the god.

"Arkons all," said Gabriel. "I fear that the power of this wizard is beyond our guardsmen. I would take Thetan, of course, since he's seen the wizard. So too will I conscript Azrael, Uriel, Raphael, Steriel, Tolkiel, Blazren, Hogar, Dekkar, Bose, and Arioch," he said, all of whom stood nearby.

Azathoth nodded. "Twelve Arkons," he said, his voice, solemn. "A number that carries power. So be it."

"And I will go as well," said Mithron.

"You too, first Arkon?" said Azathoth. "You too will join with this group?"

"The palace must be secured," said Mithron,

336

"and quickly. We cannot have wizards or their familiars lurking about, threatening your safety. The wizard must be found immediately, questioned and then killed for his treachery. I will entrust this duty to no one without my oversight, not even our best. It's too important. While we rout out the wizard, Bhaal, Mikel, and Mammon will plan our assault on the northmen. We cannot simply sit here and wait to be besieged."

"Here, here," said the Arkons.

"Hecate and Guiron will marshal the palace's defenses," said Mithron. "The palace complex must be locked down to insure no other uninvited guests enter or leave. We must be ready for anything in these dark times."

"Indeed we must," said Azathoth somberly. Azathoth spoke loudly and slowly now, as if every word were of great import. "But never fear, my Arkons, for I am always prepared, always vigilant. There is little that escapes me. Very little."

"With your leave, my lord," said Gabriel as he drew to attention and turned to depart. The other conspirators followed. Gabriel, Thetan, Mithron, and the rest had gone but a few steps when Azathoth spoke again.

"Thetan," said the lord. "There is one small matter that we must address."

Thetan stopped in his tracks. They all did. Thetan's eyes shut tightly for a moment, a pained expression on his face. That expression was gone when he turned back toward Azathoth.

"Is there something that you want to tell me?" said Azathoth. "Something that hangs heavy upon your heart, that troubles your conscience?"

Thetan's fingers fidgeted at his sides and his breathing quickened. He paused a moment, as if waiting for Azathoth to say more, though he did not.

"I am sorry, my lord," he said. "I failed you. The wizard should not have escaped me. I feel ashamed." He stared down at his boots, jaw clenched. "But I vow that I will bring him to heel. He will not elude me. Even if he has fled the palace, I will track him down and learn all that he knows, I promise you." Thetan started to turn away, but Azathoth's hand came up signaling him to freeze.

And he did.

They all did.

"There is something more that you withhold, Thetan," said Azathoth, his voice sharper now.

Thetan shook his head.

A disappointed look filled the god's face. "Speak now," he said. "Let not guile and deceit fill your heart. Confess and your transgressions will be forgiven."

Azathoth stared at Thetan. Moments passed in silence. Thetan's men paled but did not move. The other gathered Arkons seemed confused. The tension in the room was palpable.

"Beloved Lightbringer, greatest of all my chosen people, you who are like a son to me, I gift you this one last chance. Unburden your conscience and repent. Do so now in truth and in good conscience, and all may yet be forgiven. All will remain as it always was and always should be."

Thetan took a deep breath before he spoke.

338

His eyes hardened. His jaw set. His left hand fell casually to his sword's hilt. "I have acted alone. I have..."

"Lies," boomed Azathoth. And with that single word sprang forth a sonic blast from Azathoth's mouth that shook the room and sent the Arkons flying from their feet.

63

JUTENHEIM
TUNNELS OF SVARTLEHEIM

YEAR 1267, 4TH AGE

FREM SORLONS

"**O**h shit," spat Frem when he looked down and saw the creatures pouring over one another to get into the shaft. They'd definitely seen him. And they were coming after him — angry and hungry, bent on tearing him to pieces. No way to know how many were down there, but Frem guessed no fewer than a dozen.

In the shaft's confines he couldn't effectively fight them; he couldn't stop them. He wanted to throw a torch down, hoping they'd scatter and flee from it, but he couldn't afford the time to free the torch from his pack or light another.

He kept climbing as fast as he could, now throwing all caution aside. Up and up he went. Sixty feet from the bottom. The creatures had closed to within thirty feet of him.

They were too fast. He'd never make it to the top before they reached him. There was no chance of it.

He halted. Flung open his pack. Grabbed the last torch. Lit it from the dangling one. Dropped it onto the lead creature's face — now but ten feet

340

away.

The thing screeched - the loudest wail he'd yet heard. In a panic, it fell. Dropped onto its fellows. Knocked some of them loose. Those farther down arrested their falls. The whole mass of them screeched and howled.

Frem grabbed the brandy bottle from the pack. Upended it, spilling its meager contents onto the squirming creatures below — the burning torch still amongst them.

Frem enjoyed a bit of luck – for the brandy struck the torch's flame and flared up, burning all about and on the creatures.

They panicked. Went wild. The whole mass of them lost their grips, fell, and crashed to the tunnel floor far below.

Frem started climbing again, fast as he could move. He figured they'd be at him again soon enough.

Seventy feet up.

Eighty.

Then he heard the things climbing again. Maybe the same ones, maybe others. They raced up the shaft at three or four times Frem's best pace. High as he was, he still didn't think he could make it.

By the time Frem had reached the ninety foot mark, they were almost on him again. He was only ten or fifteen feet from the top of the shaft — but that was too far.

He reached down. Ripped free the dangling torch. Threw it down at the closest creature.

But it dodged.

The torch missed it.

The thing kept coming. The ones farther down howled in fear and pain as the torch fell amongst them, but whether it knocked any loose, Frem couldn't tell. And it didn't matter, because the lead creature was still coming on fast.

In but a moment, it lashed out at Frem's legs. The first strike missed. The second battered his calf, which mercifully was still well protected by his armor.

Frem kicked the creature. Hit it hard in its foreleg to no effect.

The thing braced itself against the shaft walls with its other legs, while its two forelegs went after Frem. It swung its forelegs from side to side, powerful strikes that slammed the shaft walls like hammers, but impeded by the narrow width of the shaft.

Frem kicked it — struck it over and again, though the creature ignored even the most powerful blows.

Escape seemed impossible. Frem thought about jumping –- about letting go of the shaft walls and crashing down atop the creature — using his weight and bulk to send it, and all those below it, straight to the bottom. Frem figured he'd die from the fall, or be crippled by it, but he'd take the bastards with him. Then again, he couldn't crush the skull of the first one he'd wounded down below in the tunnels, not even with a dozen clean kicks. Their armored exoskeletons were as hard as steel. The fall might not kill them -- but it would probably kill him.

Instead, he inched upward, kicked at the thing, pulled himself up another step.

Repeat, over and over.

He hit the creature with all his strength, but couldn't dislodge or dissuade it.

But so far, he kept it from getting a grip on his legs, though they were sorely battered.

Only a few feet to go.

He must've kicked the thing two hundred times while climbing those ten feet, and yet it still kept coming, still kept attacking. It pounded his armor, tearing off pieces, slicing into his flesh. Frem knew one good blow that shattered an ankle or severed a tendon, and he'd be done. But so far, his legs still worked, though the pain and burning was terrible.

Frem knew he was bleeding. He feared, badly. His strength, ebbing. Sweat poured from his brow. His heart pounded in his chest. His breathing, labored.

But he had to keep going.

He couldn't stop.

His only chance, to reach the top.

But what in Helheim would he do then?

He didn't know. He didn't have time to think or plan. He just had to get out of there. If he was going to die, he'd die in the open air with the sun on his face, not in some godforsaken tunnel.

And then he was at the top. Grabbed the very lip of the shaft, direct sunlight on his fingers. One last kick at the cave creature's face, and he pulled himself up and over the rim. A single glance told him the ground was a ways down, and he was high on a hillside – the shaft stuck up out of it like a chimney pipe.

If the thing hadn't been on his heels he'd have

tried to climb down or lower himself slowly, as best he could, but there was no time for such caution.

He had to jump.

But the thing was on him. By the gods, it had his leg. He'd been too slow. A firm hold, dragging him down. Frem's last dagger came out of its sheath. He slashed the creature once, twice, a third time – sparks flying as it dragged him farther down into the shaftway.

Frem lunged downward, keeping firm hold of the shaft's rim with one hand, his dagger's tip aimed for the creature's face — for its eyes. Even as he thrust, he knew he couldn't reach the thing's face. But simultaneous to his strike, the creature surged upward at him with open maw, trying to bite him. And his fate turned on that, for the last tenth of an inch of the dagger's blade punctured the creature's eye. The thing screeched, reared back smashing against the shaft's wall, and let go of Frem.

Then with one final leap, Frem threw himself up and out of the shaft.

And then he was falling.

"Oh, shit."

64

LOMION CITY
THE TOWER OF THE ARCANE
THE VIZIER'S CHAMBERS

YEAR 1267, 4TH AGE

THE VIZIER

The Vizier sat behind his desk in the circular domed chamber that stood at the apex of a grand turret in the Tower of the Arcane's tallest spire. The room once belonged to Grandmaster Pipkorn. Its perimeter, lined with bookcases overflowing with tomes and scrolls, ancient and obscure: history, religion, politics, treatises on every form of magic, on animals, plants, rocks, and minerals. The walls, what little were visible, were of white stone tiles, polished smooth. Every few feet stood a tall narrow window with multiple little panes of glass -- some of the clearest in all Lomion. Much of the domed roof was filled with curved stained glass lites, eliminating the need for lanterns or candles during the daylight hours. Though the Vizier oft kept a window or two ajar, the place was always musty and a bit too warm.

"You're certain that no one saw you coming here?" said the Vizier, barely visible behind a stack of books, a quill in his hand, papers scattered

345

before him and atop the books.

"I'm certain, my master," said Par Gatwind, a man so wide that he blocked the full width of the window he stood before and then some. "Plumes of smoke dot the horizon. The farms to the west and to the south are ablaze."

"They're burning them all," said the Vizier. "The north and the east fare no better. We've lost all contact with the surrounding villages and towns. Everyone has fled, or else, they are already dead. The trolls are thorough, and there must be a great many more of them than we have yet seen."

"How fared the Church Knights?" said Gatwind. "Did they break through to Dor Caladrill?"

"They had to turn back. Lost half their number. But did worse to the trolls. They are the first force we've put to the field that gave better than they got, but they were too far outnumbered."

"Why hasn't the Council put a full Corps on the field before the city?" said Gatwind. "Skirmish after skirmish we've had our hats handed to us, but we're sitting on the largest army in the world. Why don't we use it?"

"Would you use it?" said the Vizier. "You're an old military man. If you'd stayed in the service you'd be commanding a battalion out there. Mayhap a full corps. Would you put it to the field against those things?"

"Of course I would," said Gatwind. "I would take the fight straight to them. Archers and cavalry out in front. I would mow them down and have my footmen finish them. Have we no one but cowards in charge?"

"And what if we put that full corps to the field, just as you've suggested? And what if the trolls break it? What if they utterly destroy it, just the way they've destroyed every town, every company, every platoon, every regiment we've sent against them? What do you think would happen then?"

"Are you saying that the rest of our men wouldn't fight?" said Gatwind. "That their spirits would break?"

"The people's spirits would break," said the Vizier. "Wives and children would beg their husbands and fathers not to go to the field, imploring them to stay with them, to protect them from the troll incursions. And the men would wonder, *would my fate be any different than those who went before me?* If we lose a single corps on that field, we lose this war. What do you say to that?"

"If what you say is true," said Gatwind, "then we only have two choices before us. Sally forth with our entire army and fight them to the end, win or die."

"And the second option?"

"Hunker down. Settle in for a siege. Fight them from the most secure buildings and redoubts. When they finally come over the walls, safeguard our people behind stone and steel. Bleed the trolls until they give up. Until they go away. Outlast them."

"As did the Eotrus? That strategy did not work well for them?"

"Then what?" said Gatwind.

"This morning, a third option presented itself in the form of a man called Baron Jaros. He says he can save us from the trolls. Wipe them out. Send whatever survivors scurrying back to the mountains. Says he has the forces to do this."

"I've never heard of this man. Is he a southerner? A mercenary?"

"Odin knows who or what he is. But I don't believe he's brought an army to our doorstep unnoticed."

"Then a liar?" said Gatwind. "If so, who cares?"

"There is something about him," said the Vizier. "Some power about him. An aura. Something...unnatural. He is more than he seems."

"A disguise?" said Gatwind. "A spell, much like our own?"

"No, it is not magic, at least not of that sort. His appearance is what it is."

"But is he a wizard?" said Gatwind.

"I don't think so," said the Vizier. "But neither is he a common Volsung. He is...something else — what, I do not know. I want you to find out."

"That I will, my master," said Gatwind.

"Tell me of your preparations for the purge," said the Vizier.

"I've concentrated on the principal threats amongst the Freedom Council, just as we discussed," said Gatwind. "I've developed plans to deal with all of them, though some of those plans are not yet complete. I have in hand Grandmaster Mardack, Grandmaster Spugnoir, Par Triman, Baron Morfin, Lord Smirdoon, and of course, Harringgold. Only the whereabouts of Pipkorn still elude me. He must have an array of concealment spells cast in a dizzying web about him and everything he touches. Eventually, I will find him."

"We can't move on the others," said the Vizier, "until you know where Pipkorn is. He is the greatest threat of all. He must be contained. And he must be destroyed. I'm relying on you. I cannot act directly in this, for reasons complex and political."

"In any case, is it wise that we act with the city in peril?" said Gatwind. "If these trolls are as formidable as has been reported, and they do breach the city walls, every wizard will be worth a hundred soldiers, mayhap a thousand. It may be wise to wait until this war is over."

"You're assuming we're going to win," said the Vizier. "Have you so much confidence in this Jaros too?"

"Jaros or no," said Gatwind, "I don't believe any herd of animals, however vicious, can overcome the greatest city in the world. It's unfathomable. Perhaps our men have lost skirmishes, perhaps even a battle or two. But losing the city? No, Master, I do not believe it's possible. What is possible, is perhaps some of them will get through the walls one way or another. There will be chaos in the streets and people would die. That's the real danger."

The Vizier smiled. "Where there is chaos, my apprentice, there is opportunity. If the trolls come over the walls and run rampant in our streets, anything can happen. Any loss of life could be ascribed to wild trolls. Especially if those killed are just the type of men to go out and meet the trolls in battle. When the trolls come, that is when we must launch our strike."

"Opportunity indeed," said Gatwind raising an eyebrow. "Did you have something to do with these trolls coming here, Master?"

The Vizier smiled an evil smile. "You see now the problem that Baron Jaros presents, do you not?"

"If he stops the trolls before they breach the walls," said Gatwind, "there will be no chaos, and no opportunities that derive from that chaos."

"And how will you handle that?" said the Vizier.

"It appears, I shall have to add the good Baron to my enemies list," said Par Gatwind, "and come up with a plan to rid ourselves of him as well."

"He must sit at the apex," said the Vizier. "Even above Pipkorn. We must strike swiftly, before he disrupts my plans. But do not be hasty. Surveil him first, find out a bit more about him. I want to know what his forces are, whether soldiers or magic. We need to size up those forces. Determine what threat they represent to us before we do away with him. Otherwise, we blunder blindly into the unknown. I don't operate that way. First, I want you to take his measure, and learn what you can from that, and from all our agents. But you must act swiftly. I need the answers within a day or two at most. Put all our agents on it. And see to the hard parts yourself."

"Your will, will be done, my master."

65

MOUNT TROGLESTYRE TROLL CITY OF GOTHMAGORN

YEAR 1267, 4TH AGE

ECTOR EOTRUS

Ector and his officers marched up to a knight captain — one Sir Mattix from Highmount Hold. "What's this door that's giving you so much trouble, Captain?" said Ector.

"It's here, my lord," said Mattix. "We can get through it, that's not the issue." It was an iron door, heavily barred and reinforced. "Whatever is behind there," said Mattix, "is locked up tight. They don't want anybody getting to it."

"A treasure vault?" said Indigo.

"Maybe," said Ector. "Or mayhap more of their royals are back there."

"Cowering in the darkness," said Indigo, "hoping that we'll go away?"

"Whatever or whomever is in there – it's something valuable," said Ector, "at least to them."

"I thought you should know before we busted through," said Mattix.

Ector stepped up to the door. "First iron door

I've seen in this place."

"It looks old," said Indigo.

"Chained on this side," said Ector. "An odd thing. What are those, some kind of padlocks?"

"Aye," said Mattix. "We're bringing up tools to cut through them. It won't take long."

"Maybe it's a vault," said Ector.

"Who knows what treasures these things have,"said Indigo. "Who am I kidding, probably filled with a pile of bones or some other useless junk."

"Could be a pile of gemstones," said Mattix, "or gold ore. These mountains are full of both, or so the stories go."

"Bunk and bother, more likely than truth," said Indigo.

"But if it's a hidey-hole," said Ector, "then whoever is in there is not getting out. Not without help."

"Unless there's a back door," said Indigo.

"Let's look for that, that back door," said Ector.

"I've already got men on that, sir," said Mattix. "Four squadrons."

"With all the tunnels in this place," said Indigo, "it may take a goodly while to find it, if even it exists. And it may be secret. Hidden in the tunnel walls. We still don't know how sophisticated the trolls are."

"We've found no traps or secret doors so far," said Mattix.

"Make certain your men stay together," said Ector. "We risk losing more men to these caverns than to the trolls if we're not careful."

"So what do you want us to do about the

door?" said Mattix.

"Cut the chains," said Ector. "I want to see what's back there.

"Before we go bursting in, let's have a stout force in place here to back us," said Indigo, "just in case."

"Just in case," said Ector.

***

Ector, Pellan, and Indigo watched the men work on the door. The iron chains were thick and proved difficult to cut even with the best tools they had on hand. Slow going was it, but only a matter of time.

"I've got reports of five similar doors so far," said Pellan, "scattered all about the cavern complex. All in the deep tunnels, the way downs, just like this one. And all with multiple chains and crossbars set from the outside. And wedged shut to boot."

"Less and less likely that they're treasure vaults," said Indigo. "Not that we could be that lucky. We haven't found anything of value in this place. The trolls had next to nothing. And it seems they made almost nothing."

"Their drawings have a certain skill and beauty to them," said Ector. "And they're everywhere. There's hardly a wall without a painting or two. I don't have half the skill needed to copy them."

"Maybe that's just art," said Pellan, "or maybe that's how they mark their history. There are no books to be found here. They didn't have the

353

sophistication for that. So mayhap they tell their stories using wall paintings."

"You noticed the symbol over the door?" said Ector gesturing toward the portal. "Do the other doors have the same symbol?"

"I haven't seen the other doors myself," said Pellan. "I'm not certain that it matters, since we've no way of knowing what the symbols mean."

"The writing looks like runic script," said Ector.

"The reports coming back," said Indigo, "suggest that these tunnels are endless. They wind down through the mountain, sometimes in gradual slopes, sometimes in stairs hewn into the rock, sometimes in straight shafts that no man could ever climb down. I talked to two companies that went down passages for no less than three or four miles before they gave up and turned around. A lot of these passages go on like that, it seems. As many men as we have, it's not near enough to search this whole place. Not unless we want to camp out in here for days or maybe even weeks on end."

"There could be anything down here," said Ector.

"Or nothing," said Indigo.

"The important thing is," said Pellan, "if we hadn't immediately attacked when we saw the trolls enter this place, they could've fled down these tunnels and we never would've found them."

"No doubt, some of them did flee," said Ector. "Maybe a lot of them."

"We have to stay on our toes here," said Pellan. "No fewer than a full squadron of men should ever be off on their own in any of these tunnels. It would be too easy for a group of trolls to jump us. Our plan to wipe out the troll has already gone to shit."

"I fear that you're right," said Ector.

The men cut through the last of the chains and prepared to remove the crossbars. Pellan got the troops ready. She insisted that a full company of their finest be on hand to safeguard Ector when they pulled that door open.

Even with the chains cut and the crossbars removed, the door was stuck fast. The men took hammer and chisel at the top and bottom and both sides to try to break through. Eventually, the stone at the top of the door, which seemed to be the culprit, finally gave way, and it, and the runic symbol etched on it, went crashing to the tunnel floor. The men below narrowly escaped being hit. They cleared the debris and pulled again on the door. This time it opened, but jammed after it had moved less than a foot.

Indigo was at the portal. He had no interest in missing anything. He stuck a torch through the opening.

"It's a passage," said Indigo. "Empty as far as I can see. Stale air. No one's been in here in a long while."

"Can you get it open?" said Ector.

Indigo pulled on the door and the men stepped up with levers and hammers. A few minutes later they forced it open two thirds of the way, plenty of room for a man to move through with ease.

And just as they did, there came a rumbling and crunching sound from overhead.

The men froze.

Looked up.

The rumbling continued, grew louder. Dust and stone fell from the ceiling.

"Cave in," shouted Pellan. "Everybody, run for it. Run for your lives."

And they did. Moments later, the room's ceiling collapsed, as did a portion of the passage that led to it. A dozen men didn't get out fast enough. They were buried in the rubble.

The passage quickly filled with choking dust from the collapse. To escape it, the men rushed as fast as they could back to the nearest large cavern. Only once there did they halt their retreat. And when they did, they heard another rumbling. This time, from far off.

"Is this whole place coming down on us?" said Indigo.

"That was no coincidence," said Pellan, breathing heavily. "The roof collapsing just as we opened the door – that was a trap. And I bet that other rumbling we just heard was another room collapsing when its door was pulled open by our men."

"Send word down the line," said Ector, "pull the men back from those iron doors. Don't open another one."

"We've done all we can do here," said Ector. "We set out to destroy the trolls, and that's what we did. I don't care if a few stragglers got away. Or more than a few. The trolls are finished."

"Let's not forget about their army," said Pellan. "They are still out there and just as dangerous as ever."

"They're Lomion City's problem now," said Ector.

"An army without a homeland," said Indigo. "Without supply lines. Only what they can steal from us and what they carried on their backs. Ector's right. They're finished. It's only a matter of time."

"Unless there's enough of them to sack Lomion City," said Pellan.

"That's the Council's battle, not ours," said Indigo.

"I'll have to give that some thought," said Ector. "We're done with this place. Let's get on the homeward road."

"There's not much here, save stone and such, Master Ector," said Indigo, "but we should burn whatever there is. Leave nothing for them to come back to."

"I agree," said Ector. "Burn it all."

***

Some hours later, there was movement in the pitch black tunnel behind the iron door that Ector's men had pulled open. A tall figure walked stiffly down the passage toward the open door. It moved slowly but with purpose. When it reached the door, it reached its hand out to where the door was when it was closed, as if expecting resistance, but found none of course, because the door was ajar. The figure stepped forward and felt for the open door. It pulled itself through the portal and climbed over the stone rubble. It searched about the chamber in methodical fashion. Searched for an exit. The rubble was high and uneven but the chamber was not filled of it. Eventually, the figure found the opening that led to the exit passage. It climbed through and continued on until it reached the edge of the rubble, after which it was free to continue down the passage unimpeded.

"Ha, ha, ha," it laughed in a loud deep voice raising up both arms. "Free! I am free. Free at last!"

66

JUTENHEIM
NEARING ANGLOTOR

YEAR 1267, 4TH AGE

CLARADON EOTRUS

A Stowron bashed its staff into Claradon's shield, once and then again. Coming from so small a man, Claradon was shocked at the power of those blows – his arm shuddered with the impact. And then a swing caught the top of his helmet, wrenched his head around, throwing him off balance. He staggered to the side, bumping hard into Artol. His neck immediately went stiff and throbbed with pain.

A Stowron slipped between he and Glimador, leading with a wicked-looking black dagger that glistened along its curved expanse – drenched in blood or mayhap dipped in foul poison. Claradon had only a moment to react before the creature tested its blade against his leg's armor.

But a great hand intervened – Little Tug's hand. It came down atop the Stowron's head and gripped it with such crushing force that the Stowron's arms flailed limply at his sides, its black dagger dropping useless to the ground. Tug lifted the Stowron with that one hand, which had no doubt already crushed its skull, and tossed its limp body a dozen feet back into the ranks of its fellows who gasped and cursed at the sight.

Off to both flanks, Claradon saw Stowron vaulting over the Eotrus line to land amidst the men farther back. They sprang from a standstill like deer, jumping seven, eight, even nine feet into the air. Many got over the Eotrus front line, so surprised were the men by that preternatural agility. But soon, the Northmen were ready for them. Pikes and spears caught many as they leapt, arrows and crossbow bolts took more. Undeterred, the Stowron kept up the tactic throughout the battle. That caused continual chaos amongst the Eotrus ranks, but through it all, the Northmen held their lines, maintained their formation. And that was all that kept them alive, so terribly outnumbered were they.

Claradon kicked an onrushing Stowron in the jaw, then bashed his sword's pommel to the top of the man's skull. In the din, he didn't hear the crack of the skull, but he felt the bone give way, and he saw the man drop limply to the ground. Claradon grunted and winced — the horror of killing a man like that, it was almost more than he could bear. But he threw that thought aside as quickly as it came. He had to keep fighting, keep focused – he had to kill, or else be killed. Such was the way of war.

Claradon shield-bashed the face of the next Stowron that accosted him. This time, he couldn't feel the breaking bones, but from the strength of the impact, he knew that the man was done, out of the fight.

On came another, their numbers, seemingly

endless. He shield-bashed that one as well, but only landed a glancing blow. So he hit him again. And then he brought his sword's blade down atop the man's head. For a moment, he feared he couldn't pull the blade free. That he'd lose his sword. He couldn't afford that in that wild melee. He wrenched the weapon free just in time to parry the blow of another Stowron's staff. That strike was so powerful, he barely kept a grip on the sword. Claradon's next strike cut that staff in two. Then he sliced the Stowron across the chest; that was their biggest weakness, for they wore no armor. They were clad merely in cloaks of strange material. Whatever it was, offered little protection against sword, axe, or mace.

Throughout the battle, above the incessant clang of weapons, Claradon heard the cries of wounded and dying men.

And time and again, he heard Ob cursing at the Stowron, though he never caught sight of the old Gnome.

So too did he hear the unmistakable sound of Old Fogey crushing Stowron to pulp.

And once or twice, he thought he heard Theta's booming mantra, "*Doom!*"

One soldier, a few spots to Claradon's right, went down – Claradon couldn't tell who it was. The Stowron pulled him into their midst and piled atop him, stabbing and clubbing in a wild frenzy.

A man to Claradon's left suffered the same fate.

Twice more Claradon called on the *Militus Mysterious*. Each time, he called up a lesser sorcery – with power enough to knock back or slay a single Stowron immediately before him. That's all he dared do, and even that, only when he was sorely beset.

That was all the sorcery he dared call down for fear that it would weaken him. Slow him. And that he'd fall victim to some Stowron strike and be pulled down and torn to pieces. He had to conserve his strength, his energies. And hold his magic back unless and until it was sorely needed to preserve his life. Or those of his fellows. The problem was, there seemed no end to the Stowron. On and on they came, how many hundreds, how many thousands, Claradon could not imagine.

67

VAEDEN
AZATHOTH'S PALACE

THE AGE OF MYTH AND LEGEND

THETAN

As the Arkons scrambled to their feet, dazed and confused, Azathoth shouted at Thetan, "Speak the truth," his voice now filled with anger.

There was grumbling and murmuring amongst the gathered throng of Arkons. They stepped farther from Thetan, fearful of the lord's wrath. The Einheriar moved closer, in force, though by what command Thetan did not notice.

"You ordered us to kill children," said Thetan speaking loudly and slowly. "To pluck them from their mothers bosoms and bash in their skulls or cut out their tiny hearts. Time and again, you command us to do evil and you call it good."

"You must have faith," said Azathoth.

"I had faith," said Thetan. "I had it for ages. And I feel the fool for it. My conscience can no longer bear the deeds that I have done in your name. Never again. Never again will I do evil."

"My plan is long and deep and—"

"Your plan is madness," shouted Thetan as he marched toward Azathoth. "And you are--"

"Do not break my heart," shouted Azathoth,

his hand outstretched as if to hold Thetan back. "Do not do what cannot be undone."

Thetan pulled his sword from his scabbard as he broke into a charge.

A gasp rose up from around the great hall. There was motion all around as men sprang into action.

Azathoth's eyes turned red, as did his face. His aspect darkened and he grew in stature, seven and then eight feet tall, in but the blink of an eye.

Thetan moved faster than any mortal man could move.

But Azathoth's hand was the faster. The god's arm came up level to his shoulder, his palm facing outward toward Thetan.

When Thetan was but one stride away, his sword already on its downward swing toward the lord's head, a beam of red light, of heavenly fire, erupted from the center of Azathoth's palm.

It blasted into Thetan's chest.

The preternatural impact flung Thetan across the room as a man might swat a fly. The Arkons dived this way and that to avoid any impact.

Thetan crashed to the floor a hundred feet from where he began.

He lay unmoving.

The Arkons stared at his crumpled form in disbelief.

"Bhaal," said Azathoth, "arrest Mithron and his squadron, for they conspired with the traitor Thetan to betray me, to betray us all."

"If they resist," said Azathoth, "slay them where they stand. Spare only Arioch, for he alone has remained loyal."

Bhaal's eyes went wide. "Yes, my lord," he said reflexively. He drew his sword. The other Arkons pulled their weapons. The Einheriar did the same, blocking any possible retreat.

Arioch drew his sword, and kept it at the ready, between him and Mithron's men.

"*You* betrayed us?" said Mithron to Arioch.

"My loyalty is and ever has been to the lord," said Arioch. "It is you who have betrayed. It is you who are traitors to all we have ever held dear. Thetan clouded your minds with falsehoods and mad notions. Renounce him now. Put down your weapons and beg for the lord's mercy. Please, my brothers. I would see you redeemed and repentant, not dead. The lord will show you mercy, I am certain."

Mithron, Gabriel, and the others looked from side to side, as if gaging their chances, but they were sorely outnumbered, more than twenty to one, by the Arkons alone. More Einheriar flooded into the throne room, though called by what alarm, none could say. Few, if any, of the Arkons and none of the Einheriar would stand with them after Thetan's fall.

And then Thetan scrambled to his feet.

The Lightbringer's armor was scorched but intact. He was in one piece. His sword, still in hand. There was fire in his eyes; anger in his aspect.

"By the shards of Pythagoras," said Azrael, "the Lightbringer lives."

"To arms, my brothers," said Mithron.

"This cannot be," boomed Azathoth. "By holy fire and godly might, I smote you down.

"I smote you.

"Nothing should be left save ash and crumbled bone."

"And yet here I stand," said Thetan as he charged anew, his men beside him.

This time, Azathoth raised both his arms, palms outstretched. And he did not hesitate. He rose up now, ten feet tall, his skin, fiery red, his eyes, pitch black and blood red, no whites to be found; his face, frightening to behold, a sight to make any mortal's blood run cold.

Shaking with rage, Azathoth let fly his holy fire, fire that had consumed cities. Fire that had destroyed worlds. It roared from his hands with a sound like thunder, the light from it as blinding as the midday sun.

Bhaal and all the gathered Arkons fell back from him and shielded their eyes.

Azathoth's holy fire engulfed Thetan and his men. The lord's fire was no quick blast, no momentary impulse of energy, however immense and powerful. It was a lasting beam of death.

Azathoth shook with rage as he flung it, his face a fiendish caricature of its normal aspect. His conflagration roared on and on, even as his loyal Arkons and his Einheriar fled in all directions, more than a few with clothing afire, several fully engulfed.

Azathoth's own followers, his closest minions, had dared take up arms against him.

They dared to try to kill him.

To slay him in his own palace. In his own throne room. His closest servants. His beloveds. Traitors. Vile, deceitful traitors, one and all.

And when at last Azathoth's anger ebbed, or his power faltered, the holy fire finally stopped.

Azathoth's hand fell back to his side. Red tears dripped down the lord's face.

Of Thetan and his men there would be nothing left. Not after that blast.

Nothing at all.

Not even ash.

Such was the lord's rage.

68

JUTENHEIM

YEAR 1267, 4TH AGE

FREM SORLONS

Luckily for Frem, the ground was but ten feet from the top of the shaft and consisted of loose sandy soil and gravel. He landed on his feet, rolled once and then again, and planted his feet and hands to stay his slide down the slope. He slid several feet before halting, then sprang up ready for action, his dagger out, and his eyes locked on the top of the shaft, now high above him. Frem took a deep breath and braced himself, ready for battle, though the ground was poor for it — a single step might send him tumbling over and sliding uncontrolled down the steep slope.

The cave creature stuck its jittering tentacles out of the shaft. Its front legs and the rest of its head followed, but as they did, it shrieked and ducked back into the shaft.

It feared the direct sunlight, thank the gods. Whether the light merely stung its eyes or truly injured it, Frem did not know. He heard raucous clicking and screeching from within the shaft, but none of the creatures dared poke their heads out again.

Frem's legs bled badly from several deep

abrasions and the sole of one of his boots was damaged, nearly bitten off.

He glanced around. He was atop a hillside, mostly rocky and barren, the slope steep but walkable with care. Numerous rocky chimneys like the one he'd climbed dotted the top of the hillside and other hills nearby. No one was about. No signs of civilization. There was forest a few hundred feet down the hill on all sides.

Out of immediate danger, Frem dropped to his rump and then lay on his back, exhausted.

He had to get up. He knew it. He couldn't lay there. Couldn't chance a sleep, however brief, for if the creature decided to brave the sun, or if a large enough cloud passed overhead, it might emerge, who knows how many of its fellows with it. Frem was in no shape to fight them — to fight anything. He was more exhausted, physically and psychologically, than he'd ever been in his life, or so it seemed at the moment. The sweat poured off him. Moisture he couldn't afford to lose. He needed water. He needed a safe place to rest, to bind his wounds, and fix his boot. He had none of that.

"Well done, Frem Sorlons," said a woman's voice. "Well done."

Frem rolled over at lightning speed, dagger in hand, his wounds and fatigue forgotten. A few feet from him stood a woman he knew — the crone of Jutenheim — grinning at him, this time absent her boy and her wolf.

She'd appeared from nowhere.

Frem looked from side to side, and all about, but saw no one else. He narrowed his eyes and stared at her for a moment before he spoke, making certain that she was real -- not some figment conjured up by dehydration and lack of sleep. But she seemed real and looked exactly as he remembered: exceptionally tall for a woman but stooped and aged, with long gray locks, and a walking stick as tall as she. "How are you here?"

"Where needed, I go," said the crone, "and where I wish."

"I could've used some help down there," said Frem pointing to the chimney. "Did you see that thing poke its head out? That bug? A whole hive down there. Man eaters."

"Ha, ha, no help did *you* need, Frem Sorlons, for escape the chitterites you did, all by your only." She leaned in close to him. "A brave hero you be. Brave, brave, brave. Strong as an ox you be, ha, ha. But a bit of help now, I think you do need. Stand up and walk with me."

"How did you get here? We are far from Jutenheim Town."

"I have my ways, now walk with me, ears open, mouth closed."

"If you've something useful to say, my ears *are* open. But I've no strength for a stroll. If you want to help me," he said looking her over, "a bit of water would be best, some food if you have it. If not, just point me in the direction of civilization and I'll be in your debt."

"Food and drink I have to offer, but walk with me to get them you must," she said, her voice a bit sterner. "The sun will not restrain the chitterites for long, Frem Sorlons. You must get gone from here right quick or all your strength will

370

not avail you." She turned and began to slowly walk down the slope, her staff aiding her steps.

Frem pulled himself to his feet, shouldered his pack, kept his dagger in hand — his last remaining weapon -- save hands, feet, and a little slingshot he carried in his pack –- a lot of good that would do him unless they encountered an angry squirrel.

He caught up to the crone and walked beside her down the hill, both silent until they reached the tree line.

"This be no chance encounter," said Frem. "Or else my eyes deceive me and you are not here at all."

"No chance encounter it is, Frem Sorlons," said the crone as they continued to walk into the woods. "Never is it with me, but rest assured, I be no figment, no will-o-the-wisp, and no forest fairy princess either, ha, ha. I come to you, because…I value you. You serve a greater purpose than you know. What depths of strength you have to survive the perils of Svartleheim on your only. What courage. You've done well, but your trials are not yet done."

"Speak plainly woman, for a plain man am I."

"Ha, ha," she laughed, "about you, Sir knight, there is nothing plain. You are a most singular man, if a bit dense. Rejoin your troop you must, for they have need of you."

"They're alive, my Pointmen? How do you know that? You're telling me that they're alive?"

"Alive they be. And you've no time to waste wandering the woodland, supping with Elves, or getting chomped on by chitterites. I will point you in the right direction but your legs must carry you there and quickly. There are great deeds that must be done, Frem Sorlons, some of which *you* must do."

"The mission? I thought you were opposed to the League, a devout of Odin, are you not?

"Your memories were masked by magic before you began your mission. Have you any inkling of that?"

"My memories? I know not of what you speak. I urge you again, speak plainly, woman, for I am a simple man. A simple soldier. I wish no riddles or rhymes. Let us have clear words between us or none at all."

"To protect you, and others, your memories were tampered with. Done for good reason it was, but that reason is now past. Would you have me restore your memories? Do that, I can."

"Still you do not speak plainly. Are you saying that sorcery was used to change my memories? Someone has meddled with my mind?"

"Meddled no more than necessary, Frem Sorlons. Never fear, olden magic it was, from the days of yore — from *The Dawn Age*. Safer sorcery than the modern mischief — fewer untoward side effects and unintended consequences."

"If this were done to me, if this were true, how would you know it? You were here in Jutenheim when my company set out from Lomion, thousands of miles away."

"Perhaps a little bird told me. Or the wind. Perhaps I was there myself, and notice me, you did not. Or perhaps, I simply plucked that information from Ezerhauten's mind when I spoke to him in Jutenheim Town. I can read people, Frem

Sorlons. I can see into the depths of their hearts and souls. Know this, I think you do, from our brief encounter."

What have you done with my commander?

"We're veering off track," said the crone. "To your commander, I've done nothing. Stood before him I have not after he left Jutenheim Town with all the rest of you. Take some things on faith, Frem Sorlons, you must, for the truth is too complex for the telling, especially for a *plain* man such as you. Trust me that your memories have been altered. And in that trust would you have me restore them to what they were? For I say to you again, the reasons that they were altered are now past."

"So you wish to cast a sorcery upon me to restore my memories, is that it?"

The crone sighed. "With your leave, Sir Dense."

"And perhaps that spell will do me harm. Or perhaps *it* will alter my memories, which perhaps are just fine as they are. I do not trust you, crone. There is more to you than what I can see. This whole meeting is suspicious. Perhaps you are not the crone of Jutenheim at all."

"Perhaps I am not. But I mean you no harm. I am here only to help," she said as they waded across a stream. When they reached the other side, she halted and turned toward him. Frem filled his canteens and drank deeply, keeping an eye on the crone the entire time.

"You are safe now from those creatures of the dark," said the crone. "They fear to venture across moving water. You will be safe on this side even after nightfall. But if you had stayed on the other, which perhaps you would have done had I not appeared to you, they would've came upon you in the night, by the many. For all your skill, strength, and courage, you would have died. Now you will not. At least not by those creatures."

"We've bandied enough words here," continued the crone, "and we've no more time to waste." She waved her hand from one side to the other, her fingers passing close before Frem's face. Suddenly, all his wounds were healed. A moment later, his boot was repaired and his pack was replenished with all manner of useful supplies. In but a few moments after that, he remembered.

He remembered everything.

69

LOMION CITY TAMMANIAN HALL

YEAR 1267, 4TH AGE

The High Councilors gathered on the grand steps outside Tammanian Hall. With them stood a contingent from the Council of Lords. Crowds gathered up and down High Street for as far as one could see, the atmosphere akin to that of a parade or grand festival. The people laughed, cheered, and made merry — the first the councilors had seen of that in the three weeks since the siege began.

"They act as if we've won," said Slyman. "As if the war were over; as if the siege were broken."

"The people need a bit of hope," said Barusa. "A reason to believe that we might survive this. That we might even win this. And apparently our newfound friend has delivered them just that, if the rumors be true."

"They are true," said Balfor, "for unless my eyes deceive me, comes now the relief column from Dor Caladrill."

Astride heavy warhorses came the knights of Dor Caladrill, a lengthy column four horsemen wide. At their van, Lord Caladrill the younger. And beside him, Baron Jaros.

Lord Caladrill, Jaros, and Caladrill's senior officers halted before Tammanian Hall's steps. The bulk of the column marched on to where they'd be stationed. Barusa led the greeters in a round of applause.

Formal pleasantries completed, the High Councilors withdrew to their chambers, a number of prominent lords following. It was there that Jaros and Caladrill gave their report.

"Lord Caladrill, we feared that your forces would not make it through to us," said Barusa. "Several attempts we made over the last weeks to keep the route open proved futile. How did you break through the troll lines?"

"I can take little credit for that," said Caladrill. "The troll had us tied up in the valley, five miles west. Three days we were stalled there. The trolls were relentless. Harassing us all day long, worse at night. Whenever we tried to march forward, they crashed against our line. My losses were heavy. Three of my own House felt in those skirmishes, including my youngest nephew."

"You have my sympathies, my condolences," said Barusa. "The loyalty and sacrifices of your House shall not be forgotten by this Council or by the realm. When we called, you answered."

"And I stand before you now, ready to fight," said Caladrill. "More than that, I will send for more troops. All that I have. I fear that it will take that and more to stop these trolls. But with our new ally," he said looking toward Baron Jaros, "it may go the easier."

"How did you finally break through?" said Marshal Balfor.

"We didn't break through," said Caladrill. "Jaros's men broke the troll's back and sent them fleeing into the woods. We heard the howls in the middle the night, but in the black, not knowing what went on, we dared not advance. I feared a sorry group of pilgrims had stumbled into the troll ranks in desperate effort to flee Lomion city. I felt for them, I did, but I was not about to lose half my men trying to rescue them. It turns out, it was no helpless pilgrims out there. It was Jaros's fighters. And apparently, they needed no help from me."

"So you took no part in the battle that repelled the trolls?" said Balfor.

"I wish I had, but no, I did not."

"Did you see any bodies?" said Balfor.

"That I did," said Caladrill. "What was left of them. Jaros's men hacked them to pieces. Damn tough bastards."

"But did you see *them*?" said Barusa. "Jaros's men?"

"Of course," said Caladrill. "Though only a company of them remained by the morning."

"I believe the good councilors give me more credit than I deserve," said Baron Jaros. "They imagine me a powerful wizard that turned the trolls to toads or some such. I have no such esoteric powers, my friends. What I have are good fighters. Great fighters. Ah, here they come now."

Into the audience hall marched a group of folk carrying large canvas bags, two folk to each. These people had a strange air to them, but of what that was, was hard to say. They were dressed all in black, head to toe, with deep black cowls overhanging their foreheads. They carried swords and longbows. By their shapes, many of them were women. And that was an odd thing, indeed. The Lomerian army had always accepted capable women into its ranks, and treated them the same as men. But there were always few of them; very few. But in Jaros's army, women numbered half the force, perhaps more. Or perhaps that was just for show for some reason or another. When Jaros gave the signal, the soldiers upended their bags all at once and out dropped the heads of the fallen trolls. Two hundred or more stained the chamber's floor.

The councilors gasped at the gruesome sight. The smell, even worse.

"One has to take their heads," said Jaros, "or the troll will heal at a phenomenal rate and rise up again to strike you down. Only when its head or spinal cord is severed, or it's burned to ash, will a troll stay down."

Barusa, Balfor, and curiously, Bishop Tobin, walked down the steps to the petitioner's hall to get a close look at the troll heads.

After they'd studied the remains, Jaros spoke again. "As you can see, my forces have destroyed a large contingent of trolls that even a column of your best knights could not break through. I've opened the western pass, albeit perhaps temporarily, which also you have been otherwise unable to do. And I brought you proof of both," he said pointing in turn to the heads and toward Caladrill. "I trust that these actions, these victories, serve as sufficient proof to prove my worth. And to cement the bargain that we discussed."

Bishop Tobin kicked the head of one troll.

The other councilors, up upon their mezzanine, were silent, waiting for Barusa to respond. Even Harringgold had nothing to say.

Smiling at Jaros, Barusa stepped up to him with outstretched hand, and shook it warmly; held it. "You have proven your worth, indeed," said Barusa. "I thank you. This Council thanks you. Lomion City thanks you." Barusa stepped closer and put his arm around Jaros's shoulder and embraced him tightly. When he pulled back, his eyes were wet. "You saved us, Baron. You saved us, praise Odin."

Baron Jaros smiled. "Let us not rejoice too quickly, my friends, for there is much work yet left to do. But know well, it will be done. The trolls will be destroyed just as I have promised. I will see to it. Now, what of the writ?"

"I will be the first to sign it," said Barusa.

"And you, good general?" said Jaros.

"I will sign it too," said Marshal Balfor, though he seemed less than enthusiastic.

"And I," said Bishop Tobin.

"Then we have a bargain," said Jaros, loud and strong -- to make certain that all the councilors heard him.

"We do," said Barusa, just as loudly.

And across the hall, amid the throng of lords and ladies of the court, her identity concealed by her own cowl, Mother Alder nodded her head slowly and muttered to herself, "*Well played, Firstborn. Well played.*"

70

JUTENHEIM NEARING ANGLOTOR

YEAR 1267, 4TH AGE

CLARADON EOTRUS

Claradon pulled his shield closer to his body, pulled his sword the closer too. Fatigue growing, his shield's effectiveness, in both attack and defense, decreasing by the moment. He chose his sword strokes carefully, not swinging at all except when certain of a hit. He had to preserve his strength, for the battle was far from over.

Another Stowron came on and Claradon bashed it back: three strikes to its chest and head -- the first, battered its arms aside, then came the death blows. It fell away, but a moment later, another Stowron took its place. His strength ebbing, Claradon bashed that one too – once and then again.

Were these new foes or the same he'd already beaten back, coming back for more, still some fight left in them?

Claradon didn't know, the battle too wild to tell.

And besides, with those formless black cloaks and concealing cowls, all the Stowron looked alike. How they saw well enough to fight, their faces covered as they were, Claradon had no idea. Yet somehow, evidenced by the precision of their strikes, they did see, or else, they employed some sense beyond Claradon's ken to guide their hands.

Claradon's breathing went fast and heavy, almost panting. Sweat poured down neck and cheeks. No doubt, his shirt was soaked through. Probably his pants too. All the finesse, gone from his strikes. Half the strength behind them, gone as well. All he wanted was to lay down, close his eyes, and breathe. Rest. Sleep. He needed the battle to be over. Or at least, for Odin's sake, some pause to catch his breath.

But that wasn't happening. He had to keep fighting. Keep moving. Keep his sword up, his shield too. Remember his training. This wasn't the first time that he was breathless and arm weary – he'd been there a hundred times. All those days on the Dor's practice field, when Ob, Gabriel, Sarbek, and Stern drilled him in swordplay, hours on end. Drilled him until he dropped, and then made him get up for more.

He knew how to keep going. To fight through the pain and fatigue. The training had taught him that. Had given him that confidence. He kept going in training to avoid little more than scolding words and minor punishments. Here, he had real motivation – to stay alive. To keep the Stowron from bashing in his head.

And so on he fought. Pushing through the fatigue, ignoring the pain, just as he'd been taught.

Thank the gods for his large shield and small opponents, for he could plant the shield's base in the dirt instead of holding it up, yet maintain much of its effectiveness.

He heard the men panting around him. All were winded. Spent. The Eotrus men all had the same training as he. They'd fight until their last breath. But he feared for the others: the Alders, the Harringgolds, and even the Malvegils. Well trained all. Good soldiers. Tough fighters. But no soldiers in all of Lomion, save a few militant orders, underwent the grueling training that was routine at House Eotrus. Whether enough Eotrus men were left to see the others through, Claradon didn't know.

The Stowron bodies piled in heaps about the Lomerians, yet more rushed toward them in endless waves. And so the battle raged on and on, no respite and no reprieve, no retreat and no surrender.

Tanch conjured another fireball and threw it at the Stowron. This time, he lobbed it closer to the Eotrus ranks, not fifty feet beyond their front line.

No man amongst them kept his feet after that concussive blast hit them. Stowron flew through the air, in whole and in parts – many burning wildly, blue and yellow fire consuming them to the bone in but moments. The Northmen were all bowled over, flopping and sliding across the field from the blast, but no fire touched them.

The air blast that hit Claradon was irresistible: hot like an oven, and with the impact of a hammer. It lifted him into the air, and dropped him down several feet from where he had stood, and then, he slid along the ground, coming to rest mayhap ten feet from where he started. Thank the gods, only the air blast hit him. Some of the others were not so lucky. Many Stowron bodies crashed into the Northmen. Some of those Stowron were already dead, most on fire, some had some fight still left in them.

Claradon took a quick glance around. Everyone was down, Stowron and Northman alike for as far as he could see. Though the mystical fire did not burn the Lomerians, the concussive blast hurt all the same.

Claradon scrambled to his feet. By then, Theta was already up, his sword swinging swift and unforgiving. DeBoors was up too. Artol pulled himself to his feet next to Claradon. And Dolan sprang up in the distance, over by Theta.

The Northmen quickly reformed their line.

So did the Stowron.

Claradon estimated that that blast alone had dropped two hundred Stowron. Many were blasted to ash, many others lay still, their bodies afire. Still more rolled about the dirt, screaming.

The Stowron ranks were decimated. At best, they now numbered no more than 150 men in fighting shape.

Claradon knew not how many men he had left. How many of his had fallen. He had no time to assess. He and the others nearest him — Glimador, Artol, Tug, Kelbor, and The Bull -- closed ranks, shoulder to shoulder, shield to shield, and braced against the next Stowron charge. Claradon had lost track of Ob. And Kayla. And so many others. He didn't even know whether they were still alive, or if they were injured and needed help. And that was maddening.

He couldn't go look for them; he couldn't even turn around to try to catch a glimpse of them, to make certain that they were alright. He had to put them from his mind and stay focused on the fight in front of him. That was so hard to do. But he had to. And he did.

Claradon and his squad fought on together. They stood their ground. They didn't stop. They didn't give up.

Until the end came.

And just as with many battles of legend, the skalds marked that skirmish with a bit of verse rooted in truth, and set to rhyme.

Stab and swirl,
Spell and spite,
Onward charged
The Children Of the Night,
Endless berserker hordes they were
Clouding the Northmen's weary sight,
But which fierce side
Was in the right?

Axe and mace,
Frenetic pace,
Slice and slash,
Hack and bash,
The battle raged,
Noon till night.
The Harbinger of Doom
His wrath to right,
Death on all sides,
Fire and fright,

Until at end
The Northmen's might
Slew the last
Lonely
Child of the Night.

—-The Fifth Scroll of Cumbria
Chapter 12, Verses 17-18.

71

VAEDEN
AZATHOTH'S PALACE

THE AGE OF MYTH AND LEGEND

AZATHOTH

Azathoth's gaze was surely obstructed by the heavy smoke and haze, his nostrils assailed by the burning scent that hung heavy in the air.

He waited, transfixed.

Staring through the gloom.

He would not move until he witnessed the byproducts of his wrath — the scorch marks and wisps of ash -- all that remained of the traitors that he'd once loved.

From the far corners of the great chamber came howls and cries of pain. Burned men, Arkon and Einheriar both. A few were down, their fellows dousing flames that licked clothing or armor. Azathoth was oblivious of it.

And when the haze cleared, not twenty steps from the lord stood Thetan the Lightbringer. Sword still in hand, his armor and clothing singed and smoking but not aflame, his flesh intact, the fire still in his eyes. And behind him stood Mithron, Gabriel, Uriel, Azrael, and all the rest, the traitors. Each one alive, though by their expressions, they knew not how or why. Except for Thetan. His face was confident now; his expression, hard as stone; his eyes, colder and than the iciest peak.

Azathoth's mouth dropped open in shock. His own eyes wide. And he diminished. In but two heartbeats, his form shrunk back to his normal size, though his skin remained bright red, his eyes still black and bloody.

He stumbled backward, nearly fell.

What had happened could not happen.

Human flesh, Arkon or not, could not withstand his power. No creature of Midgaard could. It was impossible.

*****

THETAN

While Azathoth stood perplexed, Thetan lifted his sword's point toward the chamber's domed ceiling high above. His lips moved, whispering words unknown. A continuous beam of blue energy, sparkling and translucent, erupted from his sword's tip, a sharp hum following in its wake. It shot upward faster than any arrow could fly and struck the ceiling, its energy spreading radially outward upon contact. At first, nothing happened, but after a few brief moments shards of stone dislodged from the ceiling where the beam was centered. Two seconds later, the ceiling exploded. Huge chunks of stone fell everywhere. There was a great groaning and creaking, and then the very structure of the dome, great iron ribs, bolted and banded, began to pop and break. His beam extinguished, Thetan turned toward his fellows. "Run," he shouted. "Run!"

They ran toward the main doors, stones great and small falling in their midst. Shrieks of pain and anguish rose up from all corners of the great chamber as men were hit, injured, and killed. In the chaos, their path was open until they reached the great doors. A clutch of Einheriar met them there, braced and ready, weapons leveled. The two groups crashed together, sword, hammer, and axe. Brave as they were, the Einheriar had witnessed what the traitors had withstood. Fearful looks filled their faces. But yet they stood. A wall of muscle and steel that would not yield. It had to be broken. To be torn asunder. Mithron led the charge against them, Gabriel and Hogar beside him.

Thetan turned as the group engaged the Einheriar. Far across the hall, he saw the lord, still standing at the same spot, seemingly oblivious of the collapsing ceiling. As best Thetan could tell, Azathoth stared directly at him. The lord's arms were upraised, palms facing the heavens. Though it was too far to see, Thetan imagined more red tears streamed down his face. A face no longer filled with anger, but with sorrow. And then the largest stones fell from on high, the great iron girders with them, and in but a few moments, Azathoth was gone, buried beneath untold tons of rubble.

Thetan's breath caught in his throat. His sword arm tingled, trembled, and burned. All his limbs felt weak. His mind in a fog. His spirit, broken. What had he done? What had he done?

He prayed that no Einheriar or loyalist Arkon would come at him, for he knew not if he had the strength to resist. His men fought like demons all about him. Hacking and slashing with skill beyond that of all lesser men. For all their mettle, the Einheriar could not withstand them. Thetan's Arkons punched through the cordon of steel and breached the great doors. Thetan spied Bhaal, Arioch, Mikel, and Hecate, supported by dozens more Arkons dashing towards them, dodging falling stones as they ran. Thetan's men closed the doors behind them, but that was of little use, for those doors locked only from within.

They dashed through the palace halls. To Thetan, that trek was a blur. Uriel ran beside him. Gabriel too. The others were up ahead, crashing through anyone or anything that dared block their path. But out in the palace proper, few knew what had gone on inside the throne room. No one knew to bar their path, if any would even have dared. Uriel shouted something about a flight of Targons waiting for them. That had not been part of the plan. They anticipated no need to flee from the palace. That meant that Uriel had come up with his own contingencies. That was his way and thankfully so. Thetan tried to push the thoughts from his head. He had to focus on the now. And he did. Just as he always did.

72

LOMION CITY

YEAR 1267, 4TH AGE

PAR GATWIND

Baron Jaros walked down the stone steps as he exited Tammanian Hall after his latest meeting with Lomion's Council of Lords. Several bodyguards accompanied him.

Par Gatwind awaited him at the base of the steps, dressed in wizardly robes – a formal sign of his station. He'd donned them to make certain that Baron Jaros would not pass him by.

After exchanging pleasantries and introductions, Gatwind began his questioning. "The esteemed members of the Tower of the Arcane are very pleased at your arrival at so opportune a time. We've been puzzled however, over why you have not visited *us,* and yet have spent so much time here at Tammanian Hall."

"Is this not the seat of government of Lomion City, of the realm?" said Jaros. "I thought the wizards held no official power. Am I mistaken?"

"Oh, you're quite correct. The wizards hold no official power, but some would say, we hold all the power."

"And do you come to me as a representative of the Tower or are you here to speak only for yourself?" said Jaros.

"I represent the interests of many amongst the tower wizards. Many who are curious to learn more of our fair city's apparent savior. I entreat you, please indulge me a few questions, and a bit of your time."

The Baron nodded.

"By magic or might do you propose to stop the troll?"

"By might," just as I've told your government. "I am no wizard. But I command a force of soldiery that's up to the task of dealing with these trolls. I reached suitable arrangement with the government to act on their behalf in eliminating the threat."

"We've seen no such soldiery, Baron. We've seen only a handful of cloaked folk, lightly armed and armored. What weapon did you use to destroy those trolls? What is your secret?"

Jaros smiled. "If I had a secret, Par, I would not disclose it to you, would I? All you need know, all anyone in Lomion need know, is that I will save you from the trolls. Be grateful for now. Good day to you."

"Did you bring the trolls down upon us, Baron? Is that why you can rid us of them? Because they've been under your control from the start?"

"No, I have not brought the trolls down upon you. I am here to help you be rid of them." Jaros studied Gatwind closely, staring into his eyes, overlong. Gatwind didn't flinch. He would not be intimidated.

"Walk with me," said Jaros. As he began to stroll down the street, Gatwind followed. "It occurs to me, that we may be able to help each other."

"I'm intrigued," said Gatwind. "Please explain."

"There may be some in this fair city that might not want to be rid of the trolls," said Jaros. "That might find some advantage to the...disarray that they're causing."

"Any that felt that way, I'd mark a traitor," said Gatwind.

"Would you?" said Jaros. "I'm glad to hear that. I would as well. My concern is that some of those folk might want to stop me from stopping the trolls. I could use your help, and the help of your brethren, to protect myself from such threats. I know how to deal with trolls. I have the people for that. But assassins, that's a bit outside my realm. Especially if any wizard got such a notion. Perhaps we could come to some arrangement, me and your brethren?"

"Since you're here to save our city as you say, your safety is of paramount importance to all good citizens of Lomion. So if I or my fellow wizards can be of service to you, we *must* help you."

"I'm very happy to hear that, Par Gatwind. We must speak more of this, delve into the details, come to a proper arrangement — a business deal of course, proper funding for your expenses in providing the appropriate security of a...magical nature. Let us retire to a quiet pub that I know of down the way -- my men discovered it the other night. They've a private room in the back where we can speak unheard and set these matters down well and proper."

"Sounds like an excellent idea," said Gatwind.

They turned down the next alley, narrow and dark. No one was about save their little group. When they reached mid alley, Jaros turned to Gatwind. "I'm so very happy that we met today." A heartbeat later, Jaros's dagger sliced across Gatwind's throat. Blood spurted everywhere. One of Jaros's men grabbed Gatwind from behind and clamped his hand over the wizard's mouth, not that he could speak any longer, but just to be certain. Another man grabbed his arm which was going for a dagger.

"Why?" said Jaros, asking the question that Gatwind could not. "I'm not a wizard, Par Gatwind, but I *can* read your mind. I knew your plans the moment you brought them to mind, and they cost you your life."

Gatwind dropped to his knees.

Jaros's four bodyguards dropped to the ground, on hands and knees, and lapped up the blood that pooled around Gatwind's legs.

Jaros leaned in.

Clamped his teeth to Gatwind's throat.

And sucked the spurting blood from his veins.

73

JUTENHEIM

YEAR 1267, 4TH AGE

SERGEANT PUTNAM

The last of the Juten Lugron went down after Putnam's sword slashed across his neck, blood spraying through the air. Nearly thirty of the Lugron's fellows lay dead or dying on and around the unpaved road upon which the Pointmen traveled. The two groups, the Pointmen and that clan of local Lugron had both been moving so silently -- the Pointmen, along the road, the Lugron, through the woods -- that neither group saw the other coming. They blundered into each other, unawares.

The battle, brief but bloody. The Lugron came on like madmen. Berserkers. Even as the Pointmen cut them down, the rest did not flee. They fought to the death. To the last man.

The Pointmen fared far better: fourteen entered that battle; fourteen survived it, though more than a few left with bruises and scars. None were grievously wounded, and all mobile, and for that, Putnam was grateful. But they were spent, one and all. The skirmish had sapped much of their remaining strength. They needed a good long rest, a hot meal, and sleep, but none of that was forthcoming. An hour of rest and a few bites of fruit that they'd gathered along the trail was all they could afford. And they were happy even for that. Wise veterans that they were, their eyes and ears searched for other threats even as they caught their breaths and dressed their wounds.

Less than half an hour later, they heard more men approaching. This time, from whence they came. Someone had been following them.

"Fight or flee?" said Putnam to the lieutenant.

"I've not wind enough to run overfar," said the lieutenant. "Let's lay low, well back in the trees. They may yet pass us by."

"With bodies fresh," said Putnam, "they'll search."

"Woe to them unless they have the numbers," said the lieutenant.

"Woe to us if they do," said Putnam.

Putnam gave the signal, and the Pointmen slipped back amongst the trees and undergrowth on the western side of the road, the sun generally to their backs. After but a score of heartbeats, no trace of the Pointmen could be seen or heard from the road. Putnam took position behind a patch of thick bushes that concealed him quite well, but yet afforded a decent view of the road. He lay on his belly, the lieutenant to one side, Moag to the other. Putnam could see only a few of the others from where he lay. But he knew that every Pointman that had a bow, had an arrow nocked and ready. The rest would have throwing daggers primed to loose. Then they'd go in hand-to-hand: sword, axe, hammer, and mace.

A few minutes later, what walked into view was

not what Putnam expected. He anticipated another Lugron troop, mayhap kin to those they'd just defeated. Or else, some other Juten locals, equally unfriendly.

Instead, what he spied was a troop of Volsung warriors, battered and battle hardened, knights mostly, of varied signs and sigils. It took only a moment for Putnam to mark them as Lomerians by the style of their armor and cut of their cloth.

That could only mean one thing: that the Leaguers' fearful whispers of pursuit by a bogeyman and his minions were well founded. They called him the Harbinger of Doom — the very same one known from myth and legend. Putnam considered the whole business no more than bunk and bother, a tactic used by Ginalli and Thorn to keep their lackeys in line. But there they were, several of their knights of huge stature, some to match Frem, some even the larger. He wondered if the Harbinger was one of them. If he were real. The Leaguers warned that those men would stop at nothing to thwart them from opening the doorway to Nifleheim. That's why Ginalli had hired Ezerhauten and the Sithians. It wasn't to babysit them down the Hudsar or bodyguard them across Jutenheim. Ginalli had Archwizards for that. The Sithian Company was hired to slay the Harbinger's minions, and to hold the creature itself at bay until the wizards or Korrgonn could put him down.

Putnam knew his duty. He had to stop those men. The trouble was, they outnumbered the Pointmen by three, maybe four, or even five to one. A tough battle that would be. One they had scant hope to win unless the Harbinger's men were much less skilled than they appeared.

The lieutenant put his hand on Putnam's forearm and shook his head. He sized it up the same as Putnam had: he didn't want to fight; the odds were too long. They'd keep their heads down and hope that the soldiers passed them by. They'd follow and jump them in the night or at some other vulnerable moment. It had to be done. There was no avoiding it. But the lieutenant was smart to prefer a way to limit their own losses. By the gods, they'd already suffered too much.

The Harbinger's men halted upon sight of the battlefield. They took up defensive positions, formed a shield wall backed by bowmen at the ready. A Gnome they had with them – an elderly character with a big mouth. A half-Elf by his side — a pale, sickly fellow. Those two crept forward, all silent and stealthy, and studied the killing field — even as Putnam studied them and theirs.

He recognized some of the sigils: Eotrus, Harringgold, Malvegil, Kalathan, and Alder. A strange alliance it seemed to Putnam, but he didn't keep close with Lomerian politics. He figured that the Harbinger had hired up a bunch of mercenaries — third or fourth or fifteenth sons of this lord or that. Men that had to make their own way in the world, despite a name that otherwise meant something — at least to their fathers and older brothers. Maybe they were just hired hands much like the Sithians –- or else, mayhap they were true believers in the Harbinger's cause. Not that it mattered much. He had to kill them, all the same.

The Gnome and the Elf soon returned to their

ranks and conferred with several tall knights what wore fancy armor.

And then the Elf spun toward Putnam as if he stood in plain sight.

A bow in hand.

Arrow flying.

Faster than fast.

Putnam made to duck but the arrow slammed into his helm.

Snapped his head back.

Motion all around.

Putnam pulled up his shield.

Wondered why he wasn't dead. Why everything still worked. Felt the wet hot trickle of blood stream down his forehead.

The second arrow slammed into the top half inch of Putnam's shield just as he pulled it up. Had it come a half heartbeat earlier, it would've caught him in the throat.

The third arrow hit the shield before he made his feet.

The fourth, before he'd taken a single step.

Nobody could shoot that fast.

The Harbinger's men shouted their war cries. They charged forward — all to the west side of the road. All right towards the Pointmen.

The Pointmen loosed their arrows. Threw their daggers. Crashed forward through the brush.

Ready to meet their fate.

Putnam blinked through the blood that streamed into his eyes. Clenched his jaw, sword and shield high and ready. He barreled forward. The lieutenant and Moag did the same.

The Elf charged straight at him — sword in

hand.

The Elf swung first but Putnam parried the blow. He shield bashed the Elf with all his strength. Caught him hard on the shoulder and blasted him from his feet.

Two steps behind the Elf charged a man as big as Frem — a blue-armored knight with a wickedly wide sword.

"Valhalla," shouted Putnam. The last thing Putnam saw was Theta's piercing blue eyes as their swords came together.

VAEDEN
AZATHOTH'S PALACE

THE AGE OF MYTH AND LEGEND

Much of the domed ceiling had come down — stone slabs and iron girders both. They lay in great heaps about the hall. A thick dusty haze filled the air. The cries of men, broken and wounded, came from here and there about the room. Arioch and three score Arkons scrambled about the edges of one great pile of debris, moving stones as big as a man, sliding them from the pile, straining with all their might. Searching for their lord — Azathoth. Buried somewhere beneath that heap.

And then from the rubble came a sound. Humming. A vibration of rocks and metal. It grew stronger. And the Arkons withdrew, backing clear of the rubble in fear and confusion.

The great stones shifted; the great iron beams slid aside — not in a wild blast or explosion, but a slow measured shifting of debris. A shifting whose origin was within the debris pile itself — as if a hundred hands with the strength of the greatest giant pushed back the wreckage.

When the center of the pile parted, from within its depths appeared Azathoth, the one true god.

He glowed with a soft golden light from head to toe. His hands and arms were at his sides, palms facing forward. He rose up from the pile, floating upon the air, red tears dripping down his cheeks.

The stones continued to part about him though he touched them not. He hung there in the air gazing down upon the destruction of his throne room, his eyes taking in all there was to see.

He floated down until he stood next to Arioch. The other Arkons, all that remained in the chamber, all that did not give chase to the traitors, gathered quickly around in awe and wonder.

Azathoth's face was sad. His cheeks sunken. But his robes were of pure white glowing with golden trim. No dirt or dust marred them. Neither his clothes nor his face or his hands. No injury afflicted him. None that could be seen by the human eye.

The Arkons dropped to their knees, one after another. They bowed their heads. Many wept.

Azathoth placed his hand on Arioch's shoulder. He then walked past him, up to the railing at the overlook's edge. Far below he saw a flight of Targon taking to wing, each one bearing an Arkon.

Arioch stepped up beside his lord. "It's them," said Arioch. "The traitors."

The sun full upon them, only the Targons' wings were visible — and so it appeared as if the traitorous Arkons themselves were winged. That they flew. An illusion that oft served them well when dealing with the common folk, as each Arkon appeared as a god floating through the heavens.

"Your orders, my lord?" said Arioch.

"You are my First Arkon now," said Azathoth. "Your skills and loyalty deserve no less." In Azathoth's hand appeared a large coin of silver with the likeness of Azathoth's face emblazoned upon it. It had the weight of thirty common pieces of silver and hung from a silver chain. "A small reward for your loyalty. Let it serve as a symbol of your new station. But fear not, though now you be my right hand, I will not send you after the traitor and his minions. I know they were as brothers to you. I know the pain that your loyalty has cost you."

"No, my lord," said Arioch. "Only say the word, and I shall be after them. It will bring me no pleasure, but I would bring them to heel, or whatever punishment you decree."

"You have no need to prove your loyalty any further, beloved," said Azathoth. "It shall fall to Bhaal to bring me the traitors' heads. He shall go forth with my legions and bring them down. All of them. We must cleanse Midgaard of their evil."

Azathoth focused his gaze on Arioch as that flight of Targons disappeared into the distance. Azathoth's eyes glistened. "And when that cleansing is over, I shall weep for a hundred years, for my heart is broken. Though I created you all from the very stuff of my own being, I will never understand you. And that is both your greatness and your demise. Have Bhaal and the others set forth at once."

"But how will we catch them?" said Mammon. "The Targons have already taken them far beyond our sight. Before Bhaal and our forces are ready, they will be long gone."

"I know where they are going," said Azathoth.

"Where?" said Mammon.

"They go to Wotan," said Azathoth. "They go to the camp of the barbarian king as has been their plan from the start. All that remains unknown to me, is whether the barbarian commands the traitor, or whether the traitor commands the barbarian. In the end I suppose it matters little, for they must both be purged of this world."

"We shall see your will done, my lord," said Mammon.

"I shall see it done myself," said Azathoth. "I will take to the field, for I fear that Wotan and his sons are beyond even Bhaal or you, Mammon. It is my sword that shall bring them down and the traitor too, if he dares to face me again."

"You must not risk yourself," said Arioch.

"What risk?" said Azathoth. "Neither sword nor stone nor steel nor any craft of man can bring me down. I am the Lord. Invincible. Invulnerable. Omniscient. Omnipotent. You need have no fear for me."

His voice grew cold.

"You need only have fear *of* me."

END

Thanks for reading *Drums of Doom*.

EXPERIENCE MIDGAARD LIKE NEVER BEFORE

Are you ready to take up your sword and stand beside Theta, Ob, Claradon, Tanch, and the rest? If so, pick up your copy of the **Audiobook** for *Gateway to Nifleheim* today and begin your epic journey. Grammy award-winning narrator Stefan Rudnicki's magnificent performance will transport you to Midgaard and drop you straight into the fray! You'll feel like you're shoulder to shoulder with the heroes. Your heart will race when the fiends of *The Nether Realms* accost you. But never forget, in Midgaard, nothing is as it seems.

Get the Audiobook here:
http://smarturl.it/Nifleheim_Audio (US Link)
http://smarturl.it/Nifle_Audio_Foreign (Non US Link)

AND DON'T MISS THIS!
Join my VIP Newsletter group and receive a FREE copy of my Ebook, *The Keblear Horror.* Click here: http://smarturl.it/Keblear_signup

Already have that book? Join my VIP Newsletter group to be eligible for other giveaways and be notified about my new book releases and other news about my writing.
http://eepurl.com/vwubH

I hope that you enjoyed *Drums of Doom*, and that you will consider taking a few moments to return to where you purchased it (http://www.glenngthater.com/thank-you.html) to leave a brief review. Reviews help my work gain visibility and provide me with valuable feedback about what my readers enjoyed and didn't enjoy about the story.

Thank you again, and please check out the other books in the Harbinger of Doom series.

ABOUT GLENN G. THATER

For more than twenty-five years, Glenn G. Thater has written works of fiction and historical fiction that focus on the genres of epic fantasy and sword and sorcery. His published works of fiction include the first eleven volumes of the *Harbinger of Doom* saga: *Gateway to Nifleheim*; *The Fallen Angle*; *Knight Eternal*; *Dwellers of the Deep*; *Blood, Fire, and Thorn*; *Gods of the Sword*; *The Shambling Dead*; *Master of the Dead*; *Shadow of Doom*; *Wizard's Toll*; *Drums of Doom*; the novella, *The Gateway*; and the novelette, *The Hero and the Fiend*.

Mr. Thater holds a Bachelor of Science degree in Physics with concentrations in Astronomy and Religious Studies, and a Master of Science degree in Civil Engineering, specializing in Structural Engineering. He has undertaken advanced graduate study in Classical Physics, Quantum Mechanics, Statistical Mechanics, and Astrophysics, and is a practicing licensed professional engineer specializing in the multidisciplinary alteration and remediation of buildings, and the forensic investigation of building failures and other disasters.

Mr. Thater has investigated failures and collapses of numerous structures around the

United States and internationally. Since 1998, he has been a member of the American Society of Civil Engineers' Forensic Engineering Division (FED), is a Past Chairman of that Division's Executive Committee and FED's Committee on Practices to Reduce Failures. Mr. Thater is a LEED (Leadership in Energy and Environmental Design) Accredited Professional and has testified as an expert witness in the field of structural engineering before the Supreme Court of the State of New York.

Mr. Thater is an author of numerous scientific papers, magazine articles, engineering textbook chapters, and countless engineering reports. He has lectured across the United States and internationally on such topics as the World Trade Center collapses, bridge collapses, and on the construction and analysis of the dome of the United States Capitol in Washington D.C.

CONNECT WITH GLENN G. THATER ONLINE

Glenn G. Thater's Website:
http://www.glenngthater.com

To be notified about new book releases and any special offers or discounts regarding Glenn's books, please join his mailing list here: http://eepurl.com/vwubH

BOOKS BY GLENN G. THATER

THE HARBINGER OF DOOM SAGA
GATEWAY TO NIFLEHEIM
THE FALLEN ANGLE
KNIGHT ETERNAL
DWELLERS OF THE DEEP
BLOOD, FIRE, AND THORN
GODS OF THE SWORD
THE SHAMBLING DEAD
MASTER OF THE DEAD
SHADOW OF DOOM
WIZARD'S TOLL
DRUMS OF DOOM
VOLUME 12+ *forthcoming*

THE HERO AND THE FIEND
(A novelette set in the Harbinger of Doom universe)

THE GATEWAY
(A novella length version of *Gateway to Nifleheim*)

HARBINGER OF DOOM
(Combines *Gateway to Nifleheim* and *The Fallen Angle* into a single volume)

THE DEMON KING OF BERGHER
(A short story set in the Harbinger of Doom universe)

THE KEBLEAR HORROR
(A short story set in the Harbinger of Doom universe)